PRIOR BAD ACTS

Bantam Books by Tami Hoag

PRIOR BAD ACTS

KILL THE MESSENGER

DARK HORSE

DUST TO DUST

ASHES TO ASHES

A THIN DARK LINE

GUILTY AS SIN

NIGHT SINS

DARK PARADISE

CRY WOLF

STILL WATERS

LUCKY'S LADY

TAMI HOAG

PRIOR
BAD ACTS

DOUBLEDAY LARGE PRINT HOME LIBRARY EDITION

BANTAM BOOKS

This Large Print Edition, prepared especially for Doubleday Large Print Home Library, contains the complete, unabridged text of the original Publisher's Edition.

PRIOR BAD ACTS
A Bantam Book / April 2006

Published by Bantam Dell
A Division of Random House, Inc.
New York, New York

Bantam Books is a registered trademark of Random House, Inc., and the colophon is a trademark of Random House, Inc.

ISBN-13: 978-0-7394-6543-1
ISBN-10: 0-7394-6543-0

Printed in the United States of America
Published simultaneously in Canada

This Large Print Book carries the
Seal of Approval of N.A.V.H.

With thanks to Lynn, who,
despite all protests to the contrary,
has a mind nearly as twisted
as my own.

Brainstorms R US.

PRIOR BAD ACTS

Prologue

He knew before he entered the house that day that something was very wrong. It was July. The sky pressed down like an anvil—ominous, dark, gray. The afternoon was over, evening not yet begun. Time had ceased to mean anything.

The air was still, as if the day were holding its breath in anticipation of what would come. Dead calm. Lightning ripped across the western sky. Thunder rumbled, a distant drumroll.

In his memory there were never other houses around the foursquare clapboard house with the peeling green paint and the porch that bowed midway across the front of the building like a weary smile. Everything else receded, slipped into the trees, dropped over the horizon. He saw the house, the yard—turned weedy and straw colored by the lack of rain. He saw the trees back by the train tracks, leaves turned inside out.

No one was around. No cars on the street behind him. No kids ripping up and down on their bikes. There were no dogs, there were no birds, there were no squirrels or rabbits. There was no sound but the thunder, drawing ever closer.

In his memory, he didn't draw near the house. The house advanced on him.

Bang!

His heart stopped. His head snapped to the left.

"You better get in the basement! Tornado's coming!"

The neighbor, whose dreary ranch-style cracker box had crept back onto the periphery, stood on his back deck. He was a guy with Elvis sideburns and a gigantic beer gut. He held a camcorder. He pointed to the west.

A storm was coming.

The air was electric. Colors were sharper, crisper. Everything seemed in hyper-focus. His eyes hurt taking it in.

The house lunged at him. He tripped on

the first step and stumbled onto the porch. The hinges on the screen door screamed as he drew it back and stepped inside.

Crack! Boom!

The lightning was so bright, it seemed to fill the living room. He called out. No one answered.

In his memory his feet never moved, but he was suddenly in the dining room, then the kitchen, then the TV room at the back of the house. The room was small and dark, wrapped in cheap wood paneling. The heavy curtains at the windows were old, and they didn't hang right. They had been made for some other window in some other house, and cast out when the fashions changed. Light seeped in around the edges and down the center, where the panels didn't quite pull all the way together.

The television was on. Storm warning. Outside the house, the wind came in a gust. Lightning flashed.

He found the first body.

She was sprawled on the couch, propped up like a giant doll, eyes open, as if she were still watching television. A wide strip of duct tape covered her mouth and circled her head. Her hair had been chopped off with a scissors or a knife. Coagulating blood marked gouges in the scalp. Her clothing had been cut down the center and peeled back, exposing her body from throat to crotch.

Storm coming.

Crack! Boom!

She'd been cut down that same line. Through skin, through muscle, through bone, like a fish to be gutted. Drooping daisies had been planted in her chest.

Bile rose in his esophagus at the same time that his throat closed. Terror wrapped two big, bony hands around his neck and squeezed. He stumbled backward, turned and ran into a floor lamp, jumped sideways and tripped over a footstool, fell and hit his head on the corner of the coffee table.

Crack! Boom! Crack! Boom!

Dizzy, weak, scared, he scrambled to get his feet under himself and get out of the room. A strange mewling sound squeezed up out of his throat, like a dog that had been beaten.

He ran to the kitchen. He ran out the back door. He couldn't stay in the house, couldn't get away from it fast enough. The world had taken on a weird green cast. There was a roaring sound coming, coming, like a freight train. But when he looked at the tracks, there was no train, or if there had been one, it had been swallowed whole by the huge black funnel cloud that had touched ground and was chewing up everything in its path.

This had to be a nightmare. None of this could really be happening. But he felt the debris hit him. Slivers and splinters and dirt pelted him. He threw his arms up around his head to protect his face. The roar was deafening.

The old storm cellar door was open and clinging to the frame by a single hinge as the wind tried to rip it free. He all but threw himself down the concrete stairs and kicked in the door to the basement itself. It was old and rotted with damp, and it split away from the frame on the third kick.

The basement was as dank as a cave, and smelled of mildew. He couldn't find a light switch.

Above him, the old house had begun to shake. He had the impression of it pulling upward as the tornado tried to rip it from its foundation.

The rain came in a deluge. The bullwhip crack of lightning. Thunder drumming. The basement was illuminated in bursts of stark white light. The darkness between was absolute.

He curled into a ball on the floor—cold, wet, sick at the thing he had seen upstairs, sick at the smell of the basement.

He didn't know how long he stayed there. It might have been five minutes or five hours. Time meant nothing. All he would remember later was the dawning of awareness that everything had gone silent again. So silent, he thought he might have gone deaf.

Random flashes of lightning still illuminated the night beyond the high basement windows, but he couldn't hear the thunder.

Slowly he rose from the cold, wet floor. Something like a hand touched the back of his neck, and the sweat coating his skin turned to ice. Something nudged him in the back as if to make him turn around to see a surprise.

Lightning burst outside the windows like the flash of a camera, and the image was forever imprinted on his brain. A memory that would never fade, never lessen in its impact or in its horror: the bodies of two children hanging from the ceiling beams, their lifeless eyes staring sightless into his.

1

Fifteen months later

"He slaughtered a mother and two children."

Hennepin County prosecutor Chris Logan was a man of strong opinions and stronger emotions. Both traits had served him well in the courtroom with juries, not always so well in judges' chambers. He was tall, broad shouldered, athletic, with a thick shock of black-Irish hair now threaded with silver. Forty-five years old, Logan had spent twenty of those years in the criminal court system. It was a wonder he hadn't gone entirely white.

"I'm sorry," said the defense attorney, his sarcasm belying the expression of shock. "Did I miss something? When were we suddenly transported to the Dark Ages? Aren't the accused in this country still innocent until proven guilty?"

Logan rolled his eyes. "Oh, for Christ's sake, Scott, could you spare us the act? We're all adults. We all know each other. We all know you're full of shit. Could you spare us the demonstration?"

"Mr. Logan . . ."

Judge Carey Moore gave him a level look. She had known Chris Logan since they had both cut their teeth toiling as public defenders—a job neither of them had the temperament for. They had moved on to the county attorney's office as quickly as they could, and both had made their names in the courtroom, prosecuting everything from petty theft to rape to murder.

Sitting in the other chair across from her desk was another cog in the public defender's machine. Kenny Scott had gone in that door and had never come out, which made him either a saint battling for justice for the socially disadvantaged or a pathetic excuse for an attorney, unable to rise out of anonymity and go on to private practice. Having had him in her courtroom numerous times, Carey suspected the latter.

He looked at Carey now with the eyes of

a mouse in a room full of cats. Perspiring, nervous, ready to run, scrambling mentally. He was a small man whose suits never fit— too big in the shoulders, too long in the sleeves—which somehow emphasized the impression that he was overwhelmed by his job or by life in general.

By the luck of the draw, he had gotten stuck with the job of defending the most hated man in Minneapolis, if not the entire state: a drifter named Karl Dahl, accused of the most heinous murders Carey had encountered in her career.

The scene had been so gruesome, one of the uniformed officers who had responded to the original call had suffered a heart attack and had subsequently retired from the force. The lead homicide detective had been so affected by the case, he had eventually been removed from the rotation and put on a desk job, pending the completion of psychiatric counseling.

"Your Honor, you can't allow Mr. Logan to circumvent the rules of law," Scott said. "Prior bad acts are inadmissible—"

"Unless they establish a pattern of behavior," Logan argued loudly. He had the fierce expression of an eagle.

Kenny Scott looked like he wanted nothing more than to bolt from the office and run for his life, but to his credit, he stayed in his seat.

"Mr. Dahl's previous offenses have nothing to do with this case," he said. "Criminal trespass? That hardly establishes him as a violent offender."

Logan glared at him. "What about possession of child pornography? What about breaking and entering? Window peeping? Indecent exposure?"

"He never killed anyone with his penis," Scott said.

"It's an escalating pattern of behavior," Logan argued. "That's what these pervs do. They start small and work their way up. First they get their jollies whacking off while they look at little kids in their underwear in the JCPenney catalog. When that doesn't do it for them anymore, they move on to window peeping, then to exposing themselves. Next they need to have physical contact—"

"And they jump from weenie wagging to evisceration?" Scott said. "That's absurd."

He turned back toward Carey. "Your Honor, there is nothing violent in Karl Dahl's record. The information regarding his prior convictions would be prejudicial and inflammatory. The jury would be ready to convict him based on Mr. Logan's theory, not fact, not evidence."

Logan ticked his facts off on his fingers. "We have his fingerprints at the scene. We have a complaint filed by one of the neighbors, reporting him for looking in her windows. We know he knew the victims, that he'd been hanging around the neighborhood. He had the victim's necklace in his possession at the time of his arrest—"

"He was doing odd jobs," Scott said. "He admits to having been in the Haas home the day of the murders. Mrs. Haas paid him thirty-five dollars to install some curtain rods. He stole a cheap necklace. Big deal. Other than the one neighbor, no one in the neighborhood had any complaint against him."

Logan rolled his eyes dramatically. "Every one of them said the guy was strange, that he gave them the creeps—"

"That's not against the law—"

"Good thing for you," Logan muttered.

Carey warned him again. "Mr. Logan . . ."

He gave her a familiar look from under the

heavy dark eyebrows. "An eyewitness puts him at the scene—"

"At least five hours after the murders had been committed," Scott pointed out.

"Coming back to review his work," Logan said.

"That doesn't make any sense. Coming back that late in the day, when people would be arriving home from work—"

"So he was back to kill the father and the oldest kid—"

"Just where did you get your crystal ball, Logan?" Scott asked. "Maybe we can all run out and get one. Maybe the state can buy them in bulk and distribute them to every law enforcement agency—"

Carey arched a brow in disapproval. "Put the sarcasm away, Mr. Scott."

Logan jumped in again. "This is a clear exception to the rule, Your Honor. The man is a serial killer at the front end of his career. If we don't stop him now—"

Carey held up a hand to stave off any more arguments. Her head ached as if it had been crushed by a millstone. Through law school and the years working her way up the ranks, her goal had been to sit in these chambers, to wear the robes, to be a judge.

At that moment, she wished she had listened to her grandmother and honed her secretarial skills as a fallback should she not land a suitable husband.

Presiding over felony proceedings was a responsibility she had never taken lightly. Because she'd come from a successful career as a prosecuting attorney, people expected her to be biased toward the prosecution—an expectation she had worked hard to dispel.

As a prosecutor it had been her job to vigorously pursue the conviction of defendants. As a judge, her job was to preside fairly, to take no sides, to keep the scales of justice in balance so that every verdict was reached based solely on the relevant facts and evidence presented.

Carey couldn't take sides, no matter what her personal feelings might be. In this case she had her work cut out. Two children had been brutalized, tortured, murdered, left hanging by their necks from the ceiling of a dank basement.

She was a mother herself. The idea of someone harming her daughter evoked an emotion so strong there were no words adequate to describe it. She had viewed the crime scene photos and the videotape. The images haunted her.

The children's foster mother had been raped, sodomized, tortured, her body sliced open from throat to groin. The coroner had determined that the woman had died first, though there was no way of knowing what might have taken place before her very eyes prior to her death. She might have been made to watch while unspeakable acts were committed on the children. The children might have been made to watch while unspeakable acts were committed on her. Either way, a nightmare from the darkest, most primal, fear-filled corner of the human mind.

But as a judge, Carey couldn't attach those atrocities to the defendant on trial before her. Her decision on the matter before her now couldn't be swayed by her own fears or disgust. She couldn't worry how people would react to her ruling. A criminal trial was not a popularity contest.

A fine theory, at least.

She took a breath and sighed, the weight of the matter pressing down on her. The attorneys watched her. Kenny Scott looked like he was waiting for her to pronounce sentence on him. Logan's impatience was palpable. He stared at her as if he believed he could influence her mind by sheer dint of will.

Carey quelled the sick feeling in her stomach. *Move forward. Get it over with.*

"I've read your briefs, gentlemen," she said. "And I'm well aware of the impact my decision will have on this case. I can guarantee neither of you would want to be sitting in this chair right now."

Logan would have argued that, she knew. Bias was a way of life for him. "Right with might" was his motto. If he believed something, then it was so—no arguments. But he held his tongue, held his breath, poised to leap out of his chair. Carey met his gaze full-on.

"I don't see an exception here," she said.

Logan opened his mouth, ready to rebut.

"You'll allow me to finish, Mr. Logan."

His face was flushed red with anger. He looked at the wall.

"Mr. Dahl's prior acts may point in a particular direction, suggesting a possible path of future criminal behavior," she said. "However, he has no history of violent crimes, and this court can't foresee what Mr. Dahl might do in months or years to come. At any rate, we aren't allowed to try people for crimes they have yet to commit."

"Your Honor," Logan said, his voice tight from holding back the need to shout. "Violent criminals are made over time. Mr. Dahl's record—"

"Is inadmissible," Carey said.

If people could have been put away for crimes they had yet to commit, Chris Logan would have been led away in handcuffs. The fury in his eyes was murderous.

Kenny Scott barely contained himself from leaping out of his chair and doing a victory dance. Carey stared at him, and he slouched back down and swallowed the joy of his victory. He wouldn't think it was such a good thing after the news hit the press, Carey thought.

People generally demonstrated less loathing for public defenders than headline defense attorneys. They were, after all, civil servants toiling away for low wages, devoting their lives to helping the unfortunate. But as soon as her ruling was made public, Kenny Scott would suddenly become an enemy of the state. Defending the indigent was one thing. Getting an accused murderer off was quite another.

"Your Honor," Scott said, ready to strike while the iron was hot. "In view of your ruling, I don't see that the prosecution has enough evidence to support the indictment—"

Logan came out of his chair.

Eyes popping, Scott looked at the man looming over him. "I move that the charges be dismissed," he said, talking as fast as he could, trying to get all the words out of his mouth before Logan could grab him by the throat and crush his larynx.

"Motion denied," Carey said with a calm that belied her inner tension. "Sit down, Mr. Logan, or I'll have you removed."

Logan glared at her, defiant. He didn't sit, but he moved away from Kenny Scott and went over by the wall, his hands jammed at his waist, nostrils flaring as he tried to gather himself.

"But Your Honor," Scott argued, "the state has no direct evidence linking my client to the crimes. No fingerprints on the murder weapons—"

"He wiped them clean," Logan growled.

"No blood evidence on his clothes—"

"So he ditched the clothes."

"No DNA evidence—"

"He used a condom—"

"Not so much as a hair—"

"The guy doesn't have any," Logan snapped. "He shaves his body clean so he won't leave any hairs behind. What does that tell you?"

"He does it for hygiene reasons," Scott said. "The guy's a transient. He doesn't want to pick up lice."

Logan made a rude sound and rolled his eyes dramatically.

Carey turned to him. "Well, Mr. Logan? What *do* you have on Mr. Dahl?"

"I'm supposed to lay out my entire case in front of *him*?" Logan said, incredulous.

"Do you have a case to lay out?"

"He's got conjecture, supposition, and coincidence," Scott said.

"I've got a grand jury indictment," Logan said.

"And the Cracker Jack box it came in?"

"It's good to know you have so much respect for our criminal justice system, Mr. Scott," Carey said without humor.

Scott stammered, tripping backward, trying to cover his mistake. Carey held up a hand to forestall the attempt. She wished the earth would open and swallow Kenny Scott and Chris Logan and this entire nightmare case.

"The indictment stands," she said. "A jury can decide if the state has a case strong enough to convict your client, Mr. Scott."

She gave Logan a look she knew he recognized from their years together on the same side of the bar. "And if you don't, Mr. Logan . . . God help you."

She rose behind her desk and nodded toward the door. "Gentlemen . . ."

Kenny Scott bounced up from his seat. "But Your Honor, shouldn't we revisit the idea of bail?"

"No."

"But my client—"

"Should consider himself damned lucky to have a guarded building between himself and the public," she said. "Considering the climate of the community, bail would not be in your client's best interest. Quit while you're ahead, Mr. Scott."

Scott bobbed and nodded. "Yes, ma'am."

"Don't call me ma'am."

"No. I'm sorry, Your Honor. I meant no disrespect."

"Please leave."

"Yes, ma— Of course."

He held up his hands as if to concede his stupidity, then fumbled to grab his briefcase and nearly tripped himself on his way out the door.

Logan remained for a moment but didn't say a word. He didn't need to. Carey knew exactly what was going through his mind. Then he huffed a sigh and walked out like a man with a purpose.

The bottle of scotch in his bottom right-hand desk drawer.

"Have one for me," she muttered.

2

The best time for a controlled release of bad news to the public is Friday afternoon. Taxes are going up, the economy is going down, more troops are being deployed to some third world hot spot—the announcements are made on Friday afternoon. People are busy ending their workweek, getting ready for a few days of freedom, getting out of wherever early for a weekend at a lake. There's a good chance a lot of attention will be anywhere but on the news.

Detective Stan Dempsey knew how the world of politics worked. He'd been on the shit end of it much of his life, in the army, on the police force. He had a great loathing for the people who held those positions of power. People who were able to wave a hand, shrug a shoulder, raise an eyebrow, and alter the lives of those beneath them without a care or afterthought. People like Judge Carey Moore.

It was difficult for him to think of her as being in a position of authority, holding sway over cases he had built. She seemed too young, looked too pretty. His soul was as old as dirt. He had been wearing a police uniform when she was a child.

He had dealt with Carey Moore when she had been working her way up through the county attorney's office. A good prosecutor. Tough. Demanding. Despite the big blue eyes and turned-up nose, she had never been anyone's patsy or pawn.

Dempsey didn't know what had happened to her since she'd become a judge. Cops had believed they would have someone on the bench who wouldn't take any crap from defense attorneys, wouldn't have any time for the dirtbags on trial before her. They had practically expected automatic convictions—Do not pass Go, Go directly to jail.

That wasn't what had happened at all. She had become a different person on the bench, entertaining ridiculous defense motions, allowing the work of the police force she had once relied on to be questioned and ridiculed. As far as sentences went, if she had a book, she sure as hell wasn't throwing it at anybody.

And so Stan Dempsey shouldn't have been surprised that Friday afternoon when the news broke. Court wasn't even in session. The meeting had gone down in Judge Moore's chambers.

With nothing better to do, he had left the desk job, where he'd been stuck for all these months, and walked across the street to the Hennepin County Government Center.

The department brass had worried he wasn't stable enough to be on the streets after the Haas murder investigation. They had worried he was a liability risk, that he might go off at any time on anyone the way he'd gone off on Karl Dahl in the interview room the night Dahl had been arrested.

In his own heart, Dempsey didn't know that he wouldn't. He was a different person now. In the twenty-eight years of his career, he had been an exemplary cop—in a uniform and in a suit. Never a complaint filed against him. The Haas murders had changed who he was. He'd gone into that house that summer evening in the eerie calm between thunderstorms, and hours later he had come back out a different man.

The department had sent him to a shrink, but beyond his official report and his statements to Logan in the prosecutor's office, he had never talked about what he had seen. He had never spoken to anyone about what he felt. Twice a week he had gone to the shrink's office, stretched out on the couch, and stared at the wall for forty-five minutes, saying nothing.

The truth was, he was too damned scared to say anything. If anyone had known the kind of thoughts that filled his head, he would have gotten shipped off to a secure mental facility. Images of the crime scene were lodged in his brain like pieces of jagged glass. At any given moment a blinding spotlight could hit any one of the images, transporting him back there. He could smell the mildew of the basement and the unmistakable stench of violent death. The sour, acrid smell of terror.

The deaths of that woman and the two children had been horrible. The tortures they had endured, unspeakable. For the very first time in his career, Stan Dempsey had committed the cardinal sin of letting a case get under his skin. He had allowed himself to imagine the last, terrifying hours of the victims' lives, to feel their fear, their helplessness.

Those emotions had burrowed down into the core of his brain like some kind of weevil. A sense of toxicity had filled him. He had difficulty sleeping, mostly because he feared the violent dreams of vengeance that plagued him. The dreams had become particularly strong recently, as the trial of Karl Dahl drew near.

His lieutenant had been more disturbed than perturbed by the reports from the shrink regarding his twice-weekly lack of cooperation. That was because his lieutenant was a woman, and women always wanted to open up the heads of men and drag their thoughts out into the light like a tangled mess of string to be sorted out and rolled up neatly.

She herself had tried to get him to talk. She had expressed concern for his well-being. She had tried to find out if he had a wife or a family member she could talk to in an attempt to end his stubborn silence.

But Stan didn't have anyone anymore.

People he had been close to over the years had drifted away from him. His wife had divorced him because he was so emotionally closed off, and she needed someone who took an interest in her and in what she needed.

His daughter lived in Portland, Oregon, with her "life partner." She called on Christmas and Father's Day. He hadn't known how to keep her close. He didn't have the tools, as the shrink told him. He wasn't open or demonstrative or communicative. He only had the job. And now he barely had that.

The powers that loomed over him had pressed for him to take his retirement and go. They didn't see that any use he had left in him was worth the risk of having him around. If he snapped one day and beat some skell to death, or drew his weapon and fired into a crowd, he would cost them millions in lawsuits.

Bastards. He was that close to his thirty years and full retirement benefits. He had served the department well and faithfully. And now they wanted to screw him over on his pension because he had suddenly become an inconvenience to them.

No. He would sit at that goddamn desk, go to their shrink and stare at her wall, and time would crawl by, and his career would die on schedule, and he would take his full pension and . . . and . . . Nothing.

The thing that kept him going these days was his focus on the Haas case, the pending trial of Karl Dahl. And so he got up from his desk and went across the street and went into the criminal courts side of the building. He positioned himself where he would see the attorneys coming away from Judge Moore's chambers.

Word was she would rule as to whether or not Karl Dahl's prior bad acts could be entered into evidence at trial. Logan would fight hard for it. They didn't have a hell of a lot of direct physical evidence against Dahl. The case was largely circumstantial— knowing that Dahl had been in the Haas home, that he had been there that day, that an eyewitness had seen him enter the house, that he had left a fingerprint on the telephone, that a neighbor had made a complaint about him to the police just days prior to the murders.

But he was the guy, Stan had no doubt, and the murders were something Dahl had been working toward for a long time. He had probably been living that fantasy in his head for years, planning what he would do, inuring himself to any extreme emotional reaction that would come during the commission of the act so that he wouldn't make mistakes. Stan Dempsey believed that down to the marrow of his bones.

He sat on a bench, crossed his legs, and wished he could smoke a cigarette. A person could hardly smoke anywhere these days. There was even a movement to make it illegal to smoke outdoors in public spaces. Just another little bit of personal individuality being chipped away.

People came and went up and down the hall. No one paid any attention to him. He was unremarkable in his homeliness, a thin gray man in a baggy brown suit. Sad eyes that stared at nothing.

Kenny Scott, the public defender assigned to represent Karl Dahl, burst into the hall, looking like a man whose execution had been stayed.

Logan followed him a moment later. Logan was a force of nature—big, commanding, full of fury. His brows slashed down over his eyes. His mouth was set in a grim line. He leaned forward as if he were walking into a stiff headwind.

Dempsey stood up. "Mr. Logan?"

For an instant, Logan glared at him, then slowed his march and veered toward him. "Detective."

"I heard maybe a ruling was coming down on Karl Dahl."

Logan glanced away and frowned. His tie was jerked loose at the throat, collar undone. He pushed his coat open and jammed his hands at his waist.

"She didn't dismiss the case," he said.

"There was a chance of that?"

"Look, Stan, you and I both know Dahl butchered that family, but we don't have a hell of a lot to prove it. His lawyer has to move to dismiss—that's his job."

"What about Dahl's record?"

Logan shook his head. He was clearly pissed off. "Judge Moore seems to think it's inflammatory and prejudicial."

"Being on trial for a triple murder isn't?" Stan said. "A lot of folks figure if he's sitting in that chair, he must be guilty."

"It's a game, Stan," Logan said bitterly. "It's not about right or wrong. It's about rules and fairness, and making sure no one has the common sense to form an opinion."

"Can you appeal?"

Logan shrugged, impatient. "We'll see. Look, Stan, I've got to go," he said, reaching out with one big hand to pat Dempsey's shoulder. "Hang in there. We'll get the son of a bitch."

Dempsey watched him go, feeling defeated. He looked back down the hall toward Judge Moore's chambers. He wanted to go in there and talk to her. He thought he would tell her in great detail the things he had seen, and the terrible waves of emotion that bombarded him all day, every day, and all night, every night.

He could see her sitting behind her desk, looking cool and calm, the desk acting as a buffer between them. He would politely introduce himself (because he never expected anyone to remember him). He would tell her how disappointed he was in her ruling.

But then he saw himself exploding, raging, storming behind the desk. Eyes huge with shock, she bolted, tripping as she scrambled to get out of her chair and run.

He trapped her in the corner, her back against a cabinet, and screamed in her face.

He wanted her to feel the kind of terror Marlene Haas must have felt that day when Karl Dahl had come into her home and tortured her and her two children over the course of several hours before he had butchered her.

Rage built and built inside him like a fire, searing his organs, melting the edges of his brain. He felt huge and violent and monstrous inside. He saw himself wrapping his stubby hands around her beautiful white throat, choking her, shaking her.

But no one passing by Stan Dempsey saw anything but a bony man, with a heavily lined, expressionless face, loitering at the end of the hall.

He cleared the images from his mind and left the building to have a cigarette.

3

6:27 P.M.

I'm a coward, Carey Moore thought, staring at the clock on her desk. Not for the ruling she had made but for hiding from it.

After Logan and Scott had left her office, she had instructed her clerk to tell all callers she had gone for the day. She didn't have the energy to deal with reporters, and even though it was Friday afternoon, she knew they would be lying in wait. The case of *The State v. Karl Dahl* was too big a story to blow off for an early weekend.

She wanted to close her eyes and, when she opened them again, magically be home with her daughter. They would cook dinner together and have a "girls' night in" evening of manicures and storybook reading.

David had left a message that he had a

dinner meeting with a potential backer for a documentary comparing the gangsters who had run amok in the Twin Cities area in the thirties and the gangs that ran the streets in the new millennium. Once upon a time Carey would have been disappointed to lose him for an evening. These days it was a relief to have him gone.

All day, she carried the weight of her work on her shoulders, the Dahl case being the heaviest thing she had ever been called on to handle. And every evening David was home, the tension of their relationship made Carey feel as if she were living in a highly pressurized chamber and that the pressure was such that everything inside her wanted to collapse. There was no downtime, no release.

Over the decade of their marriage, their once-good ability to communicate had slowly eroded away. Neither of them was happy now, and neither of them wanted to talk about it. They both hid in their work, and only truly came together for their daughter, Lucy, who was five and oblivious to the tension between them.

Carey walked around her office, arms crossed, and looked out the window at the city below. Traffic still clogged the streets of downtown Minneapolis. Headlights and taillights glowing. The occasional honk of a horn.

If this had been New York, the horns would have been blaring in a cacophony of sound, but even with constant growth and an influx of people from other parts of the country and other parts of the world, this was still the Midwest, and manners and courtesy were still important.

There was an order to things here, and a logic to that order. Stability. Life made sense. Which made something like the Haas murders all the more horrific. No one could make sense of such brutality. Random acts of violence undermined the foundation of what Minnesotans believed about their society.

The office door opened and Chris Logan filled the space, looking like an avenging angel.

Carey stared at him, her outer calm belying the jolt of unpleasant surprise that shot through her. "You've just dispelled my theory that Minnesotans are still polite and mannerly."

"Everyone's gone," Logan said, as if the

lack of a monitor in the outer office excused his behavior.

"I'm just leaving myself," she said, opening the closet where she had hung her coat.

"I can't believe you're doing this, Carey."

"You shouldn't be here, Chris," she said firmly. "I'm not having an ex parte discussion with you about this case. If you leave now, I won't report you to the disciplinary committee."

"Don't try to throw your weight around with me," Logan snapped. "That so pisses me off, and you know it."

"I don't have to *try*," she pointed out. "I'm a judge, and you're a prosecutor with a case before me. It's improper for you to come in here and question my decisions."

"I've already questioned them outside on the courthouse steps."

"I'm sure you have. You wore your good suit. The rumpled hair and the tie askew are a nice touch. You'll probably get marriage proposals called in to the television stations after they run the piece on the news."

"Don't play that card with me, Carey," he warned. "This isn't about politics. This is about what's right."

"A fair trial is right."

"Putting away the sick son of a bitch who killed that family is right."

"Yes," Carey agreed. "That's your job. Make the case good enough to stick. If you really think the outcome of this trial hangs in the balance of this one issue, then I'm inclined to agree with Kenny Scott—you barely have enough to sustain the indictment."

"You want me to make my prima facie case right here, right now?" Logan challenged. Anger slashed red along his cheekbones. It was never difficult to read him. If the glare in his eyes didn't give him away, his pale Irish complexion did.

"No," Carey said. "I'm just warning you, Chris. If you rush this before a jury to soothe the public outcry, and you lose—"

"I have enough to convict him."

"Then why are you here?" she demanded. "Would you barge into Judge Olson's chambers? Or Judge Denholm's? No. You're here because you think you should have special privileges, that I should knuckle under and bend to your will because we used to be colleagues and because I'm a woman. If I were a man—"

"I never would have slept with you." Logan completed the sentence.

Carey stepped back as if he'd slapped her. He might as well have. During the years they had worked together, there had always been something between them, an attraction both had felt but neither had acted on, with the exception of one night.

They had been putting in long hours, preparing for a trial—her last before her appointment to the bench, as it had happened. Carey had been drained of energy from fighting with David about her long hours, about her lack of support for his career.

With David every issue was turned around until it was about him. Her career was interfering with his spotlight. Never mind that when he was working on a project she sometimes didn't see him at all for weeks at a time, and it was only on a rare occasion that he included her in any part of the process. It never failed that when she needed his support—as she had on that last case—he was never there for her.

But there Chris Logan had been, understanding and sharing the pressure of the upcoming trial, strong and passionate. . . .

"You'll leave this office now," she said, her voice hard and tight with emotion. "Or I'll call a deputy and you can deal with the consequences."

She went to the door and yanked it open, stared at Logan with eyes as fierce as his.

He looked away and down. "Carey, I'm sorry. I shouldn't have said that."

"No, you shouldn't have. And you will *never* say it again."

"No. I'm sorry," he backpedaled. "It's this case. It's just getting to me," he said, shaking his head, raking a hand back through his thick hair.

"Don't try to give me an excuse," Carey snapped. "There is no excuse. You're pissed off and you're trying to undermine my authority, and I won't stand for it. If you come within a yard of that line again, I'll have you removed from this case, and think about what that would do for your public image. Get out."

He didn't look at her. She wanted to think he was too embarrassed by his own behavior, but that probably wasn't the case. He was regrouping, switching tracks to a wiser course of action. Logan's passion for his work was a thing to behold in the courtroom. Defense attorneys of no small caliber were routinely blown out of the water and crushed. But he had never learned to completely control it when he needed to, and so his strongest asset was also his Achilles' heel.

"You've seen the crime scene photographs," he said quietly. "You know what was done to that woman, to those two little kids, foster kids. They didn't even belong there, really. It was just the luck of the draw that they ended up at that house.

"I look at those photos every day. Can't get them out of my head. I dream about them at night. I've never had a case affect me the way this one has."

"Then you should stop looking at the pictures," Carey said, despite what she had been thinking about the photographs herself. "There's no point in it. You can't make a trial be about your own personal obsession, Chris. You'll lose your perspective; you'll make mistakes. Like this one. Go. Now."

He sighed and nodded, then met her gaze with genuine apology in his eyes. "I am sorry."

Carey said nothing. He turned and walked

out, shoving his hands in his pants pockets, the wide shoulders slumping a bit. If this had been a movie, she would have run after him and forgiven him, and they would have ended up in each other's arms in a mad embrace. But it wasn't a movie; this was the real world. She had a job to do, she had a husband, she had a child. She couldn't have Chris Logan, and she knew better than to want him.

What she really wanted was someone strong to hold her, support her, shelter her. But she didn't have that. As lonely as it was, she'd learned a long time ago to handle her battles and her insecurities on her own.

Carey put her coat on, slung her purse over one shoulder, and picked up the large old leather briefcase her father had carried when he had sat on the bench as a judge in this same building. She wished she could have gone to him for advice, as she had for most of her life. But Alzheimer's had stolen her father away from her in the last few years. He no longer recognized her, and so all she had of him were things, his gavel, his briefcase, photographs, and memories.

Feeling hollow and beaten, she left the office. The press would still be waiting outside, hoping in vain that she would come out the main doors.

Instead, she took the skyway across the street to the garage where she parked her car. Afraid to lose the impressive background shot of the Hennepin County Government Center, none of the television people had decamped to find her elsewhere. She braced herself for confrontation with a newspaper reporter, but the skyway was empty, and most of the cars were gone from the level where Carey had parked.

She would have to consider a uniformed escort now that the news of her ruling had broken. And she felt even more of a coward for thinking it, because she pictured herself hiding behind a deputy, trying to avoid the fallout of her own decision.

Lost in her thoughts, she fumbled to dig her keys out of her purse, while her Palm Pilot and a lipstick tumbled out. She sighed heavily, set down the briefcase, and bent awkwardly to scoop up the things she had dropped.

As she began to straighten, something hit her hard across the back, stunning her, knocking her breath from her. A second blow sent her sprawling forward.

The rough concrete tore at the palms of her hands. Her knees hit the surface like a pair of hammerheads. She tried to draw breath to scream, but couldn't. Her purse flew out ahead of her, its contents spewing out, skidding and rolling.

Her assailant swung at her again, just missing her head as Carey shoved herself to the right, one hand outstretched to try to snag her keys. Some kind of club. She couldn't really see it, was just aware of the sound as it struck the concrete. Her assailant cursed.

"You fucking bitch! You fucking cunt!" Not shouting, but a harsh, hoarse, rasping sound full of venom.

He fell on her, bouncing her head into the floor like a basketball. Did he mean to kill her? Rape her?

Carey flailed at the car keys, breaking a nail, scraping her fingers, catching hold.

Her attacker grabbed her by the hair, yanked her head back.

Did he have a knife? Would he slit her throat?

She fumbled with the key to her BMW, frantically pushing the buttons. The car's alarm screamed, and the lights began to flash.

The voice behind her swore again. He slammed her head down. What little breath she had regained huffed out of her as he kicked her hard in the side.

Then everything went terrifyingly black.

4

Sam Kovac stood in front of the mirror in the john down the hall from the Criminal Investigative Division offices, his shirt half-off. He needed to go to the gym, except that he hadn't been in a gym since he'd been in a uniform. A long damn time ago.

Now that he was on the downhill side of forty, he was beginning to wonder if he shouldn't do something about that. But the notion of sweating and making a fool of himself in front of the young hot bods that populated health clubs, an obvious and pathetic display of midlife crisis, was enough to make him leave his jockstrap in the drawer. Nor was he interested in hanging out in the weight room with the muscle-heads who wore the Minneapolis PD uniform, the guys who reeked of testosterone and couldn't buy shirts off the rack. Bunch of freaks. Probably most of them were trying to overcompensate for small dicks, or homosexual tendencies, or the fact that they used to get the snot pounded out of them for their lunch money every day when they were kids.

Kovac assessed himself with a critical eye. He looked like an old tomcat that had taken his share of licks in alley fights and had dished out plenty of his own. A scar here, a scar there, a cranky expression, a twice-broken, high-bridged nose. His hair was equal parts brown and gray and had a tendency to stand up. Partly from his Slovak heritage and partly because he never paid more than ten bucks for a haircut.

But overall, he didn't think he looked that bad. No beer gut. No hair sprouting out his ears. Women had never run screaming at the sight of him. At least none that weren't wanted for something.

At his last department-mandated physical, the doctor had preached at him that it wasn't too late to reverse the damage he had done to himself smoking and drinking and living on a steady diet of sodium, fat, and job stress. Kovac had told the doctor if he had to give up all that, he might as well eat his gun, because he wouldn't have anything left to live for.

The men's room door swung in and Nikki Liska stepped inside.

"Jesus, the least you could do is go into a stall," she said.

Kovac scowled at her. "Very funny. What the hell are you doing in here? This is the men's room, for Christ's sake!"

"So where are they?" Liska challenged, crossing her arms over her chest. "The least I could get out of this is a sneak peek at a little throbbing manhood."

Kovac felt his cheeks heat. Liska had been his partner for enough years that he should have been immune to her mouth, but she never ceased to outdo herself. Her personality was her loudest, largest feature. The rest of her was five-five with big blue eyes and a white-blond pixie haircut. To the unsuspecting, she looked sweet and perky. But the last guy to call her that had gone home from the party with a limp.

Her eyes narrowed. "I don't believe it."

"Don't make a big deal," Kovac warned.

"You, Sam Kovac, are an optimist."

"No, I'm not."

"Yes, you are."

"I'm a pragmatist."

"You're full of shit," Liska said, marching into the room. She walked right up to him and smacked him on the arm. "The patch!"

"Ouch!"

"Don't be such a baby."

She admired the fresh nicotine patch affixed to his upper arm. Kovac pulled his shirt back on and started doing the buttons, grumbling under his breath.

Liska leaned back against the counter. "I thought you told the doctor to take a hike."

"I told him I have shoes older than he is," Kovac groused. "It's got nothing to do with him. You know I try to quit once a year. It's an annual event. It's like a holiday."

He had only tried quitting more times than he could count. It never lasted more than a few weeks, a month at the outside. Something always happened that made him think he should just enjoy himself, because in any given moment he could become a statistic. He was a homicide cop. A sunny outlook didn't come with the job.

"Nothing to do with Tim Metzger having a heart attack last week," Liska said.

Kovac didn't answer her. He focused on

tying his tie. It was hard enough to face mortality on his own terms. If he had to share his feelings with Liska—or anyone else—he would sooner have thrown himself in front of a bus.

Liska looked up at him, speculating. "Are you seeing someone and not spilling all the details to me?"

Scowling, Kovac straightened the knot in his tie and snugged it up against his collar. "Did you come in here for some other reason than trying to see a dick?"

"We're up," she said.

"That's what I get for hanging around to do my paperwork. What is it?"

"Assault," she said. "In the government center parking ramp. Get this. Our vic is none other than the Honorable Judge Moore."

"Moore?" Kovac said with disgust. "Can't we just leave her for dead?"

5

Friday night in the Hennepin County Medical Center ER could resemble a violent punk rock Halloween party, but the evening was young. The ghouls and gangbangers were still home, primping their nose rings and polishing their tattoos.

"Sam Kovac! Fuck me sideways!"

"He can do that?" Liska asked. "A man of hidden talents, our Sam."

Kathleen Casey, trauma nurse and ER pit bull, waved a hand in dismissal as she marched up to them. "The hell if I know. But I'd rather find out than deal with these people."

She rolled her eyes toward the waiting area, where reporters and camera crews were perched on the furniture like a flock of vultures. "God save us from the media. Give me your average street scum any night."

As if on cue, several of them spotted Kovac and started toward him.

"Kovac!"

"Detective!"

"Do you have any leads—"

"Do you know what prompted the attack—"

"Did this have anything to do with the ruling on the Dahl case?"

The usual cacophony. Rapid-fire questions they knew damn well he wouldn't answer. Kovac held up a hand to ward them off. "No comment."

Casey took an aggressive step toward them and shooed them with her hands. "Back to the chairs with you before I break out my Taser."

Casey had been through the wars. Kovac called her the Iron Leprechaun. Five feet nothing, with a hedge of maroon hair and a sweet-Irish-mother kind of a face that drew people to her so they could confide in her, then implode in some spectacular way.

Kovac had known her forever. She was a longtime veteran of HCMC, with a brief stint at a small-town ER in the Minnesota hinterland, also known by Kovac as Outer Mongolia. He tried never to venture south of the airport, east of the river, west of the 494 freeway, or north of downtown.

"So what's the story with our vic?" he asked as they started down a side hall at a quick clip.

"Resident Pain-in-the-Ass will want to fill you in ad nauseam," she said. "Quick and dirty: Someone beat the ever-living-crap out of her."

"Sexual assault?" Liska asked.

"No."

"She's conscious?"

"Yes, but she hasn't had a lot to say."

"I wish we could have said that earlier in the day," Kovac muttered.

They had all heard about Judge Moore's ruling on Karl Dahl's past criminal record. Carey Moore had been a kick-ass prosecutor, but on the bench she had earned the motto "Moore is less," giving perps a benefit of the doubt no cop in town believed they deserved, and they felt betrayed because of it.

The resident making notes in Judge Moore's chart looked like she had probably been the president of the science club in high school—last year. Drowning in her lab coat, stringy brown hair scraped back into a ponytail, and black plastic rectangular glasses.

Liska shoved a badge in her face and got aggressive. "So? Spill it, sweetie. I want to get home before menopause sets in."

It was always fun to set young doctors back on their heels before their egos could metastasize and take over their humanity.

This one used a lot of fifty-dollar words to explain that their victim had a mild concussion, a couple of cracked ribs, and a lot of nasty bruises and abrasions.

The uniformed cop who had answered the initial 911 call had filled in Kovac and Liska on the details of the assault as they had walked the crime scene. Moore had been on her way to her car in the parking ramp adjacent to the government center. The assailant had hit her from behind, knocked her down, smacked her around. Apparent motive: robbery. If anything more had been on the agenda, there hadn't been time. Moore's car alarm had gone off, and the mutt had run away with her wallet.

Kovac looked over the top of the doctor's head and into the examination room. Carey

Moore was propped up on a hospital bed, looking like she'd gone five rounds with one big, badass dude. The bruises hadn't turned blue yet, but Kovac had seen more than enough victims of beatings to read the damage and predict what would greet the vic in the mirror the next morning. There was a contusion on her forehead crowning a lump the size of a golf ball. One eye, the flesh around it already swollen, was going to turn black.

A short line of stitches crawled over her swollen lower lip like a black ant. She had a cell phone pressed to one ear. Alerting the scavengers out in the waiting room, or complaining to the mayor how people weren't safe on the streets, no thanks to her.

He moved past the doctor without acknowledging her, walked up to Judge Moore, took the phone out of her hand, and clicked it off.

"What do you think you're doing?" she demanded.

"I'll need your undivided attention, Judge Moore. That is, if you want your assailant caught and prosecuted to the full extent of the law. You might care about that more now than you did a couple of hours ago."

She snatched the phone back from him and turned it on, never taking her glare off his face. "I was on the line with my nanny, letting her know I'm going to be late and not to let my daughter see any news on television. I don't want her to find out from strangers that her mother has been attacked.

"I don't care what you need, Detective Kovac," she said. "You aren't more important than my child."

Kovac arched a brow and took a step back. So much for her weakened physical state. She looked like a tigress ready to tear his throat out. "My mistake."

"Yes, it is."

She looked down then, touched a hand to her forehead, and winced as her fingers brushed against the angry red abrasion. Flesh v. Concrete.

"I'm sorry, Anka. We got cut off. Please get Lucy in her pajamas and put a movie on for her." She was silent for a moment, listening to the nanny. "Yes, all right. Put her on. . . . Hi, sweet pea," she said softly, tears welling in her eyes.

Kovac turned a little away from her in

order to look like he wasn't eavesdropping, even though he was.

"No, honey, I won't be home before you go to bed. I'm sorry. . . . I know I promised, but I had an accident and fell down, and I'm at the doctor now. . . ."

She closed her eyes, and a couple of tears squeezed out from between her lashes. "No, honey, I don't know what time Daddy will get home. . . . Why don't you have a slumber party with Anka?"

She touched a knuckle beneath the blackening eye to discreetly wipe away the tears.

Kovac scowled and turned away completely. He didn't want to feel sorry for Carey Moore. She was no friend to him, certainly no friend to Stan Dempsey, who would never be right again after working the Haas murders. He couldn't even imagine what Wayne Haas and his son were feeling after hearing about the judge's ruling against the prosecution. The last thing Kovac wanted was to feel sorry for her.

"I'll see you in the morning, sweetheart. . . . I love you more. . . ." Her voice strained, she said good night and ended the call.

Kovac waited. Liska joined him.

"Did you make her cry?" she whispered, accusatory.

"I didn't do anything!"

"And you wonder why you're single."

"I know why I'm single," he grumbled. "And I know why I'm going to stay that way."

"Let's get this over with." Judge Moore had her voice and her composure back.

Kovac shrugged. Liska gave him a look of womanly disgust and pushed past him.

"Judge Moore, I'm Detective Liska—"

"I know who you are," the judge said. "Can we cut to the chase, Detective? I want to go home."

The resident piped up then. "No, I'm sorry, Judge Moore. You have a concussion. We'll need to admit you overnight for observation."

Carey Moore raised her chin and gave the young doctor a glimpse of the steely look she had leveled at many a difficult witness in her days as a prosecutor. "I'm going home to my daughter. I'll sign a release. Why don't you get that process started?"

The science club president looked like she didn't know whether she should be offended or afraid. She disappeared into the hall.

"You might want to reconsider that, Judge Moore," Liska said. "Someone attacked you."

"I was mugged. It's over."

"With all due respect, you don't know that."

Kovac watched her set her jaw as best she could, considering the split lip. She wanted to believe what she wanted to believe.

"You managed to piss off a lot of people today, Judge," he said. "Maybe someone decided they needed to express themselves in person."

"He stole my wallet."

"Bonus."

"He?" Liska said. "Did you see him?"

"No. He was behind me. The voice was male."

"Young, old? Black, white?"

"Angry. That's what I remember. Angry. Full of rage."

"What did he say?"

"'You fucking bitch. You fucking cunt,'" the judge said without emotion.

"Did he use your name?" Kovac asked.

"No."

"You didn't recognize the voice."

"No. Of course not."

"So, he knocked you down, grabbed your purse. That was it?" Kovac said, knowing that that wasn't so.

She closed her eyes briefly, started to sigh, winced again, and tried to cover that up. Tough cookie, he thought. The mutt had done a number on her. She had to be in a considerable amount of pain, and he knew from experience docs didn't dole out the good narcotics to people with concussions. They had probably given her some Tylenol. Big deal. Like putting a Band-Aid on a shark bite. She had to have one mother of a headache.

"I was going to my car—"

"Did you see anyone in the parking ramp?" Kovac asked.

"No."

"In the skyway?"

"No. I went to pull my keys out of my purse—"

"You should have had them out before you left the government center."

She flicked an annoyed look at him. "I dropped my Palm Pilot, bent to pick it up, he hit me from behind, hard across the back, with some kind of club. He kept hitting me, cursing me. I was trying to grab my car keys."

"Where was your wallet?"

"I dropped my purse when he knocked me down. Everything spilled out of it."

Kovac and Liska exchanged a glance.

"And he was calling you names, hitting you?" Liska said.

"Yes."

"'You fucking bitch, you fucking cunt,'" Kovac said.

"Yes."

"And when did he go for your wallet?"

"I don't know. I hit the alarm on my car key. He slammed my head down. I lost consciousness."

"He took your wallet as he left," Kovac said.

"I guess."

Then the wallet hadn't been his first objective. Purse snatchers snatched purses. Muggers hit and ran. This guy had been focused on his victim, personalized the attack by calling her names, prolonged the attack, grabbed the wallet as an afterthought as he took off.

"He knocked you down from behind and he kept hitting you?" Kovac said. "Where was he? Standing over you?"

"No. Closer. I remember he grabbed my hair and yanked my head back. I felt his weight on me."

"So he was on his knees? Maybe straddling you?"

She knew where he was going, and she didn't want to hear it. Carey Moore had prosecuted more than her share of violent crimes—assaults, rapes, murders. She didn't want to admit that someone might have tried to rape her, kill her.

"Was your driver's license in your wallet?" Liska asked.

"Yes."

"Is the address on the license your home address?"

"No. I've known better than that for a long time, Detective."

"Was there anything in your purse that might have had your home address on it?"

She didn't answer for a moment, staring down at her hands, which had been scraped badly on the concrete. Several fingernails were broken and jagged.

"No. I don't think so," she said at last, the

strength in her voice draining away. "I'm very tired. I want to go home. I didn't see the man who attacked me. I can't tell you anything that will be of any use to you. Can we wrap this up?"

"Did you have anything with you besides your purse?" Liska asked.

"My briefcase. Did someone pick it up? I have work to do over the weekend."

"No one at the scene said anything about a briefcase," Kovac said. "They have your purse and the stuff that came out of it. What was in the briefcase?"

He could see a little panic creeping in around the edges of her composure. "Briefs, reports, letters regarding sentencing recommendations."

"Something every mugger would want," Kovac commented with sarcasm.

Carey Moore ignored him. "The briefcase was my father's. It's important to me."

"Any paper in it regarding *The State v. Karl Dahl*?"

She refused to look at him, pissed off because he was proving her wrong in her assumption the attack was random. He couldn't really blame her. Nobody wanted to think of themselves as a specific target of violence.

"Yes."

"We'll also need to know what other cases you've presided over in the recent past," Liska said. "Who might have a grudge. Who's up for a stiff sentence. Cons you sent up who've been recently released. Anything."

"Yes," said the judge in a voice that was barely a whisper. The adrenaline had burned off, and she was headed for the lowest of lows, Kovac knew. He'd seen it a thousand times. He'd been a victim of it himself once or twice.

"Can your husband come and get you, Judge Moore?" Liska asked. "You can't drive yourself."

"I'll call a car service."

"You don't seem in any shape to go anywhere," Kovac said, wondering where the hell this husband was. His wife had been assaulted. There was a better-than-even chance that the attack could have been an attempt on her life. "He's out of town, your husband?"

"He's at a business dinner. I can manage."

"Does he know you're here? Have you called him?"

"He's at dinner. He turned his phone off."

The jaw was tightening again. She didn't want to talk about the absent husband. She would rather scrape herself out of a hospital bed, deal with a concussion, some cracked ribs, and an emotional trauma by herself, than try to find the one person who should have made it to the hospital before Kovac and Liska had.

"Where's the dinner?" Kovac asked. "If you're going home, you need someone to be there with you. We can call the restaurant, or send a couple of uniforms to tell him."

"I don't know where the dinner is," she said curtly. "There's no need to interrupt him. My nanny lives in."

Kovac glanced at Liska and raised an eyebrow.

"I'll drive you home, Judge Moore," he said. "As soon as you've signed your way out of here."

"That isn't necessary."

"Well, I believe that it is, and that's what's going to happen," he said flatly. "You're a target, and you're smart enough to know it.

I'll take you home, see that your house is secure."

Carey Moore said nothing, her gaze fixed stubbornly on her hands. Kovac took her silence as acquiescence.

"Good to know you haven't lost all your common sense," he grumbled.

"We can't say the same thing about you, Detective, or you wouldn't be treating me like this," she said.

Kovac sniffed. "Like what? I'm not treating you any differently than I treat anyone."

"I guess that explains your lack of advancement in the department."

"Maybe," he admitted. "But unlike some people, my career isn't about ambition. It's about catching bad guys."

6

Liska distracted the press in the waiting room with a brief statement and a lot of "No comment" and "I can't speak to that at this point in the investigation."

Kovac rolled Carey Moore in a wheelchair through a warren of halls to a little-used side exit, where an orderly had brought Kovac's car around. The judge had nothing to say as he helped her into the passenger seat and drove out onto the city streets.

"Where do you live?" he asked.

She gave the address in the same short, clipped tone she might use with an anonymous cabdriver. Her home was a short distance and a world away from downtown Minneapolis, in an area of large, stately houses overlooking Lake of the Isles. He had ten minutes—fifteen tops—to get something useful out of her.

"You'll have one hell of a headache tomorrow," he said.

She stared straight ahead. "I have a hell of a headache right now."

"You don't think that the attack seemed personal?"

"By definition, a physical assault is personal, wouldn't you say?"

"You know what I mean. Leave the lawyer bullshit on the side, Judge. You've been in the system long enough to know better."

"Oh? You don't believe lawyers are too obtuse and egomaniacal to pick up on the fact that not all cops are mentally challenged?"

Kovac shot a glance at her. Every time they passed a streetlight, the harsh white light swept over her face, pale as a ghost.

"I think there wasn't enough time between news of my ruling and my departure from the building for a disgruntled citizen to formulate a plan to kill me," she said.

"Never underestimate the capabilities of a really determined scumbag."

"I'll stitch that on a sampler while I'm recuperating over the weekend."

"People knew you were going to rule on Dahl's past record today. Maybe someone anticipated the worst. I know I did."

"So where were you between six-thirty and seven, Detective Kovac?"

"Doing a bunch of bullshit paperwork on an assault case you'll probably dismiss next week."

"I will if you haven't done your job properly," she said.

"Are you saying Stan Dempsey didn't dot all his i's and cross all his t's on the Haas murders?"

"I'm saying my job is more complicated than you choose to believe. I don't make rulings based on whim. Being a judge is not being a rubber stamp for the police department or for the county attorney's office. I don't have the luxury of bias anymore."

Her temper was bubbling just under the surface. He could hear it in her voice. He'd been in the courtroom to testify when she had been a prosecutor. Cool, controlled, but with a sharp edge and an aggressive streak beneath the veneer of calm, she had been fun to watch. Exciting, even. And the fact that she was attractive hadn't hurt anything, either.

She had known how to use her looks, too, in a way that was subtle, and classy. Many a man in the witness box had fallen for the trap and come away from the experience mentally eviscerated without even quite realizing how it had happened.

"You think I'm not appalled by the murder of Marlene Haas and those two children?" she said. "You think I don't see those crime scene photos in my sleep? Those children mutilated and hanging by their necks like broken dolls? You think I don't want their killer to pay? To pay more than this state's justice system can dole out?"

There were tears in her voice now. She was wrung out, her ability to keep emotions at bay worn away in the aftermath of being attacked.

Kovac pushed at her limits. "Then why don't you have the guts to do something about it?"

"I should make rulings in favor of the prosecution so they can be immediately overturned on appeal?"

"The buck has to stop somewhere."

"It does. It stops with me. I want convictions to stand up on their own, not lean against personal prejudices, not be open to debate or attack."

"So you let defense attorneys just have their way? You let these dirtbag rapists and killers have more rights than the people whose lives they've ruined?" Kovac said, his own temper rising.

"I do my job," she snapped. "I'm going to be sick."

"Me too."

"No. I'm going to be sick. Now."

Kovac glanced over at her. She was leaning forward and breathing too quickly. "Oh! Jesus!"

He swerved the car to the curb and hit the brakes too hard. Carey Moore pushed the door open, turned, and fell out onto the pavement, retching.

Christ, Kovac thought as he shoved the car into park and bolted out the driver's door, this was all he needed, to be responsible for further injuring a judge. That could go on his record right above insubordination.

She was on her hands and knees, half in the gutter, half on the sidewalk, heaving. Kovac knelt down beside her, not sure if he should touch her.

"Are you all right?" he asked stupidly.

In a stronger moment she would have decapitated him for being an asshole. Now she simply drew herself into a ball, shaking, and, he thought, maybe crying. He began to wish he'd stayed behind with the press and let Liska drive her home. He barely knew how to handle women when they weren't crying.

Fumbling, he dug a handkerchief out of his hip pocket and held it out to her. He put his other hand on her shoulder.

"It's clean," he said. "Let me help you up."

The judge took a blind swing at him. "Leave me alone!"

She took a couple of shaky breaths and pushed herself up, sitting back against her heels. "Just take me home and leave me the hell alone!"

A little way down the street, a couple of hookers stood outside a tattoo parlor, smoking Christ knew what and staring. The tall one in red took a couple of steps toward them.

"Honey? You need a cop?"

Kovac scowled. "I'm a cop."

"I wasn't axing you." She took a couple of steps closer. NBA tall, with an Adam's apple the size of a fist. Transvestite. "I'm axing the lady."

Carey Moore held up a hand. "I'm fine. Thank you. He's fine. He's driving me home."

"Looks like he's been driving you with a golf club, sugar."

"She was mugged," Kovac said.

The transvestite sniffed in disbelief. Kovac dug out his badge and held it out. "You want to get in the car too? I can give you a ride to Booking."

"For what? Standing up?"

"For pissing me off."

"Kovac, shut up," the judge snapped. "I want to go home."

The transvestite went back to the tattoo parlor as Kovac helped Carey Moore to her feet. As wobbly as a newborn fawn, she tried to steady herself with a hand on the roof of the car, but started to fall again as her knees gave way.

Kovac caught her against him. "Easy. You should have stayed in the hospital. I'm taking you back."

"You're taking me home," she said stubbornly. "I can vomit without a medical professional supervising."

"You're dizzy."

"I have a concussion. Of course I'm dizzy."

Kovac helped her ease back down into the passenger's seat and squatted down in front of her so he could see her face in the glow of the streetlight and the neon in the window of the pawnshop behind him. She looked like she might have been an extra in *Dawn of the Dead,* but there was still a glint of determination in her eyes.

"You're a hell of a tough cookie, Judge. I'll say that for you. But that's not always the smartest thing to be."

"Just take me home," she said. "You can come back and visit your girlfriend later."

Kovac recognized the glow two blocks before they came onto the source. The brilliant white lights the television news people used to create the impression that the sun had crashed to earth.

"Oh, fuck this," he growled as the vans came into view. It wasn't going to matter a damn whether the perp had gotten Carey Moore's address out of her wallet or her briefcase. He could get it now, sitting at home in his underwear, watching the god-damn news. "They double-teamed us."

He glanced over at the judge. She looked as stunned as she had probably looked when she got hit from behind in that parking ramp.

"Looks like one of your neighbors ratted you out," Kovac said, just to be cranky. The truth of it was, it isn't all that hard to find people. *The State v. Karl Dahl* was a huge case that had garnered national attention. Newspeople could have been trailing Carey Moore since the day the trial was assigned to her. Anyone could have.

A couple of police cruisers were parked cockeyed in the street, the uniforms trying to keep the newsies corralled in a manage-able space, a job about as easy as herding cats.

"Oh, my God. This is my home," the judge said, mostly to herself.

"All's fair in the news business," Kovac said. "These people would plant themselves in the devil's asshole if they thought they could get a jump on the competition."

"I don't want them here."

"Yeah, well, good luck with that. Is there a back way in? An alley?"

"No."

"Duck down before they see you," Kovac said. He turned the wheel and glided the car in along the curb, running his window down.

"Hey!" he shouted at a reporter and a cameraman who had snagged a prime spot in the judge's driveway with a wedge of the house as a backdrop. "Get the fuck out of the driveway! You're on private property!"

He turned to Carey Moore and lowered his voice. "Let's hope they were rolling live. Their producers flip out if someone uses the F word."

Kovac put on his game face, got out of the car, and approached the news crew, holding up his badge. "Pack up your toys and get out in the street with the rest of your kind."

He recognized the reporter, a perky blonde with too much blush. Mindy. Mandy. Cindy. She stuck a microphone at him. "Detective, Candy Cross, Channel Three News. What can you tell us about Judge Moore's condition?"

"Nothing. Pack it up and get out of the way."

"We're here to speak with Judge Moore—"

"I don't care if you're here for the Second

Coming, princess," Kovac said. "You're on private property, and I can have you removed and charged for that. How would you like your pals out there to roll that film at ten?"

The mob was now moving toward them, handheld lights bobbing up and down, red lights glowing on cameras. They sounded like a pack of dogs at dinnertime, all barking at once, each trying to drown out the others.

"Move it or lose it," Kovac said, starting back toward the car. "I'm driving up to this garage, and I don't care if your shit's in the way."

The second team, Kovac thought as his gaze scanned over the herd. The stations had sent their first teams to the hospital at the news of Carey Moore's attack. The second teams had ended up here.

He held up a hand to ward them off. "I got nothing to say. Lieutenant Dawes will have a statement for you tomorrow."

They went back to shouting questions as if he hadn't spoken at all. Kovac shook his head and went to the nearest pair of uniforms.

"Get them off this property," he instructed. "They can go to the other side of the street. I've got Judge Moore, and if I see one flashbulb go off in her face as we go into this house, I'm gonna shoot somebody. Got it?"

"They don't use flashbulbs anymore," the younger officer said as if that would change everything.

Kovac glowered at him. "Are you brain damaged?" He turned to the older partner. "Is he brain damaged?"

The partner shrugged. "Maybe."

Kovac shook his head. "Just get them out of here."

"Will do, Detective."

As he turned toward his car, Kovac saw no sign of Judge Moore, and had a second's flash of panic. Then he realized she had slid way down in the seat and covered herself with her coat.

"Stay right there," he murmured as he slipped into the driver's seat. "They'll be out of the way in a minute."

Carey Moore said nothing. Kovac took a peek under the coat to make sure she hadn't expired. She hadn't, but she looked like she might welcome death soon. Her skin was gray, her face pasty with sweat. She looked like she was maybe going to be sick again.

"Hang in there," Kovac said, his eyes on the reluctant migration of the media. As he waited for the reporters to retreat, he took a moment to check out the judge's digs.

Her home was a well-lit, impressive red-brick colonial with a couple of white columns flanking the front door. Kovac figured his whole house and garage combined was maybe half the size. The shrubbery was clipped, the leaves had been raked, a trio of uncarved pumpkins sat beside the glossy black front door. A tasteful wrought-iron gate kept the riffraff from going up the walk.

It was the kind of place where a person would want to go in and expect to feel warm and welcome. Kovac would go home to a dark, square box that needed paint.

He put the car in gear, pulled up into the driveway at an angle to minimize the view of the passenger's side. He went around to open the door and helped Carey Moore out of the car, keeping her coat pulled up high around her face. With an arm around her shoulders to support her, he shielded her as they went through the side gate and up to the front door.

As they stepped up onto the stoop, the judge rang the doorbell and leaned against the sidelight, peering into the house.

"Where are your keys?"

"I don't know," she confessed.

"You had them with you before the attack?"

"In my purse."

"You'll change these locks tomorrow. First thing."

"Yes."

"And you'll have a radio car sitting out front until that happens," he told her. "What else did you lose that you haven't told me about?"

"Nothing," she said, but he knew she was lying. The perp probably had her phone numbers, her mother's maiden name, and half her credit cards. He would get a list of the cards and alert the credit card companies. If the perp was using them, he was leaving an electronic trail.

The door swung open and a gorgeous blond twenty-something in a pink velour tracksuit looked wide-eyed at the judge. She said something in what Kovac figured was Swedish or Norwegian or something else from one of those Scandinavian places where everyone looks like they've been designed by computer as models for the master race.

"Oh, my God, Mrs. Moore!"

"It looks worse than it is," Carey said quietly. "Please don't make a fuss, Anka. Is Lucy asleep?"

"Ya. Just a little while ago," the nanny said.

Kovac helped the judge with her coat, and the nanny took it from him, but she never took her worried eyes off her boss. "But she is worried about you. She didn't want to go to bed. And she made me leave on the light on the side table."

The judge slid down onto an antique carved chair and closed her eyes for a moment. Kovac introduced himself to the nanny, Anka Jorgenson.

"You've been here all evening?" he asked.

"Ya."

"Have there been any strange phone calls? Hang-up calls?"

"No. There was a wrong number," Anka said as an afterthought. "About an hour ago."

"Who did the person ask for?"

"Marlene. I told him there was no such person here."

The judge opened her eyes at that and looked at Kovac. If she could have gotten any paler, she would have.

Marlene, as in Marlene Haas? Kovac thought. The woman Karl Dahl had opened up from throat to groin. He had planted fresh-cut daisies in the gaping wound as if she had been some strange and macabre sculpture in a surrealist gallery. Carey Moore was probably thinking the same thing.

"Was the caller a man or a woman?" Kovac asked.

"A man. He was very polite," the nanny said as if that meant he couldn't have been a bad person. "He apologized for the mistake."

"Has anyone come to the door this evening?"

"No."

"Have you heard any strange noises outside?"

The nanny's eyes filled with tears as she looked back and forth from Kovac to her boss. "Do you think this man who hurt you will come here? Who is Marlene?"

"Just being cautious," Kovac said. "Don't open the door to anyone you don't know. I don't care if they tell you their mother is lying bleeding to death in the street."

"You're scaring me," Anka said, sounding almost angry or resentful.

Kovac nodded. "Good. Does this phone have caller ID?"

"Yes," Anka said. She picked up the handheld off the hall table, scrolled through the caller list, and held it out to Kovac.

"Can you write the number down for me?" he asked. "I'm going to help Judge Moore upstairs."

"I can manage," she said, using the table to help herself to her feet.

Kovac put an arm around her shoulders and guided her toward the staircase. "Stop being such a goddamn pain in the ass. I'm helping you, and that's the end of it. You fall and break your neck on my watch, my head goes on the block."

He wanted to pick her up, toss her over his shoulder, and carry her like a sack of potatoes, but he didn't want to have to explain the complaint that that would bring to his lieutenant.

"Don't even think of saying the word 'coincidence,'" he warned as they slowly went up the stairs. "Marlene isn't that common a name, and even if it was, the odds of someone calling here by mistake and asking for someone with the same name as the victim in a case you're trying have to be astronomical."

She didn't say anything at all, but she stopped in the bathroom at the top of the hall, dropped to her knees in front of the toilet, and vomited again.

Kovac dampened a hand towel and gave it to her. She accepted it in silence and sat there on the floor for several moments with her face buried in it.

"Can I assume you have an unlisted phone number?" Kovac asked, sitting down on the edge of the bathtub.

"Yes, of course."

"We'll need to set up a trap on your line. This won't be the only call you'll get."

"Why do you think that?"

"Because the call came after the attack. If we're talking about the same mutt, then he's in this for more than your wallet."

She didn't look at him. She was staring at nothing, her expression bleak.

"You should lie down," Kovac said, reaching out once again to help her to her feet.

She paid no attention to him and stopped at the door to her daughter's room, which was adorned with a fanciful painted fairy touching a magic wand to a sign that read: "Princess Lucy's Room." Leaning against the doorjamb, she turned the knob carefully and peeked inside. Kovac looked in over her head.

Princess Lucy was sleeping the sleep of the innocent in a bed with pale pink sheets and a confection of white quilts and comforters and bed skirts. Cute kid. Maybe four or five, with a mop of wavy dark hair and a mouth like a rosebud. A small lamp with a ruffled lavender shade glowed softly on a table across from the bed.

Carey Moore watched her daughter sleep for a moment, her cheek pressed to the frame of the door, one hand pressed across her mouth. Kovac imagined she was realizing the decision she had made in her chambers today had ramifications that were rippling out far beyond the government center and beyond herself. Someone had reached out over a phone line and invaded her home, the place she should have felt most safe, the place her daughter should have been safe.

People never had a clue what an illusion their sense of safety was. A security system could be gone with the snip of a wire. A security building with a twenty-four-hour doorman still had a garage with a gate that stayed up long enough for a stranger to drive in behind a resident. A perimeter wall could always be scaled. Every e-mail ever sent could be retrieved with a couple of mouse clicks. One wrong set of eyes glancing at a social security number on a form, and an identity became a commodity for sale. One phone call and a sanctuary became a cage.

Kovac reached around the judge and drew the door closed.

"Let's get you to bed before you fall down," he murmured.

The Moores' master bedroom looked like it belonged in some five-star hotel. Not that Kovac had ever set foot in one. The places he stayed usually had disposable cups, one working lamp, and suspicious stains on the creepy polyester bedspread. He had, however, been known to watch the Travel Channel on occasion.

The room was a cocoon of heavy, expensive fabrics, warm, rich shades of gold and deep red, thick carpet, antiques, and spotlit art. Mementos were clustered on her nightstand—a silver-framed photo of a rosy-cheeked baby; a gold-leafed keepsake box with a top encrusted in tiny, exotic shells and seed pearls; a black-and-white photo of herself in a graduation cap and gown and a tall, handsome, well-dressed man with silver hair. Her dad, Judge Alec Greer. Neither of them could have looked more proud as they gazed at each other.

Kovac placed one of his business cards next to the photograph.

"Are you sure you don't want me to track down your husband?" Kovac asked as the judge eased herself back against a mountain of elaborate pillows on the bed.

There were no photographs of Carey Moore with her spouse. Not on either night table. There might have been one on the bookcase on the far side of the room, but it couldn't be seen from the bed.

"There's no need," she said quietly.

Kovac shrugged his shoulders. "Suit yourself. I just know if you were my wife and I knew you'd been attacked, I'd damn well be here. I don't care if I was having dinner with the president."

"You'll make some lucky woman a good husband someday, then," she murmured, closing her eyes, closing him and his opinions out.

"Well, I haven't so far," Kovac muttered as he left the room.

He was a two-time loser in the marriage-go-round. And still he knew enough to want to be with his partner if she was hurt and frightened. It was a husband's job to protect and reassure. Apparently, Carey Moore's husband didn't know that.

The nanny was standing at the top of the stairs, wringing her hands, uncertain what to do.

"Has Mr. Moore called at all tonight?" Kovac asked.

"No, he hasn't."

"Is that the usual for him? He goes out, doesn't check in with anybody? Doesn't call to tell his daughter good night?"

"Mr. Moore is a very busy man," she

said. Defensive, her gaze just grazing his shoulder.

"How often is he gone in the evenings?"

"I wouldn't know."

"You live here, don't you?"

"It's none of my business."

"Well, it is my business," Kovac said. "Is he gone a lot?"

"A couple of nights a week," she said grudgingly. "He's a very—"

"Busy man. I know."

He handed the girl his card.

"Will you call me when Mr. Moore gets home?" he asked. "No matter what time it is."

She frowned at the card. Kovac imagined they didn't have much crime in the Nordic countries. It was too damned cold, and the people were too polite and too damned good-looking. She was probably contemplating the next plane to Stockholm.

"Don't let Mrs. Moore sleep for more than a couple of hours at a time," he instructed as he started down the stairs. "She has a concussion. It's important to wake her up during the night and make sure she knows her name and where she is."

The nanny was still staring at his card

when he turned to look at her from the front door.

"Tell her I sent you," he suggested. "She's already pissed off at me."

Karl Dahl was a watcher. He never had much to say. He never had any friends. People didn't notice him, as a rule. He had learned long ago to melt into the background.

Over the years different people had given him the nickname "Ghost." He had always been pale, with a sort of a strange gray cast to him. His eyes were gray. His skin had a certain grayness to it.

Different people in his growing-up years had suggested he had maybe gotten lead poisoning or mercury poisoning or some other kind of poisoning. Karl had always figured none of that was the case, else he would have been dead or sickly.

He'd been in jail before. A few times. Jail was not a place to draw attention. Especially not for men with certain proclivities. After his first brutal experience, he had managed to more or less stay out of harm's way the next time, and the next. But he couldn't be anonymous this time.

This time everyone in the jail knew who he was and what he had been accused of doing. Everyone in the place hated him. Guards and hardened criminals alike hated him enough to want to hurt him, kill him. Other inmates spat at him when they got the chance. Some shouted threats. It had been made clear that if he fell into the hands of the general population, he wouldn't come out alive.

Today had been worse than most. Judge Moore had ruled on his "prior bad acts," as the lawyers called them. News of her ruling had gone through the place like wildfire. The prosecution wouldn't be allowed to talk about anything he'd been accused or convicted of prior to the Haas murders. That would be a good thing for him, except he didn't believe a jury would acquit him, no matter what. One of the guards called him Dead Man Walking, and Karl figured that was about right if he stayed in jail.

He had his own cell on the suicide-watch

row. Still, he didn't feel safe. Jail was only meant to keep the common folk safe from criminals. On the inside, nobody gave a shit if a man lived or died, especially a man like Karl himself.

At least he had an attorney who was trying to do a good job for him. Knowing his lawyer would come from a pool of public defenders, Karl had expected the worst—to get some bored and bitter underachiever who would so hate the idea of defending him that he would all but hand him over to the Department of Corrections.

Kenny Scott was a decent enough guy. Karl thought Scott almost wanted to believe he was innocent.

A guard with a buzz cut and no neck opened the door to the interview room. "Time's up, Dahl. Let's go."

Karl thanked his attorney, shook his hand, and rose from his chair. Scott had come to fill him in on the particulars of Judge Moore's ruling and what would happen next.

"Let's go," the guard said in a stronger tone.

Karl shuffled out into the hall, his gaze on the floor so as to avoid eye contact. Like wild predators, the guards took eye contact as a sign of aggression and retaliated accordingly.

"You know, it's not gonna make any difference," the guard said. "You got lucky pulling Judge Moore, but no jury in this state is gonna let you off."

Karl said nothing so he couldn't be accused of giving lip.

"It's just a damn shame we don't have the death penalty," the guard went on. "Bunch of goddamn liberals in the state government. You go outside the Twin Cities and ask the average person on the street, they're gonna say you should be hanged in public. And you should be tortured first. Let Wayne Haas have an hour with you in a locked room."

The guard punched a code into a security panel beside the door that led them back into the cells. A loud buzzer sounded. A red light flashed. The steel door unlatched with an audible clank. The guard opened it and Karl walked through ahead of him. The eyes of the inmates were on him instantly.

"Hey, you sick fuck!" one of them shouted.

"Put him in here with us, Bull! We'll deal

with that piece of shit," said the cell mate, an angry-looking black man with a hundred zigzag braids in his hair. The rolled-up sleeves of his jail-issue jumpsuit revealed numerous gang tattoos up and down his arms.

Another inmate was walking ahead of Karl, being escorted to his cell by another guard. He walked with a swagger, even in shackles his head held high, defiant, arrogant. He was tall and heavy, a white guy with a tattoo of a snake crawling up the back of his bald head. A biker. He glanced back over his shoulder at Karl. A swastika had been inked onto his cheekbone. Prison tat. Aryan Nation.

"Hey, you Nazi limp-dick!" Zigzag called. "Here's your honey. A chil' rapist, just like you, you fuckin' pervert. Master race, my ass! Why don't y'all just fuck each other!"

Snake looked at the inmate but said nothing. He never even broke stride. In the next step, he swung his hands sideways, caught his guard just under the chin, and clotheslined him, the blow yanking him off his feet and knocking him backward into Bull. Bull stumbled back into the bars of a cell, and a roar went through the place. The inmates were cheering and shouting.

Karl froze for a precious instant as Snake came at him, eyes bugging, chains rattling. Too late, he turned to try to lunge toward the door.

Snake's clenched fists came down before his eyes, arms closing on either side of his neck. The links of the handcuffs caught Karl just above his Adam's apple, and he made a raw, retching sound as Snake yanked him backward off his feet.

Black lace crept in on the edge of Karl Dahl's vision. He couldn't breathe. As he tried to raise his hands to claw at the hold on his throat, Snake slammed him sideways into the bars of Zigzag's cell. His temple cracked against the iron once, twice, three times, and blood ran down through his right eye.

The black gangster spat in his face. Karl could no longer hear the shouting, only a loud, whooshing roar inside his head. He seemed to have no command of his arms or legs, flailing like the limbs of a rag doll in the mouth of a rabid dog. His body was nothing but limp weight, hanging him on the bracelets of his killer.

He was vaguely conscious of the red light flashing over the door to the outside hall, the door swinging open.

Snake beat his head against the bars again and again.

The guard called Bull was coming at him, swinging a baton.

Blood sprayed through the air as the baton connected with something—some*one*.

Karl fell to the floor, tangled in the arms and legs of his attacker, still choking.

The last thing he remembered thinking was that his father would have just stood there and shaken his head and said he should have done it himself years ago.

8

"You think somebody tried to kill her?"

"I can't comment at this time. It's not my job to speculate."

Kathleen Casey made a loud raspberry.

Liska looked at the nurse sideways as she took a long drink from a can of Red Bull, raised her free hand, and lazily raised her middle finger.

Casey gave a weary chuckle. The press had cleared out as soon as they had realized they were never going to see or hear from Judge Moore. Liska and Casey had slipped into the lounge for a moment's solitude.

"I hate the press," Liska said. "It's always like trying to explain to a group of four-year-old children why the sky is blue."

"Because it is," Casey said.

"But *why*?"

"Because God made it that way."

"But *why*?"

"So he can weed out all the bad children who say 'But why' and send them to hell."

Liska cocked an eyebrow. "Do I have to send Children and Family Services to your house, Casey?"

"Too late. I already got rid of the bodies," the nurse said, then winced. "Bad joke, all things considered."

An ambulance siren wailed in the distance.

Liska pushed her drink aside on the table and shook her head. "I think about what that Karl Dahl did to those children, and I can't help but think of my own boys when they were that age. They were so innocent, so trusting. So vulnerable."

She still thought of them that way, as far as that went. Kyle, her serious one, was almost thirteen, as he liked to point out every third day of the week. Almost a teenager, which still qualified him as a child, Liska reminded him.

R.J., her youngest, was still a little boy. He had inherited his father's charming but frustrating Peter Pan qualities. It was a good bet he would be a boy until he was toothless and living in a rest home.

Nikki was fiercely protective of them both. If something were to happen to them . . .

"I'd go insane," she said. "Stark raving."

"Think about Wayne Haas," Casey said. "How he must have felt hearing about Moore's ruling today."

Wayne Haas would be one of their first calls, Liska thought. Kovac would handle him, mano a mano. He would side with Haas against Judge Moore. Damned liberal judge. He would try to be Wayne Haas's pal, all in the attempt to get Haas to say something self-incriminating.

Liska would take the son, Bobby, seventeen. She would ask the question "Where were you between six-thirty and seven?" As if they hadn't been put through enough. Now they would be questioned as possible suspects. They would be angry, feel insulted. Who could blame them?

But it couldn't matter to her or to Kovac. Carey Moore was their victim. And Wayne Haas and his son had the biggest ax to grind with Carey Moore.

The siren was coming closer.

Liska looked at her watch. Kovac should

be calling soon. They still had a long night ahead of them. All she wanted was to go home and hug her boys.

"Do you think Dahl will get off?" Casey asked. She was already moving out of her chair in anticipation of what the siren would bring.

"Not a chance in hell, Judge Moore or no Judge Moore. The only way Karl Dahl has out of this is to be beamed up by aliens."

"We just sent a guy up to the psych ward who could probably arrange that."

The sudden explosion of sound beyond the employee lounge jolted Liska out of her chair.

A bloodcurdling roar sounded, followed by someone shouting at the top of their lungs, "Hold him down, goddammit! Get on his chest!"

Casey nodded toward the door. "They're singing my song."

Liska followed the nurse into the work lanes of the ER. People were everywhere, rushing, shouting. Red-faced deputies, docs in green scrubs, EMT crews wheeling gurneys in from the ambulance bay. Liska grabbed one of the deputies by the arm and shoved her badge in his face.

"What's going on?"

"Riot at the jail."

An orderly yelled for them to get out of the way. Liska jumped back against the wall as a gurney zipped by, its passenger in an orange jail jumpsuit. Another gurney rolled in behind it, its passenger spraying the room with a fountain of arterial blood.

A third gurney sagged beneath the weight of an inmate the size of a walrus. He was strapped to a backboard with a deputy sprawled on top of him, trying to hold him down. Both of them had bloodied heads and faces. The inmate was bellowing like a madman.

A doc was calling for security, further restraints, IV Valium. Casey moved toward the big guy, with a syringe in hand. The inmate was bucking hard against the restraints and against the deputy. The gurney skidded sideways and slammed into a cartload of supplies. Momentum unseated the deputy, and he fell hard to the floor.

The inmate let loose another roar, and Liska saw a leg restraint pop like a string, and a boot the length of her forearm drop over the side of the cart.

Liska pulled her tactical baton from the

pocket of her blazer and extended it with a snap of her wrist. Before she could decide whether to move in or stand back, the inmate flipped himself, backboard and all, off the gurney, landing on top of the deputy.

"Grab his arm!" Casey shouted, trying to move in with the needle.

Even as another deputy descended on the inmate, the inmate got his feet under him and came up, twisting and struggling against the remaining restraints. He had one arm free and used a fist the size of a five-pound sledgehammer to backhand the deputy, knocking him on his ass and sending blood spraying from his nose.

Liska couldn't get close. The guy was staggering around with the backboard on him, like Frankenstein's monster in a rage. A deputy standing between him and the doors to the ambulance bay drew his weapon.

The ER was full of staff and patients and people waiting in chairs; people shouting, screaming, a baby wailing. If the deputy discharged his weapon . . .

Ducking below the inmate's line of sight, Liska dashed toward him and swung her baton. She felt the satisfying jolt of contact. She hit the floor and rolled. The inmate dropped to one knee, howling. A deputy barreled into him from behind, hit the backboard, and they both went sprawling.

The deputy with the gun rushed in and jammed the nose of it against the inmate's temple. Every guy in a uniform was screaming, "Down on the ground! Freeze, motherfucker!"

Kathleen Casey rushed in as one of the deputies pinned the inmate's arm against the floor. Liska winced as she watched the needle jab into a bulging, pulsing blue vein.

The inmate was crying and howling. "My leg! Oh, God! Goddammit! It's broke! Get off! Jesus Christ!"

Casey stepped back, syringe still in hand. Liska got to her feet and straightened her blazer.

"Men are such wimps," the nurse said with a sniff.

"Yeah," Liska said. "Men drool, short chicks rule."

She tapped the end of her baton against the floor, and it released and fell back into itself as she raised her hand. The deputies were rolling their monster over onto his back. He was quieting now as his heart pumped the Valium through him.

One of the ER docs dropped down beside the man, cut the bloody leg of the orange jumpsuit to reveal a jagged shard of shin-bone sticking out through the skin.

"Shit," Liska muttered, shoulders slump-ing. "Paperwork."

Casey shook her head. "You don't know your own strength, girlfriend."

"Where's Dahl?"

Liska's head snapped toward the deputy who had asked the question. He was al-ready moving toward the gurney down the hall.

"Dahl?" she asked, hustling toward the bed, her heart rate picking up.

One of the other deputies ran past her and down the hall, weapon drawn. Behind her she could hear someone get on a radio and call for backup.

"Dahl?" she said again, with more ur-gency. "Karl Dahl?"

The deputy near the gurney was cursing. It was empty, abandoned, the white sheet rumpled and stained with blood where its occupant's head had lain. "Shit! Fucking shit! He's gone!"

9

No one had wanted to go near the Haas home on the north side of Minneapolis since the murders. Kids rode past it slowly on their bikes during the day, morbidly fascinated with the place and the idea of something as evil as murder. They dared each other to go up to the windows and look inside, especially the basement windows. Every once in a while some kid would take the challenge. More often, they all spooked and ran.

No one wanted to go near the Haas home, which was why Wayne Haas and his son from his first marriage still lived in it. The "For Sale" sign had been standing in the front yard for more than a year. No takers. The only people who looked, looked out of the same morbid fascination as the children who sat on their bikes out in front on the street.

No one wanted to buy a home where a woman and two children had been tortured and murdered, their bodies desecrated in sickening, unspeakable ways.

If any place should have been haunted, it should have been that house. The evil that had lived inside it that terrible day surely must have permeated the place—the walls, the floors, the ceilings, the foundation—the same way smoke from a fire could permeate, and never leave.

Wayne Haas was not a man of means. He worked in a meat-packing plant, hanging carcasses and loading trucks. He made a decent living, but he couldn't afford to buy a different house without selling the one he had. And nobody wanted the house he had.

Kovac and Liska pulled into the cracked concrete driveway, which led to a detached garage. Erratic lights flashed in the front window of the otherwise dark house, indicating someone inside was watching television. Still, the place had a weird, vacant quality to it. The yard was bad, weedy and bald in spots. There once had been a big oak tree in the front, but the tornado that

had come on that same fateful summer afternoon as the murders had torn it up by the
roots, leaving the lawn naked and the house
exposed. A photograph of the scene had
taken up half the front page of the newspaper the next day.

"I couldn't live in this house," Liska said.
"I don't even want to go inside."

"I'd live in a garbage Dumpster behind a
fish market before I'd live here," Kovac said.

He mostly didn't believe in superstitions,
but even he drew the line at living in murder
scenes.

For one thing, in all his twenty-plus years
on the job, he had never gotten used to the
smell of death. There was nothing else like
it. It hung in the air at a death scene, so
thick and heavy that it was a presence. And
though he knew logically that the smell
would disappear shortly after the corpses
had been removed and the cleaning crew
had come through, he believed the memory
of it never left and that every time he returned to the place, the stench would fill his
head and turn his stomach.

Kovac's second wife had never allowed
him into the house wearing the suits he
had worn to murder scenes. His "corpse

clothes," she had called them. He had had to take them off in the garage and leave them there and walk through the house in his underwear to get to the shower. Then, instead of sending the clothes to the cleaners or throwing them into the trash, she would box them up and take them to Goodwill. Like the disadvantaged people of Minneapolis didn't have enough going against them, they had to go around smelling of corpses.

After the disappearance of three suits, he had wised up and kept a change of clothes at the station and made friends with the guy who ran the dry cleaners down the street.

Liska sighed. "Let's get it over with so I can go home and lie awake all night feeling guilty that I had to question these people."

Wayne Haas came to the front door looking like he wanted to hit somebody. He was a rawboned man with big hands and big shoulders from moving beef carcasses and slabs of meat. Stress and grief and anger had cut such deep lines in his ruddy face that it looked as if it had been carved of redwood.

"What the hell kind of show are you people running?" he demanded, glancing at the

ID Liska held up for him to see. "It's all over the TV. That murdering son of a bitch is running loose. How the hell could you let this happen?"

"I can imagine how you must feel, Mr. Haas," Kovac started.

"The hell you can! You're not the one walked into this house and found half his family butchered! And now the bastard is running around loose, free to kill—"

"Every cop in the city is looking for him," Kovac said.

"That's supposed to make me feel better? You people lost him in the first place!"

Kovac didn't bother to tell him it was the sheriff's office that had lost Karl Dahl, not the police department. Wayne Haas wouldn't appreciate the difference. The only thing that mattered to him was the end result.

"You're right," Kovac said instead. "I'm pissed off about it too. It was the cluster fuck of the century. Believe me, my partner and I sure as hell didn't want to come here tonight and tell you Karl Dahl escaped. We didn't even want to come here to tell you about Judge Moore's ruling on that evidentiary hearing."

Haas shook his head and stepped back a little from the door. Kovac took advantage and moved inside. Liska, who was the size of a minute, slipped in behind him and around him and did a quick survey of the place.

"What's wrong with that woman?" Haas asked. "How could she say what Dahl did in the past didn't have anything to do with this? It just proves what a sick bastard he is. The jury should hear about it."

"I know," Kovac said. "I'm with you. The guy didn't just wake up one day and decide to kill. These mutts work their way up to it."

"It's a goddamn nightmare," Haas said, almost to himself.

"We can put a squad car on the street in front of your house if you're worried about Dahl coming back here," Liska offered.

Haas looked over at the television, where a reporter was coming live from outside the ambulance bay at HCMC. Amber, blue, and red lights from the cop cars and emergency vehicles gave the scene a carnival atmosphere. But it didn't look to Kovac like any of it was registering on Haas. His mind had gone somewhere else, probably somewhere worse.

"I don't want anything from you people," he said at last.

"Mr. Haas?" Liska asked. "Is your son at home?"

"He went to a basketball game at his school. Why?"

Kovac grimaced and looked embarrassed. "This stinks. Believe me, we know it. If it was up to me, I wouldn't ask, but we have to answer to the higher powers."

Haas looked suspicious but said nothing, waiting for the other shoe to drop.

"I'm sure you heard, Judge Moore was attacked in the parking ramp at the government center earlier tonight," Liska said. "We need to ask you and your son where you both were at the time."

"Get out of my house," he said quietly, though the rage was building visibly inside him.

"It's routine, Mr. Haas," Kovac said. "No one really thinks you had anything to do with it. We just have to put it on paper."

"Get out of my house," he said louder. His neck was red, and Kovac could see a big vein pulsing on one side. "Get out of my house, goddamn you!"

He went to the front door and yanked it

wide so hard that it hit the wall and rattled the front windows.

Bobby Haas stood on the front porch, looking bewildered and worried, brown eyes wide. "Dad? Dad, what's wrong? Who are you people?"

"We're with the police," Liska said, but the boy was looking at his father as Wayne Haas raised a hand to his temple and gritted his teeth.

"Dad!"

"Mr. Haas?" Kovac moved toward him at the same time the kid did. Haas bent forward in obvious pain.

"Get him to a chair," Kovac ordered, and he and the boy each took an arm and moved Wayne Haas to a worn green armchair a few feet away. Kovac looked at Liska. "Call an ambulance."

Even as Liska was pulling her cell phone from her coat pocket, Haas was waving off the order.

"No. I'm fine," he insisted.

"You don't look fine," Kovac said.

Bobby Haas squatted down beside his father. "It's his blood pressure. It spikes like that when he gets upset. He'll be okay in a minute. Right, Dad? You're gonna be okay."

Haas blew out a couple of big breaths and nodded wearily, his eyes focused on the floor. He was pale now, and damp with sweat.

Kovac looked at the boy. "Why don't you get your dad a glass of water?"

Liska followed him down the hall.

Kovac knelt down on one knee by Wayne Haas's chair so he could see the man's face more clearly. "You're sure you don't want to go to a hospital?"

"Just go," Haas whispered. "Just go away from here."

"I'm sorry we upset you like that," Kovac said. "There are some times this job sucks, and this would be one of them. But the questions have to be asked. If we don't touch all the bases, a case can get dismantled. You've seen for yourself, the system isn't there to help guys like you or cops like me."

"I just want this all to be over," Haas said. "I wish I'd died that day too."

"You've got a son to live for."

Haas just hung his head.

Bobby Haas and Liska returned then, and the son handed the father half a glass of water. Liska gave Kovac a look and nodded toward the door. They stepped out onto the porch, and Kovac drew the door shut behind them.

"The kid's going to get our answer and come out here," Liska said. "I figured that would be a hell of a lot easier than us making the guy stroke out before our very eyes."

"What does Junior have to say for himself?"

"He hung out with a buddy after school, and they went to a basketball game tonight. He's worried about his dad, says his health isn't good. The stress of it all has taken a toll on him."

"Poor bastard," Kovac murmured, digging a finger in an inside coat pocket. Jackpot. He pulled out a cigarette and rolled it between his fingers like he was rubbing a rabbit's foot for luck. "What about the boy? How's he holding up?"

"He's rattled. Could be because of his father. Could be because of us. He's seventeen, he has a penis, definitely qualifies him for being stupid enough to mug a judge."

Kovac cut her a look of annoyance. "Don't take your shitty love life out on me, Tinks. You ought to know better than to go out with a lawyer."

"Just shows how desperate I am," she muttered. "Scraping the bottom of the barrel."

"Nah . . . You haven't dated me yet."

"Maybe I should. You're the only guy I know who returns my calls." She flicked a glance at his hand. "Didn't you quit smoking, like, three hours ago?"

Kovac scowled. "Three days, and I'm not smoking it."

Liska craned her neck to get a peek into the living room to see what was going on between the Haas men. Wayne Haas was still in the chair with one hand covering his eyes, the other grasping Bobby's shoulder. The son patted his father's knee, a very adult gesture of reassurance.

"All things considered, the kid seems pretty well adjusted," she said blandly. "I'm sure that means he's seriously screwed up."

"Who isn't?"

"Speak for yourself. I'm a pillar of mental health."

"Right," Kovac said, looking at the cigarette. "Me, I'm fucked up and proud of it. I worked hard to get to this level of neurosis."

"He's coming out," Liska whispered.

Bobby Haas slipped out the front door

and onto the porch, careful not to let the old screen door bang. He was a nice-looking kid with a head of soft, dark, curling hair, and earnest brown eyes. In no way did he resemble his father. Where Wayne Haas's face had been cut from stone with a rough chisel, the boy's face was smooth and soft, with small, almost feminine features. He had the lean build of a cyclist and stood three or four inches shy of six feet.

The boy had discovered the bodies of Marlene and the foster children, just moments before Wayne Haas had arrived home from work. By the accounts of the uniforms who had responded to the scene first—and later Stan Dempsey and his partner—Bobby had refused to leave the house, refused to leave his father. He had stayed on the front porch for hours as the forensics people and the medical examiner's people went in and out, carrying evidence, rolling out the body bags.

Bobby Haas had stayed on the front porch, crouched in a corner, sobbing and retching, rocking himself with his arms banded around his knees. Inconsolable, terrified. The advocate from Victim Services had sat beside him, trying to calm him, trying to convince him he needed to go with her to the police station. Finally, he had been taken to HCMC for his own protection and stayed the night, sedated in a bed in the psych ward, where he was kept under observation for the better part of a week.

Kovac knew the shock of seeing the horrors one human being could inflict on another. He was a grown man with twenty-plus years on the force, countless murder investigations under his belt, and still there were cases so unspeakably horrible they shocked even him and lingered in his brain like shadows. Bobby Haas would have to live with the memories of finding those bodies in his head and in his nightmares for the rest of his life.

"Is he all right? Your dad?" Kovac asked.

The kid kind of shrugged, kind of nodded, looked away. He was upset and worried, and glanced back through the front window at his dad. "He said to tell you he came straight home after work and he hasn't been out. What's going on?"

Kovac didn't answer.

"It's really hard on him, you know?" the boy said. "The judge's ruling."

"If you were hanging out with a friend after school, how'd you hear about Judge Moore's ruling?"

"People were talking about it. Me and Stench went to a Burger King."

"How did that make you feel, Bobby?" Liska asked. "Judge Moore's not letting in Karl Dahl's record. Does that piss you off?"

"Shit, yeah," he said, trying to look tough. He couldn't quite pull it off. He planted his hands at his waist, and the oversized black Vikings-logo jacket he wore crept up around his shoulders and neck like a turtle's shell. "How could she do that? The guy's a psycho!"

"So where was this Burger King?" Kovac asked.

The boy looked at him, suspicious. "Downtown. City Center, I think."

"You think? You were there. How come you don't know?"

"All those buildings are hooked together down there with the skyways and all. We were in a lot of places. I didn't pay attention."

"What were you doing downtown at all?"

"Hanging out. What's the big deal?"

Kovac just looked at him.

"We'll need to speak with your friend, Bobby," Liska said, good cop with a twist of mother. "Judge Moore was attacked tonight. We need to know where you were when that happened."

Bobby Haas looked at them like they'd each sprung an extra head. "You're kidding. You can't be serious. You think I did it?"

"Did you?" Kovac asked.

"No!"

"We don't know who did it, Bobby," Liska said. "But we need to account for your whereabouts so we can take you off the list."

"And my dad too? What kind of sick people are you?" he asked, a fine sheen of tears rising in his eyes. "Don't you think he's been through enough?"

"It's procedure," Kovac said. He finally hung the cigarette on his lip, flicked a lighter at the end of it, breathed deeply, and directed the smoke just to the right of Bobby Haas's face. "Standard op."

Liska frowned at him, then turned back to the boy. "We know this has been a nightmare for you and your dad, Bobby. I'm sorry we have to ask these questions, but we do. We have to cover all the bases, just like the cops on the murders covered all the bases to get Karl Dahl."

The boy rolled his eyes, turned away, turned back. "Yeah. Look how great that turned out."

"We'll need your friend's information," Kovac said with blunt impatience. "His name, for starters. I have to think his parents didn't name him Stench."

"Jerome Walden," Bobby Haas said grudgingly. "We didn't do anything."

"Then you don't have anything to worry about. But you can see why we have to ask, Bobby," Liska went on calmly. "We have to cover the people who have the biggest ax to grind with Judge Moore. Like it or not, that would be you and your dad."

"So we ask you a few questions and that's the end of it," Kovac said. "Provided you didn't do it."

"We didn't do anything!"

Liska glared at Kovac. "Don't you have some calls to make, Detective?"

Kovac made a face, tossed the cigarette down on the chipped, painted floorboards of the porch, and ground it out with his toe. He cut a final, flat look at Bobby Haas. "Chicks. What're you gonna do?"

Then he walked off the porch and over to the latest piece-of-crap car they had been assigned from the department pool. He slid into the driver's seat and waited.

They had agreed Liska should take the kid. Even at seventeen a motherless boy was just that: a boy. There was a better chance of his relaxing with Liska, letting his guard down. If he had acted out of hurt and rage and taken it out on Judge Moore, there was a better chance he might feel guilty with a woman who was giving him compassion and understanding.

Kovac thought about Carey Moore, lying in her bed on the other side of the tracks. She'd taken a beating delivered with more emotion than the average mugger bothered to exhibit. Smack and grab. Knock 'em and rock 'em. It didn't pay to hang around.

There had been rage behind that attack.

Liska handed Bobby Haas her card, patted his arm, and left the porch.

Kovac started the engine.

"What do you think?" he asked as she buckled her seat belt and heaved a big sigh.

"I think I want to go home and hug my boys."

10

Karl hunkered down in his nest and chewed on a cold slice of sausage pizza. It hurt to swallow, on account of being choked, but he needed the energy food would give him.

He hurt all over his body, especially his head, where Snake had banged him into the iron bars of a cell over and over. When he tried to touch the wounds, his skull felt squishy, a mess of crushed skin and clotting blood. His brain hurt bad, and he figured he maybe had a skull fracture. But he was alive and he was free, and those were the only two things that mattered.

It wasn't the first time he had hidden himself in a Dumpster. Dumpsters were warm places on cold nights, if a man could stand the smell and there weren't rats. If folks had discarded enough trash during the day, a person could cover themselves up real well.

The smell was a benefit, really. If the police brought out dogs and had something to scent from, a man was pretty much done for. But time spent in half-eaten pizzas and rotten eggshells, coffee grounds and wasted restaurant meals hid a man's natural scent pretty well. Enough to throw the dogs off, if he was lucky.

He wasn't more than half a block from the hospital, down an alley behind a diner where the special of the evening had been liver and onions. Karl crouched down in a corner of the container, one at the front side where a shadow would fall across him if someone lifted the lid.

The sirens of cop cars were wailing all around, swarming like bees, out to get him. He was the most important man in town tonight. That was something that hadn't happened very often in his life.

He heard a car coming, creeping slowly down the alley. No siren, but Karl made himself as small as he could, ducked his head down, and went under layers and layers of crumpled paper and food scraps. The lid on the Dumpster was dented and bent and didn't close properly. White light seeped in and filtered down through the paper, illuminating his strange little world. The security light hanging over the back door of the building on the other side of the alley. Then the light was tinted blue, then red.

The car stopped. Doors opened.

"Hey, fellas. We're looking for somebody. You seen anyone back here this evening?"

"Just stepped out for a smoke, Officer."

Employees from the diner. Karl had heard them come outside a while ago. They'd been chatting sporadically about nothing much—what they would do after work, how some friend had gotten a new car, what football teams they would bet on Sunday.

"Who you looking for?"

"Karl Dahl."

"That killer?"

"Yeah. He escaped custody. You know what he looks like?"

"Seen him on the news. Damn, he's running 'round loose?"

"Sheriff's deputies had him at HCMC. They lost him. You haven't seen anybody back here?"

"Just that raggedy old crazy guy works up

and down this alley, collecting cans and shit. Eats out the Dumpsters."

"Where is he now?"

"How would I know? He's a crazy old street dude."

"I seen him sleeping once under the stairs behind that upholstery shop down the block."

Shoes scuffed on pavement. Closer . . . closer . . .

Karl held his breath.

The hinges on the lid of the Dumpster squealed as someone raised it.

Karl imagined himself as being invisible.

The container rocked as someone pulled himself up to get a better look inside. One of the cops, he figured. Confirmation was a nightstick stabbing down through the garbage three inches from his head. The stick came down again and again, gradually moving away from him.

"Careful the rats don't pull you in there headfirst, Doug." The other cop.

"It's clear."

"You officers want some coffee or somethin'?"

"Who are you, Jamal? King of the damn

world? Boss kick your ass, givin' away shit."

"That's okay, fellas. We've got to keep moving. Thanks anyway."

The Dumpster lid lowered.

"You see this guy, call 911."

"Damn straight."

Karl didn't breathe right until he heard the cruiser continue its way down the alley. And then still he didn't move.

"Man, that's one bad dude, that Dahl," Jamal said. "Killed them kids. Cut that woman."

"Crazy motherfucker."

There was silence for a moment while they finished their smokes, then went back into the diner.

Still Karl waited before he dared to poke his head out and look down the alley. The cruiser was gone. There was no one in sight.

Careful not to make a sound, he climbed out of his hiding spot and made his way down the alley under the cover of shadows. Toward the end of the block on the left-hand side, he could see a broad landing and steps leading down from the back door of a business.

If the homeless man the restaurant workers had spoken about slept under those stairs regularly, there was a good chance he kept his stuff stashed under there.

Karl slipped across the alley. He could see a grocery cart loaded down with the stuff homeless people keep—soda cans and beer cans they gathered for the recycling money, filthy blankets and clothes.

He needed to get rid of the jail jumpsuit and into a disguise. No one looked twice at street people if they could help it.

The owner of the cart was nowhere in sight. Like as not, he was still working his alleys, or panhandling on the street in front of restaurants with no valet. The night was young.

Karl began to dig through the stuff in the shopping cart. A garbage sack full of cans. Another with beer and liquor bottles. Wedged down into the folds of an old blanket, he found a bottle of bourbon with two fingers' worth in the bottom and helped himself to it, hoping it would numb his pounding head and aching throat.

"Hey! That's my stuff!" The indignant voice came from beneath the stairs, under a pile of discarded upholstery fabric. The fabric rustled and moved, and a dark lump of rags and matted hair emerged.

"You can't have it! Pope Clement gave that to me!"

The man came at Karl, arms flailing, mouth tearing wide to shout. Without hesitation, Karl swung the bourbon bottle downward and hit the man in the head as hard as he could.

Without a sound, the ragman dropped straight to his knees, his momentum carrying him into Karl and knocking Karl backward. Regaining his balance, Karl was on him in an instant, hitting him again and again, feeling bone give way and splinter beneath the heavy glass of the bottle. He kept pounding away, as if the bottle were a hammer, over and over until there was no skull left to break.

Spent, he sat back on his heels, trying not to wheeze. He was sweating and shaking and dizzy. He wiped a hand over his face, and it came away sticky with the ragman's blood and brain matter.

Karl pulled the carcass back under the steps, stumbling over another bottle, this one with something clear in it. Karl opened it and sniffed. Grain alcohol. He used it to wash the blood off his face and hands, then drank the last swallow.

Methodically, he pulled off the dead man's coat and shirt and T-shirt. He stripped off his own jail jumpsuit and dressed in the dead man's clothes, which reeked of body odor, bourbon, urine, and feces.

The man had stashed his money down the front of his undershorts, taped against his scrotum. Karl took it, still warm from the body heat of his victim, peeled off a couple of bills to put in his pocket, then stashed the rest the same way the dead man had.

Hiding the jumpsuit beneath it, he covered the body over with the musty remnants of upholstery fabric that had made the man's nest, then went back to dig through the shopping cart for anything else he might be able to use.

He found a steak knife with a good blade and slipped it in the coat pocket. He found a knit cap and pulled it on, wincing as the wool settled onto his wounds. The idea that it was probably infested with lice made his skin crawl, but he had no choice. He had no choice about anything if he wanted to stay alive.

He rubbed his hands on the filthy pavement, then rubbed them over his face, working in the grime. Hide in plain sight. He knew how to do that. He knew how to be invisible. He was an unremarkable man with a forgettable face devoid of expression. It was easy for people to look right through him.

It would be impossible now for him to try to leave the city. The police would be all over the bus stations, the train depots, the truck stops. They might set up roadblocks and checkpoints. They would be expecting him to run. His picture would be everywhere, a picture of him clean-shaven and bareheaded. But he would no longer be that man, and no one would catch him running.

In fact, it seemed to Karl the best thing for him to do right now was stay put. The cops had already been down this alley. They had already been told about the homeless guy living under these stairs. He couldn't say for certain, but he imagined the police had checked out the spot on their way down the alley. They had maybe even spoken with the ragman long enough to know that he communicated regularly with Pope Clement.

Knowing he was in as safe a place as any, Karl crawled back under the stairs and stretched out beside the dead man's still-warm body to catch some sleep.

11

It was after midnight by the time they had interviewed Jerome "Stench" Walden. The kid's mother had come to the door, drunk and smoking a cigarillo. A charming woman.

Jerome had looked embarrassed that he was stuck in a crappy house that smelled of sour beer and fried onions and cheap tobacco. In a clean set of gray sweats, the T-shirt bearing the initials *USC* in maroon block letters, he looked as incongruous in his setting as Bobby Haas had looked kneeling at his father's feet, trying to comfort him. Not surprisingly, Jerome's story of the after-school and evening adventures matched Bobby Haas's version of events.

Kovac didn't believe them, but then he rarely believed anyone. He was too accustomed to being lied to. Everybody lied to the cops, even the innocent. He wouldn't have believed his own grandmother without a corroborating witness.

The security videotape from the government center parking ramp was on Kovac's desk when they arrived back at the CID offices. They went into a conference room, watched the oft-copied-over tape, and drank some bad coffee.

They had run out of desire for conversation on their way in but had been partners long enough that they were comfortable with their silences. Neither of them said a word as they watched the tape through the first time.

The tape was so grainy that if Kovac hadn't known they were looking at Carey Moore, he couldn't have positively ID'd her. She walked into the camera frame, proceeding toward her car, a black 5-series BMW sedan. She was carrying a handbag slung over one shoulder, and a large briefcase that looked heavy. Her father's briefcase.

She stuck her hand into the purse to dig out car keys and dropped a couple of objects on the floor. Stopping, she set the briefcase down and bent to pick up what she had dropped.

At that moment the assailant came from the left of the screen. Difficult to make out size, due to the angle of the camera, which was pointed down from above them. Dressed in jeans and a dark coat with the hood up. Impossible to make out a face.

He hit her hard across the back with some kind of a club or baton, maybe a small baseball bat. The attack was fast and violent, and it looked to Kovac that the assailant was more interested in hurting her than in taking anything.

They knew from what Judge Moore had told them that she had managed to set off her car alarm, at which point the perpetrator got off her, took the time to kick her hard in the side, then grabbed up her wallet. He spun around and snatched the briefcase she had set down, and ran out of the frame, going for a staircase, Kovac assumed. According to the garage attendant sitting in the pay booth on street level, no car had come squealing down the ramp at the time of the assault in a big hurry to leave.

Liska rewound the tape and hit the play button. "This sucks."

"Yeah. What's the point in having these cameras if they're going to use the tapes so many times we might as well be trying to watch cartoons from the moon?"

"They need to go digital."

"Costs money."

"Yeah? Well, if I had to park in that ramp all day every day, I'd have to take a second mortgage on my house. I think they can afford it."

In the morning one of them would drop the tape with the video geek in the lab and see if she could enhance the images to the point of being useful, but Kovac doubted that would happen.

He tossed out the question to get their brains rolling. "Who do we look at besides Leopold and Loeb?"

"They seem like decent kids."

"So did the aforementioned," Kovac pointed out. "So did Ted Bundy."

Liska shrugged. "It'll be hard to corroborate their story. Who would notice either one of them? They're too normal. And there was only one guy on the video. Where's the sidekick?"

"I want the tapes from the entrances to the garage, see if either of their cars rolls in sometime before six-thirty. They could have left a vehicle there, taken a staircase down to the street, then come back after all the hoopla to get the car. Make sure the uniform who took down all the tag numbers runs them through the DMV."

"They could have parked anywhere downtown," Liska said. "It would have been stupid to park in that ramp."

"They're a couple of seventeen-year-old boys. Forethought is not a big priority at that age."

"Thanks for the tip. I'm going to go home and lock my eldest in his room for the next ten years or so."

"I think we can rule out Wayne Haas," Kovac said. "He's too big to be the guy on the tape, and he doesn't look built for speed either. He's got plenty of motive to hate Judge Moore, but I don't like him for this."

"Me neither. Could be an ex-con with a grudge," Liska said. "Could be any nutjob following the Dahl case."

"What do we know about the parents of the foster kids?" Kovac asked, frowning as that train of thought slipped into his head.

"The mother's in jail on a narcotics

charge. Dad's got a sheet too, assault being the big prizewinner for us."

"Is he running around loose?"

"He is."

Most crime was simple and straightforward. A killed B because B had something of value, or B cheated A in a drug deal, or B did A's girlfriend while A was out of town. The obvious suspects almost always turned out to be the perps. Twisted conspiracies were the stuff of novels and movies.

"We'll need to talk to Dempsey."

"He'll be a good source."

"He's a pretty good suspect too," Liska said.

Kovac gave her a sharp look. "What's that supposed to mean?"

"Come on, Sam. Dempsey has a lot riding on convicting Karl Dahl. You know the department has just been trying to keep a lid on him until it's over. They won't fire him and give the defense more ammunition than they already have against him. But as soon as that trial is over, it's *adios* Stan. He can't be the president of the Carey Moore fan club."

Kovac chewed on a thumbnail, scowling at the possibilities. He could hear the allegations. The lead detective was obsessed. Dempsey couldn't be in the field, because he'd had a breakdown. He wanted Dahl to be his guy; Judge Moore's ruling was a slap in the face of his investigation . . .

All that would be fodder anyway. The department hadn't fired Stan Dempsey because they would have looked bad in the media and because they were afraid Dempsey would sue. Poor old Stan was screwed no matter what.

"Jesus," Kovac muttered, rubbing his hands over his face and back through his hair. "I don't like it."

"Since when is this job about what we like?" Liska asked.

"I mean, talk to him, yes. Nobody knows the players in the Dahl case better than Stan."

"We have to look at him, Sam, and you have to be the one to do it," Liska said. "You know him. He's old-school. He'll take it better from you."

Kovac heaved a sigh, pushing himself up out of his chair. "All right. But you get Mutt and Jeff and their alibi. Looks to me like they both need a mother figure anyway."

Liska rolled her eyes. "Yeah, that's me.

Mother Earth packing heat. I'm a B movie from the fifties."

She got up from her chair and stretched, her sweater rising up above the waistband of her slacks to show the Glock 9mm she wore on a belt holster. "I'm outta here, Kojak. I'll see you in the morning."

"It already is morning."

"Don't tell me that. I'm gone."

Kovac prowled around the office for a while after she'd gone. He was always restless on the front end of a case. He wanted to work around the clock. Get on it. Get after it.

Homicide cops in the Minneapolis PD had a window of about three days on a murder before the next murder or assault case came along and the last one got shuffled to a back burner. Or maybe he was that way because there was no need for him to be any other way. The job was his life. He had nothing to go home for.

He put his coat on and walked out of the building to stand on the wide front steps that led up the big Gothic stone building that was the color of raw liver. He wanted a smoke, but he didn't take it. The one he'd had on the Haas front porch had been for effect.

The streets were mostly empty on this end of downtown. All the Friday-night excitement would be at the other end, where bars and clubs crowded around the Target Center, home of the NBA Timberwolves. Night life. There was a concept.

Kovac walked down to the parking ramp where he left his car every day. The facility had been named for a cop who had been murdered back in the late eighties for no other reason than that he wore the uniform. Sitting in a pizza parlor, the guy had been minding his own business, probably thinking about the fact that he was about to retire, when some gang punk pulled a piece and shot him dead in front of a dozen witnesses.

The guy had lived with the potential and real dangers of being a cop every day he was on the job, survived to retirement, only to be gunned down, off duty, having a pizza.

No one planned on becoming a victim.

Marlene Haas hadn't gotten up on that fateful day thinking of the horrors that would take place in her home in a matter of hours.

Carey Moore had been headed home,

thinking of her little daughter, maybe thinking of the absentee husband, maybe thinking about the shitstorm she had just un-
leashed with her decision on Karl Dahl's
prior bad acts. And bam, out of nowhere,
some mutt knocked her flat and beat the
crap out of her.

Kovac scowled at the bent his thoughts
were taking—poor Carey Moore. He didn't
want to think of her as a person with problems and issues and emotions. Still, when
he drove out of the ramp onto the street, he
didn't head for home. He turned the oppo-
site direction and drove toward Lake of the
Isles.

12

Carey lay in bed, half-awake, desperately longing to sleep, pain keeping her from shutting down. It hurt to take more than a shallow breath, because of her ribs. Her head was pounding and felt swollen to the point that she wished she could open her skull and let the pressure out. She was still dressed, having refused to let Anka help her out of the gray pin-striped suit, not because of modesty but because the least movement set off waves of dizziness and nausea. Her slacks were torn at one knee. A shoulder seam had split on the jacket during the struggle, a button was missing, and one elbow was ripped out.

She concentrated on these things—the damage to her clothing and the fact that it was one of her favorite suits and she was angry to have to trash it—because in truth none of it was important. She didn't want to think about the fact that someone had attacked her, had possibly meant to kill her. She didn't want to think about what that would have meant, never seeing her daughter again, not being there for her father as his life drew to a close.

Guilt gnawed at her for not having included her husband in the list of people she would miss. She didn't hate him. He wasn't a bad guy. He was a wonderful father, when he was home, which had been less and less over the last year. It was just that what had been good between them had worn away. All they had now were pretense and tension.

Carey had realized their marriage was over a long while ago. David knew it too. He was as miserable as she was, but they both preferred to ignore the situation. Their marriage had become the elephant in the room that nobody wanted to talk about. If they talked about it, they would have to deal with it, and with the fallout that would rain down on their child.

Instead, they each stayed busy with their work. Carey had a full load with the Dahl trial looming. David, who had been a promising young documentary filmmaker at the start of their marriage, continued trying to drum up support for his latest project idea. He spent much of his time wining and dining, bowing and scraping to the kinds of people who could get films made. Unfortunately, the backing never seemed to come through, and he had had to lower himself to making the occasional local TV commercial.

Carey knew that he resented her success, and his lack thereof. He had become touchy and snappish on the subject of his career. She had tried to be supportive and patient, knowing that his self-esteem had taken a beating. But David had grown too comfortable with playing the victim, with making her walk on eggshells around his ego. She was tired of it, and her own resentments toward him had begun to grow like warts on the ends of her nerves.

If he knew how many times she had bitten her tongue to cut him a break, to give him the opportunity to be a man . . . and how many times he had failed . . .

The pressure of the tears behind her eyes made her head throb all the harder. Carey tried to blink them back. If she was going to cry, she would end up having to blow her nose, which would probably be so painful she would pass out.

Maybe that wasn't such a bad idea.

The numbers 1:13 glowed green on the alarm clock that squatted on her night table. Still no sign of David.

Potential backers, my ass, she thought. She suspected he was having an affair, and was almost relieved at the idea. He hadn't touched her in months. She hadn't wanted him to. His touch only made her feel impatient and irritated. At the same time, the idea of his cheating on her pissed her off no end, because she could too easily imagine him doing it out of spite.

She brought her hands up to her face, wanting to rub her cheeks and forehead, sucking her breath in as her fingers brushed ever so slightly over an abrasion, wincing at the pain in her ribs from taking too deep and too sudden a breath.

Anka tapped softly on the bedroom door and let herself in.

"The detective told me to check on you," she said quietly.

"I'm fine, Anka."

"You don't look so fine."

"No, I suppose not," Carey said. "Has Mr. Moore called?"

"No. I heard your cell phone ringing a while ago. Of course, I didn't answer it."

"Would you bring it to me, please?"

The nanny frowned. "You should be sleeping."

"You just came to wake me up," Carey pointed out. "I only want to check my messages."

Looking unhappy, muttering something unpleasant in Swedish, the girl went away, and came back with the phone.

"Thanks," Carey said. "Go to bed. Get some sleep. I promise not to lapse into a coma."

Anka sniffed her disapproval at her employer's sense of humor but left the room.

Carey touched the key to retrieve her voice mail, entered her password, and closed her eyes as the messages played through.

A call from Ted Sabin, Hennepin County's version of a district attorney and her former boss, expressing his concern for her, having heard about her attack. He promised to bring the full force of his considerable power to bear in the apprehension and prosecution of her attacker.

A call from Kate Quinn, an old friend from her days in the county attorney's office, calling for the same reason, telling Carey to call her and she would be there ASAP. Kate had worked as a victim/witness advocate. Carey had never imagined she would ever call on her friend in her professional capacity.

Then Chris Logan's voice was in her ear, anxious, upset, full of bluster, the usual way he reacted to unpleasant news over which he had no control. "Carey, goddammit, I just heard. Are you all right? Are you in the hospital? Why the hell didn't you take a deputy to the garage with you? Jesus, I should have walked you out, pissed off or not. Call me."

She deleted the message and put the phone down beside her on the bed. A feeling she couldn't quite identify rippled through her. A blend of regret, sadness, loss. It would have been nice to have someone strong and protective to turn to now. Someone she trusted. A shoulder to lean on.

But she didn't have that. After their one brief interlude, she had never called Logan in search of that kind of support. Not that she hadn't been tempted. After what he'd said to her in her chambers, she would never want to again. She felt betrayed by him for taking the cheap shot about their one night together, and now she wouldn't trust him.

She had never really quite trusted him, she admitted. Not absolutely. That was why there had been no other nights shared before or since. Logan was a big package of single-minded ambition. He cared about winning, about seeing justice done, no matter the cost to himself or those around him. They had been friends back in their days working together, but Carey knew he had also seen her as a rival, and that had never sat well with her.

Her father would have been there for her, as strong as the Rock of Gibraltar, as he had been all her life. But for all intents and purposes, her father was dead. His body had yet to get the message, but the essence of him was gone. The shell of him sat in a rest home, waiting to shut down.

Feeling alone and adrift, Carey closed her eyes and fell into a shallow sleep disturbed by menacing dreams. Dreams of her attacker, of who he might be. In the dark theater of her mind, she lay on her back on the cold concrete, struggling against a man she couldn't see. At first, his face was nothing but black, blank space, and then gradually it became clear.

The images flashed in her mind like lightning, a different face in each blinding burst. Karl Dahl. Wayne Haas. Chris Logan. David. Marlene Haas, her face partially decomposed, dead eyes bulging from their sockets.

Carey jerked awake, crying out, trying to sit up. The pain knocked her back, and she rolled to her side as the nausea crashed over her again. She was sweating, shaking, breathing too quickly.

The cell phone beneath her hand rang, startling her. David, she thought, half hoped, though she wasn't sure whether she wanted him to say he was coming home or that he wasn't.

"David?"

There was silence on the other end just long enough to raise the hair on the back of her neck.

When the caller spoke, she didn't recognize his voice. It was a low, hoarse whisper,

the words stretched out, strangely distorted.

"I'm coming to get you, bitch" was all he
said.

13

Kovac had just pulled up to the curb across the street from Carey Moore's house when his cell phone rang.

"Kovac."

"It's Carey Moore."

Her voice was quiet, composed, but he could hear an underlying tension.

"I just got a call. A man. He said, 'I'm coming to get you, bitch.'"

"I'm right across the street from your house. I'll be right there."

"Come to the door, but don't ring the bell. I don't want to wake Anka and Lucy."

She hung up. All business. Used to being queen of her domain, even in times of crisis.

Kovac crossed the street to the prowl car parked at the curb with two uniforms inside. The driver ran his window down.

"You guys see anything?" Kovac asked.

"Nope. All's quiet."

"You've been around the house?"

"Couple of times. The place is locked down."

"Did the husband show up?"

"Nope."

It was almost one-thirty in the morning. What the hell kind of business dinner ran until one-thirty in the morning?

Kovac patted a hand absently on the roof of the cruiser.

"You married, Benson?" he asked the officer behind the wheel.

"Twice."

"What would your wife do if you stayed out until one-thirty in the morning without checking in with her?"

"She'd hang my balls from the chandelier, and I wouldn't be attached to them."

"Right."

Kovac was willing to bet Carey Moore hadn't even bothered to call her husband to find out where he was or when he was coming home or to tell him she'd been attacked, or anything else.

He went up to the gate and heard the lock release. The judge was looking out at him through one of the sidelights. She opened the front door as he came up onto the landing.

She was still wearing the pants and blouse she'd worn home from the hospital. The pants were torn. The silk blouse was bloodstained and missing a couple of strategically placed buttons. He caught a glimpse of blue lace and a curve most other judges he knew didn't have. But if she gave a damn that he could see her bra, she didn't show it.

"You need to sit down, Judge," he said. "Looks to me like that door is the only thing holding you up."

"I'm—"

Kovac held up a hand. "Don't even."

She closed the door and leaned back against it for a moment, white as paste. Gathering herself and all the strength she could scrape together, she eased away from the door and turned to lead him into a den off the hall.

A table lamp cast an amber glow over leather chairs and the hand-waxed pine paneling. The judge slowly lowered herself into one corner of a dark green leather love seat. Kovac sat in the chair adjacent, moving it closer to her until their knees were almost touching.

"What time did the call come?" he asked, pulling his small notebook and a pen out of his pocket.

"One-twenty-two. I looked at the clock."

"Your house phone or your cell?"

"Cell."

"Can I see the phone?"

She handed it to him. Her hand was trembling.

Kovac brought up the menu and found his way to the call list. "Same number as the call to the house—the call asking for Marlene."

"Were you able to trace it?"

"Prepaid cell phone. The modern criminal's best friend. We might be able to trace it to the manufacturer, maybe to a list of places in the Twin Cities area where that manufacturer distributes. But you know as well as I do, that's a lot of territory, and the damn things are everywhere. Tracking down this one phone . . . you'll die of old age before we find the mutt who bought it."

She stared into the dark end of the room as if waiting for a sign from another dimension.

"Who are you looking at?" she asked.

"I shouldn't get into that."

The judge laughed without humor and shook her head. "Excuse me, Detective, but I'm not your average vic, am I? I've been a part of the criminal justice system since I clerked for my father when I was a student. Here's who I think you'll look at: Wayne Haas, Bobby Haas, Stan Dempsey—"

"No offense, Judge, but that's not even the tip of the iceberg of people who hate you right now."

"You should check on the relatives of the foster children who were murdered."

"I know my job."

"I know you do."

She looked away again, wrestling with something. She rested her forehead in her hand and sighed. "I'm not very good at being a victim," she admitted. "I don't know how to do it. I don't know what I should feel, what I should think, what I should just try to shut out. I still can't believe this happened to me."

A tear rolled over her lashes onto her cheek. She caught it with a scraped knuckle and swept it away. "I only know how to fight. Go on the offensive. Make something happen."

"There's nothing wrong with that," Kovac said. He wondered if part of the reason she wasn't able to accept she'd been victimized was that she had no one to fall back on, no one to take the offensive for her.

"There isn't a good time to tell you this, so I'm just going to do it," Kovac said. "Karl Dahl escaped custody tonight."

Carey Moore stared at him for so long without saying anything that Kovac began to wonder if she'd understood a word he'd said. Head injuries could have some pretty weird effects on people.

Finally, she said, "*Escaped?* What do you mean *he escaped*? How could he escape?"

"There was some kind of fight at the jail. Things got out of hand. Prisoners and jailers had to be taken to the hospital. Someone fucked up royally. Didn't cuff Dahl to the gurney. He basically just got up and left when nobody was looking."

"Oh, my God," she said with the same kind of anger and disgust every cop in town was feeling.

A triple murderer was loose on the streets because some dickhead in a uniform had blown it. Kovac knew from experience it wouldn't matter who the dickhead was specifically, and it wouldn't matter which agency he worked for. Every cop, every deputy sheriff in Minneapolis, would take heat for it from the public, from the media, from department brass.

"The public will love it," Kovac said with his usual sarcasm. "Now they have two branches of the justice system not to trust."

Carey Moore closed her eyes but didn't succeed in blocking out anything but the light. "Has someone told Wayne Haas?"

"I had that pleasure."

"How did he take it?"

"How do you think?"

She didn't answer him. Both her question and his had been rhetorical.

As they sat there in the Moores' beautiful den, it was so quiet in the house that the sound of a key unlocking the front door seemed as loud as a gunshot. Kovac had a direct view of the entry. He rose from his chair, at attention, and waited, feeling a strange mix of curiosity and aggression.

David Moore walked in, his tie askew, shirt collar undone. He was a good-enough-looking guy, Kovac supposed. Medium height, blondish conservative haircut. He might have been the athletic type once, but he was going soft, and his face and neck had a slight doughy quality that suggested indulgence. He wore a rumpled brown suit and a petulant expression.

In other words, in Kovac's vernacular: asshole.

Kovac took an instant dislike to Carey Moore's husband before one word came out of his mouth.

"Carey? What's going on?" the husband demanded, coming into the den. "What happened to you?"

Not said with loving concern, but almost as if he was offended that she looked the way she did.

"I was mugged in the parking ramp."

"Oh, my God."

"Your wife was attacked, Mr. Moore," Kovac said. "We believe it may have been an attempt on her life."

David Moore just stood there like a moron, looking from his battered wife to Kovac. "Who are you?"

Kovac showed him his badge. "Kovac. I'm a detective with the Homicide division."

"Homicide?"

"We also handle assaults. Assaults are the homicides of tomorrow," he said with a hint of sarcasm he knew David Moore wouldn't get. It was an inside joke. It always seemed like the department was more keen on solving the assaults, because there were more of them, and clearing them kept the violent-crime stats down.

Moore dismissed him, tossed his jacket on a chair, and finally went to his wife.

"Are you all right?"

"Does she look all right?"

Carey Moore gave Kovac the skunk eye.

The husband sat down on the love seat. "My God, Carey. Why didn't you call me?"

"Why don't you check your messages?" she said with an edge in her voice. "I did call you. I called you from the emergency room *six hours ago*."

Moore had the sense to look guilty. "Oh, shit. My battery must be dead."

"Or something," Kovac muttered.

The husband looked at him. "Excuse me?"

"I have to ask you some questions, Mr. Moore. It's just routine. Where were you between the hours of six and seven o'clock tonight?"

The judge glared at him. "Detective, this isn't necessary."

David Moore stood up, outraged. "Are you implying I might have attacked my own wife?"

"I'm not implying anything," Kovac said calmly. "I'm asking you a question. Do you have some problem with giving me a straight answer?"

"I don't like your attitude, Detective."

"Nobody does. Lucky for me, I don't give a rat's ass."

Moore flushed an unhealthy shade of red. He jammed his hands at his waist. "My wife is a respected member of the bar—"

"I know who your wife is, Mr. Moore," Kovac said. "Who are *you*? That's what I need to know. And so far, just from observation, I'm not coming up with a lot of flattering adjectives here."

Moore drew breath for another diatribe of indignation. His wife cut him off.

"David, stop it. For God's sake, just answer the man's questions. He's doing his job."

The husband clearly didn't like being chastened. He went a darker shade of red with embarrassment or anger, or both.

"Carey, he's not being respectful of you."

She looked away from him and shook her head with an *I'm so sick of you* sigh.

"I'm not trying to be a hard-ass here, Mr. Moore," Kovac lied. "But it's going on two o'clock in the morning. Your wife has been beaten, and she's received two threatening phone calls since. I don't have the patience to tiptoe around your ego.

"So let's try this again. Where have you been this evening?"

Moore clearly wanted to turn on his heel and storm out of the room. The big, dramatic exit for the put-upon hero of his own story.

The bruising and swelling was coming out in his wife's face. She was beginning to look like something that might live under a bridge in a horror movie. One eye was nearly swollen shut. The lump on her forehead looked like a horrible deformity. Her lower lip was twice its normal size. The stitches had pulled, and the split was beginning to bleed again.

David Moore hadn't so much as offered her a reassuring touch. He'd asked for no details of her attack, had made no comment on Kovac's suggestion it might have been

an attempt on her life. He hadn't even in-
quired if she might have been raped.

"I had a business dinner," Moore said.

"Where?"

"That new place in the IDS Tower next to
the Marquette Hotel, Buffalo Grill."

"What time was your reservation?"

"Seven-thirty, but we met for drinks first."

"When was that, and where?"

Moore looked away. "Why don't I just give
the name of the business associate I was
meeting? You'll want that anyway, won't
you?"

Kovac gave him the flat cop eyes. "Why
don't you just answer the question I asked
you?"

"Gentlemen?" the judge said abruptly. "I'm
not feeling well. I'd really like to go lie down
now. Feel free to continue without me."

She started to get off the love seat under
her own steam. The husband finally moved
to help her, taking hold of one elbow to
steady her.

"I'll help you upstairs."

She didn't thank him.

Kovac watched them go, trying to read
their body language. The judge was stiff and
limping, but forcing her back as straight as

she could. She kept her chin up, and she didn't lean on her husband, even though he was now trying to appear as solicitous as possible.

Kovac would have loved to hear the conversation between them as they went up the stairs, but they kept their voices to themselves. Instead, he took the opportunity to prowl around the den, looking for hints of who these people were, but there were more signs of who their decorator was than what made the Moore family tick.

The room seemed to belong predominantly to the husband. A lot of electronic toys—big plasma screen TV on the wall above the fireplace, stereo equipment, satellite radio setup. A couple of framed award certificates with Moore's name on them.

Kovac found the lack of family photographs and incidental personal touches telling. No one was in the middle of reading a novel or knitting a sweater. There were no toys or storybooks that would have belonged to Princess Lucy. A pricey, large flat-screen computer monitor sat in the middle of an immaculate desk. The bookcase behind the desk held books about the film industry, biographies of people Kovac had heard of and more he had not. A lot of videotape cases.

"They should have kept her in the hospital," David Moore complained as he came back into the room.

"She wouldn't stay," Kovac said, pulling a videotape off a shelf and pretending to study its title. "She wanted to come home, be with her family, except for you, of course."

"What the hell—?"

"She knew you weren't here," Kovac went on. "And she didn't want us tracking you down. Why do you think that is?"

"I don't think I told her where the dinner was," Moore said. "We're both very busy people. The details sometimes get lost."

"What are you so busy with, Mr. Moore? These business associates you were with— what kind of business are they in?"

"I'm a documentary filmmaker. The people I was with are potential financial backers for a film I want to make juxtaposing the gangsters of the thirties with street gangs of today."

"And why didn't you want to talk about these people in front of your wife?" Kovac asked, ambling closer to Carey Moore's husband. "Why didn't she want to stick around for the rest of this conversation?"

Moore tried to look confused. "I don't know what you mean, Detective. I was just trying to be helpful. I knew you would want their names—"

"But you didn't want to say where you met them for drinks?"

"I never said that."

"Uh-huh."

Flustered, Moore huffed a sigh. "We met in the lobby bar of the Marquette. Nothing suspicious about that, is there?"

Kovac shrugged. "Depends. Who are these cohorts of yours?"

"Edmund Ivors," Moore said without hesitation. "He's a businessman. He made his fortune in multiplex theaters and likes to give back to the industry by helping talented filmmakers."

"Like yourself."

"Yes."

"Should I have heard of you?" Kovac asked, deliberately rude.

A muscle flexed in David Moore's jaw. "I'd be surprised if you had," he said tightly.

"You don't strike me as the intellectual type."

Kovac raised his brows, amused. "Whoa. Go easy there, Sport. I'm not as dumb as I look. You really don't want to poke a stick at me, Dave," he said, smiling like a crocodile. "I'll feed it to you the hard way. But hey, points for showing some balls. Who else was at your little soiree?"

Moore sulked. "An associate of Mr. Ivors. Ms. Bird, uh, Ginnie Bird."

"Associate?" Kovac arched a brow. "Is that anything like being his *niece*?"

"I don't know what you're talking about," Moore said impatiently.

"You don't know what a euphemism is?" Kovac said. "I'll be blunt, then: Is Ms. Bird about work, or is Ms. Bird about fucking somebody?"

Moore glared at him. "Who the hell do you think you are, speaking that way—"

Kovac got in his face and backed him off a step. "I'm the homicide dick who's half-past sick of your attitude, pal. I think you didn't want to say in front of your wife that one of the people you spent the last six hours with, having the longest business dinner in recorded history, was a woman. And I think the reason that is, is that your wife doesn't trust you, and you know it."

Moore breathed heavily in and out of his nose, furious. Kovac figured the guy wanted to lay him out flat right there and then but didn't have the guts or the muscle to do the job.

"This conversation is over, Detective," Moore said, his jaw set tight. "I won't be treated like a criminal in my own home. You'll leave now. And in the morning, I'll be making phone calls to people who will make your life unpleasant."

A nasty smile curved Kovac's mouth. "Is that a threat, Mr. Moore?" he questioned softly. "Are you threatening me? You know people who'll do that kind of job for you? That would send you straight to the head of my shit list of suspects."

"My wife is a very well-connected woman," Moore said. "Connected to people who have the power to pull your strings."

Kovac chuckled like a predator with one paw already holding down his next live snack. "And you think she'd really do that for you? That's funny. I'd tag her for one of those ladies who wants her man to get out from behind her and fight his own battles."

"Get out of my house." The hate in David Moore's eyes was electric.

Kovac knew he was pushing a line, but he was enjoying himself too much to back off. He leaned against the side of an armchair the size of a small rhinoceros and crossed his arms.

"You know, you haven't asked one single question about what happened in that parking ramp. Is that because you don't need to or because you don't give a shit?"

"Of course I care!" David Moore rubbed his hands over his face and looked up at the ceiling as he moved away. "Carey insists it was a mugging. Do you really think someone tried to . . . meant to . . . harm her?"

"I've seen the videotape from the garage," Kovac said. "I think this mutt would have beaten her to death if she hadn't managed to hit her car alarm and spook him. There'd been one menacing call to the house before I got her back here from the hospital, and she just had an out-and-out threat on her cell phone. 'I'm coming to get you,' the guy said."

"Jesus," Moore said under his breath. "Can't you trace the calls? Can't you get an identification from the video? Clean it up, enhance it, zoom in on the guy's face—"

"We traced the number. That's a dead end. As far as magically making a bad video good—Hollywood doesn't write real crimes, Mr. Moore. And they don't budget real police departments. The teenager next door in this neighborhood probably has more sophisticated electronics than our Bureau of Investigation.

"We'll do everything we can to run this mutt to ground, but your wife is in serious danger," Kovac said. "It's partly my job to see that nothing worse happens to her, and I take my job very seriously, Mr. Moore.

"My victim is my first priority. You see, I don't get that many live ones. If I seem a little overprotective, a little too aggressive, that's why. Nobody else ranks above the judge while I'm on this case. Not you, not the chief of police, not the pope, not God Almighty. That's how I work.

"You'll have twenty-four-hour surveillance on your house. A technician was here already, to rig up your house phones so we can trap and locate call origins and so we have recordings of all calls in or out."

Moore dropped down onto a big square

leather ottoman, braced his elbows on his knees, and put his head in his hands. "I can't believe this is happening."

"Your wife made a very unpopular ruling today on the case against Karl Dahl," Kovac said. "Were you aware of that?"

"Yes, of course."

But it hadn't seemed important enough to him that he would forgo a business dinner in order to be there with her for support.

"This is an emotionally charged case, Mr. Moore. People have strong opinions, mostly that Karl Dahl should be boiled in tar, strung up in front of the government center like a piñata, and everyone in the state should get a few swings at him with an ax.

"Your wife made a ruling in his favor today, and tonight the son of a bitch broke jail. A triple murderer is running loose in the streets, and people are going to blame Judge Moore for that, even though she didn't have a damn thing to do with it."

"He escaped?" Moore asked, alarmed. "Do you think he was the one?"

"No," Kovac said. "But I think everyone in the Twin Cities is going to believe your wife is Karl Dahl's patron saint, including Karl Dahl."

Adrenaline ebbing, Kovac sighed and pushed away from the chair. He pulled out a business card and dropped it onto the ottoman next to David Moore's thigh.

"I'll leave now," he said. Now that he was good and ready.

He shook his head at himself as he walked out into the night. For guys, life was nothing but one big pissing contest. It was a pure damn wonder women didn't take over the world while men were busy trying to prove who had the biggest dick.

He raised a hand to the uniforms in the prowl car down the street as he got into his own car. He looked across the street at the Moore house, at the upstairs room with the light burning in the window, and wondered what the rest of the night was going to be like for Carey and David Moore.

14

With rare exceptions, Stan Dempsey had not slept for more than an hour at a stretch since he had walked into the Haas home on that fateful August evening, now more than a year ago. What sleep he got was fractured with nightmare images and emotions so strong he had no idea what to do with them.

He had been a simple man all his life. Quiet to the point that kids in school had thought him damaged in some way. He had really never had a friend in the way most people thought of friends. No slap-on-the-back buddies to drink with and watch sports with. Those things held no interest for him.

From childhood he had wanted to be a police detective like Joe Friday on *Dragnet*. He had been a voracious reader of detective stories and had starred in many of his boyhood daydreams. He always got his man.

He had served in the army and taken two years of junior college. When he finally made it to the police academy, he had worked harder than anyone in his class. The day of his graduation had been one of the proudest days of his life. The day he had made detective had been the pinnacle. His only dream had come true.

That his dream had now soured into this broken, bloodstained nightmare that was his life crushed him. Crushed his spirit, his sense of self, his sense of order in his world. He felt as though a huge black iron anvil had fallen from the sky and landed on him, and the feelings he had always kept so neatly contained had been forced from their box and were trying to come out through his eyes, his ears, his mouth, the tips of his fingers.

His superiors in the department worried that he might have an anger-management issue, that he might have a nervous break-down. They would have been terrified to know the things that really went on in his brain—thoughts of retribution, brutal vengeance, striking out at anyone he perceived to be on the wrong side of what was right. As his anxiety increased with the approach of the trial, the less he felt able to control those thoughts and the emotions that went with them.

News that Karl Dahl had escaped had reached him via the ten o'clock news Friday night. Stan could hardly remember the next couple of hours. He had gone into a rage. The pressure in his brain had been such that he had believed his head was going to explode, that he would be found that way on the floor of his living room, and everyone would assume he had killed himself.

He had overturned furniture. He had kicked a hole in a wall. He had gone into a closet and brought out every gun he owned. He had emptied his service weapon into his couch. That none of his neighbors had called the police was testimony to how his neighborhood had gone down over the years.

Between outbursts, he had fallen into fitful bouts of sleep wherever he happened to be in the house—on the living room floor, at the dining room table—only to wake and find the rage hadn't spent itself yet.

Karl Dahl was loose in the city, and there wasn't a damn thing he could do about it. Hell, no one had even thought to bother to call and break the news to him. Every cop in the city would be out beating the streets for Dahl, except for him. The brass had sat him down at a desk. He might as well have been chained to it.

Stan prowled restlessly through his small house, breathing too hard, the pressure building in his head again. The night was over. Saturday was breaking.

Stan looked at the television set on his kitchen counter. Channel 11 had dumped their usual Saturday-morning lineup of fishing shows and light local interest in favor of covering the escape of Karl Dahl and the beating of Judge Moore.

A news reporter stood in the street across from the county jail, explaining the way the riot had begun with another inmate attacking Dahl. All hell had broken loose. Ambulances had been called. The situation, the condition of some of the inmates, had been such that corners had been cut on procedure and safety. Somehow no one had cuffed the unconscious Karl Dahl to the gurney that he rode to HCMC.

Cluster fuck, Stan thought. The most important collar of his career was being ruined by stupidity and carelessness. Evil had been set loose to move at will through the community. Good people and their children were vulnerable.

Stan pulled a box of cereal from the cupboard and set it on the counter, going through the motions of making breakfast just to do something normal, just to expend a little energy, like opening a pressure valve ever so slightly.

On the television, they had gone from the jail to a scene of police cars prowling the dark streets, to a shot of the government center, to a shot of the parking ramp adjacent to it, to a head shot of Judge Moore.

She wore the robes and a serious expression that made her seem aloof. Her eyes were the color of a winter sky—a cold, piercing blue-gray. Stan knew she could use that look to make a man feel like he was nothing more than a cockroach crawling at her feet.

A reporter live in the parking ramp was talking about the assault on Judge Moore. The scene was still taped off, and numbered markers on the concrete showed where possible evidence had been discovered, bagged, and tagged.

Judge Moore, fresh from ruling for the defense in the matter of Karl Dahl's prior bad acts, had entered the ramp from the skyway. The perp had come out of the shadows, attacking her from behind. He had knocked her down and struck her and struck her and struck her. . . .

Stan felt himself flush not only with anger but with excitement. A part of his mind he didn't recognize came with the thought that she'd gotten what she deserved. She needed some sense knocked into her. She needed to know what it was like to be a victim, to feel that helpless, to be that terrified.

Stan had never been a violent man, but neither had he ever been the man he was now, in the wake of the Haas murders. He felt himself enjoying the idea of striking Carey Moore, venting his rage and frustration on her. And the rage and frustration doubled because she could make him feel these feelings, which went against the nature he'd had most of his life.

These thoughts swarmed in his brain as Stan tried to open the new box of Total with raisins. He couldn't get his blunt-tipped fingers under the edge of the flap. He had no fingernails to scratch at it.

He felt his head start to pound. He could hear it in his ears, a roaring that sounded like the sea was inside his skull. He could feel the pressure building and building.

The television was showing Judge Moore's home on Lake of the Isles. A brick fortress for the princess safe behind her gate, safe inside a security system. She had probably believed the Karl Dahls of the world could never touch her.

The box top wouldn't give. Stan dug at it with his fingers, fumbled the box, dropped it to the floor. As he bent to pick it up, the pressure in his head nearly made him pass out.

He flung the box down on the counter, grabbed a knife, and began stabbing the box over and over, his rage boiling over the rim of his control.

He jabbed the knife down again and again with such force that the tip was biting into the old linoleum countertop. He was aware that that sound was coming out of him and that it was a raw, animal call that came from a place so deep and primal inside of him he knew no other way to access it.

Cereal flew in all directions. He knocked the milk carton sideways, and milk spewed out of it. The knife stuck hard into the countertop, and he cut himself trying to pull it out. He grabbed the sugar bowl and threw it and smashed it, and sugar went everywhere.

All because of Carey Moore.

All because of careless jailers.

All because of Karl Dahl.

His life was out of control, all because of people who didn't care anything more about him than if he was a speck of dirt on the floor. His life meant nothing. All the good he had done in his life meant nothing.

Clamping his hands around his head, tears streaming down his face, Stan Dempsey slid down to the kitchen floor and sat there with his back against the cabinets and his mouth torn open as if to scream. But no sound came out of him now, and no one was there to hear it if it had.

Karl had catnapped beside the ragman off and on during the night, stirring at the least sound coming down the alley. He would awaken and sit up for a while to listen. He passed the time absently sawing long clumps of matted hair from the ragman's head, using the steak knife he'd found in the shopping cart.

The police car had not come back, and no one had come looking for his dead friend under the stairs behind the upholstery shop.

Anonymity had come with darkness. Now the new day was at hand, and with it a keen tension at the idea that he would be out among the public. But people would glance over him, not see who he was but what he was. And in their minds people would dismiss him as being beneath their notice. After all, they had more important things on their minds—an accused triple murderer was walking their streets.

Karl felt he should move, slowly begin to put some distance between himself and the hospital, and between himself and the corpse under the stairs.

The first order of business was to relieve himself, then find something to drink. His throat hurt something awful from the choking Snake had given him. He could feel it was all swollen inside. His voice box didn't feel right, and he could barely swallow. The mother of all headaches was banging inside his damaged skull.

He crawled slowly out from under the stairs on his hands and knees and worked his way up to standing. A rusted old van with faded blue paint sat parked off to the side of the small loading dock behind the upholstery shop. It looked to have died there. One tire was flat to the rim. The radio antenna had been fashioned from a wire coat hanger.

Karl went over to it and relieved himself on the far side of it, then turned the side mirror so he could see himself. The whites of his eyes had turned bloodred, the blood vessels bursting as he had struggled for air during the attack. His face was bruised and swollen, his lip split and crusted with blood. He didn't look himself at all, and that was a very good thing for a man in Karl's current position.

Taking one matted rope at a time, he shoved the hair he had cut from the dead man's head halfway up under the wool cap, letting the ends trail down his forehead and down the sides of his face, giving himself one more layer of disguise.

Pushing the ragman's shopping cart, Karl

made his way down the alley, checking in the trash along the way. Some worker had left half a bottle of beer sitting on a vegetable crate behind the diner. Karl helped himself, then climbed up on the Dumpster he had hidden in, and scored a pork chop bone with some meat still on it and a piece of liver that had dried to the texture of shoe leather. He sunk his teeth into the cold, greasy meat of the pork chop.

"Hey! Get outta my trash!"

A squat man in a dirty apron and dirtier thin white undershirt came out the back door of the restaurant. He wore a dingy white knit cap on his head, rolled up on the sides, and a lot of blue tattoos on forearms roped with muscle.

"Get out, you crazy old lice head! Get the fuck outta here!"

Karl threw the pork chop bone in his direction, turned, and left, his shopping cart rattling over the pitted, uneven pavement of the alley. At the end, he turned the corner, went around to the front of the block, parked his shopping cart where he could see it, and went inside the diner through the front door.

A large woman with jet-black hair up in a

bun, and a face like a cigar store Indian, came away from the counter with a ferocious expression and a damp rag in one hand.

"Hey, you! Out!" she shouted. She had an accent he thought might be Greek.

Karl pulled a twenty out of his coat pocket and shook it at her. For the first time since he'd been choked, he tried to speak. His voice was as rough as the back of a rasp, and it hurt like hell to use it.

"I got money," he said. "All I want is a cup of coffee, ma'am, and maybe some eggs. I got money. Please, ma'am?"

The woman stopped a good ten feet away from him and gave him the eye.

"I'm down on my luck, ma'am," he said. "I don't mean no harm. You can take the whole twenty if that's it. I just want a square meal. It ain't often I can afford to have one someone else ain't throwed out first."

She was still glaring at him, her arms crossed beneath her ample bosom. "You can't eat here. You scare my customers."

There were no other customers in the place.

"Please, ma'am? Just a cup of coffee. A biscuit. Anything . . ."

The woman appeared unmoved, but the fact that she hadn't started screaming at him seemed a good sign to Karl.

"If you could be so kind, ma'am," he said softly. "The Lord loves them what helps the down-and-out."

The waitress snorted at that, turned on the heel of her orthopedic shoes, and walked off.

Karl wondered if she would go into the kitchen and tell the squat man to come run him off. Until he would find out, he watched the news on the television that was bolted to the wall above the diner counter.

He was the news. His escape, the search for him, the warning to citizens not to approach him but to call the police if they thought they had spotted him. Larger than life, Karl thought, and it pleased him. It wasn't often in his life that he had been considered important.

When the newspeople moved on to the next story, it was of Judge Carey Moore. She had been attacked in a parking ramp last night and rushed to the Hennepin County Medical Center. Karl wondered if she had been there at the same time he had. That would be something, he thought, that the woman who had championed him that very day would be in the same emergency room as him, and maybe even because of him.

She had been the talk of the county jail. Much of it lewd and crude talk, because she was a beautiful woman and all men in prison tended to think about—besides getting out—was having sex. The notion that she was a judge excited them all the more. To take a woman in a position of power and dominate her was a very erotic fantasy. Karl felt it working on him as he watched file footage of Judge Moore giving a press conference.

Her eyes were large and unblinking, her expression very serious. Her mouth was every man's wet dream—the upper lip a perfect Cupid's bow, the lower one full and slightly down-turned, as if she was on the verge of a pout. Her neck was smooth and pale and elegant.

Karl had never known a woman like that, not in any sense of the word. She was an angel. She was *his* angel.

The television was showing a picture of her home. A live shot, the crawler on the bottom of the screen said. It was a beautiful brick house with a neat yard and a black iron fence. Not a mansion, but the kind of a house a lady would live in.

The reporter talked about how people in that neighborhood were never bothered by terrible crimes, but a crime had been visited upon one of their own. How one of their own was paying the price for siding with a murderer.

Live near Lake of the Isles, Candy Cross, Channel 3 News.

Lake of the Isles . . . What a fine-sounding place . . .

The large Greek lady came across the room of empty tables, still scowling, but with a styrofoam carton and cup. She set them on the table and stepped back before Karl's lice could jump on her.

"Here," she said. "But you can't eat here. You scare my customers. Go away."

"God bless you, ma'am," Karl whispered, and handed the woman the twenty.

She folded the bill and stuffed it down her cleavage.

She didn't come back with change.

15

Kovac woke to a pounding he thought was inside his head. The clock read 7:32. In the morning. On Saturday.

He rolled out of bed, naked as the day he was born, and went to look out the window. On the roof of the house next door, his idiot neighbor was swinging a hammer. The sound reverberated in the otherwise-still morning air like gunshots.

Kovac shoved the old double-hung window open. "Hey! Elmer Fudd! What the hell are you doing?" he shouted.

The neighbor looked over at him, hammer cocked in his hand like he might throw it. The guy was seventy-plus, with mean, piggy little eyes and more hair growing out of his ears than on his head. Not that his head could be seen. He wore his favorite red plaid bomber cap with the flaps tied up on top of his head. The ends of the ties stuck up like antennae.

"Getting a jump on the Christmas lights!" he said.

"At seven-fucking-thirty in the morning?"

The old man frowned deeply. "You've got a filthy mouth on you!"

"I'm not even warmed up," Kovac said. "Are you out of your fucking head? Christmas? It isn't even Halloween!"

"Shows what you know!" the old man shouted. "*Farmer's Almanac* says it's an early winter. Could be a blizzard by Halloween."

"Could be I'm gonna shoot you dead off that roof if you don't stop with the hammer."

The neighbor gave him a face. "I'm within my rights. City ordinance says I can bang all I want after seven-thirty A.M."

Dismissing Kovac, the old man teed up a nail and smacked it into his roof. Every year it was the same thing—the most god-awful array of mixed holiday messages filled the man's yard, crowned his roof, hung from the eaves, lit up the trees. Santa Claus bringing gifts to the baby Jesus. The herald angel beaming down on an army of plywood snowmen. All of it illuminated with more wattage than the whole of Times Square. For eight weeks it was like living next door to the sun.

"You ever hear of common courtesy, you rancid old fart?"

The old man stuck his tongue out.

Kovac turned around and mooned him.

So began his day. A shower. The patch. Coffee. A couple of doughnuts, just to perpetuate the stereotype. The local morning news was all about Karl Dahl's escape and the public outcry caused by it. The attack on Carey Moore was a distant second. Half the city probably thought she deserved it. Now that the newsies had all but announced her home address, there would probably be a steady stream of cars driving by to egg her house.

Or worse . . .

Kovac sighed, rubbed a hand over his face, and tried to decide where to start. He or Liska would have to speak to the judge's clerk. See if she had any hate mail on file. Cross-reference the phone number from the two threatening calls with the judge's phone logs. They needed to get a printout of any recently released felons Carey Moore had put away in her capacity as either prosecutor or judge.

They had to meet Lieutenant Dawes downtown at nine so she could impress upon them what her boss had no doubt already impressed upon her, and right up the food chain to the chief, who had already been read the riot act by the mayor, and the county attorney, who had heard it from the state attorney general. Kovac and Liska would be lectured on the gravity of the situation, like they were morons who hadn't managed to figure that out for themselves.

Christ, how he hated the politics of the system. He had always wanted to line up the brass monkeys, ask those who hadn't worked on the street in the last decade to take a giant step back, and have them drop into a big black hole.

If he could avoid that meeting, postpone it until, say, the case was solved, he would.

He needed to speak with Stan Dempsey.

Man, you are desperate.

Kovac had never balked at going after a bad cop. A wrong guy was a wrong guy, badge or no. He'd even toughed out a stretch working Internal Affairs a million years ago. He hadn't liked it, but he'd done it. But Stan Dempsey wasn't a bad cop. Kovac felt nothing but pity for the man.

Stan Dempsey was a guy who had plodded along through life mostly under the radar. A decent cop, but no one the brass would take notice of until they decided he was a liability. He was a guy who really didn't have any friends, because he was odd and quiet and antisocial. Stan Dempsey would probably have been more comfortable working in the morgue than on the streets, but he was a cop, and that was probably all he had ever wanted to be.

Kovac doubted that anyone Dempsey had ever partnered with knew much of anything about him. But everyone knew Dempsey had lost it in the interview room when they had first questioned Karl Dahl for the Haas murders. Dempsey had exploded into a rage that was three times bigger than he was. Totally out of his head. It had taken two other detectives to pull him off Dahl. Ranting, eyes rolling back in his head, practically foaming at the mouth. He had had to be sedated.

Kovac tried to imagine Stan Dempsey lying in wait for Carey Moore in the parking garage, rushing out at her, knocking her down, hitting her again and again.

You fucking bitch! You fucking cunt!

The rage was there. Pent up behind that hangdog face and emotionless demeanor. Kovac grabbed a pen and a receipt from Domino's Pizza and scribbled a note to see if the video geek could zoom in somehow on the weapon. If it was a police baton . . . that wouldn't be a good thing.

Stan Dempsey lived maybe a mile away from Kovac. His house was a small story and a half with gray shingle siding and white trim. The yard was scattered with stray leaves that had drifted across the sidewalk from a maple tree on the boulevard.

Kovac went to the front door and rang the bell. The house was silent. No barking dog, no Stan. He rang the bell again and waited.

Where would Stan Dempsey go this early on a Saturday morning? The supermarket for his groceries. He struck Kovac as the kind of guy who would eat liver and onions . . . and hash . . . and all those kinds of food that normal people wouldn't eat. Tongue . . . oxtail . . .

Still no Stan coming to the door. Kovac tried to turn the doorknob. Locked.

He could have gone for a walk. Maybe he'd gotten out of town for the weekend. An old fragment of memory made Kovac think Dempsey was a fisherman. Maybe he had a cabin on one of Minnesota's ten-thousand-plus lakes.

Kovac moved off the front step and went to the picture window that faced the street. The drapes were closed. He couldn't see inside.

Around the side of the house, a lace curtain hung in a window that might have been a dining room. But the window was shorter vertically than the picture window, and Kovac wasn't tall enough to look in.

He went around to the back of the house. A charcoal grill was in its place near the back door. Inexpensive white plastic furniture sat on a concrete patio. A single chair and a small table. A lonely tableau. Kovac grabbed the chair and went back to the window with the lace curtain.

What he expected to see, he didn't know. But he hadn't expected what he found. A small traditional dining room, the walls painted a weak mint green. A traditional

cherry buffet. A traditional cherrywood dining room table . . . with an arsenal of
weapons laid out neatly on top of it. And a
video camera sitting on a tripod, pointed at
the one chair pulled out from the table.

"Oh, shit," Kovac said under his breath as
his stomach dropped.

"Can I help you?"

Kovac looked over his shoulder to find a
tiny old lady in a lavender flowered house-
coat and slippers that had been made to
look like white rabbits with floppy pink-lined
ears.

"I'm a police officer, ma'am," he said, getting down off the chair. He pulled his badge
and ID out of his coat pocket and showed
them to her.

She squinted at them. "Mr. Dempsey is a
police officer too," she said. "A detective."

"Yes, ma'am, I know."

"I'm his neighbor. Hilda Thorenson."

He wanted to tell Hilda it wasn't a good
idea to approach a stranger who might have
been looking to rob the place, but now was
not the time.

"Do you know if Mr. Dempsey is home?"
he asked.

"Oh, no. I wouldn't know that. Why? Is something the matter?"

"Maybe," Kovac said.

His mind was racing. Visions of Stan Dempsey eating his gun flashed through his head. He didn't want to find that. He'd handled a couple of cop suicides in his career. He didn't want to look at another dead cop and think: *There but for the grace of God go I.* He didn't want to have to tell another wife, child, girlfriend that their loved one had chosen to end his life because the emotional pain of that life had been just too much to bear.

Family never understood the why of that. Why hadn't their husband/wife/girlfriend/ boyfriend/father/mother come to them to unload that pain? Why hadn't he or she gone to a minister, a priest, a rabbi, a shrink for help? They didn't understand that cops felt no one understood them but other cops. And still, cops didn't confide in one another about the problems they had. They didn't want to seem weak to their peers, didn't want to give superiors a reason to look at them.

Kovac felt guilty all of a sudden that he hadn't made more of an effort to get to know Stan Dempsey over the years. Maybe if he had, the guy would have had at least two white plastic chairs in his backyard.

"I need to get inside Mr. Dempsey's house," he told Hilda Thorenson. "I'm afraid something might have happened to him."

The old woman looked alarmed. "Oh, dear!"

Kovac went to try the back door. Locked. *Shit.* He was too damned old to be kicking doors in.

"I have a key," the neighbor said. "For emergencies. Wait here. I'll go get it."

Kovac watched her go at something slightly more than a snail's pace. She had to be eighty if she was a day. Dempsey might have been in the house at that very minute, sitting on the toilet, trying to work up the courage to pull the trigger.

He had already been feeling desperate, trapped at a desk while other people took over the case that had pushed him to the breaking point. He would have been upset about Judge Moore's ruling, maybe to the point of acting out against her. And Karl Dahl's escape would surely have pushed him over the edge.

Kovac couldn't wait for a key.

He went to the back door and blocked the screen door open. He grabbed a bug candle in a small galvanized pot and smashed one of the old glass panes in the door. Ten seconds later he was in the house, calling for Dempsey.

Without even trying to take in the scene, Kovac dashed through the small house.

"Stan? It's Sam Kovac. Where are you?" he shouted as he pushed open the door to the small bathroom off the hall. Empty. Dempsey's home office. Empty. He took the stairs two at a time, bracing himself mentally for the sound of the shot.

"Stan? Where are you? We need to talk."

Bedroom one. Bedroom two. Empty.

Taking a deep breath, Kovac rested his hand on the doorknob of the bathroom. This was where they did it, often as not, in the bathroom, where the mess could be steam-cleaned.

Kovac pushed the door open.

Empty.

A second's relief.

He ran back down the stairs and out the back door, nearly mowing down the nosy neighbor.

Garage.

Carbon monoxide.

But the small detached garage sat empty. No Stan Dempsey. No car.

Shit.

"What's happening?" the old lady asked. "Is Mr. Dempsey hurt?"

"He's not here, ma'am," Kovac said.

"Well, I don't know where he'd go," she said, as if she couldn't possibly imagine Stan Dempsey having a life.

Kovac rubbed the back of his neck and sighed heavily. "Ma'am, I'm going to have to ask you to return to your home. The police will be sealing off this residence."

The woman looked confused and frightened as she backed away.

"Oh, dear."

"Thank you for your help," Kovac said. He stood there until the old lady turned away and retreated, the bunny ears of her slippers bobbing up and down as she went.

The basement of the Haas home had been where the murdered children had been hung from the ceiling. There was a certain logic to thinking Stan Dempsey might have chosen the basement, might have hanged himself down there.

Kovac went back inside and flipped on the light leading down to the basement.

"Stan? It's Sam Kovac. I'm coming downstairs," Kovac warned, going slowly, taking one step at a time.

The basement was finished with knotty pine paneling, cheap green carpet, and a yellowed acoustical tile ceiling that had absorbed years of cigarette smoke. No walls divided the space. A laundry area in one corner. Storage took up one end. In the remaining quarter Stan Dempsey had set up his own command center.

Several freestanding bulletin boards were covered with photos from the Haas murder scene, photos from the autopsies. Copies of reports, copies of Dempsey's own notes. He had taped white butcher paper to the wall above the bulletin boards with time lines sketched out—who was where, when; what time the bodies had been discovered; the approximate time of death as stated by the ME. Boxes on an old card table held copies of files on the case.

None of it struck Kovac as being particularly unusual. He had a basement full of old case files and notes himself. Most of the detectives he knew did. They hung on to them for various reasons—superstition, paranoia, in case an old case got overturned on appeal, in case the station burned to the ground and the originals were destroyed. He had laid out cases himself in his home office so he could ponder and stew over them in his off hours.

The thing that bothered Kovac about Stan Dempsey's basement was the chair. A single straight-backed wooden chair sat front and center by the board with the photographs. An oversized red glass ashtray sat on the floor beside it, full of ashes and butts.

Kovac could imagine Stan Dempsey sitting in that chair for hours on end, staring at the carnage. Images straight out of the darkest nightmares anyone could imagine. The brutality stark and cruel, frozen in time. The faces of the victims, blank and staring. The mind didn't want to accept the idea that these had been real people, living human beings, only hours before the photographs had been taken. Or that in those hours prior to death, these people—this mother and two small children—had been subjected to unspeakable tortures, that they had experienced choking fear, that they had probably known they were going to die.

If a person's mind allowed those realities to sink in, then it became too easy to hear the screams, to see the sheer terror in those now-blank faces. It became too easy to see the events unfold like the worst kind of horror show.

If a cop allowed that to happen, if he made a case like this one personal, if he allowed logic and procedure and a professional distance to be overrun by emotion and empathy and reaction . . . thereon lay the road to madness.

A terrible feeling of foreboding lay like a stone in Kovac's gut as he climbed the basement stairs. This time he took in everything as he went through the house.

The kitchen was a mess. Cereal flakes were all over the counter, all over the floor, as if the box had exploded. Raisins were scattered throughout like rat turds. The milk carton had been overturned. Milk puddled on the counter and dripped over the edge.

The cereal box looked to have been slashed several times with a knife. The countertop had received similar treatment—multiple stab wounds. The knife was not in sight, but there was some blood.

Stan Dempsey lost his mind in this room,

Kovac thought as he looked around at the chaos. A small television sat on the counter. The local news was running, but the sound was off. Karl Dahl's mug shot and his physical description were up on the screen.

Considered extremely dangerous.

Do not attempt to approach.

Call 911.

Kovac moved into the dining room. From the dining room, he could see the living room, which was also trashed. The old brown couch had been shot to death. A floor lamp had been knocked over. The coffee table had been overturned.

What the hell went on here?

Kovac briefly considered the notion of an intruder, but the house had been locked up tight. No. This was Stan Dempsey's rage. This was what had been building inside that homely, quiet, strange man in the months since Stan Dempsey had been called out on a triple homicide one stormy night in August a year past.

The array of weapons laid out on the dining room table was impressive. Shotguns, a deer rifle, several handguns, some that appeared to be World War II vintage. Knives of various lengths and blades. An old leather sap—a leather sack filled with sand or buckshot. Coppers used to carry them in the old days before the Miranda rules had come down. A smack behind the ear could take down a big guy instantly if it was done right. Nobody carried them anymore. Not legally, anyway.

And lined up neatly in a row above the weapons: medals. A Purple Heart. A Bronze Star. Several commendations from the police department. All laid out on display, as if Stan had fully expected people to come into his home. These were the things he had wanted seen, the awards that had marked his life into segments—the army, war, the police department.

On the buffet behind the table stood a couple of framed photographs. Stan in a bad suit from the seventies and a too-wide tie. Standing beside him, a homely woman with beauty-parlor-blond hair teased and sprayed into a sheer helmet circling her head. A girl of maybe five or six sitting in front of them, the only one smiling, a black hole where one front tooth had been.

The family. Kovac hadn't known Dempsey had ever been married. It was difficult to picture. He had seen no evidence of a woman living in the house. No clothes in the closets, no woman stuff on the dresser or nightstand. The wife was gone, by either divorce or death. The little girl was grown and long gone by now.

Finally, with a sense of dread heavy in his chest, Kovac looked at the video camera perched on its tripod, pointing at the lone chair pulled out from the table. He stepped behind it, looking how to turn the thing from RECORD TO VCR

Stan Dempsey came on the small screen, walking in front of the camera, seating himself in the chair. When he began to speak, there was no emotion whatsoever. Very matter-of-fact. He talked about the things that had gone on in his life, how all he'd ever wanted to do was become a cop, a detective. He talked about how much he had loved the job over the years. He talked about a couple of cases he'd worked that he was especially proud of.

In the background Kovac could see through the doorway to the kitchen to a cookie jar in the shape of a pig sitting on its ass on the counter. He looked up from the video screen, through the doorway into the kitchen. There was the cookie jar, a silly, stupid thing completely incongruous with its owner. A simple, normal thing completely in contrast to the creepy, dark tone of the videotape.

The whole thing seemed surreal. Dempsey was too calm on the video. The kind of calm that came to people when they had made a difficult decision and felt at peace. He picked up a knife and stroked the blade lovingly while he explained what kind of knife it was, what its purpose was.

He put the first knife down and picked up a broad, gleaming hunting knife with a deadly-looking serrated blade. He explained how it could be used to cut the throat of an animal, how it could be used to gut the animal, to skin the animal.

He picked up a boning knife and explained the process of removing bones and cutting the meat from them. The job took a very sharp knife, he said. Stan talked about how he oiled and honed the blades of his knives himself and took great pride in his work.

The hunting knife and the boning knife were both absent from the table now, Kovac noted.

On the tape, Dempsey picked up a long

two-pronged fork, the kind that came with barbecue sets.

"Depending on how a person used this," Dempsey said in his flat, monotone voice, *"this could be a very effective tool."*

Jesus God.

He talked about his guns, how the first two of the collection had been his father's, his own pistol from WWII and another he had taken off a dead German.

He talked about the Haas murders, how hard he had worked that case, the rage he had felt in the interrogation room looking at the man who had tortured and murdered a woman and two little children. He talked about how angry he'd been when the lieutenant had pulled him not only from the case but from the rotation, and stuck him on a desk.

". . . and now the judge has ruled Karl Dahl's prior bad acts can't be admitted into evidence. The jury might find that evidence too significant. The buildup to a triple homicide, the making of a killer. Judge Moore found that to be prejudicial and inflammatory. Well, that's the whole idea, isn't it?" Dempsey asked. *"Are we supposed to pretend Karl Dahl was a damn Boy Scout be-*

fore he butchered Marlene Haas and those two children? Of course he wasn't. He was a criminal and a pervert, but the jury won't hear about that."

Dempsey shook his head slowly. *"That's just not right. It's not right for a judge to take away the prosecution's case. Judge Moore's decision puts Karl Dahl one step closer to walking on a triple murder, and she should be ashamed of herself.*

"I hear she has a small daughter. I wonder how differently she would feel if her daughter were raped and sodomized and hung up from the ceiling like a slaughtered lamb. I think she'd sing a different tune."

Holy Christ.

Kovac felt sick.

"Of course, it doesn't matter now," Stan Dempsey said. *"Karl Dahl is out, running around loose. Escaped. I don't know how that could happen, but it did. And I have to do something about that. Someone has to take responsibility. That'll be me. I'll do that. The guilty have to pay.*

"The guilty have to pay . . ."

The screen turned to snow.

Stan Dempsey was gone.

16

Carey was surprised when she woke Saturday morning, because she didn't believe she had slept all night. She had hovered in the strange twilight between consciousness and unconsciousness, denied the rest of sleep, still subjected to the nightmares. She had felt as if she were underwater on a moonlit night, being held under by a hidden force. Dark images of violence had drifted before her, and she had fought to free herself from them, breaking the surface into consciousness, gasping for air, only to be pulled back under moments later.

David had not come to bed. When he had walked her upstairs, he'd told her he would stay in the guest room so she could have the bed to herself and not be disturbed by him moving around. Carey thought he had probably been as relieved as she not to be sharing the bed. As much as she would have liked someone to comfort her, that someone was not her husband. David wasn't good at taking the role of defender-protector. She was supposed to be strong and self-reliant so he didn't have to be.

Slowly, carefully, painfully, Carey eased herself up to sit for a moment with her feet over the side of the bed. A little dizziness buzzed around her brain, but not as bad as she had thought it would be. The next step was to stand, and she managed that. Both knees were sore from landing on the concrete when her assailant had knocked her down. She walked like a ninety-year-old woman, shuffling her way into her bathroom.

The face that greeted her in the mirror was a horror. Black eye, bruised swollen knot on her forehead, stitches crawling over her lip like a centipede. Most adults would be startled to see her. The idea of her daughter seeing her this way for the first time upset Carey more than seeing herself had.

Lucy was only five. She didn't need to be told anything more than that someone had knocked Mommy down. If she had been a little older, Carey would have worried about what the kids at school might say to her, having overheard their parents' comments. But at five, children were still mostly interested in innocent things that existed in their immediate orbit.

An overwhelming sense of protectiveness rushed through her, and Carey wanted to take Lucy in her arms and hold her tight and not let anything bad come into her life. The things Carey had seen over the years, as a prosecutor, as a judge . . . The horrible things she knew one human could do to another for no reason at all . . . She wanted to shield her daughter from all of it.

She thought of the two foster children found hanging in the basement of the Haas home and wondered if their mother had ever had the same desire.

Moving in slow motion, Carey undressed, dropping the torn slacks and ruined silk blouse on the floor to be discarded later. She took a warm shower, wincing as the water droplets touched the torn skin of her knuckles and her knees. She supposed she should have called Anka to help her, but she was too private a person. David should

have been there. Even if he thought she
didn't want him there, he should have been
there to offer help and sympathy and
comfort.

She wondered what Kovac had made of
the scene last night. He was a good cop,
and a good cop was a quick study of people and the dynamics between them. He
had taken an instant dislike to David; that
much had been clear. He had all but accused her husband of having been with
another woman when he should have been
with her. The fact that that was probably
true had been more than Carey wanted to
deal with. And she knew Kovac hadn't
missed that either.

She pulled on an old pair of baggy gray
sweatpants and a favorite black cashmere
cardigan sweater that had been washed
and worn so many times it felt like a child's
security blanket wrapped around her.

A quick peek out the front window told
her the media had not given up interest in
her. Vans from all the local TV stations were
parked across the street, their dish antennae standing at attention.

The radio car Kovac had promised sat at
the curb in front of the house like a very

large guard dog. This wasn't the first time in her career Carey had needed police protection. Her life had been threatened more than once when she had been prosecuting gang murders. Going head-to-head with gang criminals and their sleazy attorneys was not about winning friends.

Sitting on the bench was no different. A criminal trial always ended with one side unhappy, angry, bitter. The judge was considered a friend only by the winning team.

Turning away from the window, Carey noticed for the first time that the house was silent. No TV blasting Saturday-morning cartoons. No sounds of people having breakfast. It was early, but Anka was an early riser, and Lucy was never far behind her, even on the weekend.

She opened the bedroom door and listened. She could smell coffee, but it was so quiet she could hear the downstairs hall clock ticking. The door to Lucy's bedroom was open. She could see a corner of the bed, already made. The door to Anka's room was closed. Carey knocked softly but got no answer.

She checked in the guest room, expecting the bed to be torn asunder. David had never made a bed in his life, or picked up a shirt or a sock. He left a room looking like it had been ransacked by thieves. There was no sign of his having been in the room at all.

"Hello?" she called down the stairs.

The house was empty. Everyone had gone, just left her without a word, probably assuming she would want to sleep in.

Even knowing that was the logical explanation, Carey felt apprehension and anxiety swell inside. Residual effects of the attack. Irrational fear even while in a safe environment. The sense of dread that the people she loved were in danger and would be hurt. The fear that she was alone and her attacker would come back.

"I'm coming to get you, bitch . . ."

The memory of that low, menacing voice was like a finger tracing down the back of her neck.

Carey shook off the sensation and slowly, carefully, painfully descended the stairs to the first floor.

In the den she found evidence of David. He had spent the night on the love seat. A gold chenille throw was lying on the floor. A heavy crystal tumbler—empty, save for a desiccated wedge of lime—sat on the end table without benefit of a coaster to protect the antique that had belonged to her father.

Carey picked up the glass and rubbed a thumb over the damp stain it had left. The glass had held gin. The slightly sour, astringent smell lingered.

She was the one who had been beaten and threatened, and he was the one drinking.

Exhausted from what little she'd done, Carey sat down in the leather executive's chair behind David's desk. The silence of the room rang in her ears, and dizziness swooped back in and around her head like a flock of sparrows. She waited it out, focusing on the items on the desk—the IBM flat-screen monitor, the telephone, the notepad.

During one of her wakeful moments in the night, she had thought she heard David talking to someone. The memory came back to her now, and she wondered if it had really happened or if his voice had been part of a dream. Who would he have been having a conversation with at three in the morning? Had Kovac stayed that long? She didn't recall his voice. Only her husband's.

She looked more closely at the notepad

on the desk. David was a nervous doodler when he was on the phone. The top sheet of the pad was clean, but with some indentation marks. She couldn't make out any words. But lying on top of the garbage in the leather trash container beside the desk was a wadded-up piece of the same paper.

There was no hesitation. Carey felt no twinge of guilt. She reached into the trash and retrieved the note, handling it with the same detachment she would have used as a prosecutor examining evidence.

Most of the scribbling on the page was of dark geometric shapes, boxes, rectangles, quadrangles. In the center of the page was a monetary amount, twenty-five thousand dollars, with three harsh lines drawn beneath it for emphasis.

Maybe he had found a backer for his project after all.

But if the note was related to the half conversation she believed she had heard, the call had come or been placed in the middle of the night. No business deals happened at three in the morning, unless David had suddenly tapped into investors in China.

Late-night conversations in hushed voices were between lovers, or associates whose business couldn't be conducted in the light of day.

Twenty-five thousand dollars was a lot of money. Twenty-five thousand dollars in the middle of the night was a payoff, a bribe, blackmail. . . .

Carey folded the note and tucked it into the pocket of her sweater, and wondered what the hell her husband had gotten into.

She stared at the telephone, considering the step she was about to take. She was about to open a door and walk through it onto a path that would very probably take her to the end of her marriage. But she had already conceded her marriage was over. There was no point in feeling nervous or hesitant or in dreading what she was going to find.

Without allowing herself to feel anything—no guilt, no sadness, no anger—she picked up the handset and keyed the scroll button to the last call received. The mystery number. The caller who had asked for Marlene. The same caller who had whispered over her cell phone: *I'm coming to get you, bitch.*

If David had been on this phone, the call had been outgoing.

She touched the redial button, waited as

the phone on the other end rang unanswered, then picked up and played a recording of the operating hours of Domino's Pizza.

Twenty-five thousand dollars was a lot of pizza.

David hadn't used this phone for any late-night clandestine call. If there had been any such call, it had to have been made or received on his cell phone.

Carey opened the upper left-hand desk drawer. The drawer was a catchall for things they used day-to-day—extra check blanks, stamps, address labels, things they both used. It was where they kept tickets to events, and paper clips, and bills to be paid. No one using that drawer had an expectation of privacy.

She walked her fingers through the different divided sections of the drawer. Tickets to an ice show. Carey smiled just enough to pull at the stitches in her lip. Lucy's current passion was figure skating. She was looking forward to taking her daughter out.

Had been looking forward to . . . The show was just two days away. It was doubtful either the bruises from the beating or the public resentment for her position on Karl

Dahl's prior bad acts would have faded by then.

The smile slipped away. She didn't want to put Lucy in a position where she might be frightened or upset because of the way strangers felt about her mother. That wasn't fair to her child. Carey would end up giving her ticket to Anka, and the Moore family outing would be comprised of daughter, daddy, and nanny.

Pushing the disappointment aside, Carey continued her search, methodically moving toward the back of the drawer, looking for David's cell phone bill. She checked the amounts due on all the other bills in the drawer, looking for one in the amount of twenty-five thousand dollars. There wasn't one.

There was, however, a note written in David's hand with a list of phone numbers and corresponding names. *Elite, First Class, Dream Girls.*

Carey picked up the phone and dialed the last number, getting a sexy voice mail message.

"Dream Girls Escorts make your dreams come true. Leave a message at the tone,

and we'll fulfill your fantasies as soon as we can."

Nausea churned in Carey's stomach. Her husband was using the services of prostitutes, apparently on a regular basis. The fact that she shared a bed with him made her want to go and take a shower. The fact that she had no idea how long this had been going on or whether or not he had put her at risk made her angry. Their sex life had dwindled to nothing months before, but for all Carey knew David had established this habit long ago. Months. Years, even.

This is unbelievable, she thought. This had been going on right under her nose, and she hadn't seen it. She hadn't looked for it. The truth was, lately she hadn't cared what David was up to. She hadn't wanted the distraction of caring. And he had to have known it. Why else would he have felt so comfortable that he would leave this list in a desk drawer where she might have come across it on any given day?

Or maybe he had wanted her to find the list, either to get her attention, to hurt her, or to push her into taking an action he didn't have the guts to take.

Carey made a copy of the list and added it to her growing pile of evidence.

Slowly, she swiveled the desk chair around to face the built-in cabinets and pulled open a file drawer. David was organized to the point of being anal. There was a file for everything—bank statements, receipts, paid bills broken down into smaller categories: electricity, gas, etc.

The job of bill paying and record keeping had been assumed by David from the start of their marriage. He had taken on the responsibility willingly, and with an air of self-importance. He had a better head for business than she did. Lately, he had complained about being made to feel like a secretary, as if it was beneath him to write a check and stick a stamp on an envelope or click a few keys to pay bills electronically. And yet when Carey had suggested that Anka might like to do the job for some extra cash every week, David had accused her of belittling his role in the family.

Carey had refrained from snapping back that his role in the family had become largely ornamental.

She pulled the file with the paid phone bills and lifted out her husband's last cell phone bill. There were a lot of calls to numbers she didn't recognize, not that she had expected to recognize any of them. David had associates and acquaintances in his own world, and he rarely shared that world with her. A lot of repeat calls to one particular number. A lot. Maybe fifty or more on this one bill.

She picked up the phone and dialed the number. A machine answered with a woman's breathy voice.

"I can't take your call right now. I'm busy having fun. Leave a message. Bye."

A girlfriend, Carey supposed, but she didn't feel anything as the thought crossed her mind. No jealousy, no hurt. It was as if she were looking into the affairs of a stranger.

She ran the phone bill through the fax machine to make a copy, put the original back, and replaced the file.

With the same sense of detachment, she pulled the credit card statements and receipts for David's business account, sat back in the chair, and started going through them.

Legitimate expenses, and plenty of the other kind. Restaurant tabs, bar tabs.

Seventy-five dollars to a local florist. Fifty-three dollars to the same florist. Forty-five dollars, same florist. Sixteen hundred dollars charged as a gift certificate to a gym in Edina, ten minutes away. Some gift. Forty-three hundred dollars to Bloomingdale's. Four hundred ninety-seven dollars to the Marquette Hotel. The receipt was dated the day before.

"*. . . Where have you been this evening?*" *Kovac asked.*

"*I had a business dinner.*"

"*Where?*"

"*That new place in the IDS Tower next to the Marquette Hotel. . . .*"

A strange, hollow feeling opened up in Carey's chest, as if her ribs were being spread apart. While she had been lying in a hospital bed, David had been lying in a hotel bed with another woman.

Setting that thought aside, she copied the credit card statements, then looked through the canceled checks. No twenty-five-thousand-dollar checks, but a monthly check to a property management company for thirty-five hundred dollars going back at least eight months.

Housing for the girlfriend? His own secret

hideout for entertaining prostitutes? That son of a bitch. He hadn't made a profit on his business in four years, but he was shelling out thousands of dollars a month of their—*her*—money to keep a roof over the head of his illicit activities.

Carey pulled a file of bank statements, looking for a deposit or withdrawal in the amount of twenty-five thousand dollars. Nothing listed for any of their accounts, but the latest statements were almost a month old.

It was Saturday. She couldn't call the bank and ask them. She knew David did a lot of their banking via the computer, but she didn't know how to access the account.

A car door slammed outside. Carey's heart tried to jump out of her chest. Her hands were shaking as she shoved the credit card statements and receipts back into their file and put the file back into its place in the drawer.

She stood up too quickly and her head swam. She didn't care if David found her at his desk. She cared that she might frighten her daughter, looking the way she did. But when she pulled back the drape and looked out the front window, Kovac was coming up the sidewalk to the door.

He looked like an unmade bed, thick hair standing up from a finger combing, rugged face drawn, mouth frowning. Like most street cops Carey knew, Sam Kovac had never been in any great danger of gracing the cover of *Gentleman's Quarterly*. He bought his suits cheap, cut his hair cheaper. He was a no-muss, no-fuss kind of a guy. It was a safe bet he had never spent forty-three hundred dollars at Bloomingdale's on himself or anyone else. And she knew without asking that he held nothing but contempt for the politicians and police brass who ranked above him.

Carey imagined he hadn't gotten any more sleep than she had. Maybe less. He had a case to run, and with a judge for a victim. The powers that ruled the city would be coming down hard on the police department. Not because any of them cared particularly about her personally but because of the media attention and because they had constituents to answer to.

He didn't look surprised to see her as she cracked the front door open before he could ring the bell.

"Judge . . ."

"Detective. I'm guessing you haven't come for the all-you-can-eat brunch."

He blinked at her, taken aback that she still had the energy for sarcasm. "No appetite," he said. "Do you have coffee?"

"Yes."

"I need some. How about you?"

"Make yourself at home," Carey said dryly as Kovac brushed past her and went in search of the kitchen.

"Where's the husband?" he asked, snooping through the cupboards. He found the mugs on the second try. The coffee was already brewed. Half the pot was gone. Two mugs were resting upside down in the drainer rack at the sink. David and Anka. The morning paper had been left spread out on the breakfast table.

"Out."

Kovac shot a look at her. Carey felt as if he could see past her clothes, past her external self, straight to the part of her that held her secrets. It wasn't a good feeling.

"You don't like David," she said, easing down onto a chair.

Kovac poured the coffee. "No," he said bluntly. "I don't. Do you?"

"He's my husband."

Again the look, the flat cop eyes. Tigers probably had that same look in their eyes when they faced their prey. He sat down at the kitchen table with her and put one of the steaming mugs in front of her.

"You didn't answer me."

"I don't have any reason to discuss my marriage with you."

"You don't *want* to have any reason to."

Carey's mouth pulled at one corner. "As you so graciously pointed out last night: There is no shortage of people who hate me right now. David only resents me. And he has an alibi."

Kovac didn't say anything, though Carey knew what he was thinking. The cheating husband gives himself an alibi and pays someone else to do the dirty work. She would have categorically denied the possibility except for one thing.

Twenty-five thousand dollars.

"You have better suspects to look at," she said.

"I have other suspects."

His choice of words was not lost on her, but she refused to take the bait.

The kitchen table sat in a nook with a bay

window looking out onto the backyard, where the lawn was awash in fallen leaves, and Lucy's swing set stood as a monument to childhood. Such a normal Saturday-morning kind of thing: sitting, chatting, having coffee.

"He's cheating on you," Kovac said.

Carey continued to stare out the window.

"I don't get it. You're a strong, independent woman. Why would you put up with that?"

She still didn't look at him. "You have no direct evidence David is cheating on me . . . do you?"

"Don't try to play me, Judge. I'm not stupid, and neither are you."

Carey was silent for what seemed like a long time. Finally she said in a very soft voice, "Maybe I'm not as strong as you think."

It was Kovac's turn to be silent. She could feel him watching her and wondered what he was thinking. That she was in denial? That she was pathetic for staying with a husband who had so little respect for her? She was past denial. On the other count, she pled the Fifth.

"Karl Dahl is still at large?" she asked.

"Yeah. That's nothing you have to worry about as far as him coming after you," Kovac said. "He's got no reason to hurt you. You being his new best friend and all."

Carey ignored the jab. "Have you been able to enhance the video from the parking ramp?"

"Not yet."

"Just why are you here, Detective?" she asked, arching a brow. "Not that I don't enjoy your pleasant company."

Kovac let go a long sigh and looked at his coffee for a moment. "Stan Dempsey—the lead detective—"

"I know who Stan Dempsey is. What about him?"

"I went to his house this morning. You know, he's never been right since those murders. I wanted to talk to him about yesterday. He's got as good a motive as anybody to call you a fucking cunt and try to beat the shit out of you."

"And?"

"And he wasn't there," Kovac said. "He had trashed the place. Shot up the furniture, tipped over tables, smashed stuff. Basically went ape shit, by the look of it. He left a videotape of himself talking about the Haas case, talking about his frustration, his anger. He went on about you, about your rulings. About how he needs to take matters into his own hands and make sure the guilty pay."

"The guilty," Carey said. "As in Karl Dahl."

"And you."

"Did he threaten me?"

"Not in so many words, but I have reason to believe he could be a danger to you, and possibly to your daughter."

Carey sat up straight, her pulse quickening. "My daughter? What did he say about my daughter?"

"He's aware you have a small daughter, and he thinks because of that you should be more sympathetic to the victims, for what they must have gone through," Kovac said, but he didn't quite meet her eyes.

Carey slapped a hand down hard on the table. "Don't treat me like a child, Detective! I'm not some naive little soccer mom. What did he say about my daughter?"

He looked her in the eye then. "He wondered how differently you'd feel toward Karl Dahl if your daughter had been raped and sodomized and hung up from the ceiling like a slaughtered lamb."

A chill went through Carey like an icicle

stabbing her through the back. Tears filled her eyes. The images from the Haas murder scene photos flashed in her head.

"Oh, my God," she whispered.

The fear that had shaken her earlier came back. Lucy was gone. David was gone. Anka was gone. She had no idea where they were or what might be happening to them. Lucy was who she lived for, who she would die for. The thought of her being hurt, being tortured . . .

She got up from the table and rushed across the room for the telephone. Dizzy, sick, shaking, she leaned against the counter and punched David's cell number into the handset.

The phone on the other end rang . . . and rang . . . and rang.

"Goddammit, David! Answer the fucking phone!"

Kovac stood up but didn't seem to know what to do.

Carey cut the call off and dialed again, in case she'd transposed a number the first time. But still David's phone rang unanswered. The voice mail kicked on and informed her that the customer's mailbox was full. He wasn't there for her, just as he hadn't been the night before, when she'd been in the hospital, and he'd been fucking some whore at the Marquette Hotel.

"Dammit!" she shouted, and hurled the handset against the wall.

She was crying now. Huge, gulping sobs. Fury and helplessness and weakness washed through her in waves, all of it crashing into her—the attack, the pressure of the case, the sense of being in it all alone, and now the knowledge that her child was vulnerable to harm because of her. She put her hands over her face and bent forward as if she had been kicked in the stomach.

"Hey," Kovac said quietly, touching her arm. "You need to calm down. Nothing's happened. We've got an APB out for Dempsey's car."

"How do you know he hasn't been here already?" Carey demanded.

"The uniforms outside would have seen him."

"Not if he parked up the street or around the corner. He could have been sitting there, waiting. He could have seen David's car leave the garage. He could have followed them," she went on. "Why didn't you call me the instant you found out Dempsey was missing?"

"So you could have been hysterical half an hour sooner? What good would that have done?" Kovac asked. "I immediately notified the units on this block.

"There's nothing you could have done that we hadn't done already," Kovac said calmly. "I didn't want to dump this on you over the phone."

Carey's anger dropped out from under her. She didn't have the strength to sustain it. The worry and the fear were drowning out all else.

"I want my daughter," she whispered. "I need to find my daughter. I need to find David. Why can't he be here just *once* when I need him?"

Her voice cracked and she coughed, trying to hold back a sob.

Kovac's arm wrapped around her shoulders. "Come on," he whispered. "Let's sit you down. We'll find your daughter."

"I can't believe any of this is happening," Carey said in a choked voice. For just an instant she leaned against him, needing to feel the solid support of someone stronger than she was. He smelled of sandalwood soap. The faint scent of cigarette smoke clung to his coat.

"I'm sorry," she whispered, embarrassed to meet his eyes as she stepped away from him. "I'm sorry."

"Don't worry about it," Kovac said as he herded her back toward the table. "So, you're human after all. Your secret's safe with me."

Karl figured there likely were no homeless people in the part of town where he was headed. It was a sunny, warm fall day, warm enough that he could discard the ragman's coat, which he did in a Dumpster behind a closed printing shop. He kept the matted dreadlocks and knit cap, though his head was itching something fierce and he couldn't stand the feeling. He had no doubt that the ragman's clothes were full of lice.

He wanted a hot shower, and to shave himself. He imagined he could feel the hairs pushing their way up through the skin on his chest and groin. The idea made his skin crawl.

Checking out his reflection in the printing shop's barred back window, Karl was pleased enough. The ragman's pants were baggy on him, on account of Karl's not being a large man. If he had been a woman, he would have been considered petite. There really was no equal word for a man that he knew of.

He put his hands in the pants pockets and slouched into a sort of lazy S profile. That was a good look, lazy, not in any hurry to get anywhere. No one would think he was running from the law if he didn't move faster than a shuffle.

Digging through the ragman's cart, Karl found several pairs of sunglasses, some scratched and broken, some not. He tried them on until he had a good fit, covering the bloodred of his eyes, which would call attention and people would remember.

He studied himself in the window and liked what he saw. But he wasn't satisfied. He hadn't changed the appearance of his jawline or his mouth, and a lot of people looked there first when they looked at somebody. Everyone in Minneapolis was looking at his picture on the news and in the paper.

He had the five o'clock shadow. That was helpful, but not enough. He had the bruises from the night before. He reached into his mouth and took out his bridgework, leaving a couple of black holes in his smile. Better, but he still wasn't satisfied. He rummaged through the junk in the ragman's cart, looking for something that might spark an idea.

Street people kept the damnedest stuff. This one had a collection of near-empty aerosol cans, mostly spray paint and hair spray. For huffing the fumes, Karl knew. A cheap high. There were half a dozen one-off shoes that all looked to have been run over in the street. There was a trash bag with some aluminum cans and glass beer and liquor bottles. These were probably the source of the money Karl now had in his pocket and taped to his privates. There was a claw hammer, which Karl took and strapped to his ankle with shoestrings under his pant leg. There was a pliers.

Karl picked it up and studied it, ideas turning over in his mind. He put a fingertip in the mouth of it and squeezed a little.

Standing in front of the store window, he tugged up the T-shirt he wore and put it over his lower lip. Then he took the pliers and very methodically began to squeeze the lip hard, hard enough to bring tears to his eyes. From one corner of his mouth to the other and back again, he pinched his lip with the pliers.

When he started to get faint from the pain, he stopped and looked at himself in the glass once more. The lip was already swelling, there were some lines from the teeth of the pliers, but he had only broken the skin a couple of times.

He was a satisfied man. This would do for now.

Slouched and shuffling, fat lip sticking out from his face, Karl abandoned the ragman's cart and went back out on the street. The day was glorious. The sky was an electric shade of blue, and the air was warm—well, fairly warm for this place with fall slipping away. But there were hardly any people on the streets. Nothing much happened on Saturdays in this part of town. Businesses were closed. People had no call to be walking up and down.

The lack of people, however, did not stop the city buses from running. Karl sat at a bus stop, slumped, and waited. Some lonely soul before him had left a newspaper scattered in sections on the bench. On the front page was a mug shot of himself, and a photograph of Judge Carey Moore in her judge's robes, sitting up on the judge's bench, overseeing some trial or another.

Karl's heart pumped a little harder. His picture and the picture of his angel on the same page. His mother would have said it was a portent, a sign. Karl didn't believe in signs, except for now. Carey Moore had taken a beating on account of him, because she had ruled in his favor. He couldn't imagine any other judge doing that. Everyone in the state wanted him dead.

She was a woman with the courage of her convictions. Karl found that idea excited him. A strong and passionate woman who wouldn't back down from anybody.

The city bus rumbled up to the curb and groaned and hissed like an old man letting a fart. Karl folded up the newspaper and got on, heading toward his heroine.

18

Stan drove out of the city in the 1996 Ford Taurus he had owned since it rolled off the assembly line in Detroit. It ran well, got him from one place to another. He'd never seen a reason to trade it in. He wasn't one to need status symbols.

Now that he had decided on a plan of action, he needed a base. When one of his fellow detectives came to question him at his home about the attack on Judge Moore— and they would—they would find the videotape, and they would be looking for him.

It had been important to him that he left it, that they found it. It was important everyone understood who he was and what he stood for and how he had come to be the man he was now. What this case had done to him. The overwhelming sense of impotence, sitting behind a desk; sitting in the office of a shrink, staring at the wall; knowing all the power to put Karl Dahl away or put him back on the street was in the hands of other people. People who didn't understand what evil was.

In better days, Stan had been quite a fisherman. The lake had been his escape from the job and from the silent disappointment of his wife. He enjoyed the solitude, the time alone, without noise, without voices, without the pressure of having to interact with other people.

The country west of Minneapolis and its suburbs was marshy and peppered with lakes large and small and tangles of woods all connected by narrow, twisting roads. The lake Stan fished was too small to be of interest to weekenders with powerboats and too difficult to find for the casual fishermen. He had been fishing that lake for nearly forty-five years.

His uncle owned a small cabin on the southwestern shore. Nothing to brag about, just a little tar-paper shack with a small kitchen and a smaller bathroom with a tin shower stall. It had a tiny cellar and a screened porch where a person could sit on summer evenings without being devoured by mosquitoes. And there was a big shed where Stan kept his little fishing boat during winter and where his uncle's old Chevy pickup sat.

This place had been Stan's hideaway since he was a boy. His uncle was elderly now and had been in poor health for years. When he died, the place would pass on to Stan.

He stopped at a country store and bought supplies—food, water, cigarettes, toilet paper. The clerk was a fat girl with a ring in her nose and jet-black hair streaked with yellow in front. She had no interest in Stan. She looked right through him, same as most people did.

The lake was glistening like blue glass in the sun. The rushes and reeds had dried to a golden alabaster shade. The far shore was dotted with clumps of paper-white birch trees, their remaining leaves bright gold. Maples and oaks made up the woods beyond, an artist's palette of reds, oranges, and bronze. As far as Stan could say, this was the most beautiful place on earth.

A couple of huge old trees anchored the yard of his uncle's property and kept the grass thin and sparse. The cabin looked the same as it always had, with the exception of bars on the windows and the door. Places like this one—which were occupied infrequently and mostly on weekends—were a target for vandals and thieves. Local kids with nothing better to do with their time.

Stan unlocked the door and took his groceries inside. The place always smelled vaguely musty. The damp seemed to seep in through the tar paper and drywall and settle into the cushions of the old couch, which also served as a bed.

He went back out to the shed, unlocked the big padlock, and rolled the door open. He popped the hood on the pickup and hooked up the cables of the battery charger, then went back to moving in.

From the trunk of his car, he lifted out a couple of black duffel bags and took them into the cabin. Tools and things he had packed, not knowing what he might need for the job he was setting out to do. A couple of handguns. A couple of knives. Handcuffs. Duct tape.

In a part of his mind, Stan watched himself examine these items with a weird, calm sense of horror, but it was not so strong that he made any attempt to stop himself. His decision was made. For the most part, he went about his business methodically, on autopilot, as if this were routine and normal, preparing to take the law into his own hands.

After he had made himself a few bologna sandwiches, he chose several close-range weapons, packed his essentials, and left the cabin, locking up behind himself.

The pickup battery had charged. Stan loaded his stuff in the back, inside the camper shell that enclosed the truck bed. He drove the truck out of the shed, replaced it with his car, slid the big door shut, and locked the big padlock.

No place was ever fully immune to a break-in, but Stan knew from long experience that criminals were lazy and put forth as little effort as possible. Deterrents like locks and bars could make a thief or vandal move on to an easier target.

He wondered how things might have turned out if Marlene Haas had locked her doors that fateful day. Would Karl Dahl have moved on, unwilling to put forth the effort or risk being seen breaking in?

Or had he been too fixated, too bent on

living out his fantasy, to let something as simple as a dead bolt turn him away?

Stan believed the latter. That Karl Dahl had lived out his dark fantasies in his mind too many times not to make them reality.

He now understood what that was like.

He felt exactly the same way.

19

"The brass are pulling out all the stops on this."

Homicide lieutenant Juanita Dawes sat back against the front edge of her desk. She was in full on-camera dress: hair done, makeup done, a smart navy blue suit with the perfect accessories. The press conference would start in the chief's office in half an hour.

Dawes had jumped up the PD food chain by leaps and bounds. She was forty-one. Liska knew this because every time Dawes's name appeared in the newspaper, her age was always mentioned as if it were actually a part of her name. Lieutenant Juanita Dawes Forty-one.

Liska's theory was that the brass thought they were getting an equal-opportunity publicity triple whammy with Juanita Dawes—a black Hispanic woman. It wouldn't matter to them that Juanita was not actually Hispanic. What the chief and everyone else in his stratosphere cared about most was appearance.

Not that Dawes wasn't qualified. Liska felt she was the best lieutenant they'd had in a long time. And however she had climbed the ladder, more power to her.

Liska had dragged herself out of bed early to go through the same pregame ritual as Dawes: hair, makeup, a steel gray suit that accentuated the blue of her eyes, simple black pearl earrings, and a fine silver chain necklace threaded through a single black pearl.

She looked like a million damn dollars. Maybe she would get marriage proposals after the press conference aired on every television in the Twin Cities.

"We've got someone going over the video from the parking garage. With luck you'll have an enhanced version to look at shortly," Dawes went on. "I've pulled in El-wood and Tippen. They'll be compiling information on any recently released cons who had Judge Moore preside over their cases. They're already talking with the judge's clerk to find out if she's had any hate mail."

"We'll need phone records too," Liska said. "We've got the number the calls last night came from. It's untraceable, but at least we can establish a pattern or a time line."

"That's already happening," Dawes said. "And you'll need to track down the father of the foster kids who were killed in the Haas massacre. Has there been any activity on the judge's credit cards?"

"Not yet," Liska said. "I guess I get to be the one to call attention to the elephant in the room."

Dawes frowned. "Stan Dempsey."

"He has to be at the top of the hit list in light of what Sam found this morning."

Dawes looked genuinely sad. "I hate to have to think in that direction, but it looks like we've got a very real possibility in Dempsey. Kovac said he all but openly admitted he wants to make Judge Moore pay for ruling in Dahl's favor."

"But here's what doesn't make sense to me," Liska said. "If Dempsey attacked Judge Moore last night, why wouldn't he take the credit on the tape he made this morning? I mean, why play coy about it? According to Sam, he wasn't shy on the tape talking about what he's planning to do next."

"That's a good point," Dawes said. "If he attacked the judge in his self-appointed role of avenging angel of justice, why wouldn't he say so? Why wouldn't he say something like 'I'm going to finish what I started' or 'I gave that bitch what she deserved'?"

"Of course, the guy's gone nuts," Liska said. "Who's to say what's going on in his head?"

"I'd like to get a professional's opinion on that. I'll talk to the chief about calling in the shrink Dempsey's been seeing."

"She'll cry privilege."

"She can cry all she wants," Dawes said. "But if Dempsey told her about his plans to commit a crime, she's obligated to report that to us."

"I can't see Stan Dempsey pouring his heart out to anyone about anything," Liska said. "In all the time I've been in Homicide, I don't think I've heard the guy say ten words."

"I know. He's one strange homely little

duck, our Stan," Dawes said. "I feel sorry for him. Let's try to give him the benefit of the doubt here for a moment. Who else have you talked to about last night?"

"Wayne Haas, his son, the son's buddy."

"And?"

"We don't like Wayne Haas for it," Liska said. "The son could be a candidate. He and his friend admitted being downtown late afternoon, and he knew about Judge Moore's ruling. He certainly has plenty of reasons to be pissed off at her."

"And Sam spoke with the judge's husband?"

"Yeah. He doesn't like the guy. Says he's a prick."

Dawes made a face. "Kovac doesn't like anybody. He would give his own mother the third degree."

"He's looking into David Moore's alibi today."

Dawes looked at her watch and sighed. "We'd better go up there," she said. "Chief'll chew my ass if we're late. You know what to say when they start asking you questions?"

"We can't speculate on or discuss the facts of an ongoing investigation."

"You got it," Dawes said as she pulled

open the door to her office. She tipped her head as Liska went past. "Great suit, Detective."

"Back at you, Boss."

The press conference was the usual circus of muckety-mucks who knew nothing and reporters who wanted to know everything. Liska wondered how many of either group would have shown up if Carey Moore had been a single mother who worked two jobs to make ends meet. Carey Moore rated the mayor, the county attorney, the chief of police, the assistant chief, the captain of the investigative division, Lieutenant Dawes, and herself.

The lights for the television people were harsh, white, and made her squint, which was going to confuse her possible fiancés in the viewing audience, she thought, needing a little humor to offset the seriousness of the situation. She probably looked like a Chinese woman with bleached hair. Chinese Punk Woman. Her male prospects were going to skew to Asian bad boys.

The press was in a feeding frenzy. First over Karl Dahl's escape, then over Judge

Moore's attack. The Hennepin County sheriff had to be the whipping boy for losing Dahl. As far as Liska was concerned, there was no explanation for what had happened that didn't include the words "cluster fuck."

He promised that every available deputy was out looking for Dahl. He promised that Dahl was absolutely his priority and the priority of everyone in the sheriff's office. The Minneapolis branch of the FBI had been called in to assist. His promises didn't carry much weight, seeing as how it was the sheriff's office that had been in charge of Dahl in the first place.

The PD brass focused on the need to restore public confidence in law enforcement. The top detectives in the department were on the case, determined to bring to justice the man who had struck at the very heart of our judicial system.

When Liska was called upon to answer questions, she repeated her lines perfectly. *"We can't speculate on or discuss the facts of an ongoing investigation."*

Her first stop after the press conference was the women's prison to speak with Amber Franken, mother of the two foster children who had been killed at the Haas home.

Amber Franken was a skinny, ratty-looking dishwater blonde with a pasty complexion. Her skin was so thin Liska could see the blue tracery of veins in her throat. She had rolled up the sleeves of her shirt to show off sinewy arms lined with tattoos and old needle track marks. She was twenty-two. Which meant she had started popping out kids at the tender age of fourteen. The two children who had been murdered had been ages seven and five at the time of their deaths. A two-year-old girl had been placed by social services with a different family.

She swaggered into the interview room with a sour look on her face and dropped into a chair across the table from Liska.

"Amber, I'm Detective Liska from Homicide division."

"I'm suing the police department for what happened to my kids," she said, sneering.

"Yeah?" Liska said, uninterested. "Good luck with that."

"And I'm suing social services too. They put my kids in an unsafe environment."

Liska wanted to ask Amber what kind of environment she, a junkie whore, had provided for her children. But she needed the woman's cooperation, and that required her to rein in her usually smart mouth.

Good luck with that, Nikki.

"Have you had any contact with your kids' dad lately?"

Amber laughed. "That piece of shit? I haven't had 'contact' with him since the last time he knocked me up."

"Then why is he on the visitors' log for having been here ten days ago?"

"Probably here to see one of his other sluts."

Liska leaned forward, elbows on the table, and sighed. "Look, Amber, you don't want to talk to me, I don't want to talk to you. But we're gonna sit here and enjoy each other's company until you give me a straight answer."

Again with the sneer and a snotty shake of her head. "I got nothing but time."

"That's true. But you can stay in this place for more time or less time."

"What's that supposed to mean?"

"It means if you waste my time, jerk me around, piss me off, and refuse to cooperate with a police investigation, that's not gonna look very good on your record when you come up for parole."

The girl pulled back in her chair, her face mottling, eyes bugging out a little. "Are you *threatening* me?"

"I'm telling you the plain truth, Amber," Liska said without emotion. "I'm doing you a favor telling you. If you don't straighten up and at least pretend to be a good citizen, the parole board is not going to be all that anxious to kick you back out into the real world. That's how it is.

"You're pulling real time here. This isn't county jail, where they're happy to watch your ass walk out the door because they need the bed," Liska said. "Unlike a lot of other places, the State of Minnesota has plenty of prison cells to go around.

"Am I getting through to you here? I don't want to make things hard for you, Amber. I really don't. I don't even want to be here right now. I've got two kids of my own. I'd like to be spending time with them.

"I'm sure, as a mother, you can understand that. You remember what it was like. Your kids look up to you like you've got the key to the world. That love is like no other. That bond is stronger than anything."

Amber Franken's eyes welled with tears. She looked away, arms crossed tight, as if she was trying to hold herself together.

"You miss them, don't you?" Liska said softly.

It didn't matter how unfit a mother this chick had been; absence had erased the bad memories and left her with sweet, sentimental images of time with her children. Children she would never see again.

"I can only imagine what that must feel like, knowing that they're gone. Knowing what they went through before they died . . ."

Amber began to cry in earnest. She put her hands over her face and sobbed, "I miss them so much!"

Genuinely feeling sorry for the girl, Liska sat patiently as the worst of the storm wore itself out. There couldn't be anything worse in the world than to think of your children being tortured by a sadist.

After a few minutes, Amber pulled up the tail of her shirt and wiped her face and nose with it.

Liska tried again. "Why was Ethan Pratt here to see you ten days ago?"

Amber drew in a shuddering breath. "To

talk about the lawsuits. He wants in on them, the rotten son of a bitch. Like he was ever anything more than a sperm donor. Fucking leech. I told him to hire his own damn lawyer."

"Did he say anything about Karl Dahl's trial coming up?"

She wiped her nose again, this time with the back of her hand, which she then wiped on the leg of her pants. "He said he'd want Judge Moore next time he got arrested, 'cause she cares more about the guy on trial than the victims."

"Did he seem angry about that?"

"He called her a fucking cunt, if that's what you mean."

"That's what I mean," Liska said.

20

They both heard the car roll into the attached garage. Carey Moore looked over at
the door Kovac presumed was the entrance
from the garage. Her expression was trans-
parent, even behind the bruises and swelling. Hope, eagerness, a little apprehension.

Kovac rose before she could, went to the
door himself, and locked it until he heard
the voices—David Moore, the Swedish girl,
a child. They sounded relaxed, happy. Kovac wanted to open the door and smack the
husband's smile off his face. Instead, he
opened it a crack and gave them a flat, un-
friendly look.

David Moore was unpleasantly surprised.
"What are you doing here?"

"What are you doing leaving a woman
with a concussion alone?"

"I checked on her several times in the night, Detective," the Swedish girl said, trying to be helpful. "Mrs. Moore was fine."

Kovac ignored her, holding his stare on the husband.

"We went out to breakfast," David Moore said defensively. "I thought Carey should sleep in."

A dark-haired little girl with big blue eyes sat comfortably in the crook of his arm. She had her mother's directness.

"Who are you?"

"Honey, this is a police detective," Moore said. "He's here because of your mom getting hurt last night."

She turned the look on her father. "Where's Mommy?"

"I'm here, sweetie," Carey Moore said, wedging herself in between the doorjamb and Kovac.

Lucy Moore took one look at her mother, and the blue eyes went liquid. "Mommy?"

"I look pretty bad, don't I?" Carey said softly. Kovac stepped back a little and let her past. "I'm okay, though. Honest. It's just scrapes and bruises."

Lucy didn't seem to know what to make

of the situation. She gave her father a suspicious look, then turned it on her mother.

"You look scary," she declared.

"I know."

"You should maybe put some makeup on."

Carey's eyes glazed with tears as she smiled and tried to laugh, and reached out for her daughter. "Come on. You can help me with that, and tell me all about what you had for breakfast."

The little girl wriggled down out of her father's arms and went to her mother, taking her hand and leading her into the kitchen.

"I had pancakes with blueberries in them and lots of syrup. I like syrup."

"I know you do."

"And it doesn't matter either, 'cause I brush my teeth."

Kovac watched them go through the kitchen and down the hall. The mother-daughter thing touched him in a very tender, very well hidden part of his soul. He didn't allow himself to examine the feeling. He turned back to David Moore.

"We need to talk."

"Can I take my coat off first?" Moore asked, petulant.

Kovac turned to the Swedish girl. "You too."

They went into the kitchen and sat down, and Kovac filled them in on the Stan Dempsey situation. The Swedish girl listened, wide-eyed. Stockholm in the dead of winter was looking better and better.

"You can't be unavailable," Kovac said, directing his comment at David Moore. "No cell phones turned off or ignored."

Moore looked unsettled. "You think this guy is serious?"

Kovac refrained from asking him if he had always been this stupid or if it was a recent affliction. "I *know* he's serious. You can't just take your daughter and go off to do as you please. I'd be happier if she didn't leave the house until the situation is resolved."

"Should we leave town?"

"I don't think your wife is in any condition to travel right now. She needs to get clearance from her doctor. If you just do what I'm telling you, you should be fine. I'll have officers here around the clock."

The nanny murmured something in Swedish. *Oh, my God,* or *Holy shit,* or *Fuck this,* Kovac figured. She shot a nervous glance at David Moore, who pretended not to see her. Kovac filed the moment away in his head. The nanny and the daddy? He remembered she had been defensive of Moore the night before when Kovac had asked about the guy's schedule.

Lazy bastard. He couldn't even put out the effort to get a mistress outside his own household.

"I have to go," Kovac said. "You both have my card if you need me. If you need to leave the house, notify the officers out front, and tell them where you're going and when you expect to be back."

David Moore looked unhappy. "I'm a prisoner in my own home?"

"Yeah," Kovac said. "Sorry it's such an inconvenience to you to have the lives of your wife and daughter threatened."

"That's not what I meant."

"I know what you meant. You don't want to be under my thumb," Kovac said. "What the hell have you got going on that's so damned important? You're suddenly Mr. Ambition?"

Moore narrowed his eyes. "I resent that."

"I'm sure you do."

"I'm working on a business deal."

"Yeah? Well, it's the age of telecommunication. Pick up a phone; send an e-mail."

Moore stared just to the left of Kovac's head. He was going to do whatever the hell he wanted. Asshole.

"I'll need your cell phone number too," Kovac said to the nanny.

She recited it, and Kovac wrote it down in his notebook.

"I'll let myself out," he said, and left them in the kitchen, pausing in the hall to listen in case they were stupid enough to go lovey-dovey before he was out the door.

"I'm going to make a fresh pot of coffee." Moore.

"I'm going to my room. I have studying to do." The nanny.

Kovac waited for her at the foot of the stairs. She looked surprised to see him, but not alarmed.

"Anka, I need to have a word with you."

"I don't know anything," she said. "I can't believe this is happening."

"They don't have crime in Sweden?"

"Not like here. It's crazy, evil, what that man did to that family, to those children. And now you say this other man, a detective with the police department, wants to hurt Mrs. Moore or Lucy?"

"It's pretty scary stuff," Kovac conceded. "Judge Moore is in a position that attracts a lot of attention, not all of it good."

Anka looked away, clearly upset.

"Anka, I'm going to ask you something very personal," Kovac said. "And I need you to answer me honestly. It's very important that I have a clear picture of what's going on. Do you understand what I'm saying?"

"Yes," she answered, nervous, anxious.

"Do you have something going on with Mr. Moore?"

Kovac watched her expression carefully. Shock and offense.

"I don't know what you mean," she said. "Mr. Moore is my employer."

"He's not more than that to you?"

"No. Of course not."

The answer was a beat too slow, and she didn't quite meet his eyes.

"You're not sleeping with him?"

She gave a little gasp. "No! I'm going upstairs now. I have nothing more to say to you. Good day."

Indignation. Outrage.

But she still didn't quite meet his eyes.

21

Karl got off the bus at Calhoun Square in a trendy area of Minneapolis known as Uptown even though it was actually south of downtown. The neighborhood was full of nicely redone older homes, lovely yards, and established trees on the boulevard. It was an area of young upwardly mobile families, upwardly mobile gay couples, comfortably well-off retirees.

There weren't a lot of people looking the way Karl was looking, but he planned to remedy that quickly.

He went into the Calhoun Square shopping mall, a collection of boutiques and restaurants tucked into an old brick building that had been converted from blue-collar beginnings. A bored girl at a kiosk on the first floor watched him approach, with a mix of disgust and trepidation. As he neared her, Karl thought she might run, but he held out a twenty-dollar bill and told her he needed a cap.

She eyed the twenty, and her greed got the better of her. She sold him a plain khaki ball cap and offered back no change.

As he went toward the men's room, Karl looked over his shoulder and saw her stick the bill in her purse. The dishonesty of people in general made him shake his head.

He took the cap and went into the men's room to discard the ragman's hair and knit cap.

Because it was early, he had the place to himself, and decided he would take the opportunity to wash his face and head.

Removal of the cap was a painful process. The wool had knitted into the bloody head wound he'd gotten when Snake was pounding him into the cell bars. As he peeled the cap away bit by bit, the wound opened in several places and began to bleed again. He stared at himself in the mirror, thinking he looked like something out of a horror movie, a red-eyed demon up from hell. His lip was throbbing something fierce. Grotesquely swollen and red, it reminded him in a way of the folds of tender flesh between a woman's legs.

For the briefest of moments, he imagined he could smell the musky scent of a woman who was ready for sex. He enjoyed that moment. Then he pulled his bridge out of his pants pocket, rinsed it off in the sink, and put it back in his mouth. There probably weren't many people in this part of town who went around without teeth.

The ball cap went on with the sunglasses.

He neatly rolled the sleeves of his shirt halfway up his forearms. There wasn't anything he could do about the filthy pants except roll the cuffs up. He took off his shoes and socks, threw the socks in the trash, and put the shoes back on. This would do for the moment.

Pulling the brim of the ball cap down low, he exited the bathroom, the building, and walked away into the neighborhood. Hands in his pockets, he strolled down the sidewalk like a man without a care in the world. Maybe he was just walking home from Starbucks. Maybe he'd been doing yard work, and that was why his pants were dirty.

As he walked, Karl scoped out the houses on this side of the block. Bikes on the front porch meant more than one person in the household. A couple or a family. He looked for the smaller homes—single story, or story and a half. The ones with large flower beds, now dead from the cold, told him perhaps the people, or person, who lived there had a lot of spare time. Older, retired maybe.

A small Cape Cod type of a house caught his eye. Blue with white shutters, and a picket fence around the front yard. A country-crafty wooden welcome sign hung beside the front door: "Grandma Lives Here." Karl turned the corner, then turned again down the alley.

Privacy fences blocked off the view into the backyards of most of the houses. Grandma Lives Here had a fence made of wide vertical cedar planks that had been allowed to weather to a silvery gray.

Karl slipped between that fence and the neighbor's, testing for loose boards as he worked his way to the back of the one-car garage. There were none. There was, however, a window on the side of the house, at the back, which was blocked from view from the street by a big lilac bush.

In the garage, a car started. Karl watched through the lilac bush as a late-model Volvo backed down the driveway. He couldn't make out the driver's face. A woman, he thought, based on her cautious maneuvering as she backed the car out into the street.

Grandma was leaving. Karl wondered if there was a Grandpa still inside. He looked in the side window of the garage and, judging from the absence of power tools, concluded there probably was no man of the house.

The window at the back side of the house had been left open partway to let in the fresh air this lovely fall morning. Winter was coming, and once it hit, no one would open a window for the next five months.

Several large, heavy plant pots with dead plants in them had been parked alongside the garage, between the garage and the privacy fence. Waiting to be cleaned out and put away for the winter. Karl rolled the largest across the narrow space, tipped it upside down, and used it for a step stool.

A little work with the ragman's steak knife, and Karl was able to peel the screen away enough for him to crawl inside. When he was in, he carefully pulled the screen back down and into place.

He had expected the house to be littered with Grandma stuff—porcelain poodles and old china and fussy furniture with flowered fabric and lace doilies. Instead, the space looked like something from a decorating magazine, with sage-colored walls and dark, modern furnishings.

In the kitchen Karl found the story of Grandma Lives Here. Her refrigerator was covered with photos of her with other people—friends, family, grandchildren. So many smiling, happy faces.

According to unopened mail on the counter, Grandma's name was Christine Neal.

Christine Neal was in her late fifties, trim and athletic. She ran in marathons. Went on vacations to exotic places. In several photographs, she was as bald as Karl was. A banner at one of her races called for support for a local breast cancer survivors group.

Karl pulled the refrigerator open and helped himself to an orange. It was cold and juicy and refreshing. When he had finished and thrown the peel in the trash, he wiped the handle of the refrigerator with a towel and went in search of a bathroom.

There was only one downstairs, adjacent

to what must be Christine Neal's bedroom. White and immaculate, it smelled of lavender.

In the medicine cabinet, he found mint-flavored dental floss, tore a string off for himself, and set to cleaning all the bits out from between his teeth—the orange he had just eaten, the piece of pork chop he had found in the garbage earlier. He took the toothbrush from the holder, helped himself to toothpaste, and brushed his teeth with vigor. He pulled his bridge out of his mouth, brushed it, and replaced it.

Karl undressed and threw the ragman's filthy clothes down the laundry chute, happy to be rid of them. Carefully, he removed the money taped to his scrotum. Naked, he sat down on the toilet and settled in to have his first bowel movement as a free man. What a pleasant, quiet, private experience.

He picked up a copy of *People* and leafed through it. He took very little interest in the entertainment world. He rarely looked at television, only knew about movies from the posters at the theaters.

He didn't recognize many stars. The girls all looked young and too skinny, and they dressed like whores. They shouldn't be surprised to be raped and killed, going around like that. The men were unremarkable. Half of them looked like they had dressed at the Goodwill and didn't have sense enough to tuck in their shirts. Most of them needed a haircut and a shave.

So did he, he reminded himself.

The shower was hot and had good water pressure. Karl lathered himself with Olay soap and rinsed off the top layer of grime. Then he lathered himself again, picked Christine Neal's pink razor off the shelf, and began to shave. He started with his head and worked his way down—his face, his chest, his belly. He considered himself lucky not to have a hairy back like a lot of men did, else he would have needed help.

From his belly, he skipped down to his legs, as careful not to nick himself as any woman would be. Then he helped himself to a fresh razor blade and began the very delicate task of shaving his privates. Karl couldn't stand the feeling of hair prickling out of him. It made him feel unclean.

He stroked his penis and made himself hard, making the shaving of his scrotum easier.

A woman's scream broke his concentration.

Christine Neal stood in the bathroom doorway, frozen in shock. Her eyes locked with Karl's for the briefest moment; then she bolted.

Karl leapt out of the shower, slipped on the wet tile, but managed not to fall. He sprinted down the hall and tackled Christine Neal from behind as she reached for the phone on the kitchen counter. The handset tumbled to the floor.

She was a strong, athletic woman, and she twisted, and arched her back, and kicked and scratched at him. They struggled on the floor, Christine Neal grunting and trying to scream and choking on her own breath. Her hand swung wildly along the floor and managed to grab the phone again.

Karl lunged to get the thing away from her, rolling partly off her to get it. Christine Neal scrambled desperately to get her feet under her. Before she could take a step, Karl grabbed her by the ankle, and she fell once more. She was sobbing now, hysterical, trying to call out for help.

She twisted onto her side and tried to

drag herself out of his reach, tried once more to pull a knee up under herself.

Karl reached out and grabbed her by the hair, but the hair came off in his hand, a wig. He chucked it aside and straddled her waist.

She was on her back now. His hands were around her throat, squeezing. She hit at him with her fists, tried to arch her body up beneath him to get him off. She tried to scream. The scream died under his thumbs.

Karl squeezed harder. Christine Neal was beginning to turn blue from lack of oxygen. Her tongue came out of her mouth, swollen and purple. Her eyes were bulging.

Karl fixed on her eyes, on the emotion in them. Sheer animal terror. He thought it must be horrible to die this way, looking into the face of your killer and finding no compassion, no sympathy. In his case, he imagined she didn't see anything at all.

This wasn't personal. He had no anger toward this woman, no real desire to kill her. But he couldn't have her calling the police. He was flying below the radar now. No one had any idea where he was. He was free to move about the city as he wanted. And he had plans. He couldn't let Christine Neal have an opportunity to ruin those plans. It simply wasn't practical to let her live.

The swinging of her arms became weaker and weaker, until she was doing nothing but slapping her hands against the floor . . . then just twitching . . . then nothing.

Karl did not take his hands away from her throat, didn't stop choking her. He didn't want Christine Neal reviving and having a second chance to get away or call for help. He kept squeezing until his hands began to cramp.

When he finally did let go, Karl remained sitting on top of her. Her head fell to one side, mouth hanging open, nothing in her eyes but tiny pinpoint hemorrhages. Christine Neal was gone.

Karl sighed. He rested for a moment, stretched his hands and fingers, rubbed at the aching muscles of his forearms. After a while he got up and dragged her body down the hall and into the bedroom. He removed her clothes and threw them down the laundry chute where he had thrown the ragman's clothes, then went back into the bedroom and shoved Christine Neal's body under her bed, careful to adjust the dust ruffle after.

He wiped down the bathroom with alcohol. Cleaned out the drain traps. Found a bottle of Drāno and poured it into both the sink and the tub drains. In the kitchen, he wiped down the telephone handset and placed it back in the cradle. He left no signs of the struggle.

He found the door to the basement, put a load of laundry in the washing machine—the ragman's clothes and Christine Neal's clothes—added detergent and half a bottle of bleach, and started the machine.

Back on the first floor, Karl picked up Christine Neal's blond wig and went back into the bedroom, into the walk-in closet, to dress.

From a drawer of panty hose and knee-high socks, Karl chose a pair of opaque brown tights. He put them on, taking great care not to run them, then tucked his money into the crotch and tucked his privates away as best he could. Then he chose a brown knit calf-length skirt and pulled it on.

From a drawer of underwear, he chose a bra. But it was too tight around his rib cage, digging into him. How women put up with the discomfort was beyond him.

Instead, he found a stretchy, tight-fitting

T-shirt and fashioned the illusion of small breasts with two pairs of athletic socks, each pair rolled into a ball. The tightness of the T-shirt held them in place. A boxy brown cotton sweater went over the T-shirt.

Shoes, he expected, might present a problem. But when he started comparing the length of his foot with the length of Christine Neal's shoes, Karl found that wasn't the case. He selected a pair of low-heeled brown boots and pulled them on. They fit as well as any shoes he'd had.

In the bathroom once more, he set about transforming himself. He had once worked as a stagehand in a playhouse in St. Louis and had watched the actors carefully as they applied the layers of color and shading, creating characters on the bland canvas of their own faces.

He applied foundation, concealed the bruises and shadows, created eyes with brown liner and shadow and dark mascara. With a shade called Dolce Vita, he painted his swollen lower lip and gave himself the appearance of having a fuller upper lip, using a colored pencil.

When he had finished, Karl stood back and studied his masterpiece in the mirror.

He stretched Christine Neal's blond wig over his bald head.

Just like that, he had become a woman.

Karla.

No one was on the lookout for a blond woman in a brown skirt and sweater.

His finishing touches were a brown and blue print silk scarf, which he tied around his throat to hide his Adam's apple and the red marks on his own throat where Snake's handcuffs had bitten in the night before, and a pair of large-framed brown tortoiseshell sunglasses, the kind President Kennedy's wife had always been photographed in.

Karl went back into the bedroom, bent over, lifted the dust ruffle. Christine Neal's sightless eyes stared at him; her mouth was open, her swollen tongue sticking out at him. She looked like a spare mannequin that had been discarded in the back room of a store, forgotten under other unneeded props and racks.

"Thank you, Ms. Neal," Karl said respectfully. "I'm sure you was a real nice lady."

He put the dust ruffle back in place and walked out, stopping at the coat closet in the hall to choose a brown poncho. In the kitchen, he picked up Christine Neal's handbag and car keys before he let himself out the back door.

The car in her garage was the dark blue Volvo. Nice. Leather seats and all. A car that wouldn't stand out in this part of town. She had kept it real clean too. It smelled like lemons.

Karl backed out of the garage and put the garage door down with the remote. With luck no one would come looking to visit Christine Neal over the weekend. But even if someone did, they would simply find her gone. No Christine, no car, no handbag. She was out. Shopping, maybe, or at a movie. If she worked somewhere, she wouldn't be missed until Monday at the earliest. If she didn't work, it could be days before someone noticed she wasn't around.

Days and days of freedom to use Christine's car, to do what he wanted, to go where he pleased.

He turned down the street and headed out on the next leg of his quest: to find the place that would please him most—the home of his champion, Carey Moore.

22

"No usable prints on the judge's handbag. At least half a dozen people touched the car. So far none of those prints have come back with a rap sheet," Tippen said.

He paced back and forth at the end of the conference table, tall and thin, with a long caricature of a face, all angles and hollows, craggy brow, bristly salt-and-pepper mustache. He had been a detective with the sheriff's department for years before making the move to work Homicide with the city cops.

As a sheriff's detective, Tippen had first teamed with Kovac and Liska on a multi-agency task force to solve the Cremator murders—a killer who had targeted primarily prostitutes, tortured and killed them, then set their bodies on fire in a public park.

They had worked well as a team and had become drinking buddies after.

"Judge Moore gets more than her fair share of hate mail." Elwood Knutson, another of the Cremator task force. A man roughly the size of a small brown bear, Elwood was their philosopher in a too-small porkpie hat.

"That's hard to believe," Liska said sarcastically.

Kovac said nothing.

"Her clerk has it separated by degrees: crazy, crazier, and certifiable."

"Threats?" Kovac asked.

"Veiled and not so veiled. Anything she gets that looks legitimately scary goes to the sheriff's detectives." Elwood glanced at Tippen and said, "Really, it's a wonder she wasn't killed a long time ago, considering."

"Don't look at me!" Tippen said. "In case you hadn't noticed, I changed teams."

"Then why hasn't the quality of their work improved?" Liska asked.

Tippen fired a chocolate-covered coffee bean at her. He had recently acquired an addiction to them, despite the fact that he was the last guy in the department in need of caffeine to wire himself up.

"I had all the letters copied and brought them over," Elwood went on, tipping a big hand in the direction of the file folders stacked in front of him. "A little bedtime reading, if anyone's interested."

"What about ex-cons?" Kovac asked. "Any bad guys recently released who might think they have a big ax to grind?"

"I've tracked some of the more obvious candidates through their parole officers," Liska said. "So far I don't like any of them for the assault. Despite all efforts by the Department of Corrections, it seems several of them have actually reformed, and can be accounted for by their bosses at the time of the judge's attack.

"But," she continued, "I *do* have a hot prospect in Ethan Pratt, the father of the foster kids who were murdered."

Tippen arched a shaggy brow. "He's been out of the picture since conception, but now he cares so much he assaults a judge?"

"He's of a type," Liska said. "One of those guys who only wants to be around to make the big, dramatic scene."

"An asshole," Kovac declared.

"Pratt's done jail time for minor assault.

He punched out a guy in a sports bar for being a Dallas Cowboys fan—"

"That's a crime?" Elwood asked.

"—knocked around a girlfriend. Big temper, small brain," Liska said. "He made the news when Karl Dahl was arrested, giving a loud, obnoxious statement outside the courthouse after the arraignment. Demanded the death penalty. It somehow escaped his notice that we don't have the death penalty in this state."

"I saw that," Elwood said. "Fu Manchu mustache and a blow-dried mullet."

Liska nodded. "The perennial favorite hot look for the white trash set."

"You ever have a mullet, Sam?" Elwood asked.

Kovac scowled at him. "Jesus Christ."

"He had the mustache," Liska said with mischief in her eyes. "I've seen the photographs."

"It was the eighties," Kovac defended himself. "Every cop with balls had a Fu Manchu."

"Yeah? I don't think I was born yet."

Kovac gave her a look across the table and tried not to laugh. "Don't make me come over there, Tinker Bell."

"What're you gonna do?" Liska teased. "Beat me with your walker?"

"You're just begging for a full day of misogynist PMS jokes."

"Ha! You're the one asking for it, Kojak. As you well know, you are no match for my mouth."

"I'm not touching that," Tippen announced. "It's too easy."

It felt good to open the pressure valve and release some of the job stress, Kovac admitted. They were merciless with each other, and a lot of their humor would be considered shocking, rude, and in very poor taste by normal human beings. But it was how they coped with a job that showed them the worst kind of human cruelty and depravity on a regular basis.

Lieutenant Dawes cleared her throat loudly, reining them in. "Ethan Pratt . . . ?"

Liska had the grace to look sheepish. "He's on probation. But he's not at his last known, he didn't show up for work last night, and he didn't check in with his PO yesterday. *And* Amber Franken told me he was going off on the judge the last time he visited, ten days ago. She said he called Moore a fucking cunt."

"A popular phrase with the mullet faction," Tippen said.

"Practically an endearment," Elwood concurred.

"You should add that to your repertoire, Elwood," Liska suggested. "Girls go wild for that kind of talk."

"So, he's not accounted for, he has a temper, he called Judge Moore the same thing her assailant did," Dawes said. "We need to find this guy and have a sit-down."

"It's out there," Liska said. "Be on the lookout for an asshole with a mullet."

"I'll put someone on that specifically," Dawes said. "There has to be someone out there who knows where this guy is."

"Even assholes have friends," Elwood said.

"Any word on Stan Dempsey?" Kovac asked.

He knew there was a BOLO out for Dempsey in all agencies in the entire metro area, but no one wanted to talk about it.

"He's the one running around armed to the teeth and promising justice," Kovac said dryly.

Dawes shook her head. "We have a call in

to his daughter in Portland, Oregon, but she hasn't called back."

"Dempsey has a daughter?" Elwood said with disbelief.

"Dempsey had sex with a woman?" Tippen said. "Stan, we hardly knew ye."

"Well, that's a problem, isn't it?" Dawes said. "We don't know him. We can't find anyone who knows him. We don't know where he'd go to hide. We don't know what he does outside the job."

"He used to do some fishing," Kovac said. "And there was a photograph in his house of him and the ex ballroom dancing."

Nobody knew what to say to that. They couldn't have looked more puzzled if Kovac had jumped up on the table and did the tarantella.

"Check with the county registrar," Kovac said. "Maybe he's got a shack on one of the lakes. And we should try to track down the ex, in case Stan's decided justice begins in the family."

"Good idea, Sam," Dawes said. "I'll go back further in Dempsey's file. She must have been listed as a contact at one time. And we've got Dempsey's address book from his house. She might be in there."

"If that doesn't work, find out from Dempsey's financials who his attorney for the divorce was," Tippen suggested. "He'll have the name of the wife's attorney. It's roundabout, but it works."

Dawes nodded. "We've already checked with the DMV to see if he might have another vehicle registered. There's nothing."

"So he's in his own car," Tippen said. "Or has to boost something."

"He won't steal a car," Kovac said. "It's against the law."

Liska gave him a look. "And torturing someone with a meat fork isn't?"

"He sees that as justice. An eye for an eye. That's his job. But he won't break the law to do it. For one, that would be against his principles, to say nothing of stupid and careless."

"What do we need with Dempsey's shrink when we have Sam?" Liska asked.

Kovac looked to Dawes. "It's just common sense."

"Who have you got at Judge Moore's house?" Dawes asked. "Since no one has any idea where Karl Dahl is, the judge will be Dempsey's obvious first choice."

"If he tries to get to the judge, I've got a

unit on the house and a prowl car staying within a four-block area around the clock."

"How's Judge Moore doing?" Dawes asked.

Kovac shrugged. "She's a tough cookie. She's hanging in."

"She's tough, but her sentences aren't," Tippen complained.

"Give her a break," Kovac snapped. "Someone beat the shit out of her last night."

Eyebrows went up all around the room. Kovac felt his cheeks heat.

Liska broke the silence. "He's trying to quit smoking again."

As if that would explain any strange behavior on his part.

"Oh . . ."

"Hmm . . ."

"Well . . ."

No one looked directly at him except for the lieutenant.

"Nikki tells me you don't think much of the husband."

"He's an asshole. I'm on my way to check out his alibi as soon as we're done here."

"You don't think it'll hold up?"

"He's an asshole," Kovac reiterated.

"What's the word on the videotape from the parking garage?"

Liska shook her head. "I wouldn't recognize myself on that tape. See for yourself."

She went to the television that was sitting on a cart in the corner of the room nearest Sam and started the tape rolling.

Kovac frowned. "This the best they could do?"

"Considering what they had to work with . . ."

The picture had a slightly better clarity, but the subjects were featureless.

"What's that white thing on the back of the perp's jacket?" Kovac asked.

"Some kind of logo, I suppose," Liska said, "but there's no chance in hell of ever being able to read it."

"What about the check of the license plates in the ramp?"

"Nothing so far."

"Not the Haas kid or his pal, or Ethan Pratt," Kovac said, thinking out loud. "Anyone with priors?"

"Nothing," Tippen said.

Kovac sighed, scratched his head, drank some coffee. His eyelids felt like they were lined with sandpaper. He pushed his chair back from the table and got up. "Are we done here?"

"You have better things to do?" Tippen said sarcastically.

Kovac stretched and yawned. "Yeah. I thought I'd go catch some bad guys, then maybe catch a movie or save the world or something."

Liska batted her eyelashes at him. "A superhero's work is never done."

"You got it, babe," he said. "Play your cards right, and maybe I'll let you watch me change clothes in a phone booth."

"So what was that about?" Liska asked when they were back in their cubicle in the squad room.

Kovac didn't look at her. "What was what?"

"Last night you wanted to leave Carey Moore for dead. This morning you're ready to defend her honor? What's that?"

"I feel sorry for her," he said, making a show of putting on his reading glasses to go back over his field notes. "She got the crap beat out of her while her husband is off fucking some bimbo and couldn't care less what's going on with his wife."

"You know that?"

"I know when a guy's lying about it. And she's trying to pretend it's not happening or that somehow it doesn't matter to her. I don't get that."

"She's embarrassed," Liska said quietly. "It's no fun to be the butt of the joke. Especially if you're supposed to be tough and strong and the rest of that type-A-woman crap.

"This is the voice of experience talking," she said.

Kovac pulled his glasses off and looked at her. She'd been married to a narcotics detective from the St. Paul PD long enough to have had two kids with him. They had come up through the ranks together, marrying when they were both still in uniform. The ex-husband—everybody called him Speed—was one of those bad-boy types women always wanted to reform. Liska had believed herself above that, believed she knew exactly what Speed was all about. But she hadn't counted on his not being able to handle her success.

Nikki was a good cop, and ambitious. She had a drawerful of commendations from the department. She worked high-profile cases, got her picture in the paper every once in a while. Speed was a cowboy, reckless, always living on the edge undercover, the nature of his work keeping him out of the limelight. He had cheated on her over and over. A cruel kind of revenge for not being able to outshine her.

Kovac hated the guy. Always had.

"Yeah," he said softly. "Good thing you didn't take the judge home. You would have taken one look at the husband and castrated him on the spot. He's a bastard, and she puts up with it because . . . I don't know. They have a daughter; she's got a lot on her plate being a judge. . . . Maybe she just doesn't have the energy to deal with him."

Liska narrowed her eyes. "You like her."

Kovac scowled. "I feel sorry for her."

"No. You *like* her," she said, dead serious, pointing a finger at him. "She's another damsel in distress who needs rescuing. Be careful with that, Sam. I don't want to see you get hurt."

"Jesus," he grumbled, putting his glasses back on so he could avoid her laser gaze. "There's no evidence to support your theory."

"The hell there isn't. I know you. I know your track record."

"Prior bad acts," Kovac grumbled. "Inadmissible."

"Shows a pattern of behavior," Liska argued.

"I barely know the woman."

Liska sighed and just looked at him with a familiar mix of concern and frustration. He could tell she wanted to say more, but she bit her tongue on it.

"I have to go," Kovac said, getting up from his chair. "What's next on your agenda?"

"Follow-up on Bobby Haas. Unless I get an eyewitness who can put him or his buddy at the scene, I can't connect him to the assault. I figured I would go and be supportive of him and his dad. See how they're doing. Update them on Karl Dahl, not that there's anything to report. Show Bobby what a kind, warm, and motherly person I am."

"So you can break him down and feed him into the wheels of justice?"

"Exactly."

Kovac patted her shoulder. "That's my girl."

23

Bobby Haas was in the front yard, raking leaves, when Liska pulled up to the curb in front of the Haas home. Just parking in the driveway made the skin on the back of her neck prickle, so she didn't.

She felt a little sheepish being so weird about this place. During the course of her career, she'd been to literally hundreds of death scenes, had gone back to them, had spent time in them to try to imagine the crime as it was taking place. But this place . . . She wished she had worn a religious medal.

The boy looked up as soon as Liska got out of the car. He had an expression that told her he had received too much bad news in his young life and was bracing himself for more.

"Hey, Bobby. How's your dad doing?"

"He's not feeling very good."

"Should he be going to a doctor?" she asked. "I'll try to help you with him. I know he doesn't want to go, but if he's sick . . ."

Bobby Haas looked back at the house as if he were seeking permission. When he turned back to her, he sighed. "No, thanks. He's got his medication from his regular doctor. And he's really no worse than he ever gets. He just needs to rest. I can take care of him. I don't mind."

"He's a proud man, your dad," Liska said, though she knew nothing of the sort. "You know, when something really catastrophic happens, sometimes the strongest people get hit the hardest."

"He feels responsible," Bobby said. "Like he could have prevented it. But he couldn't have. Not without being psychic. Maybe I could have stopped it from happening too, if I'd known it was going to happen."

Liska nodded. "But you didn't know. No one knew. No one could ever imagine something that evil, except the Karl Dahls of the world."

"He's still loose, isn't he?"

"Everything possible is being done to find

him," Liska said. She nodded toward the front porch. "Can we sit down for a minute?"

He looked suspicious but went with her as she started toward the porch, suggesting he didn't really have an option.

Liska took a spot on the top step. Bobby sat two steps down, leaning his rake against the side of the stairs. The brilliant fall sun cast a glow around him as if he were an angel.

Pretty, she thought. That was how to describe him, not as a handsome young man but beautiful. He had to have taken after his mother. She tried to remember what Marlene Haas had looked like, but the only picture she held in her mind was the garish, horrific crime scene photo showing Marlene Haas propped up on the sofa in the TV room, her face lifeless, daisies sprouting out of her chest.

"You know, Bobby, I'm sure you've heard this so often you don't want to hear it anymore, but I really am sorry for your loss. I'm sorry for what you and your dad have had to go through. Especially what you had to go through, finding your mother's body, finding the kids in the basement. I can't even begin to imagine what that must have felt like. Were you and your mom close?"

The boy squinted across the yard as if his mother might be standing over by the garage. "Marlene was my stepmother. But yeah, I liked her. She was a nice person. Really kind. She liked to bake. The house always smelled like cookies."

"Is your mother in the area?"

"She died when I was thirteen."

"I'm sorry. I didn't know. What happened?"

"Cancer."

"Wow, that sucks," Liska said. "You've had a really tough go of it, haven't you?"

He shrugged a little. "I'm okay. My dad and I have each other."

"You two are pretty tight, huh?"

"We used to do a lot of stuff together. Go to ball games, go fishing, stuff like that. He used to coach my youth hockey team. He taught me how to drive a car."

"You don't do so much of that since the murders."

"He hasn't been up to it. He took a leave from work when it happened, but he could only be gone for three weeks. I told him he should've quit. Retire."

He sighed heavily, the weight of his world bearing down on him. "I thought we could've moved somewhere, like Arizona, and just started over. Here, all he can think about is what happened. But we have to stay in this creepy house. He won't do anything about it."

"It's a pretty tough sell, Bobby," Nikki said. "Unless your dad is a lot better off than I am, he can't buy a house without selling a house."

"But we wouldn't need a house," the boy said. "We could just get an apartment or something. I don't get it. I mean, what happened was horrible, but we have to go on with our lives."

Frighteningly well-adjusted, this kid, Liska thought. He had dealt with his own grief, put it away, and moved on. In many ways, he was now the adult in the family, while painful memories and grief incapacitated his father. And yet he was still a boy, and he just wanted his dad back.

"Has your dad been able to work with someone from Victim Services? They can hook him up with grief counseling—"

"He won't go," Bobby mumbled, looking

down at the crumbling old concrete step. "He doesn't believe in shrinks."

"How about you? Did you go? Would you go?"

"I'm okay. I talked with a grief counselor a couple of times. She didn't really get it. But who could, I guess."

Liska watched him fiddle with the end of a shoelace, a nervous gesture. He wasn't a happy kid. She had rubbed at some sore spots, reopened still-raw wounds.

He glanced up at her. "What happened with the judge?"

"She'll be all right. We're following up on what leads we have."

"Is that why you're really here?" Bobby asked. "To ask me again if I did it?"

"I need to corroborate your story to clear you, Bobby," Liska said. "Did you or Stench happen to talk to any teachers or school staff when you were at the basketball game last night?"

"No. Why would we?"

"Just asking."

"I bumped into one of the janitors when we came in. Mr. Dorset. I don't know, maybe he'd remember seeing us."

"Did you have to pay to get into the game?"

"No."

"What time did the game start?"

"Seven."

"Were you there for the whole thing?"

"Yeah."

It was Liska's turn to sigh.

"Okay," she said, getting up from the step. "You know, I'm not trying to prove you did it, Bobby. I'm trying to prove that you didn't.

"I have a son almost your age," she said. "When I think if he had to go through all this . . . I'd want to know somebody was looking out for him. You don't have anybody like that, do you?"

He looked away. "I have my dad."

"Not really. It's more like he has you. He's lucky you're a good kid."

The kid looked down, scratched his rake in the grass. "He's my dad. I'd do anything for him."

"Bobby, do you know who Ethan Pratt is?" Liska asked, changing tracks.

Bobby Haas looked confused. "Yeah. I know his name. He's—was—Brittany and Ashton's dad. Why?"

"Has he ever come around or called?"

"No. Why would he?"

Liska shrugged. "Just covering my bases. Call me if you think of someone who can back you up about last night," she said. "I'll check with the janitor. Thanks, Bobby."

The boy didn't say anything.

Liska walked away, wondering if Bobby Haas's devotion to his father might extend to revenge.

24

Kovac was a great believer in the element of surprise. Forewarning only gave people time to get their lies straight. He didn't like to make appointments for interviews. Better to just show up. The sudden appearance of a homicide cop with a lot of questions tended to rattle the average citizen.

Of course, he knew he wasn't going to get the jump entirely on David Moore's alibi witnesses. Kovac had no doubt that Moore had been on his cell phone the minute he had gone out the door the night before. But they wouldn't be looking for him to just show up.

After Liska had gone, he ran Edmund Ivors and Ginnie Bird through the system. Both came up blank for any known criminal activity.

Ivors turned up on Google. As David
Moore had said, Edmund Ivors was an en-
trepreneur, fifty-seven, had made his fortune in multiplex movie theaters in the Twin
Cities and Chicago. He had offices downtown, a home in the pricey suburb of Edina,
and a place on Lake Minnetonka, where
mansions had dotted the shoreline for more
than a hundred years. He sat on the boards
of several film councils and half a dozen
charities. A man seemingly above reproach,
but then, in Kovac's experience, those were
the people who often had the weirdest
skeletons in their closets.

Ginnie Bird, on the other hand, did not exist. Kovac couldn't find her anywhere. He
tried running variations on her first name—
Virginia, Ginnifer, Jenny, Jennifer . . . nothing. Tried alternate spellings on her last
name. Nothing. She was not in a phone di-
rectory, didn't have a car registered in that
name. She wasn't on the list of registered
voters, nor on the tax rolls for the State of
Minnesota.

Moore claimed Ginnie Bird was an "associate" of Ivors's, so Ivors should have her
address and phone number.

Kovac glanced at his watch. His stomach

was growling like a dog. He needed lunch and a gallon of coffee, and about three packs of cigarettes. If he hadn't thought he would dislocate his shoulder doing it, he would have patted himself on the back for his restraint with the smokes. He had always run a big investigation on caffeine, nicotine, and adrenaline.

His cell phone went off before he could think too much about falling off the wagon.

"Kovac."

"Detective Kovac, my name is Edmund Ivors."

The element of surprise had just turned around and bitten him. A preemptive strike. He immediately believed this to be a sign of something rotten.

"Mr. Ivors. I guess you've spoken with David Moore."

"Yes. I heard about the attack on Judge Moore last night. I called David right away, of course. He told me you'd have some questions."

"Yeah, I do," Kovac said. "I was just on my way out. Can we meet somewhere?"

"I'm at my office. Do you have the address?"

"I'll be there in half an hour."

Edmund Ivors's downtown offices were sleek, modern, expensively decorated, as was the man himself. A small, immaculate man with a closely trimmed salt-and-pepper beard and a navy blue pin-striped suit that would have set Kovac back a month's pay. A subtly striped shirt, a purple tie and pocket square. Kovac never trusted a guy with a matching pocket square—they always thought too much of themselves. The shoes were probably handmade by blind monks in the Italian Alps.

Kovac took one look at him and thought: Asshole.

Ivors met him in the reception area with a too-friendly smile and a strong shake with a soft hand. This was the kind of guy who got manicures every week.

"Detective," Ivors said, "I'm glad I was able to get hold of you."

"Why is that?" Kovac asked. "Most people try to avoid me."

"I wanted to be able to put to rest any suspicion you might have regarding David."

Kovac raised a brow. "You're tight, you and Dave?"

Ivors smiled like a politician. "I've known David for a couple of years. He's a nice man. Couldn't possibly do anything along the lines of what happened to his wife last night."

"He was with you."

"Yes. We met for drinks in the lobby bar of the Marquette. Sevenish."

"How did he seem? Nervous, anxious, relaxed . . ."

"He seemed perfectly normal."

"Did he say anything about his wife?"

"Not that I recall. We were discussing business." Ivors gestured toward a hall. "Let's go into my office, Detective. We can be comfortable. Is there anything I can get you? Water? A soft drink? I'd offer you coffee, but I'm completely inept at making it. If it weren't for my staff, I would have to take up drinking tea. I can manage to boil water, but that's about it."

"Nothing for me, thanks."

The office at the end of the hall had a stunning view of the city. Two walls of floor-to-ceiling glass. There was a huge art deco-style mahogany desk, and a visitor's chair with a woman in it.

Kovac gave her the once-over. Ginnie

Bird, he presumed. Another preemptive strike. He liked this less and less. It was a setup, and so obvious they had to think he was as dumb as a post.

She didn't look like she would hold up to much. She was petite—thin, really, except for the store-bought breasts; attractive, but in a way that didn't appeal to him. It wasn't any one thing. She was dressed well in camel slacks and a rust-colored silk blouse. She was nicely made-up. But there was something about her that made him think *cheap*. Something in the gaunt hollows of her long face, the shape and set of her eyes, the limp blond hair shagged off at shoulder length.

Or maybe it was just that Kovac had taken an instant hatred to her because he had it in his head that this was the woman David Moore had been screwing while his wife was lying in a hospital bed.

"Detective Kovac," Ivors said, "this is Ginnie Bird. Ginnie was there last night."

"Ms. Bird."

The woman didn't move other than to offer Kovac a limp hand when he reached out to her. She didn't want to be here, and she certainly didn't want anything to do with a police detective.

The end of her nose was red as if she had a cold or had been crying.

Junkie, Kovac thought. The pallor, the thinness . . . That was it, he thought. She looked like a junkie whore someone had tried to pass off as something better, something legitimate.

"So the three of you were out on the town until two in the morning," Kovac said. "That's a long evening."

"We were talking about David's new project," Ivors said, walking over to a credenza to pour himself a glass of water from a clear pitcher with a dozen lemon slices floating inside. "He's putting together a documentary juxtaposing—"

"I don't care what it's about," Kovac said bluntly. "Are you backing it?"

"Yes."

"And, Ms. Bird, what's your part in all of this?"

She looked startled to have him turn his attention on her. As she opened her mouth to answer, Ivors said, "Ginnie is a casting director. She'll be casting the actors for the reenactment segments of the film."

"And this gets you in on the deal making?" Kovac asked, openly dubious.

"Ginnie's very talented, great instincts. I wanted her insights on the project."

Kovac stared directly at the woman. "Do her talents include the ability to speak?"

Ivors laughed, the jovial host. "I'm sorry, Ginnie. My wife always tells me I won't let anyone else get a word in sideways. I'm afraid I can't help myself."

"Try," Kovac said, unamused. He turned back to the Bird woman. "Are you new to the area, Ms. Bird?"

"No," she said, brow knitting. Her voice was as strong as her handshake.

"Newly married?"

"No. Why?"

"Well, you know, I was looking you up this morning, trying to find a phone number for you, but I couldn't find you anywhere. The State of Minnesota doesn't seem to know you exist."

"I'm from Wisconsin," she said quickly. "I live in Hudson."

Just across the St. Croix River from the easternmost commuter towns to the Twin Cities.

"Really?" Kovac said. "Nice place. I have

a buddy in Hudson. Ray Farmer. He's chief of police there. Maybe you know him?"

"No, I don't," Ginnie Bird said, glancing at Ivors. "I haven't lived there very long."

And yet she wasn't new to the area. Whatever else she was, she was a poor liar.

"Where are you from originally?"

"Illinois."

Kovac raised his brows as if he thought people from Illinois to be particularly suspect.

"You know, I checked with the restaurant," he said. "They told me they close at eleven-thirty Friday nights."

"Yes," Ivors said. "We took our conversation to their bar."

"So if I ask someone working in the bar, they'll tell me the three of you were there until closing?"

Ivors's gracious mood was starting to fray around the edges. "And why would you do that, Detective? Did we break a law I don't know about? I thought you were interested in where David Moore was at the time of his wife's attack. What does it matter to you that we were sitting in a bar until two o'clock?"

"Just covering all my bases, Mr. Ivors,"

Kovac said. "Let's say—hypothetically— that someone paid someone else to attack Judge Moore. The first guy might meet the second guy later on to pay him off."

"David would never do that." Ginnie spoke up, angry on Moore's behalf.

Kovac gave her the eye. "You know him that well?"

"He's just not that kind of person."

"I've been a cop a long time, Ms. Bird. I can tell you, I've seen people do the god-damnedest things. People you would never imagine. Someone gets pushed far enough, gets backed into a corner, you can't say what they might do. Some guys, they see someone standing between them and free-dom, or them and a lot of money, they'll take the shortest route between two points and to hell with who's standing in the way."

"You're talking about David like he's a criminal," she said, incensed.

"I don't know that he's not," Kovac said. "I don't know that you're not. That's the whole point of an investigation, isn't it? To pry open the closet door and take a look at the skeletons. Everybody has at least one."

"This is ridiculous," Ivors said, openly irri-tated. "Carey Moore was mugged in a parking ramp. Her husband was with us from seven o'clock on. That's what you needed to know, Detective Kovac?"

"Yes."

"Fine. Now you know it."

"I guess I'm being asked to leave," Kovac said.

"There's a triple murderer running loose in the streets," Ivors said. "I'm sure you have better things to do than stand around asking pointless questions."

Kovac smiled a little as he backed toward the door. "But you see, Mr. Ivors, that's the beauty of my job. No question is ever pointless.

"Thank you for your time," he said, and gave a little nod toward the Bird woman. "You've been very helpful."

25

Karl had no difficulty finding Judge Moore's house. He recognized it from what he'd seen on the news. It was a fine redbrick house with white trim and black shutters. The kind of house where well-off, respectable folk would want to raise their families and host dinner parties.

He could imagine what it would look like at the holidays, like something from a Hallmark Christmas card. There would be candles in all the windows, a big wreath on the shiny black front door, evergreen garland wound around the pair of white columns. Inside there would be a very tall, noble fir hung with colored lights and every kind of ornament.

Now it was the perfect picture of fall, with

big maple trees shedding their leaves onto the lawn. Pumpkins on the front step.

This was exactly the kind of house he would have imagined for Carey Moore. A fine house for a fine lady.

Karl drove past in the Volvo, noting the police car sitting at the curb in front of the house. He drove around the block, looking for more cops, but he didn't see any. No radio cars, no unmarked cars with men sitting in them, pretending to be waiting for someone.

There was an alley, but he didn't dare go down it. There could have been police sitting in Carey Moore's backyard. Maybe when it got dark he would park the Volvo on the street and slip down the alley on foot.

For now Karl drove to the parking lot on the north end of Lake Calhoun, which was connected to Lake of the Isles by a canal. Lake Calhoun was bobbing with sailboats, bright white against the gleaming blue water. Calhoun was huge, hundreds of acres wide between its shores. Lake of the Isles was much smaller, but very scenic, with its small islands and abundance of waterfowl, which cartwheeled in the sky above and used the lake's glassy surface as a landing pad.

Karl walked north along the paved path that followed the shoreline. Minnesotans had spilled out of their homes in droves to take in the warm sun and blue skies. The walking path was busy with people of all ages, from babies in strollers to white-haired elderly men and women. Bikers and people on in-line skates whizzed past on the outer paved path.

Karl breathed deep of the fresh air, feeling thankful and optimistic. When he could see Judge Moore's home, he found a park bench and sat down. He had stopped at a busy deli on his way over and gotten himself a roast beef sandwich with mustard, and a bottle of Coca-Cola. Now he took his lunch out of the bag and began to eat.

All around him, he could hear snatches of conversation. A woman complaining about her daughter-in-law, a woman complaining about her lumbago, a woman complaining about her husband, two men brainstorming some kind of a business deal, a young couple in a serious discussion about the future of their relationship.

Everyday life was walking past him, he

thought. People caught up in their own little dramas, unaware that the woman on the park bench they walked past was, in fact, the most wanted man in the city. Maybe in the whole country.

Karl enjoyed the joke that he was hiding in plain sight. It gave him a sense of accomplishment. As Karla Neal (Neal, after Christine Neal, as a little tribute to the woman who had supplied him with his new identity), he was viewed as harmless, just another person going about her life on a lazy Saturday afternoon. Not worth taking notice of.

As he watched the people around him—children feeding the ducks and Canada geese at the water's edge, mothers chitchatting, lovers fighting, old men talking about the escaped murderer, old women going on about whatever old women went on about—Karl imagined standing up in the midst of them, peeling off the wig, and revealing the monster they all believed he was.

He could imagine the sense of horror as something palpable in the air, brushing against him, washing over him. He would breathe it in and convert it to power. The power would make him feel like a giant. Invincible.

Of course, that would never happen. He would remain as he was: a quiet woman enjoying the lovely day, looking at the lovely home across the way, thinking of the lovely woman inside.

26

Stan drove carefully, observing the speed limit and all traffic laws. The fact that what he was planning in his head was against the laws of God and man registered in his mind in only an abstract way. The only law he was operating under was an eye for an eye.

That was his job now, his mission. To take the guilty parties and make them pay for what had been done to Marlene Haas and those two little children, for what they were allowing Karl Dahl to get away with. As if a piece of crap like Karl Dahl should have rights. What about the rights of the victims?

If the system wouldn't give them justice, then that was Stan's purpose. That would be his last job here on earth. He had no other reason to be here. His career was gone, and he had nothing else. If he ceased to be a cop, then he ceased to be at all.

In a way, that had already happened. The Stan Dempsey people thought they had known was gone, not that anyone had ever really made an attempt to know him. That part of his being had shut down, leaving him numb in some ways, but more alive than ever in other ways.

This is what it's like to lose your mind, he thought, but there was no emotion attached. No fear, no panic, no despair.

Kenny Scott, Karl Dahl's attorney, lived in an unremarkable house in an unremarkable neighborhood. The house was not unlike Stan's own, built in the fifties, a story-and-a-half rectangle like every other rectangle on the block.

The juniper shrubs were overgrown, and the grass in the yard looked poor, as if Scott never fertilized or aerated it. Stan shook his head as he parked the truck down the block. Yards needed tending. If a person let their yard go, that spoke to their lack of character as far as Stan was concerned. But then he'd already known Kenny Scott lacked character.

He got out of the truck, taking a small

duffel bag with him, and walked down the sidewalk toward Scott's house. Across the street there were some boys playing with a football in a front yard. They paid no attention to Stan. A woman struggling with a baby stroller was at the side of a minivan in the driveway of the house two doors away from Scott's. She didn't even glance at Stan as he walked past. He had always been a person no one noticed. A lot of times that had worked to his advantage.

He turned down Kenny Scott's driveway and walked around to the back of the house. There was a small concrete patio with a black Weber grill, a glass-topped round table with an umbrella sticking up through the center of it, and four metal chairs with green cushions.

Stan put his duffel bag on the table, unzipped it, and chose a handgun. A .22. Small, quiet. A lot of criminals thought they had to carry big guns, .44s, .357s. That was just crap. That was ego, idiots trying to look like big men. A .22 did the job close range, very little mess, very little noise, and it was easy for the shooter to pocket and simply walk away from the scene with.

He zipped the duffel bag and slung it over

one shoulder and across his chest, shoving the bag itself behind him, out of his way. Then he went to the back door and knocked.

A television was playing somewhere inside. Kenny Scott was watching a college football game. Stan himself was a lifelong fan of college football, the Michigan Wolverines in particular. But as with everything in Stan's life, that was something only he knew about himself, because no one else had ever bothered to ask.

He knocked on the door again.

The attorney came through the kitchen, looking puzzled. Stan could see him through the glass in the back door. Scott looked out through the glass, still confused.

"Detective . . . ?" he asked as he opened the door.

"Counselor," Stan said. "Can I have a moment of your time?"

Scott still didn't know what to think, but he took a step back, because Stan was, he thought, a known quantity. Stan stepped inside and pointed the .22 in Scott's face.

Scott's eyes went round. "What the hell?"

"Turn around, Mr. Scott."

"Are you out of your mind?"

"Yes, sir, I am," Stan said flatly. "Turn around. Up against the wall."

The reality of the situation was starting to dawn on the lawyer. Fear flashed in his eyes.

"What do you want with me?" he asked. "I haven't done anything to you."

Stan wanted to laugh out loud, but he didn't. How could Kenny Scott think his actions as Karl Dahl's attorney hadn't had any impact on anyone else?

"Turn around. I won't say it again, Mr. Scott."

Kenny Scott didn't react. He didn't believe this was happening.

Stan backhanded him across the face with the .22, snapping his head sharply to one side. Blood splattered sideways and hit the dingy beige wall. Stan thought he could see the individual droplets fly in slow motion, changing shape and dimension as they went, skittering along sideways as they hit the surface of the wall.

Sound came to him slightly delayed, then quickly caught up like some kind of strange special effect in a movie, the sound of the gun connecting with Kenny Scott's cheekbone, the attorney's grunt of pain, the thump of him hitting the wall.

Stan held him there with his gun hand, pulled handcuffs out of his left jacket pocket, and cuffed one wrist and then the other behind the lawyer's back.

"Why are you doing this?" Scott asked again.

This time Stan could hear the fear in his voice. Scott could tell this situation wasn't going to go well for him. He was probably already imagining what Stan might do to him.

Stan felt a rush of power that was exciting. This was what Karl Dahl had felt gaining control of his victims.

"Down the stairs," he said, jerking Scott away from the wall and shoving him to the right, toward the head of the basement stairs. Blood ran down the wall from where Scott's face had been. His nose was bleeding, as well as the gash on his cheek from where the sight of the .22 had cut him.

The lawyer had begun to cry. "Please don't do this."

He already believed he was going to die, which told Stan he must have felt that that was what he deserved.

"Down the stairs."

Stan gave him a little push. Scott brought his shoulder against the door frame to block himself. Stan grabbed him by the arm, yanked him sideways, shoved him forward.

The lawyer stumbled, started to fall, twisted sideways, trying to use the wall to stop his momentum.

"You feel helpless?" Stan said. "You think this is how Marlene Haas felt when your client was torturing her? Or how those children felt as he took them down to the basement?"

"Jesus," Scott said. "You can't hold that against me. I'm a public defender, for God's sake. I don't get a choice who I represent. You think I want to defend Karl Dahl?"

"You're trying to get him off," Stan said, pushing him down another few steps.

"That's my job."

"It's just a damn game to you people. You know what Dahl is, and still you try to get him off on some technicality."

"The rules are there for a reason—"

"For you to bend them around and let that sick bastard get away with what he did to those people. Let him go so he can rape and murder someone else's family?"

"Defendants are presumed innocent—"

"Innocent?"

Stan felt the rage rise up inside him like a column of fire. "He butchered that woman. He violated those children and hung them from the ceiling. I was there. I saw them. I smelled their deaths. Do you have any idea what that's like, Counselor? Have you ever been to a death scene?"

Scott didn't answer him. Of course he didn't know what it was like to stand in the place where a violent death had occurred. He had never experienced the unsettling feeling of evil lingering in the air, mingling with the last vibrations of terror. He didn't know what it was like to feel as if he could almost still hear the screams of the victims as their lives were being torn out of their bodies.

"You look for loopholes to get these scumbags off," Stan said bitterly. "You're as guilty as Karl Dahl. And you're going to pay for that."

He put his foot into Kenny Scott's back and pushed. The lawyer went headfirst down the final few steps and landed on the concrete floor with a dull thump like a bag of wet cement.

Stan stepped over the groaning lawyer and went to a workbench built up against one wall. The duffel bag went on the bench. Stan unzipped the bag, looked inside, trying to decide what appealed to him most for this situation.

"You're going on trial, Mr. Scott," Stan said, pulling his choice from the bag. "And nobody is going to try to get you acquitted."

27

David Moore, the brilliant filmmaker who hadn't made a film in years, had a Web site devoted to himself. Arrogant prick.

Back at his desk, Kovac looked it over. It wasn't a cheap deal. Sharp graphics, great color, a little slide-show montage of his work. A lot of self-aggrandizing crap about his credentials and awards he had won in the past. He certainly made himself sound like a genius.

Kovac wondered if he ever got a call off this site to produce anything or if it was just for ego. He knew nothing about the making of documentary films, except that when he watched one on PBS, they always seemed to be funded by grants from big oil companies and private trusts for the endowment of the arts. The latter of which was apparently where Edmund Ivors came into the game.

He didn't know what kind of a living a man could make doing what David Moore did. Seemed to him that if the guy only got one film made in a decade, either he made a boatload of money doing it or he was leeching off his wife.

Kovac suspected choice B. David Moore was all talk and no walk. His most recent work had been producing the occasional commercial for local television.

The best thing Kovac could see about Moore's Web site was that the jerk had included numerous photographs of himself. Photographs of him hard at work and twenty pounds thinner. Photographs of him in black tie at some awards bash.

Carey was with him in that one. She looked happier then, with a brilliant smile, her hand on her husband's arm. A knockout dress that flashed a little skin. She would have been a prosecutor at the time, trying to make a name for herself in the county attorney's office. And Husband had been at the top of his game, the man of the hour.

Cut from the same inferior materials as Liska's ex, Kovac thought. Big mouth, fragile ego. What had Carey said? That her husband resented her.

With guys like that around, it was a pure damn wonder that women bothered to associate with men at all. Not that he'd been any great catch himself, Kovac admitted. At least he couldn't say he had ever resented either of his wives when he'd been married to them. Afterward was a whole other matter.

The four-star Marquette Hotel had been designed as part of the central complex of the IDS Center, a soaring fifty-plus dramatic stories of dark glass. The hotel connected to the main office tower via the Crystal Court—a glass-enclosed 23,000-square-foot urban park with a glass ceiling 121 feet above the ground and a 105-foot cascading water fountain at its center.

The complex connected to the rest of the city by the skyway system—enclosed second-story sidewalks that linked most of the major buildings downtown. The skyways allowed you to travel by foot all over downtown without ever setting a toe outdoors, a great thing when winter temperatures dropped well below zero and the winds howled through the concrete canyons of the city.

At the front desk, Kovac showed his badge to a young clerk, who immediately went and fetched the manager, a rail-thin red-haired man with a very serious face. Brendan Whitman, his name tag said. Kovac went through the introduction business again, then showed Whitman the photograph of David Moore he had printed from the Web site.

"Mr. Whitman, do you recognize the man in this picture?"

"Yes. That's Mr. Greer," he said without hesitation.

Mr. Greer. David Moore had chosen his father-in-law's name to use when checking into hotels to cheat on his namesake's daughter. Passive-aggressive prick.

"Can you tell me if Mr. Greer was checked into the hotel yesterday?"

Whitman looked at him, suspicious. "What's this about?"

"This is about a police investigation into an assault last night. I'm sure you wouldn't want the good name of your hotel to be associated with an assault if there was no need."

"Of course not."

"So let's try this again. Did Mr. Greer check into the hotel yesterday?"

"Yes. I checked him in myself."

"What time was that?"

Whitman thought about it. "Around three in the afternoon, as usual."

"He's a regular?"

"Every other week. He's from Los Angeles. Does something in the movie industry. Was Mr. Greer injured in the assault?"

"Not yet," Kovac muttered under his breath. "Is he usually with a lady when he comes in?"

"No. Always by himself."

"Have you ever seen him here with a woman?"

"Yes. I've seen him several times with a woman in the bar."

"What did she look like?"

Whitman squinted as he thought about it. "Ummm . . . medium height, slender, blond."

"Do you keep records on your guests?" Kovac asked. "Could you, say, type Mr.

Greer's name into your computer and bring up a list of his stays at the hotel?"

"Yes, but you'll need a warrant for that," Whitman said. "If we just gave out that kind of information, it would open the hotel to lawsuits. If we can show we were compelled by the authorities to give over the information . . ."

"I understand," Kovac said, though he didn't like it.

There was no chance of his getting a warrant for David Moore's hotel records, or for his financials, which Kovac would have loved to get his hands on. To get a warrant, he had to show reasonable cause for the specific items or information he wanted. As he had been told by more than one prosecutor, Carey Moore among them, if what he wanted was a fishing license, he would have to get it from the state Department of Natural Resources.

Moore's hotel stays would be pertinent in divorce court, not criminal court. The investigation was about Carey Moore's assault, and David Moore's alibi held. Unless Kovac could come up with something that connected Moore to the actual perpetrator of the crime, he was out of luck.

Liska would have been all over him if she'd known he was even asking the questions he had asked Brendan Whitman. She already thought the warning flags were up, which irritated him. For Christ's sake, couldn't he feel sorry for Carey Moore without falling in love with her overnight? He couldn't simply dislike her husband for cheating on her?

It wasn't like he fell for women at the drop of a hat. For the most part, he'd sworn off relationships. They never worked out for him. He wasn't exactly sure why. He was a decent guy, treated women with respect. He knew the job had taken its toll on his marriages. The hours, the grimness, the stress. His better qualities apparently weren't enough to offset that.

He was a cop. It wasn't what he did; it was who he was. He could no more change that than he could change the color of his eyes, so he just didn't think about it . . . most of the time. The one woman he'd fallen for who would have understood that, because she had been a cop herself, had committed suicide right in front of him.

He still thought about her, still felt pain at the loss. He still second-guessed himself sometimes late at night when the nightmare of that scene woke him. If only he'd known the depth of her pain . . . If only he had unraveled the mystery of her an hour sooner . . . If only he could have reached her before she fired the gun . . .

Pointless to think about it, he knew. What happened, happened. No one could change that. It hadn't been in the cards for him to save Amanda Savard.

"She's another damsel in distress who needs rescuing. . . ." Liska's words whispered in his ear. Kovac shut them out and closed the door on the whole topic.

The lobby bar was empty except for the bartender, who was busy checking bottles. Kovac pulled out a stool and sat down.

"Sorry, sir," the bartender said. "We don't open till four."

"Good. I'll be out of here before I'm tempted to drink on duty."

The bartender looked over her shoulder, raising an eyebrow at the badge. She was a little thing, but tough as nails. He could see it in the fine lines around her eyes, the set of her mouth. Forty-something, he figured, dark hair scraped back into a ponytail for convenience, not cuteness. Patty, according to her name tag.

"I can make an exception for a badge," she said in a two-pack-a-day voice.

"Don't tempt me."

He put the picture of David Moore down on the bar.

"Oh, yeah," she said, rolling her eyes. "What's he wanted for? Have they finally made being an asshole a crime?"

"We'd have to build jails on the moon," Kovac said.

Patty laughed at that, a harsh cackle that would have been more at home in some American Legion post bar than in a swank hotel.

"You see a lot of him?" Kovac asked.

"Enough to know he's a cheap son of a bitch. Buys himself a label, buys the working girl house booze."

"Working girl?"

"Skirt up to her ass, neckline down to her navel ring? She ain't no schoolgirl, unless the guy pays extra, if you know what I'm talking about."

"Medium height, blond, thin?"

"Expensive tits? That's the one."

"They were in here last night?"

"They were in here around six, six-fifteen. I was trying to watch the news," Patty complained. "Hey, what's up with that psycho Dahl? Have you caught him?"

"I don't know," Kovac said. "Not my case."

"What kind of retards do they have running that jail? Jesus."

Kovac let the question ride. "So they were in here, just the two of them?"

"For a while," Patty said. "She's all over him. The postgame cozies, if you know what I mean. If I didn't think he paid for it, I'd say she's in love with the clown. She's got the big cow eyes. She's all 'Oh, David' this and 'Oh, David' that," she said in a higher, breathier voice, batting her eyelashes. In the next second, she made a face like she'd tasted something rotten.

"Made me wanna puke," she said. "Then, around seven, this older guy comes in and joins them. Real neat, kind of prissy-looking. Expensive suit, little beard trimmed just so."

She curled her lip and shook her head, disgusted. "He had that look like maybe he likes to watch, if you get my drift. At least he was a good tipper."

Patty poured two fingers of Johnnie Walker Red and set it in front of him.

"On the house," she confided. "Don't worry about it. I'll overcharge the next big asshole."

Kovac thanked her and took a long sip of the scotch and savored the smooth warmth as it went down. Just one moment of quiet pleasure. Now, if he had a smoke . . .

"And then this other guy came and joined them," Patty said, helping herself to one of the nut dishes. "But he didn't stay long."

Kovac's alarm bells went off. "Another guy?"

"Yeah. Thirty. On the small side. Longish blond hair. Kind of foxy-looking. Wiry, sharp features, narrow eyes."

"How was he dressed?"

"Dark jeans, black jacket, black T-shirt."

"And he didn't stay long," Kovac said.

"Ten, fifteen minutes. I couldn't say for sure. It had started getting pretty busy in here. Predinner crowd. But I know he wasn't here as long as they were."

Long enough to say the job was done, Kovac thought. Long enough to pick up his payoff.

David Moore, you son of a bitch.

A rush of electricity went through him, the way it always did when a piece of the puzzle fell into place. He wanted to run right out and haul Moore downtown for questioning, but he knew he wasn't quite there, didn't quite have enough. He needed to put a name to the foxy-faced guy dressed in black. The guy who had shown up here between seven and seven-thirty, a time frame that easily could have allowed him to be in that parking ramp when Carey Moore was being attacked.

To get that name, he needed to go back to the weakest link in the trio, Ginnie Bird. If he could get her alone, she'd break fast.

The fantasy was cut short by the ringing of his cell phone.

"Kovac."

"Detective. Judge Moore is leaving her house. We thought you'd want to know."

28

"I'm going to the courthouse," Carey said.

She stood in the hall at the front door, not even wanting to go the few extra feet to the den, where David had been sitting at his computer all day. She didn't want to see him, she didn't want to speak to him, she didn't want to hear his voice.

He looked out at her, perturbed. "Why? You're supposed to stay here."

"I'll take a police officer with me," she said. "I won't be going back to work for a while. I can at least do some reading and paperwork."

"Call your clerk. Have him bring it to the house."

Carey said nothing to that. Of course she could have had her clerk do it. Of course she should have. She felt terrible, and she needed to rest. The truth was that she just didn't want to be in the house with her husband. She hadn't decided yet what to do, whether she should confront him with what she knew, or wait and gather more evidence against him, or tell Kovac everything.

She didn't want to believe the worst—that the man she had loved and married could hate her enough to pay someone to kill her. But the David she had discovered that morning was not that same man. This David had a whole other life going on that she didn't know anything about. This David was a stranger. She had no idea what he might be capable of.

"I won't be long," she said.

Lucy came racing down the stairs, wearing a pink fairy costume and clutching her favorite toy, a stuffed dog she had named Marvin. "Mommy, I want to go! I want to go with you! Please."

Carey caught her daughter and hugged her tighter than the occasion called for. "Sweetie, I'm just going and coming right back."

"I want to go with you," Lucy insisted, tears filling her eyes.

She was afraid. Afraid her mother might

get hurt again, afraid she might never come home. Lucy was a bright and perceptive child. She knew something bad had happened, something worse than just her mother falling down. Carey knew she could also sense the tension between her mommy and daddy. They never argued in front of her, but the negative energy between them vibrated subtly in the air around them. Lucy picked up on that. She was probably feeling very insecure.

"Okay," Carey said. "You can come along."

An instant, beaming smile lit up her daughter's face. "Do we get to ride in a police car?"

"No. The officer will drive us in Daddy's car."

"My car?" David said. "Why my car?"

"Because mine is at the police impound yard, being processed for evidence," Carey said. "Were you planning on going somewhere?"

"No," he said, obviously scrambling mentally for a logical reason he didn't want her in his car. "I just need to get some paperwork out of it before you go."

"We'll be gone twenty minutes. Your

paperwork has been out there all day, and suddenly you can't wait twenty minutes for it. What's that about?"

"It's not about anything," he snapped, getting out of his chair. "I just realized I need it."

"Then get it," Carey said.

She wanted to add that he should be sure and get out any of his girlfriend's stray lingerie while he was at it, but she didn't.

"Fine," David said in a huff. "I'll get it."

He stomped down the hall to the kitchen and out to the garage.

Carey glanced down at her daughter. Lucy was watching her with a somber face.

"You need to have a coat on, Miss Sugar-Plum Fairy," Carey said, and turned to the hall closet to get one out.

The officer, Paul Young, parked the car at the curb in front of a "No Parking" sign and escorted them into the government center and to Carey's chambers. After looking through the offices to make certain there were no bad surprises waiting for her, he stationed himself in the hall outside to wait.

Lucy ran around behind the desk and

climbed up in Carey's chair, wide-eyed with excitement at the prospect of all the fun she might have with the stuff on the desk.

"Mommy, can I play on your computer?"

"No, sweetheart. This is where I work. The computer isn't for playing with," Carey said as she took the copies of the phone bills, the credit card receipts, the list of escort agencies out of the tote bag she'd brought with her. She pulled an empty file folder from a cupboard, put the papers in it, and put the folder in the bottom left-hand drawer of her desk. The evidence could stay there until she decided what to do with it.

"Mommy? This was Grandpa Greer's hammer, wasn't it?"

"That's called a gavel," Carey said. "Yes, that belonged to Grandpa Greer."

Lucy held the gavel with both hands. It was almost as long as her arm, and an incongruent accessory to her pink fairy costume. An impish smile curved her mouth. So precious. The one good thing to come out of her marriage: her daughter.

Carey brushed a hand over Lucy's unruly dark hair. Tears burned the backs of her eyes.

"I wish Grandpa Greer could remember me," Lucy said.

"I wish that too, sweetie."

God, I wish that too.

All her life she had been able to go to her father with anything, for any reason, day or night, 24/7. He was the Rock of Gibraltar, her foundation, her anchor.

He had never really liked David. She knew that because he had told her when she had announced her engagement to him. Not in a harsh way, but with concern for her. Was she sure that was what she wanted? Was she sure David was the one?

She had been upset with him at the time. She had wanted him to be happy for her, to be supportive of her, to approve.

David had been a different person then, confident from the success of his work and the accolades of critics. But even then her father had sensed a lack of foundation in him. And he had said to her that if this was what she truly wanted, he would give her his blessing but that she needed to know that she would always have to be the strong one in the marriage, that when the chips were down the only person she would be able to rely on was herself. He felt that David's strength would always rise and fall with the opinions of other people.

Her father had walked down the aisle with her and handed her over to the man who would be her husband. And he had never spoken of his opinion of David again.

"Don't cry, Mommy," Lucy said. She put the gavel down on the desk and stood up on the seat of the chair and hugged her mother.

Carey winced at the pain in her ribs, but she didn't tell Lucy to let go. She wanted to feel the security of being held by someone who loved her, even if that someone was only five years old.

A sharp knock at the door startled her. Before she could ask who was there, Kovac walked in with a stormy expression. He stopped short to take in the scene. He had wanted to come in with a big temper to throw at her for leaving the house, but see-ing her with Lucy, seeing her with tears in her eyes, knocked the wind out of his sails.

Embarrassed, Carey touched gently be-neath her eyes to wipe away the tears. She could probably have counted on one hand the number of people who had ever caught her crying. Kovac had managed to do it twice in one day.

"By all means, come in, Detective Kovac," she said with an edge of sarcasm ruined by the weakness of her voice.

Kovac looked from Carey to Lucy.

"How did you know we would be here?" Lucy asked, bright-eyed with curiosity.

"I'm a detective," Kovac said. "That's what I do. I find out where people are. I find out who committed crimes."

"My mommy's a judge," Lucy said proudly.

"I know."

"She puts bad people in jail."

Kovac glanced at Carey, biting his tongue on some smart remark, she thought.

"Hey, Princess Lucy," Kovac said. "I need to speak with your mom in private. Why don't you go out in the hall with Officer Young, and he'll show you all the cool stuff on his belt. He'll show you how handcuffs work."

"I'm a fairy now, not a princess," Lucy informed him. She turned. "Can I, Mommy?"

"Sure, honey."

Lucy climbed down from the chair and went around the desk to Kovac and offered him her hand. By the look on his face, she could have been offering him a live snake.

"I'm not allowed to go places alone," Lucy said. "You have to take me."

Carey motioned to the door when Kovac looked to her.

"Uh . . . okay," he stammered, taking her small hand. He walked her out to hand her over to the care of Officer Young.

When he came back, he looked a little rattled, as if he didn't know what to do with the emotions Lucy had evoked in him. Murderers he could deal with. A five-year-old child undid him.

"Do you have children, Detective?"

He hesitated a beat before he answered. "No. I'm not married."

Not that one necessarily had anything to do with the other. Like eighty percent of the cops she knew, Kovac had probably been married and divorced at least once.

"She's a doll," he said.

"Thank you."

An awkward silence hung in the air for a moment.

"I suppose you want to scold me for leaving my house," Carey said.

"I believe I did tell you to stay put."

"You can tell me anything you want."

"And you'll do whatever you damn well please."

"Wouldn't you?"

He thought about that; then one corner of his mouth crooked up. "Point taken. You should sit down, though. You look a little pale."

"I look like something from a zombie movie."

"Well . . . yeah," Kovac conceded.

Carey eased herself down into her desk chair, glad for the soft padded leather. "So is this bad news, or are you just going to lecture me?"

Kovac sat in the chair on the other side of the desk and let go a sigh. "Well, yeah, I was gonna lecture you, but . . . what's the point?"

"I wouldn't have come here alone," Carey said. "I'm not that stupid woman in every suspense movie who has to go investigate the strange sounds in the basement."

Once again he gave that little quarter of a smile that only touched one side of his mouth. He let his gaze wander around the room, seeming to not want to make eye contact with her unless he had the cop face on.

"This is a lot nicer than what the prosecutors get," he said. "You kicked ass back then. Do you ever miss it?"

"Yes, sometimes," she admitted. "But this was what I always wanted to do."

"Because of your old man?"

"Yes. My idol," she said, looking away as the emotion threatened to surface again.

"He was a good judge. What's he doing in his retirement? Golfing in Arizona?"

"He's dying," she said. "He has Alzheimer's, and . . . he's dying."

"Oh, Jesus," Kovac muttered. "I'm sorry."

"Me too."

"I never miss an opportunity to stick my foot in it."

"You didn't know," Carey said. "Have there been any leads tracking down Stan Dempsey?"

Kovac shook his head. "No sign of him. No sign of his car."

"Has anyone called Kenny Scott? He has to be up there on Dempsey's hit list."

"That's supposed to be happening."

"You didn't call him yourself?"

"Kenny Scott is not my priority," Kovac said. "I've got all I can handle with you."

Carey smiled a little and realized that she never made eye contact with him either in those moments when her guard slipped.

"Am I being difficult?"

He didn't answer right away. He studied her. She could feel his gaze on her. Finally, he said, "I think you're too brave for your own good. Why did you have to come here?"

"I wanted to get some paperwork to look at while I'm convalescing."

His sharp eyes swept over the desktop. "So where is it?"

"I forgot it's in my briefcase," she lied.

"You know, you're good," Kovac said. "But I'm better. Let's try this again, and maybe you can tell me the truth this time. Why did you have to come here?"

Carey looked down at the desk drawer where she had stashed her file on David's hobbies. She should probably have given it to him. But what was really in it? Evidence that her husband was unfaithful. Kovac already knew that. And the note—*$25,000*—could have been anything. Maybe David was thinking of buying a boat. Maybe twenty-five thousand dollars was the lottery prize that day. Maybe he was putting a down payment on a house for another one of his hooker girlfriends or for himself. Maybe he was thinking of moving out.

"I spoke with your husband's business associates," Kovac said. "The people he had dinner with last night. A man named Edmund Ivors. Do you know him?"

"No. David doesn't include me in his business dealings." *Or anything else,* she thought.

"Does the name Ginnie Bird mean anything to you?"

"No. Why?"

"I think your husband is sleeping with her," he said bluntly. "Actually, I'm pretty sure of it."

Carey didn't say anything for a moment. Kovac let her process the information.

"I'm telling him I want a divorce," she said at last.

Kovac raised his brows. "Just like that? No 'Let's work this out'? No 'Let's go to counseling'?"

"Our marriage has been dying a slow death for a long time. There isn't anything left to work out except visitation rights."

"I'm sorry."

She almost laughed. "Why? You hate my husband. You can't believe I ever married him in the first place, let alone that I stayed with him all these years."

"I'm sorry for you," Kovac said softly. "I'm sorry you have to go through it. I'm sorry I had to tell you about the girlfriend."

Carey shook her head. "No. Don't be."

She stared down at the desk drawer, then finally pulled it open and took out the file. She handed it across the desk.

"What's this?"

"Evidence. I'll be using it in court."

Kovac paged through the contents. "How long have you been saving this up?"

"Since this morning. I did a little detective work of my own. He wasn't even bothering to hide it."

"That rotten, rat bastard son of a bitch," Kovac growled half under his breath as he looked at the hotel receipts and florist bills. He picked out the list of escort agencies and turned red with anger. If David had been there, Carey had little doubt that Kovac would have punched him in the face.

He pulled out a copy of several canceled

checks made out to the property management company. "What are these for?"

"He's paying for an apartment," she said, and recited the address to him. "For himself or for one of his little playmates. I called the company this morning, pretending to be David's new accountant. I needed information. The last accountant left things in a terrible mess. Couldn't they help me out? All I needed was the address of the property."

"And they gave it up," Kovac said.

Carey nodded.

Kovac picked up the copy of the note regarding twenty-five thousand dollars. "What's this?"

"I don't know," she said softly. "It was in his wastebasket this morning."

"It's a payoff," he said.

"You don't know that. It could mean anything. A debt. Something related to his business. He's talked about buying a boat."

Everything she said sounded like an excuse. If she had been sitting in Kovac's place, she knew what she would have been thinking.

"In October?" Kovac said. "Who buys a boat right before winter?"

Carey didn't answer him.

"Carey . . ."

"David is a lot of things," she said softly, looking down at the desk. "But I can't believe he would do what you're suggesting."

"Before you found this stuff, would you have believed he was living a secret life? That he was cheating on you with prostitutes every time you turned your back? That he would use your maiden name as his alias?"

She looked up at him, startled and hurt.

"You didn't know that part," Kovac said gently. "What else don't you know about him?"

What could she say? She was married to a stranger.

"Things weren't always like this between us," she said at last, feeling the need to justify having stayed in the marriage. "We were in love once. The last couple of years, we've grown apart. He's slowly become this bitter, unhappy person. I wanted just to gloss over it, to think he was frustrated with his lack of success. I didn't want to come down on him, because I knew his ego was fragile and my career was going so well."

She brushed a thumb beneath her eyes. "And there was Lucy. She loves her daddy.

If nothing else, he's been a good father. He adores Lucy. The sun rises and sets on her.

"I didn't care that he didn't love me anymore. I had my career, my daughter. I could make that be enough."

She felt weak, was trembling ever so slightly. She didn't think she'd ever felt so defeated in her life. Kovac just sat there quietly, watching her with sympathy in his world-weary face.

"I'd like to go home now," Carey announced, pushing herself to her feet. "I need to rest up for the big scene."

"You're telling him tonight?" Kovac said, rising from his chair. "Are you sure you want to do that?"

"Why wait? I've waited too long as it is."

Kovac gently caught her by the arm as she came around the desk, headed for the door. His touch surprised her.

"I can be right there for you," he said, looking her straight in the eye.

And he meant it, Carey thought. This hardened street cop, who didn't even like her, would help her through this if she asked. And she had no doubt that he would follow through. That was who Sam Kovac was—blunt, honest, reliable—and not for any reason other than he simply believed that that was the right thing to do.

"I really don't want an audience," she said.

"I'll stay outside."

Carey shook her head. "I already have two officers sitting out front. David is as aware of them as I am. He wouldn't risk touching me. He has a whole other life to live for. I can guarantee you prison isn't on his agenda."

"I don't want you to be alone," Kovac said.

"Well, that's what I'll want to be—alone. Despite all recent evidence to the contrary, I prefer to cry in private."

He didn't like the idea at all. He wanted to protect her. What a lovely thought, someone looking out for her, someone to lean on, someone volunteering to shoulder the burden for her.

"I appreciate the thought," she said. "I really do."

"I don't trust him, Carey."

"Don't worry. David is far too passive-aggressive to hurt me himself."

"I want you to call me after," Kovac said. He still had hold of her arm and stood close enough that she could feel his breath on her cheek. Peppermint . . . and the faintest hint of scotch.

She arched a brow. "Drinking on the job, Detective?"

"Yeah," he admitted, that little tug of a smile at the corner of his mouth. "You drove me to it."

"Well, then, I guess your secret should be safe with me."

She took a step away from him, and he let go of her arm.

His expression turned serious. "Be careful. And call me. And remember: I can be there before you hang up the phone."

Carey nodded. "Thank you . . . Sam. Thank you."

She wanted to put her arms around him and hug him for being kind. Or because she wanted to feel strong arms around her, supporting her, protecting her. She felt so alone.

Instead, she thanked him again and went to the door. Lucy's face lit up.

"Mommy, I learned how to arrest somebody."

Officer Young smiled at her. "What do you say to the bad guys?"

Lucy put her hands on her hips and made her best mean face. "Assume the position!"

Carey chuckled. "We have to go now, sweetie. Thank Officer Young and Detective Kovac."

Lucy said her thanks to the officer, then went to Kovac's feet and looked up at him. "Thank you for holding my hand, Detective Kovac."

Kovac leaned down and shook her hand formally. "You're welcome, Fairy Princess Lucy. You can call me Sam."

The little girl smiled, delighted. "I like you, Detective Sam. Will you carry me?"

"Lucy!" Carey exclaimed.

Kovac looked uncomfortable and slightly terrified. He glanced up at Carey.

"You don't have to," she said.

But when he looked back at Lucy, he couldn't seem to say no. Lucy put her arms around his neck and sat in the crook of his arm, looking pleased as punch with herself.

"I'm going to pretend you're a giant," she said. She jabbered at him all the way to the car.

When he put her down on the sidewalk, he turned to Carey, his expression dead serious. "You call me, I'm there. Be careful."

Carey nodded and slipped into the back-seat of the Mercedes. All the way home, she thought of how much her father would have liked Sam Kovac.

29

"You place kids in foster homes, you worry if the foster parents are just in it for the money or if it might turn out they're abusive. You never think about some psycho killing them."

Marcella Otis had been the Family Services caseworker for Wayne and Marlene Haas regarding their fostering of Amber Franken's two children. Liska had arranged to meet her at a coffee shop on the Nicollet pedestrian mall just a few blocks from the police station. They sat at a sidewalk table, soaking up the glorious day, nursing their drinks, and talking. They probably looked as if they were just two ordinary women chatting about ordinary things. Only the people at the next table, who were quite obviously eavesdropping, knew better.

Ms. Otis was a sight to see. A woman of considerable substance in a neon green tunic and pants, an African-looking multicolored pillbox hat perched atop ropes and ropes of cornrows. She wore hip rectangular glasses and an abundance of silver jewelry.

"I was just sick when I saw it on the news. I'll never forget that night. That terrible thunderstorm. Just waiting for a tornado to take the house. It seemed like a nightmare, but it was all too real. I remember everything turned green just before it hit, the sky, the air. Freaky."

She closed her eyes and shivered at the memory.

"Had the kids' father ever surfaced before the murders?" Liska asked.

"Ethan Pratt? Ha! That's a good one. He had no more interest in those children than the man in the moon."

"But I heard he's suing the county for endangering them."

Marcella pursed her lips and made a face. "He's all interested now. Those kids are worth more to him dead than they ever would have been alive. That boy's a damn coyote, picking at their bones. He's making noise about suing what's left of the Haas family too. Like those poor people haven't been through enough tragedy."

Liska nodded. "Yeah. I talked to Bobby Haas a little while ago. He's been through more than any one person should go through in a lifetime. Finding Marlene and the two children. His own mother dying of cancer."

"Cancer?" Marcella said, arching a brow.

"He told me Marlene Haas was his stepmother," Liska said. "That his real mother died of cancer a few years ago."

"If he was talking about the first Mrs. Haas, that's just not true," Marcella said. "The first Mrs. Haas was carrying laundry down to the basement, slipped, and fell down the stairs. She died of a broken neck."

Liska sat back. "Why would he lie about something like that?"

"I don't know. I guess you'd have to ask him. Maybe he just doesn't want to think about one more person being snatched out of his life so suddenly."

"Did you know that Mrs. Haas?"

Marcella nodded. "Rebecca. A very sweet lady with a big heart. She and Wayne were talking about taking on another child. I had just been to their home to speak with them about it a day or two before the accident."

"You said *if* Bobby was talking about her," Liska said. "Who else would he have been talking about?"

"His birth mother, I suppose." She took a long sip of her chai latte.

"Bobby Haas is adopted?"

"Yes. Wayne and Rebecca took him on as their first foster child when Bobby was ten. They ended up adopting him. And now that I think about it, his birth mother didn't die of cancer either. She committed suicide." She fondled a chunk of biscotti while she pulled the memory up. "That's right. She hanged herself."

"Jesus," Liska muttered.

"If I remember correctly, she was a seriously disturbed woman. Bobby Haas had gone through the tortures of the damned before he ever became Bobby Haas."

"Does he have any history? Trouble in school? Trouble on the streets?"

"No. I hear he's an excellent student. Hasn't been in any trouble ever that I know of. Why? Is he in trouble now?"

"No," Liska said absently. "Not that I know of."

"He's a good kid," Marcella said. "If I'd gone through half of what he's gone through, I would've gone crazy a long time ago."

"Maybe he did," Liska said softly. "There are a lot of ways to go crazy. The ones who do it quietly are the ones you have to worry about most."

"You can't possibly think he had anything to do with those murders," Marcella said. "The boy was inconsolable when it happened. Karl Dahl is your killer."

"Yeah," Liska said, her mind already moving on from the conversation. "Actually, I'm looking in to the attack on Judge Moore."

The social worker sniffed and made another face. "I hate to sound un-Christian," she said, "but there are a whole lotta people in this city who would have lined up for the chance to take a whack at her."

Yes, Liska thought, but more and more she was thinking maybe Bobby Haas had been at the head of that line.

30

"So let's have the update, people."

Lieutenant Dawes stood at the head of the table in the conference room. The war room, they called it when they were working a case like this. One entire wall was covered side to side with whiteboard. Leads, questions, details were written on it in Dry Erase marker, easily wiped away for the next terrible case.

"I've been looking for any record of Stan Dempsey owning property other than his house," Elwood said. "Nothing. But I did discover there are forty-one land-owning Dempseys in the metro area. One of them might be a relative. I've got people making those calls right now."

"Did we locate his ex?" Liska asked.

"In a cemetery," the lieutenant said. "She passed away last year. Brain tumor.

"And I've heard nothing from the daughter," Dawes went on. "I reached out to the Portland PD to ask them to locate her if they can."

"Did anyone warn Kenny Scott about Stan?" Kovac asked. "As Dahl's defense attorney, he's a prime target."

"I called him," Dawes said. "Got his machine. I've dispatched a radio car to go over there and sit on his house until he shows up. Hopefully, he got out of town for the weekend."

"He might want to think of making that a permanent move," Tippen said. "If his address goes public, he's going to have angry villagers with their pitchforks and torches on his front lawn."

"He's court appointed," Dawes said. "He didn't choose to represent Karl Dahl."

"No," Tippen conceded, "but he chose to represent him with zeal."

"Minnesotans hate zeal," Elwood said. "Zeal is right up there on the list of suspicious emotional behaviors like joy and despair."

"Always err on the side of blandness," Tippen advised.

Dawes turned to Kovac. "Sam, what have you got?"

"A headache," he said. "I don't like the husband's alibi witnesses. One is too slick; the other is a hooker. Moore checked into the Marquette around three yesterday. Moore and the hooker were in the lobby bar from six, six-fifteen on. In between time he was banging the hooker, not beating his wife's head in. The slick one, Edmund Ivors, joined them around seven."

"Edmund Ivors?" Tippen repeated. "I know that name from somewhere."

"He's some kind of multiplex movie mogul," Kovac said. "The most interesting part is that they were joined briefly by a third guy. Neither Moore nor Ivors mentioned a third man when I questioned them. The bartender described the guy as thirtyish, blond, dark jeans, black jacket, black T-shirt. Was there for maybe ten minutes."

"Long enough to say, 'Hey, I tried to kill your wife. I got run off. I want my money,'" said Dawes.

"That's what it looks like to me. We'll need

paperwork to get the hotel to hand over the surveillance video."

"Did the bartender see them make an exchange of some kind?"

Kovac shook his head. "She was busy. She saw the guy talking with them; then she didn't see him. Dickhead Moore, Slick, and the Bird woman then went off to dinner and Christ knows what else. The bartender said Ivors struck her as the kind of slimebag who likes to watch."

Liska crinkled her nose. "Eeewww!"

"What's Moore's motive?" Elwood asked. "Besides that he's an asshole."

"Money," Kovac said. "She divorces him, he gets half. He has her killed, he gets it all."

"Is she divorcing him?" Liska asked, watching him with particular scrutiny.

"The handwriting is on the wall," Kovac said, avoiding her eyes. He wouldn't betray Carey's trust. No one needed to know the famous final scene was still hours away, least of all Liska. "That clown's been living off her for a while now, I'd say. He hasn't made a film in years. He's out running with the dogs while she's in the hospital with a concussion. You can cut the tension between them with a knife."

"She's got money?" Dawes asked.

"Family money," Tippen said. "The Greers of old were in the lumber business. Huge fortunes were amassed on the backs of immigrant lumberjacks. Alec Greer's father branched out to mining taconite when that was still lucrative, and got out while the getting was good. Judge Greer is well off. Unless he leaves it all to charity, his daughter should inherit a bundle."

Dawes raised her eyebrows. "Thank you, Mr. History Channel."

"I'm a Renaissance man," Tippen said. "A bon vivant. A raconteur."

"You're full of crap," Liska said, tossing a ballpoint pen at him.

Tippen fired back a chocolate-covered coffee bean. Liska squealed as it hit her in the forehead.

Dawes assumed the role of mother. "Tippen, do I have to take those away from you before you put someone's eye out?"

"No, ma'am."

"Is Judge Moore's father healthy?" she asked Kovac.

"No. On his way out. Carey is his only child—"

Liska burned a look into him and mouthed *Carey?*

"If she's out of the picture, then the old man's money would pass to his only grand-child, her daughter, Lucy. Lucy's five years old. Moore would have control of whatever she inherited."

"This is all a neat theory," Dawes said. "What do you have to back it up?"

"My years of experience and wisdom," Kovac said. "Get me a warrant and I'll prove it. A search warrant for the house and a warrant for Dickhead's financials."

"And what are you going to use to get a warrant, Detective?" Dawes asked. "Your good looks?"

"And charming personality."

Dawes rolled her eyes. "What have you got, Nikki?"

"Nothing much. I haven't been able to confirm Bobby Haas's alibi or to break it. One strange thing: When I was talking to him today, he told me that Marlene Haas was his stepmother, and his real mother died of cancer. But when I spoke to the caseworker from social services, she told me the kid's adopted, that his birth mother committed suicide, and Wayne Haas's first wife died from a broken neck when she fell down the basement stairs with a basket of laundry."

"So nobody had cancer?" Elwood said.

Liska shook her head. "No. That's a pretty weird thing to lie about, wouldn't you say?"

"How old is this kid?" Tippen asked.

"Seventeen."

"And he's had that much violent tragedy in his life?" Dawes asked. "Maybe he just wanted to eliminate one of them. How would a kid feel, having all of that in his background? The only thing my fifteen-year-old son wants is to be exactly like everybody else his age.

"This boy probably feels like people think he's some kind of a freak. At least saying his mother died of cancer is something other kids have a frame of reference for."

Liska looked at Kovac. He knew her well enough to see all the subtle signs that something about this kid was bothering her.

He shrugged. "You can't arrest the kid for saying his mother died of cancer when she didn't. And if you can't get a witness to put him at the parking ramp, you can't pin the assault on him.

"I'm putting my money on the future ex."

"I'm sure you are," Liska said.

Kovac lowered his eyebrows.

"I'm taking Dempsey," Tippen said. "He's openly crazy. He's made threats. What's beating a woman with a club to a guy who might be willing to torture someone with an electric carving knife?"

"No wagering in my presence, please," Dawes announced. "Let's all get back to it. We've got to make something happen."

"Any word on Karl Dahl?" Kovac asked as he rose from his seat.

She shook her head. "The man has vanished. The dogs never got on a scent. No one credible has seen him. We're getting the usual tips from psychics and religious fanatics and people who just call because they're lonely and they want someone to talk to. And lots of dead ends. I've got uniforms running all over town, chasing down bald-headed men."

"He's the kind of guy who lives off the radar," Tippen said. "A shadow figure on society's fringes."

"I thought that was you," Liska said, standing up.

Tippen gave her a mean look. "You're very short and perky."

"Fuck you."

As they all moved toward the door, Dawes nodded for Kovac to hang behind.

"You have that strong a feeling about Judge Moore's husband?"

"You're only seeing the tip of the iceberg of my hatred for this jerk."

"I'll make sure we get the security video from the hotel bar ASAP. Maybe we can get a line on this mystery man. We can at least compare the video to the one from the parking ramp. See if it could be the same guy."

"If I could get Moore's financials, maybe I could find evidence of payoffs for the hit."

"I don't see a judge giving us a warrant based on what we have, Sam. Do you think Judge Moore would swear out a complaint on him?"

"For what? If being a lousy husband was against the law, I'd be doing twenty-five to life," Kovac said. "Besides, I don't think she would do it. She has her daughter to consider. And her reputation. I don't see her filing a complaint on some half-baked accusation just to get the Dickhead in our box so we can break him."

Dawes sighed. "Do you have any excuse to bring him in for questioning?"

Kovac thought of the file folder he'd locked in the trunk of his car. He'd only glimpsed through it, but he knew there was plenty of evidence of Moore's infidelity. But if he brought David Moore in for that, then he tipped Carey's hand.

Maybe that wasn't such a bad thing.

"I could ask him to come in for a noncustodial interview," he said.

"Will he cooperate?"

"No," he conceded. "He won't cooperate. The first thing he'll do is squeal for a lawyer, and then we're fucked."

He looked away and sighed. "I don't know what to say, Boss. I'd throw the jerk into a snake pit if I could, but if we bring him in on what I've got, that just gives him time to circle the wagons, tip off the doer."

Dawes nodded. "All right. We can put a tail on him."

"You can get the overtime for that?"

"Already blessed from on high. The brass wants this doer's head on a silver platter."

"I mean to make that happen," Kovac said. "I'll even stick an apple in his mouth for the ceremony."

31

The trial was over. It hadn't come out well for Kenny Scott, Esquire, but justice had been done. Swift and terrible.

Stan was shaking, sweating, exhilarated. There was still a small part of his brain that was horrified and terrified of the other emotions roaring through him. But that part was smaller and smaller, weaker and weaker. With justice came strength. Might with right.

Stan's justice was pure and simple. There were no games, no loopholes, no getting off on a technicality. There was only right and wrong.

For the first time in his life, Stan Dempsey felt powerful.

To any casual observer going down the street, Kenny Scott simply wasn't at home. Stan had turned off the television before he left. He had taken Kenny Scott's car and parked it a block away, then walked back to his truck.

If his former colleagues discovered Kenny Scott too quickly, they would have a target area to look for him, and the intensity of the search would be fierce. Stan couldn't have them find him before his job was done.

He calmly drove to another neighborhood and parked his uncle's truck. In the back, under the camper shell, he ate a couple of bologna sandwiches with slices of midget gherkins in them and drank some coffee from his thermos.

He didn't think about what he had just done. He didn't try to recall the panic in the lawyer's eyes, the screams the man had to swallow behind the duct tape that covered his mouth.

The rush the memory of meting out punishment gave was a thing unique to criminals, to serial killers, to men like Karl Dahl. That reaction belonged to the criminals who indulged in cruelty because it excited them. For those men, the memories were as important as the crime itself. They would relive their exploits over and over in their minds.

Stan didn't think of himself as a criminal.

He was just doing a necessary job no one else would do.

He finished his lunch and cleaned his hands off with a wet wipe. It was time for him to move on to the next name on his list.

Carey Moore.

32

It seemed to take days for the hours to pass. Carey spent the rest of the afternoon in her bedroom with Lucy, playing nurse, taking her temperature with a toy thermometer, and giving her "medicine"— M&M's.

They napped, though Carey couldn't sleep for more than a few minutes at a time. The tension was exhausting. She passed the time second-guessing herself.

Maybe this wasn't the time to confront David. Maybe she should wait until the rest of this nightmare was over. Except that she didn't know her husband wasn't a part of it. She didn't want to stay under the same roof with a man who might have arranged to have her killed. She didn't want her daughter in the same house as him.

She worried about Lucy, who was already feeling insecure and clingy. But was there ever a good time for a child's parents to end their marriage? No.

She thought about sending Lucy to Kate and John Quinn's home for the night. Lucy loved sleepovers and was friends with the Quinns' daughter Haley. But Carey didn't want her daughter out of her control, or out of her sight, for that matter. Things were too uncertain. And she didn't want to potentially put John and Kate in harm's way if Stan Dempsey had decided to go after her daughter to make her pay for Carey's sins. He could have been watching the house, for all she knew. He could follow her to the Quinns'.

She would wait to speak to David until after Lucy was asleep. Anka would make sure Lucy didn't go downstairs in the event she woke up. Carey was very thankful the nanny had insisted on staying the weekend, even though Saturday and Sunday were usually her days off. Anka wouldn't hear of leaving. Her responsibility was to the family.

What a sad thing, Carey thought, that she could trust her nanny more than she could trust her husband.

———

David ordered Chinese for dinner. Lucy was a big fan of moo goo gai pan. David's appetite was as healthy as ever. Carey picked at her egg-fried rice, continuously rearranging it on her plate but eating only a few grains. She rested an elbow on the table and her head in her hand and stared down at the bright bits of peas and carrots dotting the rice like confetti.

"How's your moo goo, Lucy Goosie?" David asked, smiling at his daughter.

"I'm Fairy Princess Lucy now, Daddy! Detective Sam said so."

"Detective Sam?" He looked at Carey.

"He was at the courthouse, Daddy," Lucy went on. "He was my pretend giant, and he carried me all the way to the car. Isn't that nice?"

"Yes, very," David said. "Why was he at the courthouse?"

"I don't know," Lucy said with a big shrug, going back to her dinner.

"I'm his case," Carey said. "He was keeping tabs on me."

"You should have stayed in the hospital," David said for the tenth time.

"So I could not eat there?" she said too sharply. "So they could force-feed me Jell-O?"

"I like Jell-O," Lucy piped up. "I like green Jell-O best. My friend Kelly's mom puts pieces of carrots in her green Jell-O. Isn't that weird?"

Carey smiled at her daughter.

"I like pineapple in mine," Lucy said. "It's pretty."

"You look ready to collapse, Carey," David said. "And you're out running around like you think you're fine. You've exhausted yourself."

He actually looked concerned for her, and she wondered if any of that look was genuine. A part of her hoped so, even though her practical side told her no. If David cared about her, he wouldn't have been doing what he'd been doing. The more likely explanation was that he wanted her out of his hair so he could do whatever he wanted to do over the weekend. What had Kovac said her name was? Ginnie.

"Did you get your paperwork?" he asked. "I didn't see you bring anything in from the car."

"I forgot it was in my briefcase, which was stolen."

"So you went down there for nothing."

"Do I need to pay you back for the gas I used?" Carey asked with a fine edge of sarcasm.

"What's that supposed to mean?"

"Nothing."

He went to say something more but stopped himself, held up his hands in surrender, and pushed back from the table. "Excuse me, ladies. I have work to do. I'm applying for a grant for the film."

Carey didn't comment. Before this day, she would have encouraged him, tried to be supportive, even though she had long since tired of that game. The time for being David's cheerleader had passed. The time to move on had arrived.

The evening was passed with Lucy, painting toenails and reading stories. After she had tucked her daughter in bed and sat with her until she'd gone to sleep, Carey showered and dressed in a loose pair of jeans and an oversized black button-down shirt. It was one of her father's old shirts. Wrapping herself in it was like wrapping herself in the memory of her father's strength.

It was important to her to feel as strong and secure as she could. Confronting David in pajamas wouldn't do that.

Lucy had been in bed nearly an hour. Once she was sound asleep, it was rare for her to wake up before morning. The sleep of the innocent, Carey thought. She envied her daughter that.

David sat at his desk, staring at the computer screen and nursing a drink.

Carey stood outside the den, watching him for a moment before he looked up.

"I thought you went to bed."

She took a deep breath and walked into the room. "We need to talk."

The four most ominous words with which to open a conversation.

David just sat there for a moment, then clicked his mouse to make his screen go dark. The top-secret grant application. *My ass,* Carey thought. He was probably having virtual sex with one of his prostitute friends. He didn't get up, keeping the solid mass of the desk like a shield between them.

"I want a divorce," she said bluntly.

"What?" He looked more nervous than surprised. "Why?"

"Don't pretend to be shocked, David. You don't want to be married to me. I don't want to be married to you. I don't even know who you are anymore. But I do know all about your extracurricular activities with the prostitutes."

He was actually stupid enough to try to correct her. "Escorts."

"They're women you pay for sex," she snapped. "A whore is a whore, David. No euphemism is going to put a pretty face on that.

"How could you?" she asked. "How dare you."

He rubbed a hand over his face and got up from the desk.

"It was just . . . business," he said. "A transaction for a service. When was the last time you and I had sex, Carey?"

"When was the last time you were an equal partner in this marriage?"

He laughed without humor and shook his head. "And you're wondering why I would go outside our marriage for attention."

"Oh, poor, poor David," she said bitterly. "You're the victim. You've spent the last how many years contributing not one god-damn thing to this relationship—"

"So it's about my failure to make money," he said, moving a step closer to her. "Is that it?"

"Don't try to make this about money. You haven't been plugged in emotionally for years, you don't care about anyone's needs but your own—"

"I'm selfish?"

"Yes."

"And how many years were you working eighty-hour weeks, Carey, never home, always too tired—"

"We were supposed to be partners," Carey said. "Yes, I had a career. You had one too, once upon a time. And you can't tell me I haven't been supportive of that. I've been your biggest cheerleader. Even in the last few years, when you couldn't get arrested, let alone get a film made, have I even once tried to discourage you?"

He looked away.

"Do you have any idea how exhausting that's been, David? To have to carry your fragile ego around like the world on my shoulders?"

He rolled his eyes. "Well, I'm so sorry to have been such a burden on you!"

Carey looked away from him and crossed her arms over her chest. "I don't want to argue with you, David. There's no point in it. We're done. It's over."

"Oh, Her Honor the Judge has spoken and passed sentence," he said sarcastically. "I don't even get to mount a defense."

"How could you possibly defend what you've done?" Carey said, incredulous. "Fucking prostitutes every time I turn my back. How do you defend that? Paying out thousands of dollars a month for sex, for flowers and gifts, for four-star hotel rooms and an apartment I don't even want to know what for, or who for. What can you say that could make any of that okay?"

He looked at her with narrow-eyed suspicion. "How do you know all of that?"

"I looked it up. For God's sake, David, I'm surprised you didn't dedicate a file folder just to your deviant secret life."

"You went in my file drawers?"

"To look at *our* financial records. Am I supposed to have to get a warrant for that? You didn't even bother to try to hide any of it. Your list of favorite escort agencies was in the drawer where we keep checkbooks and stamps. You had to know I would go into that drawer. You probably wanted it to happen, wanted me to find you out, because you obviously don't have the balls to tell me yourself."

He held his hands up in front of himself. "I don't need this. I don't need to be lectured by you, Ms. Perfect. Perfect daughter, perfect mother, perfect lawyer, perfect everything. What a fucking hypocrite! You think I don't know you slept with someone else too?"

Carey took a step back as if he'd slapped her.

"Yeah," David said with malicious glee. "You're not so perfect after all. So don't stand there and look down your nose at me."

"Once," she said. "Once. Because I was overworked, overstressed, and all I was getting from you was a shitload of whining that I wasn't here to serve your every need."

"Right. It's my fault when you're unfaithful, but it's not your fault when I am?"

"There's no comparison," Carey said. "One night I turned to a man I knew and trusted because I needed comfort. You open the yellow pages and pick a number.

And you say it's just a *business transaction*. That's beyond sleazy.

"Can you at least tell me you used protection?" she asked. "That you didn't put me at risk? That you wouldn't put your daughter at risk if she needed a transfusion or a kidney?"

"No," he said with a smug look. "I didn't. I wanted my money's worth."

Carey slapped him across the face as hard as she could. She'd never struck another human being in her life.

"You son of a bitch," she said, glaring at him. "Get out. Get out of this house. Get out of my life. Just go!" she shouted, pointing toward the door.

"It's my house too."

"The hell it is. And if you think for one minute you're getting anything out of this divorce, you are sadly mistaken."

"Yeah," David sneered. "It's all for you."

"For me and for Lucy."

"You can't keep me from seeing my daughter," he said.

"You don't think so? A Family Court judge is not going to be impressed with your hobbies, David."

"I have been a very good father to Lucy,"

he said, his voice trembling, tears coming to his eyes. "Whatever I have or haven't been to you, Carey, you can't say I don't love my daughter, or that she doesn't love me."

Carey closed her eyes and sighed. "No, I can't say that."

"You can't possibly believe I would ever do anything to hurt Lucy in any way. You can't just cut me out of her life."

"No," Carey said with resignation. "I won't do that."

She didn't really know what she would or wouldn't do. Thinking about David's having been with prostitutes made her want to never let him touch Lucy as long as he lived. Her misgivings about the twenty-five thousand dollars made her want him to be out of both of their lives forever. But now was not the time to say any of that.

In all the years she had known him, she had never known David to be violent in any way. But she didn't know this man in front of her. He wasn't the man she had married. He wasn't even the man she thought she had been living with.

She thought of Kovac. Despite what she had told him, he was probably standing in the shrubbery, ready to smash the window in if he so much as imagined anything going wrong.

"I can be there before you hang up the phone."

She thought of the two officers in the squad car out front.

Lucy was her ace. David wouldn't do anything to her here and now, because he couldn't get away and because he would never see his daughter again if he went to prison. Lucy's guardians were Kate and John Quinn, a victim advocate and one of the country's leading experts on the criminal mind. They would never allow David to be a part of Lucy's life again.

And that knowledge only gave credence to the notion of her husband's having paid someone else to do the dirty work for him.

"I guess I loved you once," he said quietly. "I don't know how we got here."

"Please go now, David," Carey said, surprised by how much what he had just said hurt her. *"I guess I loved you once. . . ."*

"I could just stay in the guest room," he said. "I don't want Lucy to wake up and have me just be gone."

"I'll tell her you had to go away on business. I can't have you here, David. I don't trust you."

"You don't trust me not to do what?" he asked, his anger rising again. "That's Kovac telling you he thinks I paid someone to have you attacked. How could you possibly believe that, Carey? You know me better than that!"

Carey stared at him. "I don't know you at all. I don't know who you are. The man I married would never have done any of the things you've done. I have no idea who you are."

"So that's what you think of the man I am now?" he asked aggressively. "That I would pay someone to kill you? That I might kill you in your sleep myself? Jesus Christ, Carey."

"You have to go now, David," she said. "I can't have you here. I don't want you here. Don't make me call the officers in from their car to remove you. It's not like you don't have someplace else to go."

"You are un-fucking-believable!" he shouted.

"Please keep your voice down. Your daughter is asleep upstairs."

Muttering curses under his breath, David

grabbed the external hard drive from his computer and stormed out of the room and up the stairs.

Carey followed him, afraid she had pushed him too far. Her heart in her throat as David approached Lucy's bedroom, she was struck by a fear that David might try to take Lucy with him. But when he stopped at the door to the room, it was only to look in on their sleeping child.

He was red in the face, fighting tears, breathing hard as he turned away and stalked down the hall into the bedroom they had shared. He jerked a suitcase out of his closet, tossed it on the bed, and began throwing clothes at it.

Ten minutes later he was gone.

Carey stood at the kitchen door to the garage and listened as his car started and backed out. She hadn't known how she would feel after the big scene. She hadn't known if she would cry or be angry or feel sick. She didn't feel anything. She was numb. She had spent all her emotions confronting him.

Going back to the den, she walked back and forth across the room, physically holding herself together. She needed to call Kovac. She had told him not to come, but he was almost certainly there, if not in the front yard, then sitting in his car down the street. It touched her that he was concerned about her. She felt less alone.

Being a cop, Kovac was unshockable. Carey couldn't even picture herself telling anyone else what David had been up to all this time. Not even her best friend. She felt stupid and embarrassed talking about it. Kovac hadn't batted an eye. He had dealt with far worse than a cheating spouse.

Sitting down in David's desk chair, she used her cell phone to call him. She had put his number on speed dial. He answered before the first ring finished.

"Kovac."

"It's Carey. I'm all right. David is gone."

"You don't sound all right."

"I'm very tired," she said, appalled at how weak her voice sounded.

"Do you want to talk about it? Do you want me to come over? I'm not that far away."

"You're in my front yard, aren't you?"

"Yeah. You can tell me what to do," he said. "But I'll do whatever I want."

She managed to smile a little at that—her

own words tossed back at her. "Touché," she said. "I really just want to go to bed. But thank you for offering, Sam."

"I'm here to protect and serve."

"I know."

An awkward silence hung between them for a moment. Carey had the feeling he wanted to say something more, but finally he just said, "I'll call you in the morning."

Carey turned off her phone and tucked it into the pocket of her jeans, and sighed, hoping morning would come soon.

33

Kovac flicked on the dash strobe as he drove through the streets, trying to catch up to David Moore. He was betting Moore would go straight to the apartment he had been paying for. Even money said Ginnie Bird lived there.

He caught a look at the big Mercedes sedan sitting at the next stoplight and killed the strobe.

Moore went through the intersection and turned onto the ramp to the freeway. Kovac followed him, then stepped on the gas and blew past him, two lanes over. Moore didn't know his car and wouldn't be looking for him anyway. His head would still be in the scene that had just played out between himself and his wife, and on what he was going to do next.

Kovac exited the freeway and drove straight to the apartment building. It was a nice place in a pricey neighborhood. Fairly new building, landscaping, a gated underground garage. No doorman, though, no concierge.

He parked across the street, got out, and walked over to the entrance.

The tenant list was on a brass buzzer pad beside the door to the small lobby. Kovac went down the names.

Bird, V. Apartment 309.

As he debated whether or not to ring the buzzer, a white Lexus turned in at the drive. The garage gate groaned and rattled as it began to rise.

Kovac moved away from the building entrance, went back down the sidewalk, nonchalant, going for a stroll. The Lexus rolled down into the garage. He waited until the car had turned to the right in search of a parking spot, then walked down into the garage, ducking under the descending gate.

It was as simple as that to get into a building where residents believed they were secure. He checked the ceiling for cameras, but there were none.

He didn't bother to hide, but walked over to the elevator as if he lived there, and pushed the button to go up. Ten seconds later he was joined by the driver of the Lexus, a tired-looking guy with a red, runny nose and a plastic bag from Snyder Drug.

"You got that bug that's going around?" Kovac said.

The guy rolled his eyes. "I wish I was dead."

"Drink whisky."

"That helps?"

The elevator arrived and they got on. Kovac pushed the button for the third floor and glanced up at the ceiling of the car. No security camera.

"Doesn't matter," he said. "After you've had a couple, you won't give a shit."

"Good point."

"Where you going?"

"Four. Thanks."

They rode the rest of the way in silence and nodded to each other when Kovac got off on the third floor.

He didn't go down the hall to Ginnie Bird's apartment but stood there outside the elevator, waiting for the car to go back down and come back up, and the doors to open on David Moore. The hall was empty. Some-one had taped a bright orange sign on the wall beside the elevator, inviting all residents to the October meeting of the renters' association.

VOTING ON THE ISSUE OF CHRISTMAS DECORATIONS ON THE BUILDING EXTERIOR.

WE NEED A QUORUM! PLEASE COME!

Kovac considered writing his neighbor's name and phone number on the poster as a source of expertise on the subject.

Maybe five minutes passed before the elevator rumbled as it descended, then rose out of the parking garage. Kovac stood in front of the doors so that when they opened, David Moore stepped right into him.

"Hey!" Moore barked, annoyed at the obstacle, then realizing the obstacle was Kovac. The look in his eyes went from annoyance to confusion to suspicion in a split second.

Kovac hit him hard in the chest with the heels of both hands, knocked him back into the elevator car, into the back wall, and followed him in.

"What the hell?" Moore said, trying to get his feet back under him.

Kovac grabbed him by the front of his shirt and shoved him into the corner.

"Listen, you sorry piece of shit. I know all about you and your girlfriend," Kovac said. "I know all about your little tête-à-têtes at the Marquette every other week.

"What are you? One of those pervs that gets off on taking the chance of being caught?

"That'd be you, all right," Kovac sneered. "You don't have the balls to stand up to your wife. You want somebody else to tell her you're out on the town with some fifty-bucks-a-blowjob skirt. You fucking coward."

Moore pressed himself back into the corner, raised up on his toes like that would somehow make him a bigger man than the worm that he was.

"You can't treat me this way!" he blustered, red faced, more afraid than aggressive. "This is harassment and—and brutality."

Kovac curled his lip in disgust. "Call a

cop, limp-dick. I've got twelve witnesses who'll swear I was playing Parcheesi at the Moose Lodge in New Hope."

"Are you crazy?"

"Yeah, I'm crazy," Kovac said sarcastically. "I'm not the one meeting in a public bar to pay off the guy I hired to whack my wife."

"I don't know what you're talking about!"

"You make me sick." Kovac all but turned and spat on the floor. "What'd you think, David? That everyone would just assume your wife was mugged, or that some nutjob did her because of Karl Dahl?"

"I didn't do anything to Carey!"

"And you figured you were playing it smart to be seen in public at the time of her attack, that you were extra clever, using your motive as your alibi."

"What motive?"

"Your little plaything you got this apartment for. A junkie whore too stupid to think you're exactly what you appear to be—a loser with a big mouth and delusions of grandeur. You're pathetic."

The look on Moore's face was priceless. Kovac smiled like a tiger. He had opened both barrels of bullshit and actually hit some

nerves. A little knowledge and a lot of attitude went a long way toward rattling people
with something to hide. All the years of
wading hip-deep in the excrement of criminal minds had taught him more about human nature than any Ph.D. in psychology
could have.

David Moore was the kind of guy who
needed to feel important, needed people to
think he was smart. That he had to lower
himself to the standard of prostitutes to ac-
complish that wouldn't matter.

"You're thinking, 'How do you know all
that, Kovac, you dumb son of a bitch?'" Kovac said, still smiling. "I know all kinds of
things about you, Sport. I know about your
taste for hookers. The flowers, the gifts, the
expensive dinners, paying for it all out of the
family funds. I know about your biweekly
habit at the Marquette, *Mr. Greer*. You go
there to pretend you're a big shot, don't
you? Mr. Hollywood, the film executive.

"By the way, that's lower than low, using
your wife's maiden name. Freud would have
a field day with you and your issues with
women, huh? What's that all about, David?
Your mother screwed up your potty train-
ing?"

Moore was silent, seeming to be holding himself very still, as if one wrong move and his whole alternate universe would implode on him.

"What I can't figure is where Edmund Ivors fits into this sordid little puzzle. What's a guy like him have to gain acting as your beard, helping you out with your alibi?"

"I don't need an alibi," Moore said. "I haven't done anything wrong."

Kovac just looked at him, stunned to silence for a moment.

"You haven't done anything wrong? Jesus Christ, you cheat on your wife with whores, spend her money to finance your secret life. What part of that isn't wrong?"

The elevator gave a little jerk and groan and began to descend.

Kovac hit the key for the second floor and pulled Moore out into the hall with him when the doors opened. The door to the stairs was just to the right. He gave Moore a shove in the back.

"Step into my office here for a minute, Ace."

"Fuck you, Kovac," Moore said, turning around.

"Are you resisting?" Kovac asked, incredulous. "Are you resisting me? 'Cause if you're resisting, all bets are off, pal."

"Are you arresting me?"

"You want to have this conversation downtown? 'Cause I'll be happy to take you there and put you in the box for a formal questioning. Is that what you want?" Kovac asked. "You want to up the ante? You want to call my bluff? Go ahead. Then you can call a lawyer, and I can call Chris Logan, and he'll have you arraigned and toss your ass in the can. And if you think a judge is going to give you bail for trying to kill one of their own, you're even dumber than you look. Is that what you want?"

"I didn't try to kill my wife!"

The door to apartment 214 opened and a woman stuck her head out, glaring at them. "Take your fight somewhere else, or I'll call the cops."

Kovac pulled his badge out of his coat pocket and showed it to her. "This is already police business, ma'am. Go back into your apartment and lock the door."

The woman disappeared.

Kovac turned back to David Moore.

"Why didn't you tell me a man joined your little party at the bar last night?"

Moore looked away, looked confused, shrugged, spread his hands. Only the first thing was significant.

"I—I don't know," he stammered. "I didn't know the guy. Why would I mention it?"

"Because you don't leave things out when you talk to the cops, Einstein. It tends to make us suspicious when we find out after the fact. Who was he?"

"Ivors knew him. He's—uh—in the business. He's a—a director of photography. He stopped by. We talked about my project."

"What's his name?"

"Don something. I don't remember his last name."

"He drops by to talk about your project. Maybe 'cause he's interested in doing whatever he does for you, right? And you don't remember him. He didn't give you a business card?"

"It was a casual conversation. Ivors wanted me to meet him. That's all."

"So why did Ivors and your little Bird friend not say something about him to me either?"

"I don't know. They didn't think it was important. He was only there for a few minutes."

"I'm supposed to swallow this load of horseshit?" Kovac asked.

"I don't care what you believe."

"That's a very poor attitude you've got, Sport. You damn well ought to care what I think. Because I have the power to take your putrid little life apart turd by turd and poke at every slimy thing crawling under your lies.

"And now I'm gonna go upstairs and talk to the little chickadee without you being there. Did you all get your lies lined up beak to tail earlier today? 'Cause I'll be a lying son of a bitch and tell her that you talked and told me all about your plan, so she might as well too. And Edmund Ivors won't be there to put words in her mouth this time."

Moore's cell phone rang, tucked somewhere in a pocket.

"Why don't you answer that, Dave?" Kovac suggested. "That's probably her right now, wanting to know where the hell you are."

Moore didn't move.

Kovac pushed past him, took the stairs back up to the third floor, and knocked on the door of apartment 309.

Ginnie Bird opened the door immediately, her face falling as she was greeted with the unpleasant surprise of Kovac.

"Can I come in?" he asked even as he stepped inside the apartment and past her.

Moore came in behind him. "You don't have to talk to him, Ginnie. Not without a lawyer."

Kovac arched a brow. "Ms. Bird isn't under arrest. Why would she want a lawyer present?"

Ginnie Bird looked like a deer in the headlights. Dumb as a sack of hair, this girl. Her assets lay elsewhere—in plain sight. Deep purple silk and lace were artfully arranged over her unnaturally round breasts and slender frame in the form of a camisole and a thong. She wore a sheer purple robe over the ensemble for her version of modesty. It barely came to the top of her thighs. She balanced on a pair of silver stilettos. All ready to offer comfort and white-hot sex to poor beleaguered David Moore.

Kovac looked around what he could see of the apartment. Hardwood on the hall floor, white carpet flowing through a dining/living room to a small gas fireplace with a granite surround. Contemporary furnishings—chrome, glass, leather.

"Nice digs," Kovac said. "But we're a long way from Hudson, Wisconsin. You must be very good at what you do to have a place on this side of the river and the other, Ms. Bird."

"Ginnie is a casting director—" Moore started.

Kovac turned on him. "You're interfering with a police investigation, asshole. You can sit down and shut up, or I can put you in the hall facedown on the floor, hog-tied."

"You wouldn't dare," Moore said.

"Hey, you're the one who decided I'm crazy. You don't know what I might do. And you really don't want to find out the hard way, do you?"

Moore held up his hands and took a couple of steps backward into the dining room area to pace.

Kovac turned back to Ginnie Bird. "Ms. Bird, you were at the Marquette Hotel last night, having drinks with your boyfriend here, Edmund Ivors, and a third man who dropped by. Who was that man?"

Her eyes darted to Moore. Kovac moved into her line of sight.

"Don . . . something," she said. "It was loud in the bar. I couldn't catch his last name."

"What was he doing there?"

"I don't know. I wasn't paying attention."

She shifted to the left, trying to make eye contact with Moore again.

"What's the matter, Ms. Bird?" Kovac asked. "Can't remember your lines?"

"There's nothing to remember," she said. "I don't know anything that might help you."

"You don't know about the payoff? The twenty-five thousand dollars?"

He had told David Moore he would bluff a confession out of her, but Kovac knew in truth he had to tread lightly. It didn't take a very clever defense attorney to get tossed anything a client had said without first being Mirandized. A good lawyer could get a confession tossed even after the client's rights had been read to them. They would argue the police had violated the client's rights by denying them counsel, even though one of the first items mentioned in Miranda was the right to an attorney. Or they would argue that their client hadn't been of a clear mind, or some other lawyer bullshit.

"I don't know what you're talking about," Ginnie Bird said.

Her eyes were a little glassy. The end of her nose was red. Kovac glanced around the room, hoping against hope to see drug paraphernalia out in plain sight. Then he could have taken her in, questioned her at the station, put a little scare in her. But he didn't see anything.

"You don't know anything about your boyfriend here paying someone to get rid of his wife?"

"David would never do that," she said adamantly. "Never. Why can't you just leave us alone? All we want is to be happy."

"Yeah," Kovac said. "The problem with that is Mrs. Moore. And somebody tried to eliminate that problem last night. If you know who that somebody was, and you don't tell me, you become an accessory after the fact. If you knew about what was going to happen before it happened, that's conspiracy. Either way, you go to jail."

"I can't tell you anything, because there's nothing to tell," she said. "David is going to divorce her. He told her tonight."

"Did he?" Kovac said, looking at Moore. "That's an interesting spin."

"I think you should leave now, Detective," Ginnie Bird said. "I know my rights."

As explained to her by the lawyer the escort agency had sent to bail her out, back when she got paid per sex act, Kovac thought. What an idiot David Moore was, throwing away a woman like Carey, and a beautiful daughter, for this chick.

He turned to Moore, shaking his head. "Man, you have to be one of the all-time fools."

Moore said nothing.

"I'll see you around," Kovac said, ambling toward the door. "And next time I'll come with warrants. And just let me give you fair warning, Mr. Moore. If I find one shred of solid direct evidence that links you to your wife's attack, I will unleash hell on you."

Back on the street, Kovac walked down to the unmarked car assigned to tail David Moore and told the officers to call him if Moore so much as came out of the building to fart.

Back in his own car, he settled behind the wheel and just sat there, willing his blood pressure to calm down. He wanted to take

David Moore apart. He wanted the guy to be guilty. He wanted someone to cough up the real name of Don Something, the alleged director of photography, so he could put the guy under a spotlight and get him to sweat out his connection to Moore.

That was what he wanted. The problem with that was that he wasn't supposed to want anything. A good detective didn't draw conclusions until he had all the facts. Getting too close to a crime—or to the victim of a crime—was a stop on the way to madness. Or to the civilian review board. If anyone had seen him knock David Moore back into that elevator, Moore would have had a corroborating witness for his brutality charge.

Still . . . it had sure as hell felt good to do it.

As Kovac savored the moment, his cell phone started to bleat.

"Kovac."

"Liska."

"Oh."

"Don't sound so happy to hear from me. I'll get the wrong idea," Liska said sarcastically. "Who were you expecting to call you? The Queen of Sheba? Catherine Zeta-

Jones? Oxsana the Amazing Contortionist?"

"Is there a reason I'm talking to you?" Kovac asked, cranky because he had actually let himself think the call might be from Carey. And if Liska had known that, she would have given him no end of shit. Stupid, stupid, stupid.

"Yeah," she said. "You need to book it over to HCMC."

"Why?"

"Because Kenny Scott had a visit today from your friend Stan Dempsey."

34

Karl knew he couldn't stay in the park all night. He had been there for a long time as it was, though no one had paid him any mind. But the city didn't allow overnight parking in the lot.

He had spent the afternoon wandering from park bench to park bench. The day had been so pretty, people had stayed in the park to have cookouts, to watch the sun set, to squeak out every drop of good weather. The smell of meat grilling had made Karl's stomach growl. But now the warm day had given way to a chilly evening that was nipping right through his brown cashmere poncho and sneaking up under his skirt. It was time to move to a warmer hiding spot.

He stared across the street at Carey

Moore's house. One set of windows upstairs and one set downstairs glowed with
lamplight.

In the afternoon, Karl had spotted her
briefly as a black Mercedes sedan had
rolled out of the garage. She was in the passenger's seat. A police officer was driving. A
small head of unruly dark hair had bounced
up and down in the backseat. Carey
Moore's child.

Karl closed his eyes and imagined her
heavy with child. A beautiful sight. A
Madonna. His angel. He wondered what
she might be doing right at that very moment.

At one point earlier in the evening, a man
got out of a sedan parked behind the police
cruiser, went to the driver's side of the car,
and said something to the officers inside,
then walked up into the yard and stood near
the lighted downstairs windows. Another
cop. Plainclothes.

Time had stretched by and nothing happened.

As he contemplated this peculiar turn of
events, the Moores' garage door rose and
the same black sedan rolled out with only
the driver inside. A man, he reckoned, by

the size of him. The husband, he supposed. He drove away fast, like maybe he was mad about something. Another sedan had slid away from the curb to follow him. The plain-clothes cop had followed moments later.

The important thing to Karl was that the husband was gone.

Soon it would be time for him to speak to Carey Moore. To thank her for her kindness to him. To explain to her his feelings for her and how much she meant to him. In his whole life hardly anyone had ever taken his side in anything. She had risked her life to take his side in this trial.

He imagined kneeling at her feet, pouring his heart out to her. He imagined her expressing her understanding to him. In his imagination she was lit from behind with a golden light, and she stood with her arms opened, looking just like a statue of the Virgin Mary his mother had kept on her dresser. It was a beautiful dream.

Karl looked up at the stars in the clear night sky—what stars a man could see with a city all around him—and thought this might become the most perfect night of his life.

After a while, he got up and straightened

his skirt and walked back to the parking lot and Christine Neal's Volvo.

Stan Dempsey drove through Carey Moore's neighborhood, but not past her home. He knew the officers in the radio car out front would be making note of the plate numbers of every vehicle that cruised by and immediately running them through the system, looking to get a hit on a possible suspect.

Instead, he cruised up the next block, toward the Moore home, then turned in at the driveway of a dark house near the end of the street and sat there, watching.

A dark sedan backed out of the garage fast and drove toward him in a hurry. Seconds later, an unmarked car followed. Shortly after that, a second unmarked car. As it passed under the streetlight, Stan thought it might be Sam Kovac behind the wheel.

Kovac was a good cop, a straight shooter, probably the best detective on the squad. It would be difficult to pull off anything under Kovac's nose. But now he had gone from Carey Moore's house and from her neighborhood, and Stan could see a window of opportunity cracking open.

He didn't mean to get away with anything. He meant only to finish his job. When his job was finished, he would be honored to have Sam Kovac close the case.

When his job was finished . . .

35

Carey sat on the love seat in the den for a long time, doing nothing, thinking nothing, staring at nothing. The house was absolutely silent. The tension that had charged the air was gone. She felt drained, empty.

Around ten-thirty, Anka quietly came downstairs and stopped just outside the den.

"Are you all right, Mrs. Moore?"

Carey waved a hand. "No, but there's nothing to do about it. Are you going out?"

"Only to pick a movie and get some popcorn. Can I bring something for you?"

"No. Thank you, Anka."

The girl lingered at the doorway a moment longer, seeming like she wanted to say something more. But if she had, she thought better of it.

Carey went back to staring, feeling nothing.

She wondered what she would feel the next day, and the day after that. Relief? Anxiety? And she wondered how Lucy would react to her father's sudden absence.

David was a different person with Lucy. With their daughter, he was the man she had married—sweet, fun, brimming with promise. His relationship with Lucy was pure love, untainted by what the rest of his life had become. With Lucy he had no track record. She only cared that he was her daddy. Her expectations were simple. He had yet to disappoint her.

Carey purposely didn't wonder what David was feeling or doing. She told herself she didn't care. She *didn't* care. What did that say about her? About their marriage?

Restless, she got up from her seat and walked around the room. She still hurt everywhere, and her head was pounding. A Vicodin and bed sounded like the best plan.

As she walked around behind David's desk, photos of Lucy caught her eye. David's screen saver was a slide show of their daughter dressed up in her various costumes—the princess, the fairy, the ballerina.

Carey sat down in the desk chair and

watched the images float across the screen. Lucy was the spitting image of herself as a child—impish grin, bright blue eyes, an unruly mop of dark hair that had eventually given up its curls.

Oh, to be that innocent again.

The computer mouse rested on its small green pad beside the keyboard. Only vaguely curious, she moved the mouse and clicked on the AOL icon at the bottom of the screen.

What came up and filled the screen was as far removed from the innocence of a child as anything could have been.

What came on the screen was a scene of such degradation, it made Carey feel ill and dizzy, as if she'd just gotten hit in the head all over again.

A naked woman bound and gagged, hung spread-eagled from chains on her wrists and ankles, blood running down her arms. She was being raped by two men wearing leather hoods to cover their faces, one behind her, one in front of her. She appeared to be terrified.

This was what her husband had been looking at when she had come to tell him she wanted a divorce. Carey began to shake. She moved the cursor to the Web address bar and clicked on the downward arrow, bringing up a listing of every Web site David had looked at for who knew how long. Porn site after porn site.

She clicked on an arrow, and another photograph, equally violent as the first, popped up.

It took a moment for her to recover enough from the shock to process the rest of the page—the title, the graphics. It was a promotion for a movie available on DVD or VHS. The ad promised savage sadism, violent scenes of torture and rape.

The film was by David M. Greer.

36

"Whose cluster fuck is this?" Kovac demanded as he stormed into the ER and made a beeline for Liska. He had been mobbed by the press swarming all over the ambulance bay. Four large uniformed officers were keeping them from rushing the door.

"It's a fucking feeding frenzy out there," he snapped.

"I'm taking responsibility for the whole thing, Detective Kovac," Lieutenant Dawes said, coming away from a coffee vending machine across the room.

Kovac pulled up short and grimaced. "Lieutenant."

"Way to stick your foot in it, Kojak," Liska said, rolling her eyes at him.

Dawes didn't react at all.

"I personally called Mr. Scott this morning to tell him Stan Dempsey was at large, but I only got his voice mail," she said. "I then dispatched two officers to go to Mr. Scott's home and tell him in person if he was at home, and to wait if he wasn't."

"So what went wrong?" Kovac asked.

"A call went out to all units to respond to a sighting of Karl Dahl not far from where the officers were."

"They took the priority call," Kovac said.

"Which turned out to be a false alarm. But in all the confusion of trying to run down the suspect, there was a collision involving the officers' car and a minivan—"

"And the coppers are still giving their statements and filling out paperwork," Kovac said.

"One of the officers was killed," Dawes said soberly.

"Oh, Jesus," Kovac said. Add that charge to Dahl's indictment, he thought—another person dead because of that creep.

"And the ball got dropped," Dawes went on. "By the time I found out and drove to Kenny Scott's home myself, it was already dark. The basement light was on. If not for that one screwup on Dempsey's part, Scott would still be bound to a chair."

"Is he alive?"

"Yes," Dawes said, leading the way down a corridor. "It wasn't Dempsey's intent to kill. Turns out he just wanted to make a statement."

They turned into the room where Kenny Scott had been brought for treatment, and Kovac was instantly taken aback by the putrid smell of burned flesh.

Kenny Scott lay propped up on the hospital bed with an IV dripping something into his arm. His hands and feet were grotesquely swollen. Ligature marks dug deep into his wrists and ankles. But by far the most shocking injury Stan Dempsey had inflicted on Karl Dahl's lawyer was literally burned across Scott's forehead.

One word: *GUILTY.*

37

Carey slept restlessly, fitfully, turning from one side to the other, even though she had taken the Vicodin to kill the pain and knock herself out. The drug didn't seem to reach her subconscious. It couldn't shut out the disturbing images, the dark dreams that rolled through her mind like thunderstorms. Violent dreams of being chased, of being caught, of being helpless.

Neither would the drugs allow her to come fully awake, to escape the nightmares that seemed so real. Her heart was beating so fast it felt like a small bird trapped behind her ribs, desperately trying to get out.

She was being chased through the dark by a man. Running as fast as she could, but her legs were weakening. She was losing speed. He was gaining ground. She could hear him breathing hard.

She cried out as his hand took hold of her arm. She struggled to pull away but couldn't. As he pulled her back toward him, she felt he was pulling her into another dimension.

And then she realized that he was.

She was being pulled out of her nightmare and into a terrible reality.

Kicking and flailing, Carey tried to pull free and lunge across the bed. But her legs tangled in the sheets, and she couldn't get free of them. She tried to scream but didn't know if the sound ever escaped her mouth.

Then two hands were on her, yanking her backward. She was helpless to stop it from happening.

Tears were coming now, broken sobs born of terror.

A forearm came across her throat and started to choke her hard. She kicked backward. She tried to dig her fingernails into the arm that was crushing her throat, but there was a shirtsleeve preventing any real damage. Nothing she did made any difference.

Panicking, she choked, tried to get air and couldn't. Her vision began to fade. She thought of Lucy. Then everything faded to black.

38

Kovac woke to a pounding he thought was inside his head.

He had a vague memory of having had exactly that thought before. He'd gotten five, maybe six hours of sleep, but his body told him it needed more.

The pounding didn't stop.

"Tylenol," he murmured, trying to wake himself.

It took all his willpower to sit up and drop his legs over the side of the bed. He could hardly open his eyes to look at the clock. Quarter past eight.

The pounding continued.

Kovac went to the chair at the foot of his bed, pulled on a pair of wrinkled pants and a wrinkled shirt, and went downstairs. He slipped into a pair of shoes he'd left by the front door, and went outside.

Another bright Technicolor blue fall morning greeted him with undue cheerfulness. He shuffled over to his neighbor's yard, his eyelids still at half-mast. The neighbor watched him suspiciously from his perch on the roof, hammer in hand.

The old man called down at him, "Hey, what are you doing?"

Kovac didn't answer him. He went straight to the aluminum ladder that leaned against the side of the house and took the thing away, letting it fall to the side and crash in the yard. Squirrels ran for their lives in all directions. Then he turned and went back to his own house.

The old man was screaming blue murder. "Get back here! Get back here and put that ladder back!"

Ignoring him, Kovac went back inside, made a pot of coffee, carried a cup upstairs with him. He went into the bathroom, took a leak, had a long, hot shower, shaved, brushed his teeth, put on a fresh nicotine patch.

When he went back into his bedroom, the

old man was still shouting at him. The red of his face matched the red of his plaid flannel shirt.

Kovac opened the window. "You want me to come put that ladder back?"

"You'd darn well better!"

"Now is not the time to be pissy with me," Kovac said. "You'll give yourself a stroke and die up there. Not that I would give a rat's ass."

The old man sputtered and spat and called him some names.

Kovac waited for the tirade to end.

"I'll come put the ladder back," he said. "But if you get up on that roof tomorrow morning while I'm sleeping, I'll come back and take it down and leave you there at the mercy of passersby. You're an inconsiderate son of a bitch, and you think just because you're too goddamned mean to die, you ought to be able to make the rest of us as miserable as you are."

The old man scowled at him.

Kovac went to his closet and dressed for the day. The task force was meeting at nine. He wanted to swing past and check on Carey before he went downtown.

Outside, he struggled with the unwieldy

ladder to get it back up against the house. The old man scrambled down it like a monkey and got right in Kovac's face.

"I'm going to report you!"

Kovac walked away. The weatherman was promising thunderstorms later in the day. Maybe lightning would strike the old fart and fry him while he was attaching colored lights to his television antenna.

I live in hope. . . .

Everything at the Moore house appeared the same as it had the night before. The media had decamped Saturday when it had become clear they weren't going to get anything interesting. Today they were probably swarming all over the street where Kenny Scott lived. Next victim, please.

Kovac went to the window of the cruiser parked at the curb.

"Anything I need to know about?"

The cop at the wheel shook his head. "All quiet. The guys from last night said the only thing that happened after you went after the husband was the nanny going to the 7-Eleven and coming back. She drove out

again a while ago. Waved. Going to Starbucks."

Kovac yawned, straightened away from
the car, and went up to Carey Moore's front
door. He rang the bell and waited. It was still
early for a Sunday morning. After the night
she'd had, she was probably sleeping in.

He rang the bell again and waited.

There were no sounds coming from the
house. No radio or television. No voices in
conversation.

He rang the bell a third time. A fourth time.

Now his cop sense began to itch and
tremble through him. He didn't like it. Something was wrong.

He pulled his cell phone out of his pocket
and called the Moores' house number.

The phone rang unanswered until the machine picked up.

He called Carey's cell number. The call
went straight to voice mail.

Kovac walked around the house, peering
in the windows for any sign of life, or death.
He checked the doors. All locked.

His heart was beating faster.

He went around to the front yard and motioned for the uniforms to come.

The side door on the garage seemed the easiest place to get in. The officers rounded the corner. Kovac looked to the larger of the two, a strapping twenty-something guy.

"Kick it in."

"Shouldn't we have a warrant?" the young guy asked.

"We've got exigent circumstances," Kovac said. "Kick it in!"

The officer put his shoe to the door once, twice. On the third kick, the frame splintered and the door swung in, carrying the entire dead bolt mechanism with it.

The house alarm began to shriek.

The door into the laundry room was unlocked. Kovac went through into the kitchen and began calling.

"Carey? Judge Moore? Are you here? Is anyone here?"

Silence.

Kovac drew his weapon and went through the downstairs, calling, looking, finding nothing.

A sick feeling churned in his gut as he went up the stairs.

"Carey? Judge Moore?"

He knocked on the door to the nanny's room. No answer. He pushed the door open. No one. The bed was unmade. He checked the closet. No one.

"Carey! Anka!" he shouted.

The uniforms stood at the top of the stairs. Kovac ran past them, down the hall to Carey's bedroom. The door was open; the bed had been stripped to the mattress. Carey was gone.

"Check the basement," he shouted at the officers.

He thought of Kenny Scott bound to a chair, the word *GUILTY* branded into his forehead. He thought of the Haas family, of the two children left hanging in the basement.

Lucy.

Oh, Jesus.

A feeling washed over him he so rarely experienced that it took him a moment to name it.

Panic.

The little painted fairy on Lucy's door smiled at him. The things that Stan Dempsey had said on the video played through his head.

"I wonder how differently she would feel if her daughter were raped and sodomized

*and hung up from the ceiling like a slaugh-
tered lamb. . . ."*

Kovac felt like he was going to puke. He
braced himself for the worst and pushed the
door open.

Lucy's bed was empty, the covers messy.
No blood. That registered right away. There
was no blood. There was no body.

"Lucy?" Kovac called. "Lucy, are you in
here? It's me, Detective Sam."

He went to the closet and opened the
door. Nothing.

He got down on his hands and knees,
lifted the ruffled bed skirt, and peered under
the bed, his heart breaking at the sight of
the little girl. She was shaking and crying
and trying very hard not to make a sound.

"Come on, sweetheart," Kovac said gently. "You can come out now. You're safe. I
won't let anything bad happen to you."

Slowly she inched her way toward him,
crying openly now, her breath hitching, her
nose running. Kovac reached out to help
her, and her little hand grabbed hold of his
fingers and squeezed for dear life.

When she popped out from under the
bed, she threw herself into his arms, threw
her whole small trembling body against him,

wrapped her arms around his neck, and sobbed, "Where's my mommy?"

Kovac held her tight and thought, *I wish I knew.*

39

Carey didn't know how long she had been unconscious. She came out of it layer by layer, first becoming aware that she was breathing, then moving an arm, a leg. Still, she wasn't sure that she wasn't dead. She lay curled in a fetal position, disoriented, dizzy. Then she opened her eyes and saw nothing but blackness.

Panic hit instantly.

Was she blind?

She brought her hands up to her face to feel for a blindfold, even though she knew there wasn't one.

Her heart was racing. Her breathing was too quick and too shallow. She felt as if she wasn't getting any air at all.

Raw fear raked through her.

Instinctively she lashed out, pushed her

hands out in front of her, and hit something solid. She tried to straighten her legs, but there wasn't enough space.

She turned onto her back and did the same thing again, with the same result.

Her first thought was that she was inside a coffin.

Memories of old horror stories flashed through her brain. Stories of people being buried alive.

As a prosecutor, she had once worked a case where a woman had been left for dead, buried in a shallow grave. She had been stabbed multiple times, but when the ME determined cause of death, it was asphyxia. The woman had breathed in dirt particles after she had been buried. Her nose and mouth had been full of freshly turned earth.

Carey tried frantically to push at the lid of her coffin. It didn't move.

She called for help, the sound seeming to come back at her instead of traveling beyond her small, dark prison. Even so, she cried out again and again, until her throat was raw.

No one came.

Tears trailed from the outer corners of her

eyes into her hair as she lay on her back, wondering, waiting. Time lost all meaning.

Periodically, she kicked at the lid of her box. Realizing she had no water and that her mouth was already dry, she stopped trying to call out.

The power of fear was like an animal inside her, trying to escape.

She couldn't breathe.

She felt faint.

If she hadn't already, she was going to die. Lucy.

She had to keep thinking of Lucy.

Was she nearby? Had the abductor taken her daughter as well?

Carey thought about what Kovac had told her. About Stan Dempsey, about what he had said on his videotape.

"I wonder how differently she would feel if her daughter were raped and sodomized and hung up from the ceiling like a slaughtered lamb."

Tears filled her eyes once more. The idea of someone's hurting Lucy, torturing Lucy, hanging her by the neck, made Carey's stomach turn and her heart feel as if it were being torn from her chest.

She had seen the photos from the Haas

murders. She had been as horrified as anyone—more so, considering she had a child of her own and considering that the fate of the man accused of committing those crimes hung in the balance in her own courtroom.

Was that going to be her fate, the fate of her daughter? To die as Marlene Haas and her foster children had died? Or had Lucy already been killed? Was she lying in her bed at home with her throat slit to prevent her from identifying the perpetrator?

And what about Anka? An innocent in the dramas that Carey found herself in. Whatever someone might have had against her, Carey hated to think that one of the few loyal, trustworthy people she knew would be made to pay for her imagined sins.

The voice on the phone late Friday night echoed in her mind over and over: *"I'm coming to get you, bitch."*

A man's voice.

Stan Dempsey's voice. Or Wayne Haas's voice. Or the voice of any one of the thousands of people who hated her for having ruled against the admission of Karl Dahl's prior bad acts as evidence in the case against him.

Or the voice of a man twenty-five thousand dollars richer, courtesy of her husband.

The sound of a door closing startled her from her speculation. Someone who might rescue her? Or her captor?

"Help me!" she called. "Help me!"

Another door slammed, closer. The box dipped down slightly, and an engine started.

She was in the trunk of a car, and the car was backing up.

Whoever sat behind the wheel of this car probably meant to kill her. She had to do whatever she could to prevent that from happening.

She needed a plan.

She needed to focus.

She needed to live.

40

"How the *fuck* could this happen?" Kovac shouted at the uniforms. They stood in the Moores' study, out of the way of the crime scene team.

Kovac looked from one of the officers to the other.

"I don't know," the older one, MacGowan, said. "We never saw anybody go into the house. Neither did the guys ahead of us. We walked the perimeter every half hour. There weren't any signs of trouble."

Holding on to his head as if it might break in half, Kovac stalked away from them, turned, and stalked back. "You said you saw the nanny drive out."

"She waved out the car window and called out 'Coffee,'" the younger officer,

Bloom, said. "She's the nanny. What were we supposed to do?"

"You're sure it was her?"

"A blond woman driving a Saab."

"You didn't stop her," Kovac said.

"Why would we?" MacGowan said irritably, getting in Kovac's face. "She had a pass—she was family. No one said to stop family. So get the fuck outta my face, Kovac. You're in a suit, so you think you're Jesus Fucking Christ—"

"Fuck yourself, MacGowan!" Kovac shouted. "You lost a judge. You let some mutt waltz out of here with the one person you're supposed to be protecting! You're gonna be a fucking crossing guard when this is over!"

"Gentlemen?" Lieutenant Dawes walked into the room. Her voice was calm, and such a contrast to Kovac's that everyone took notice immediately. "Officers, wait in the hall, please. I'll deal with you later."

Bloom couldn't get out fast enough. MacGowan lingered, giving Kovac attitude.

Kovac shook his head. "Go sharpen your pencil, asshole. You'll be writing up jaywalkers till your teeth fall out."

MacGowan made an angry gesture and walked away.

"Detective Kovac?" Dawes said.

Kovac continued huffing and puffing, pacing back and forth. "I can't fucking believe this!"

"Sam, get ahold of yourself." Dawes put herself in his path so that he had to pull up.

When he spoke, he lowered his voice to just below a shout. "How the hell could this happen? Cops here around the clock. The place locked down like a fortress. And someone just drives out of here with Carey Moore? Is this a fucking joke?"

"I don't think anyone is laughing," Dawes said. "And we should all get out our umbrellas, because there is going to be a shitstorm raining down on us from on high soon enough. I've already had a call from Assistant Chief Harding. There's a mob of media outside. In the meantime, we need to get our ducks in a row and figure out what's really happened here."

Kovac rubbed his hands over his face and sighed, trying to will his blood pressure down. "I was here until about nine last night."

"Doing what?"

He looked away, looked back, uncomfortable. "She told me she was going to ask her husband for a divorce. I wanted to be here in case the jerk flipped."

Dawes lifted a brow. "How very chivalrous of you."

"The guy is a creep, leading some kind of a double life," Kovac said, scowling. "I didn't want to take the chance."

"Where did you go from here?"

"I followed the husband."

"We had a tail on him to do that."

"I wanted to rattle his cage," Kovac said. "He has an apartment in Edina where he's set up his girlfriend."

"I've already checked with the officers who were here last night," Dawes said. "They said the nanny left around ten-thirty to go to the 7-Eleven."

"Did she tell them that specifically?"

"Yes. She backed out of the driveway, slowed as she came near their car, put down her window, and told them what she was doing."

"Did they speak to her when she came back?"

"No. They were walking the perimeter of the property."

"Dumb and Dumber out there in the hall said she backed out of the driveway around seven this morning, said the word 'coffee,' and drove away."

"How close were they to her?"

"I don't know."

"Did she drive away from them or past them?"

"I don't know."

"Do you think the nanny could have done this?" Dawes asked.

Kovac thought about it for a moment. "I would say no. She seemed devoted to the family. But she is very protective of David Moore. She didn't like me implying he could have had his wife attacked. They seemed a little too cozy when they came back from having breakfast yesterday. I asked her point-blank if she had something going on with him."

"And?"

"And she denied it, but she didn't want to look at me when she said it."

"Do you think she could have done it?" Dawes asked again.

He tried to imagine Anka overpowering Carey.

"Physically could she do it? Probably. She's young, looks athletic. She's taller than Carey. And Carey was in no condition to fight," he said. "And if the girl had a weapon—"

"Or if she didn't have to struggle with her victim," Dawes said.

Kovac knew what she was saying. If Carey was already dead, Anka would have had to struggle only with her employer's corpse. She wouldn't have had to be careful about it. Shove the body down the stairs, drag it down the hall and out through the kitchen and into the garage.

Kovac called over the lead of the crime scene people and told him to check the stairs for hair, blood, and tissue.

"I haven't seen any blood," he said to Dawes. "I guess she could have cleaned up."

"We don't know that she didn't have help," Dawes said. "When she left last night, she might have picked up an accomplice along with her movie and popcorn."

Kovac sat back against the edge of David

Moore's desk and crossed his arms, thinking.

"If she had an accomplice, why would she leave the house this morning?" he asked. "It would make more sense to stay behind, play the victim."

"Not everyone has the sly, conniving mind you do."

"It's a gift."

"Possibilities other than the nanny?" Dawes asked.

"The house was locked tight," Kovac said. "The alarm system was set. Of course, Moore would have given up the code if he sent someone here to do the job."

He thought about that for a minute. "That's some balls to go through with a kidnapping when the cops are already all over you like a bad rash. Moore doesn't have a set like that; that's for sure. He nearly pissed himself when I confronted him last night."

"It doesn't take much nerve at all to hire out the job," Dawes said. "And he gave himself an alibi. He couldn't have come back here last night without us knowing about it. The tail would have followed him over here."

"We have to get a handle on the mystery man from the bar," Kovac said. "If I could get Ginnie Bird alone, I'd scare a name out of her in three seconds."

"And we still have Stan Dempsey running around," Dawes said.

Kovac shrugged. "Why would Stan grab the nanny? Why wouldn't he just tie her up, tape her mouth shut, and leave? He's got no beef with the nanny. It doesn't matter to him if she's a witness. He's not trying to be anonymous."

"Where's my daughter?" The demand came from the front hall. David Moore.

Kovac looked hard at Dawes. "You called him?"

"He's the little girl's father, Sam."

"He's a suspect!"

"We have nothing linking him to this or to the attack in the parking ramp."

"Kate Quinn is here. She can take care of Lucy," Kovac said. "Kate has experience with both kids and crime victims. And it turns out she knows the family."

"That's not the protocol," Dawes said calmly.

"Fuck the protocol!"

Out in the hall, David Moore raised his voice. "I damn well will come into my own home!"

"I'm sorry, sir. This is a crime scene."

Dawes went out into the hall. "It's all right, Officer Potts. Mr. Moore, could you please join me in your den?"

Moore stepped past the uniform, drawing a bead on the lieutenant. "What the hell is going on? Where's my daughter? Is she hurt?"

"Mr. Moore, I'm Lieutenant Dawes. Your daughter hasn't suffered any physical injuries. I need you to calm down and understand what's going on here before you see her."

"I don't care what you need, Lieutenant," Moore said. He was red in the face and breathing hard. "I want to see my child."

"Yeah," Kovac cracked. "Here's the fucking father of the year. Had to get out of bed with his prostitute girlfriend to come to his daughter's aid."

Dawes gave him a look. "Detective . . ."

Moore turned purple. "I want him off this case!" he shouted, jabbing a finger at Kovac. "I want him charged with harassment and brutality! He put his hands on me—"

Kovac rolled his eyes. "I never touched him."

Dawes positioned herself between them

and said to Moore, "Come with me, Mr. Moore. I'm sure your daughter will be happy to see you. She's been through quite a trauma."

"You're certain she isn't hurt?"

"She isn't hurt, but she's very upset. We don't know what she might have seen or heard."

"Oh, my God," Moore breathed, following Dawes through the house to the family room.

Kovac hung back a few steps. David Moore hadn't asked a single question about what had happened. He hadn't expressed any interest in what might be happening to his wife.

Lucy had curled herself into a little ball on Kate Quinn's lap. Kate held her tight and rocked her slowly back and forth.

Prior to Kate's arrival, Lucy had clung to Kovac like a limpet, refusing to leave his arms for the EMT who had come to look her over for injuries. She had kept her little face pressed against his neck, sobbing. It had surprised him how emotionally difficult it had been for him to let go of her. He felt an obligation to protect her, to make her feel safe.

Now Moore rushed across the room. "Lucy!"

He hit his knees as the child climbed down and raced into his arms, the tears coming again on a new wave of hysteria.

Kate rose from the sofa, five feet nine inches of gorgeous legs, and a head of lush red hair. Kovac had known her for years, had had a crush on her most of that time. They didn't come any more no-nonsense than Kate. She looked down at David Moore like he was turd on the carpet.

"She *was* calming down," she said.

"Has she said anything about what happened?" Kovac asked.

Kate shook her head as she walked over to him with her arms crossed. Kovac recognized the look. She was pissed off. He wondered how much Carey might have confided in her regarding her marriage.

"She hasn't said a word," Kate said softly. "I wouldn't count on her talking about this for a long time."

"Do you think she witnessed the abduction?"

"Part of it, anyway. She's terrified. This isn't just about waking up and not finding anybody home."

"We need to know what she knows," Kovac said. "And I don't want Moore anywhere near her when we ask those questions. In fact, I don't want Moore anywhere near her, period."

"Me neither," Kate said. "But he is her father. Whatever else David might be, he is good at that. I'm sure Lucy will want to stay with him."

Kovac looked to Dawes. "How are we supposed to get an answer out of her with Moore right there? He's at the top of the suspect list, for God's sake."

"We can't question a child without a parent or guardian present," Dawes insisted.

"Don't you need David to stay here in case there's a ransom call?" Kate asked.

"Absolutely," Kovac said.

She nodded and went back over to Moore, who was rocking his daughter back and forth as she cried. She knelt down beside them and started speaking quietly.

"David, things are going to stay crazy here all day, and probably beyond that. And I know the police are going to need you to be here in case there's a call from the kidnappers. Why don't I take Lucy to my house?

She'll be in a safe, familiar environment. Maybe she'll be able to get some rest."

Kovac tipped his head toward Dawes. "I guess that's one way to do it."

"As opposed to what?"

"Kicking his ass."

41

"He hasn't asked one question about his wife," Kovac said. "She could be in the basement, carved up like a Halloween pumpkin, for all he knows. If he's an innocent man, don't you think he would have shown a little concern by now?"

"Innocent?" Liska said. "How about just plain decent?"

"How about human?" Kovac said.

The task force had gathered in the Moores' formal dining room, a change of venue made necessary by the morning's events. With Dawes and Kovac already on scene to deal with the chaos, it had seemed easier for the rest of the crew to come to them.

The room was a far cry from their war room at headquarters. Instead of commercial carpet, white walls, long tables loaded with files and notes, they had something out of a home decor magazine. Antiques, mahogany, china, crystal. A room the family rarely used, by the look of it.

David Moore was on the other side of the house, sitting in the den with a phone gadget specialist who had been volunteered by the BCA (the state Bureau of Criminal Apprehension), waiting for a ransom call no one really expected to come.

Lieutenant Dawes gave Kovac a warning look. "Rein yourself in, Detective."

"What?" Kovac snapped as he paced back and forth at one end of the table. "He's a suspect, even if we know his whereabouts last night. He can cry 'harassment' all he wants. It doesn't change the fact that investigations into abductions are always two-pronged: outside the family and inside the family."

"I know how investigations are run," Dawes said. "But you are *not* going to be the one in his face."

"Why not?" Kovac demanded. "I'm the one that's been poking at him from the start. He's off balance with me already. It's not going to take that much more to tip him over the edge. He loses his temper, he'll say something he shouldn't. He's not smart enough to keep his cool."

"Neither are you," Liska said, raising chuckles around the table.

"He's smart enough that he's managed to live a secret life under the nose of one of the sharpest prosecuting attorneys I've ever known," Chris Logan said.

Logan had joined the team, making himself available to help with warrants or anything else the detectives needed. He looked as wired as Kovac felt. He had pulled his power tie loose and unbuttoned the neck of his shirt. He was pacing too.

"He hasn't seen me yet," Logan said. "He's going to think we've upped the ante, involving the prosecutor's office. Let me and Kovac speak to him together."

Dawes sighed. "He's not under arrest. Be careful what you ask and how you ask him."

Logan arched an eyebrow. "That's usually my line."

"Can we get warrants?" Kovac asked. "I want his financials. And I want to toss that den and the girlfriend's apartment."

"Don't push your luck," Logan said.

"Have we forgotten our strange little colleague who's running around performing his own personal version of *The Scarlet Letter*?" Tippen asked dryly. "Our man Stan left his intentions on videotape."

"But how does Dempsey get in the house?" Elwood asked. "How does he get past the security system?"

"When did he become a blond woman?" Liska asked. "That's who pulled out of here this morning: a blond woman."

"Even in a wig, even from a distance, nobody is going to mistake Stan Dempsey for a woman," Dawes said.

"So we're back to thinking it was the nanny driving out of here this morning?" Logan asked.

"Blonde in a Saab," Liska said.

Kovac stopped his pacing, his brow knitting. "The guy who joined Moore and his girlfriend and Edmund Ivors Friday night at the Marquette. He's blond, slender, fine features."

He turned back to Dawes. "Did you get the security tape from the bar?"

"It's at the station."

"But if he's the hired gun," Liska said, "where's the nanny? The cops outside saw one woman in the car."

"So he took the nanny too?" Tippen said. "Why?"

"I still say if the nanny was involved, she would have been smarter to stay here," Kovac said. "Why draw suspicion?"

"If she acted alone, she wouldn't have had any choice," Dawes said.

"But then what?" Liska asked. "If she made off with the judge, dumped the body somewhere, she can't exactly come cruising in here and tell us she's been at Starbucks all this time. How does she ever come back here?"

"Maybe she doesn't," Elwood said. "She's Swedish; she's got a passport. Say she dumps the judge, hops a plane to wherever, and David Moore joins her after the furor has died down. After he's gotten his hands on Judge Moore's money."

"Well, there's one good way to find out," Logan said. He looked at Kovac and tipped his head toward the closed dining room door.

"Okay," Dawes said. "You two go that route. Elwood, Tippen, go back to the station, get on the phones, and call all the airlines. See if this girl booked herself a flight somewhere.

"Nikki, do you still think the Haas boy and his friend might be connected to this?"

Liska shrugged. "I don't know. Assaulting the judge in the parking ramp was one thing. Could Bobby Haas mastermind a kidnapping as slick as this one? Seems unlikely."

Dawes nodded. "And what would his motive be for doing something this risky?"

"To get the Dahl trial handed over to another judge," Liska suggested. "Some hang-'em-high type."

"We have one of those?" Elwood asked, puzzled.

"Any word on the father of the dead foster children?" Dawes asked.

Liska nodded. "The reason we couldn't find Ethan Pratt is that he's enjoying the hospitality of our brethren in St. Paul. Another bar fight."

"Another Dallas Cowboys fan?" Tippen asked.

"New York Yankees."

"I'm with the lieutenant," Kovac said impatiently. "It doesn't make sense the Haas kid would risk so much. Even if he is bent on getting Karl Dahl convicted."

"And what about Karl Dahl?" Elwood asked. "Do we consider him for this?"

"Why would he want to harm Carey— Judge Moore?" Logan corrected himself. "Her ruling went in his favor. And how would he know how to get into this house? Why would he risk it with cops sitting right out front and every law enforcement officer in the metro area hunting him?"

"He's not exactly a model of mental health and stability," Tippen reminded them. "Who knows what strange creatures live in the depths of his psyche? Why would he butcher a woman and two small children? Who can explain that?"

"My money's still on the husband," Kovac said, heading for the door. "Let's go crack him like a soft-boiled egg."

Kovac and Logan walked down the hall, each closed off in his own mind, forming a plan for how this interview would go. When they stepped into the den, David Moore looked up from where he sat in one of the armchairs, nursing a drink. It was not yet noon.

"I'm not talking to you, Kovac."

Kovac arched a brow. "Was it something I said?"

Moore looked at Logan and said, "I'm not talking to him."

"That's your right, David," Logan said, matter-of-fact as he took a seat on the arm of the leather love seat.

Kovac sat back against Moore's desk and crossed his arms over his chest.

"Should I have a lawyer present?" Moore asked.

"I don't know why you would want one," Logan said. "You're not under arrest for anything."

Moore's eyes darted from Logan to Kovac, Kovac to Logan, like a mouse sizing up his odds against a pair of tomcats.

"I had nothing to do with Carey's disappearance," he said.

Logan ignored him. "How long has your nanny been with the family?"

"Uh, three years."

"She had good references when she came to you?"

"Of course."

"And you called those references and spoke with her former employers?"

"Carey did. Why? You can't possibly think Anka has anything to do with this."

Kovac raised his brows as if he was sur-

prised by the stupidity of Moore's statement. "Well, let's look at the facts. The
nanny is missing, the nanny's car is missing,
and your wife is missing."

"That's ridiculous," Moore said. "Anka
would never—"

"Just how close is Anka with the family?"
Logan asked.

"She's wonderful. She loves Lucy."

"What about with you?"

"What about with me?" Moore looked
confused, then disgusted. "Anka is my
daughter's nanny. That's it."

"She's a beautiful girl," Kovac said.
"Young, hot. She seemed very . . . devoted . . . to you."

Moore got up from his chair. "This is
ridiculous."

"Is it?" Logan asked. "If I go upstairs and
look through her things, I'm not going to
find any photographs of you, of you and
her?"

"I wouldn't know. I've never been in her
room."

"Oh, come on, David," Kovac said.
"You're leading a double life. You've
stashed one girlfriend in an apartment—
we're supposed to find it so hard to believe

that you wouldn't go for a little Swedish meatball?"

"That's disgusting."

"Why? You seem to have the moral backbone of a leech," Logan said. "Why wouldn't you be trying to screw the nanny?"

"That's it!" Moore shouted. "Get out! You can address any more questions you might have to my attorney."

"Your choice, David," Logan said, calm again. "But if you take that route, I can't play nice anymore."

"Nice?" Moore shouted, incredulous.

"Hey, Logan?" Kovac asked. "He lawyers up, do I get my warrants?"

"What do you want, Detective?"

"Search and inventory the house, starting with the room we're in; his financials—"

"Follow the money," Logan said.

"Why aren't you out trying to find my wife, instead of harassing me?" Moore asked.

He was as pissed off as Kovac had seen him. And scared. There was panic in his eyes. He moved like a caged animal, back and forth, back and forth.

"As we both know, she isn't going to be your wife much longer," Kovac said. "She was getting ready to toss you off the gravy train, Sport."

Red faced, Moore went around behind his desk and picked up the phone. The guy from the BCA looked at Kovac and Logan in disbelief. Moore was using the house phone when he was supposed to be waiting on pins and needles for a ransom call.

"It's David Moore," he said. "I need an attorney. Now."

42

Kovac walked out of the den and up the stairs, leaving Logan to deal with David Moore. As soon as Moore invoked his right to counsel, that was it. The interview was over, from Kovac's point of view. Anything incriminating Moore might say—if he was stupid enough to say anything at all—would be argued to be out of bounds by his attorney. And any evidence against him discovered as a result of such a statement would be out as well.

Despite Liska's statement to the contrary, Kovac wasn't stupid enough to push that line. As badly as he wanted to beat an admission of guilt out of Carey's husband, he turned and walked away.

The crime scene team had finished processing the nanny's bedroom. Kovac stood at the open door for a moment, looking in, trying to imagine what had gone on here.

The bed, which looked as if no one had slept in it, had been stripped and the sheets taken away to be processed for fibers and bodily fluids. The carpet had been recently vacuumed.

A lot could have happened here between the time of Kovac's last conversation with Carey and the time the nanny's car had pulled out of the driveway that morning. He couldn't help but imagine the possibilities. He'd dealt with too many violent crimes and too many violent criminals.

There had been no obvious signs of blood or semen in either bed. But murder could be committed without bloodshed. A rape could be concealed with a condom.

If David Moore had hired out the apparent kidnapping, returning the victim wasn't part of the deal. His objective was presumably to get rid of his wife, get her out of his way, and get his hands on her money. And as soon as the job had been handed over to the contractor, whatever else happened was out of Moore's control. Carey and the nanny, provided the nanny wasn't part of the scheme, would have been entirely at the mercy of a cold-blooded killer.

Kovac stepped into the room, pulled on a pair of latex gloves, and started poking around for any sign that the Swedish girl might have had an inappropriate connection to her employer.

The dresser was clutter-free. A small lamp on either end. A jewelry box. He lifted the lid. A couple of necklaces, earrings, nothing expensive.

Three small framed photographs smudged with fingerprint dust sat on the nightstand beside the bed. Anka and a couple of friends on a hiking trip; Anka and her family, half a dozen identical blond Swedes of various ages from teens to fifties; Lucy Moore and Anka bundled in winter coats, beaming smiles, kneeling beside a snowman. David Moore crouched down behind them, one hand resting on Anka Jorgenson's shoulder. Happy family. There were no photographs of the nanny with Carey Moore.

The drawer of the nightstand held the kinds of things women everywhere kept in their nightstands—a nail file, hand lotion, lip balm, a couple of pens, an address book, a journal.

Kovac lifted the journal and opened the cover, half expecting to read: *Dear Diary, I think I'm in love with David Moore.* What he found was a whole lot of Swedish. The big revelation, if there was to be one, would have to wait until they could get someone to translate. Luckily, in a state full of Scandinavian descendants, that wouldn't take very long.

Small comfort, he thought, considering they had no idea how much time they had. It could already be too late.

He went to the closet and opened the door, looking for obvious signs that the nanny had packed a bag before she vanished. But there was no telltale block of empty hangers. The closet was neat as a pin. A roll-on suitcase and a duffel bag were tucked into one corner.

Kovac closed the closet door, turned around, and surveyed the room again. No one had left this room in a hurry. No one had been forced to leave this room. No struggle had taken place here.

Years before, when he was new to Homicide, he'd come across a case of a missing woman who was found only after her body had begun to decompose. Her boyfriend had bludgeoned her to death with a claw hammer and stuffed her body under her mother's bed.

Kovac carefully lifted the bed skirt and looked. No body. A couple of long plastic storage containers full of shoes and clothes.

Down the hall, in Carey's bedroom, the crime scene unit was going over every square inch. But as with the nanny's room, the carpet had been vacuumed. The linens had been stripped from the bed. If they were lucky, they might find the sheets in the laundry. If not, their bad guy might have taken them to dispose of them so there would be no chance to get hair, fiber, bodily fluids, to put a name to their perp.

Kovac stood in the doorway of the welcoming, elegant room where he had helped Carey Moore to bed just two nights prior. Now the room gave a different feeling entirely.

Though he would never have admitted it to anyone, sometimes he thought he could feel the echo of raw emotions at the scene of a violent crime. Terror, anger, panic, intent.

He looked at the bed and pictured the scene in his mind—the room dark, Carey sleeping with her back to the door. He imagined the crime from the point of view of the perpetrator, never the victim. He could see Carey kicking and flailing as she was dragged backward from the bed. In the struggle, the heavy alabaster lamp was knocked over and fell to the floor. The framed photographs on the night table tipped over.

But as he looked at the room before him, the lamp was undisturbed, and there were no picture frames, on the stand or on the floor.

Kovac called to a squat woman plucking a piece of something off the carpet with a tweezers. "Where'd the pictures go?"

She put the fiber in a small clear plastic tube and placed a numbered evidence marker on the floor. "What pictures?"

"You didn't find any framed photographs on this nightstand or on the floor?"

She shook her head.

"No black-and-white eight-by-ten graduation photo? No baby photo in a silver frame?"

"Nope."

"You've looked under the bed?"

"Nothing under there."

Kovac looked across the room at Carey's dresser. Perfectly neat and tidy.

"Can I come in?" he asked.

"You need booties," the woman said.

Kovac pulled a pair of blue paper booties on over his shoes so that he wouldn't track in anything that would contaminate the scene. The forensics team had enough to do analyzing the legitimate evidence.

Avoiding evidence markers on the floor, Kovac crossed the room to the dresser and opened a drawer, and then another and another. All with items neatly folded.

He went to the large walk-in closet that held the rest of Carey's clothes, and looked around at the racks that held business suits, blouses, slacks, dresses. Nothing appeared disturbed.

At the back of the closet, a collection of matching luggage was neatly lined up, except that one piece seemed to be missing, leaving an empty spot in the row.

That bothered him. Of course, the piece could have been lost, or out for repair.

He looked around the closet again more closely, scrutinizing every inch of hanging space. A small gap here, a small gap there. Things might have been missing, or not.

But that missing suitcase . . .

If someone had packed a bag, that person had not been Carey Moore. No way she would have left this house voluntarily and left her daughter behind.

What the hell kind of kidnapper took a change of clothes for his victim?

Kovac could only hope that if that missing suitcase was in the possession of the kidnapper, it meant whoever had taken Carey meant to keep her alive.

He tried not to think about why.

43

Carey felt dizzy and nauseated. The oily scent of exhaust was inescapable.

She had to hope the secret destination was near, or she would die of carbon monoxide poisoning. Then again, what lay in store for her at the end of this ride would be nothing good. She would probably wish she had succumbed during the ride.

She had moved her hands around the cramped trunk, feeling for anything she could use as a weapon—a tire iron, a wrench, anything. But she found nothing.

As she turned onto her right side, something rectangular pressed against her hip bone. She felt it with her fingertips and a quick burst of hope shot through her.

Cell phone.

She remembered sticking it in the pocket

of her jeans after speaking to Kovac the night before. David had just stormed out of the house. She had called Kovac to tell him. He had been standing right outside her house, ready to come to her rescue.

When she had finally gone up to bed, she had been too exhausted to bother undressing. Or maybe it had been that she already felt too exposed and vulnerable.

Hands shaking, she fished the phone out of her pocket and punched a button to light it up.

911.

Fingers fumbled as she pressed the numbers. Misdialed. Tried again.

Her heart was banging against her ribs like a fist.

The only sound the telephone made was a series of beeps, then nothing. The lighted screen showed the message "No Service."

No service.

No signal.

No help.

44

Kovac called ahead to the Edina police to send a unit to Ginnie Bird's condo and not let her leave the premises, hoping to hell that that hadn't already happened. Since arriving at his house, David Moore hadn't been alone two seconds to make a call to his girlfriend. But whomever he had called for a lawyer—Edmund Ivors, Kovac suspected—could have given the Bird woman the heads-up to get out of Dodge.

Ginnie Bird had to be cut off from the pack. If he could get her alone, Kovac knew he would get her to talk. She wouldn't know what to do without Moore or Ivors there to put words in her mouth. She didn't have the backbone to stand up to him.

She was standing on the curb in front of

her building when he pulled up, looking very unhappy to be facing two uniforms.

Kovac walked up to them. "Ms. Bird. Are these guys bothering you?"

"They won't let me leave," she said, anxious. "They can't do that . . . can they?"

"Well, that would be my fault," Kovac said. "I asked them to detain you until I could get here."

Ginnie Bird looked up at him, suspicious. "I don't have anything to say to you. I don't know anything about what happened to David's wife."

"You knew he had a wife," Kovac said. "That tells me right there that you make bad choices, Ginnie. I mean, bad enough to hook up with a jerk like Moore if he was single. Why go to all the trouble of having an affair with a guy like that? A sneaky, spineless, petulant liar—"

"I love him!" she said emphatically. "You don't know anything about him."

Kovac shook his head. "Honey, I know all about the David Moores of the world. Why don't we go inside?" he suggested, gesturing toward her building. "I'm sure you'd rather not have your neighbors taking all this in."

"Am I under arrest?" she asked.

"No. Should you be?" Kovac arched a brow. "Do you have something to hide?"

"No!" she insisted. She glanced surreptitiously at her building, checking to see who might be peering out their windows.

"Fine," she said. "We'll go inside."

She liked her illusion of legitimacy. It was important to her that people around her believed she belonged in this tony part of town.

"No," Kovac said.

Ginnie Bird had already started to go back to the building. She turned around and looked at him, puzzled.

"No," he said again. "You know what? I don't have time for this bullshit."

"But—"

"There's a woman missing. I think you know something," Kovac said aggressively, stepping a little too close to her, his voice getting louder. "And you'd better spit it out, or we'll be talking about this in an eight-by-ten room downtown."

"I don't know anything," she insisted, but kept her voice down.

"You know who the blond guy was that

met you in the bar Friday night," Kovac
said. "I want a name."

"I don't know his name!"

"Maybe you don't know your own name,
Ms. Bird," Kovac said. "If I were to run your
prints through the system, who would you
turn out to be?"

Big tears filled her eyes, and her face
tightened into an unattractive expression.
She turned one way and then the other, not
knowing what to do or say next.

"I want a name," Kovac said again.

She put her hands over her face and
started to cry.

"Nobody feels sorry for you," Kovac said
harshly. "You're a junkie whore screwing the
husband of a missing judge. Do you know
what that sounds like? That sounds like motive. You couldn't have what you wanted as
long as Carey Moore was in the way. I have
no doubt you know plenty of lowlifes who
could do the dirty work for you."

Ginnie Bird made a sound like a siren, her
face still in her hands.

Kovac held his hands up and took a step
back. "That's it. I've had enough of this
crap."

He turned to the uniforms. "She's going in, guys."

"Donny," she sobbed. "Donny Bergen."

"How do you know him?" Kovac demanded.

She sobbed but didn't answer.

Kovac got in her face. "How do you know him!"

"He's my brother."

Liska had managed to ferret out of the department computers the incident report
from the death of Rebecca Rose Haas.
Short and sweet. A detective named
Rothenberg had gone through the motions
of an investigation. He had retired six
months later and moved to Idaho. She remembered his retirement party at Patrick's,
a cop bar strategically located halfway between the Minneapolis Police Department
and the Hennepin County Sheriff's Office.

The situation seemed cut-and-dried. Rebecca Haas hadn't had an enemy in the
world. She had simply been one of many
people who died accidental deaths in their
own homes every year.

According to Rothenberg, a neighbor had
spoken to her around two o'clock in the

afternoon. Mrs. Haas had been excited at the prospect of taking in another foster child. Marcella Otis from Children and Family Services had been there earlier that week to go over some details.

Sometime between two-fifteen and four-thirty that afternoon, Rebecca Haas had apparently taken a header down the basement stairs. She had been found on the basement floor, dirty laundry all around her from the basket she had been carrying downstairs.

Liska pulled up in front of the Haas home, parked on the street again, and went up the sidewalk to the front porch. No one answered the door. Wayne Haas's Chrysler was gone from the driveway.

She walked around the side of the house, thinking about Wayne Haas and his high blood pressure. Maybe he was inside, lying on the floor from having had a stroke.

Maybe he had decided to get the hell away from this place, chuck it all, and hop a bus to San Diego. Who could have blamed him?

She turned the corner to the backyard. Haas sat at a picnic table, his elbows on the table, his head in his hands.

"Mr. Haas?"

He raised his head and watched her cross the yard.

"I'm sorry to disturb your morning," she said.

"Are you?"

He looked smaller somehow. Pale in the bright sunshine.

"You're not coming to tell me you caught Dahl," he said.

"No. I wish I could tell you that."

"You're here to accuse me of something, then? What? I haven't been watching the television. No news but bad news."

Liska sat down across from him at the picnic table and leaned her elbows on the tabletop. She had already decided not to tell him about Judge Moore's abduction unless he brought it up himself. He would be less suspicious when she asked him questions about his son.

"Seems like it," she said. "How are you feeling?"

He tried to laugh but didn't have the breath or the energy for it. "What do you care?"

Liska sighed. "You know, we have to learn early on in this line of work not to put ourselves in the place of our victims or their loved ones. It's too difficult, too painful, warps our sense of objectivity. But that doesn't mean we don't have feelings, Mr. Haas.

"I'm sorry for what you've had to go through," she said. "I have two boys. And every day I see the things that happen, the things people will do . . . and I think about my kids. What if? What would I do? I don't think I would be able to go on."

Haas was quiet for a moment, looking off toward the wooded area at the back of his property. "You would," he said at last. "You wouldn't know how or why, but you would."

"To see justice done?"

"I don't know. What's justice? It's not what Karl Dahl was getting."

"He will," Liska said, though she had no idea if that would happen. Perps didn't always get their just deserts in this life. That was one of the reasons she kept believing in God, the hope that he would kick ass in the afterlife.

"Sometimes it's just anger that keeps you going," he confessed. "And you think if you let that anger go, then none of it means anything."

"Do you have anyone you can talk to about this?" Liska asked. "A friend? A minister?"

He tried again to laugh. "I don't have anybody. Nobody wants to know me. It's like they think it's catching, that someone might come to their house and kill their family too."

"You've got your son."

"I'm supposed to be strong for him. He takes care of me like I was an invalid."

"He loves you very much," Liska said. "I'm surprised he's not here with you."

"He stayed the night with his friend, the Walden kid. He's home too much. Sometimes I have to practically throw him out of the house, make him go be a kid. He hasn't had a lot of opportunity to do that."

"How old was Bobby when you and your first wife took him in?"

"Ten years old."

"That must have been a big adjustment for all of you."

Haas said nothing. He shook a cigarette out of a pack of Winstons and hung it on his lip. He looked past Liska as if she weren't there.

"I understand his birth mother committed suicide."

"Hanged herself," he said, lighting up. "Right in front of him."

"Oh, my God."

Liska could only imagine what that would do to a child. Ten years old and forced to watch his mother kill herself. What must he have thought and felt? Helpless. Powerless. Terrified. Angry that his mother would leave him. Guilty, because children often feel responsible for bad things happening. Because their worlds revolve around them, they think that somehow they could have prevented them. If only he hadn't thrown a baseball through the front window. If only he hadn't gotten in trouble at school. If only he had meant enough to her . . .

"And then to lose your first wife, his second mother. That must have been tough on him."

"She loved him," Haas said. "Didn't matter how difficult he could be. She just loved him."

"Bobby told me he really liked Marlene too," Liska said. "He said she was always baking cookies."

Wayne Haas smiled a little at the memory

before a cloud of grief settled over him, darker than before.

"Bobby told me you and he used to do a lot of stuff together," Liska said. "Go fishing, play catch. He misses that. He misses you."

His eyes rimmed red and he looked away from her, embarrassed he might cry in front of her.

"You need each other," Liska said. "That's the way you heal each other."

She got up from the table and put a business card down near Wayne Haas's hand, then walked away, feeling ashamed of herself for using the emotions of a broken man to get information about his own son.

At least she hadn't left any scars. Guys on the job could bully a witness or a perp, scare them into cooperating. Being small and female, she was better off relying on gentler, sneakier ways of getting information. Not having a penis was, every once in a while, to her advantage.

Jerome Walden's home was her next stop. The lovely and pleasant Mrs. Walden answered, hungover, wearing last night's makeup, a leopard-print see-through wrap over a zebra-striped bra and panties. She should have been arrested for crimes against fashion.

Liska showed her ID through the screen door.

"What now?" the woman complained. "Is this about Ray Malone? I don't know nothing but that he's a son of a bitch, and he owes me money."

"He give you that shiner?" Liska asked, referring to a black eye that was only just beginning to purple.

"I ran into something."

Like a fist, Liska thought, but she didn't pursue the issue.

"Is your son home?"

The woman looked suspicious. "Why?"

"Because I asked."

"That's not an answer."

"It's the one I'm giving you," Liska said, annoyed. That women like this one were allowed to have children was beyond her. "I shouldn't give you that much. The state this house is in, I should be calling social services."

"Oh, fuck you, Little Miss Tweed Blazer."

"You can answer one goddamn question, or I'm on the phone to report you," Liska said forcefully. "Your kid gets taken away from you, so do the family aid checks."

Jerome Walden's mother scowled at her, trying to decide if Liska was bluffing, or maybe considering how the loss of that AFDC check would crimp her lifestyle.

"He's not home," she said.

"Where is he?"

"Like I'm supposed to know that? He's practically an adult."

From somewhere in the background came a loud male voice. "Hey, babe, where are you? Come suck my dick!"

Liska arched a brow. "Duty calls."

The woman gave her the finger and slammed the door in her face.

What could she expect from a woman who mixed her animal prints?

With a mother like that, it was a wonder Jerome Walden wasn't already on the most-wanted list.

But the larger question that loomed in front of her as she got back in her car and headed downtown was where Jerome Walden and Bobby Haas were and just what the hell were they up to.

46

Carey tried the phone again. Still nothing. She kept pressing buttons to keep the phone illuminated, and tried to use it as a flashlight. She'd found nothing in her reach to use as a weapon once her abductor stopped the car.

As she moved the cell phone to the right, the light reflected off something. The plastic cover of one interior trunk light.

She felt around the cover, trying to find a way to pry under it, to pull it loose. She dug at it, pulled at it, broke two fingernails.

Closing her eyes, she took her phone and used the end of it like a hammer, beating at the plastic until it cracked.

Pulling the shattered cover apart, she felt around inside. Her fingertips snagged on something.

Wires.

To the taillights? The turn signals? Many a criminal had ended his career with a traffic violation.

Carey pulled the wires loose and prayed for a ticket-happy cop.

47

Liska walked into the war room, feeling troubled and anxious. She had called in a BOLO for Bobby Haas and Jerome Walden and for Wayne Haas's Chrysler. There wasn't much else she could do on that front. She couldn't figure the boys for the abduction of Judge Moore. That had pro written all over it. But she kept moving the puzzle pieces of Bobby Haas's life around and around in her mind, not liking any of the pictures she came up with.

The women in Bobby's life hadn't fared well. His mother had killed herself in front of him. The first Mrs. Haas had fallen to her death. The second Mrs. Haas had been murdered. Judge Moore had been assaulted, would probably have been killed if not for the car alarm scaring off the perpetrator. And now she was gone, vanished.

The idea of the boy's being involved in any of that made Liska's skin crawl. He looked so sweet, seemed so polite, so vulnerable. The fact that he had had so much sadness and tragedy in his life tripped the Mother switch in her and made her want to put an arm around him and comfort him. He wasn't much older than Kyle, her firstborn. It was difficult for her not to look at Bobby Haas and see Kyle, and want to protect him.

He had told her Rebecca Haas had died of cancer.

The lie was like a stone in her shoe—small but irritating, something she couldn't stop thinking about.

Why would he have lied?

Because he thought telling the truth to a cop would arouse suspicion?

Or was it just as Marcella Otis had said, that maybe Bobby didn't want to think about his first foster mother's violent demise? Lieutenant Dawes had suggested the boy might have felt like less of a freak saying his mom had died of cancer than being known as the kid with multiple violent deaths in his life.

"You're just in time for the movie," Tippen said.

Liska joined him, sitting on the end of the table as Elwood stuck a videotape in the VCR and turned the television on.

"Why so glum?" Tippen asked.

She shrugged. "Oh, I don't know. Maybe it has something to do with the fact that every day of my life is about death and depravity and the decline of a once-great civilization."

"Oh, stop whining," Tippen said. "It could be worse. You could be the sheriff's deputy who didn't cuff Karl Dahl to the gurney."

"Any word on him, Dahl?"

"Nada. He'll probably resurface years from now, found to be working as director of a shelter for homeless women and children in Milwaukee. Credited with orchestrating the decline in the numbers of street people."

"Well, that cheered me up," Liska said. "Excuse me while I go slit my wrists."

Elwood hit the play button, and the television screen filled with black-and-white snow, then a bird's-eye view of the lobby bar in the Marquette Hotel, date and time superimposed in the upper right-hand corner of the screen. The tape was clean, the picture sharp enough to easily make out faces. He hit fast-forward, racing through the tape to the time in question.

"There's David Moore and his amour," Tippen said, using a laser pointer to touch the screen.

"Eeww!" Liska said, wrinkling her nose at the sight of Moore's junkie whore girlfriend crawling all over him. "Get a room!"

Elwood goosed the tape ahead until Edmund Ivors joined the party, then goosed it a little more.

"Here he comes," Liska said.

Slender guy on the small side, dressed in black, fine blond hair almost to his shoulders. He could definitely have passed as a woman, from a distance.

He walked up to the table, leaned down, and shook David Moore's hand, presenting his profile.

Tippen sat up straighter. "I know that guy! That's Long Donny. Long Donny Bergen."

"Who's Long Donny Bergen and why do they call him that?" Liska asked.

"He's a porn star."

"Oh, gross!" Liska jumped off the table and looked at Tippen with disgust. "Don't tell me you're a fan! I don't want that in my head!"

"What?" Tippen asked, shrugging his shoulders. "The man is a star in his own right."

"Oh, yuck! And here I thought I already knew too much about you!"

"We know why you know him, Tip," El-wood said. "The question is: Why does David Moore know him?"

48

Ginnie Bird's brother.

Well, why not keep it all in the family? Kovac thought as he sped back toward the Moore house. David Moore wanted his wife out of the way, Ginnie Bird wanted Carey Moore out of the way, and she happened to have a brother willing to do the job for twenty-five thousand dollars. Neat and tidy. What a pack of mutts—David Moore, his junkie whore girlfriend, and her brother the hit man.

Donny Bergen was slender, with shoulder-length blond hair. The cops on surveillance had seen the nanny's Saab come out of the garage Saturday night with the slender blond nanny in it. The car had backed out of the garage in the morning with a slender blonde behind the wheel and driven away from them. They hadn't thought anything of it.

Moore would have given him the security code, which explained how Bergen gained entrance to the house without setting off the alarm.

Now the question of what might have happened to the nanny took on a more ominous tone. If Donny Bergen was willing to kill Carey, Anka Jorgenson might have been his first target. He might have killed her to get her car, to gain access to the Moore house via the garage.

One hand on the wheel, one on his cell phone, Kovac speed-dialed Liska. She answered on the second ring.

"What's up?"

"Are you at the station?"

"Yeah. Why?"

"I need you to run a couple of names through the system for me. Virginia Bergen and Donny or Donald Bergen."

"Donny Bergen is the guy on the tape from the hotel bar," she said.

"I know. How do you know?"

"Tippen recognized him. He has a frighteningly extensive store of knowledge about the porn industry."

"Porn?" Kovac said, confused. "What are you talking about?"

"Long Donny Bergen, porn star extraordinaire. What are you talking about?"

"He's Ginnie Bird's brother."

"Their mother must be so proud. Now what?"

"Send someone to his apartment. If he's there—which I doubt—pick him up for questioning."

He gave her the address he had badgered out of Ginnie Bird.

"I'll send Tippen," Liska said. "He can get an autograph from his hero."

Kovac could feel his blood pressure rising again. His head began to pound like a bass drum.

David Moore, you motherfucking son of a bitch.

David Moore, his junkie whore girlfriend, and her brother the *porn star* hit man. How much deeper into the shit could this creep go?

He didn't delve into Moore's connections to the porn industry. At the moment, he didn't care. His immediate fantasy was to drag Moore into a small room and beat the answers out of him, then beat him some more just on principle.

That fantasy played over and over in his mind, making him angrier and angrier as he drove back to the Moore house. By the time he pulled into the Moores' driveway, he was breathing hard, and his neck felt hot.

News vans had descended on the block again as news of Carey Moore's disappearance had leaked. A mob with cameras, all of them shouting at once. They sounded like a cloud of locusts swarming. Kovac ignored them, stalking past the uniforms who stood guard at the door.

Inside the house, he turned and went straight for the den, where he could see David Moore standing in front of the fireplace. Logan stood with his back to the door. A third man was talking to Logan. Moore's eyes widened as Kovac came into the room, striding straight for him.

"You spineless piece of shit!" Kovac shouted, jabbing an accusatory finger at Moore. "You fucking spineless piece of shit! You and your junkie whore girlfriend and her porn star brother are going to rot in prison till the day you die!"

Moore jumped back, knocking over the

fireplace tools and tripping on them, falling against the wall.

Logan yelled, lunged, and grabbed Kovac, banding his arms around Kovac's shoulders.

The third man ran backward out of the way.

Kovac kept on shouting, kept trying to move forward, struggled to break free of Logan's hold. "I'll fucking nail your ass to the wall! You are done! You are over!"

"Kovac!" Logan shouted in his ear.

"I don't know what he's talking about!" David Moore shouted.

"Kovac!" Lieutenant Dawes rushed into the room with two uniforms behind her.

The uniforms joined Logan in dragging and shoving Kovac back across the room toward the hall.

Dawes was shouting in his face. Kovac was so angry, he couldn't make sense of her words.

Out of the room, Logan pushed him back against a wall.

"What the hell's the matter with you?" he shouted in Kovac's face.

Kovac shoved him back. "This is all him!" he shouted, pointing at the now-closed doors to the den. "She's gonna die because he didn't have the balls to stand up and walk out—"

"That's enough!" Dawes shouted at him. "Not another word!"

Kovac held his hands up, forcing himself to lock down the fury. He was breathing hard, sweating like a horse. Logan stepped back, doing the same.

Dawes glared at Kovac. "What is this about?"

"The girlfriend's brother," he said. "The third guy at the bar was the girlfriend's brother, a porn actor."

"I don't care if he was the devil himself," Dawes said. "What's the matter with you, coming in here like that? What were you going to do? Beat David Moore to death in front of his attorney? You're out of control, Detective."

Kovac walked around in a little circle, rubbing his hands over his face. He was shaking as the rush of adrenaline recycled itself.

"Go home," Dawes said.

Kovac looked at her.

"Go home," she said again.

"This is my case."

"You need to step back, Sam. Now."

He held up a hand, still pacing. "I'm all right. I was out of line."

"You were *way* out of line. I can't have you threatening people. You'll be lucky if Moore's attorney doesn't demand you go before the civilian review board."

"Fucking slimebag," Kovac muttered. "What rock did he crawl out from under?"

"It's Anthony Costello," Logan said. "He crawled out from under a very expensive rock."

Kovac shook his head. "Great. David Moore can have his wife kidnapped and murdered. Tony Costello can soak up Carey's money to defend the asshole. And *I'm* the one in trouble. Yeah, that's how the system should work."

"You're making this personal, Sam," Dawes said. "You know better."

Kovac sat down on the stairs, put his head in his hands, and let go a shuddering sigh. "I'm fine."

"You need to take a break."

"No."

"Sam—"

"Don't send me home, LT," he said, looking up at her. "I won't go. This is my case.

Carey Moore is my responsibility. I won't walk away from that. Don't try to make me."

He looked at Logan, standing near the front door. Logan was watching him with eagle eyes.

Dawes's cell phone rang. She took the call, walking away.

"Twenty-five grand to a hit man," Kovac said. "That should buy him twenty-five to life, right?"

"Can you connect Moore to the hitter through the money?" Logan asked. "Assuming that's what's going on."

"I don't know. We need to crack open Moore's books."

"You think he's mixed up in the porn business?"

"Looks like. Has to be how he hooked up with these people. Ginnie Bird, the brother. Ivors is involved in the movie business. Moore is in Ivors's pocket. Fucking creep. Documentary films my ass."

He stared at the floor and blew out a breath. His heart was still pounding like a trip-hammer. It was all he could do to keep himself seated on the steps.

"You've had worse cases than this," Logan said.

Kovac looked at him sharply. "So?"

"So what's with the big blowup? You know Carey that well?"

"I know she's my vic," Kovac said defensively. "I know she's my responsibility. And I'm pretty damn sure that asshole in the other room made her disappear. Do I need something more than that? I'm supposed to care less because Carey Moore hasn't been raped and eviscerated and set on fire yet?"

Logan held up his hands. "No. I just . . .

"Never mind," he said, turning toward Lieutenant Dawes as she came back from her phone call. Her face was grave as she looked from one of them to the other.

"We've found the nanny."

49

Her body had been folded into the trunk of a late-model dark blue Volvo. She looked like a broken doll lying there, legs bent, her eyes wide-open, her head turned at an odd angle.

She was wearing a brown velour Juicy Couture tracksuit and a pair of pink Puma running shoes. Dressed for a Saturday night at home, kicking back to watch a movie and eat some popcorn.

"I—I didn't have anything to do with that."

Kovac looked at the guy, annoyed.

Bruce Green. Twenty-seven. Pasty white wimp with a mop of blond frizz that looked like he'd stolen it off the dead body of Harpo Marx. Bell-bottoms and a black and yellow rugby shirt. He dabbed a bloody handkerchief under his nose. His forehead was growing a big goose egg.

"I—I just glanced down," Green went on nervously. "I—I dropped my BlackBerry, and—and when I reached for it, I knocked over my latte, and—and it spilled—"

"Shut up," Kovac said sharply. He turned back to the uniform who had been first on the scene, Hovney, a woman built like the corner mailbox, with a face like the flat side of an anvil.

"He rear-ended the Volvo," she said, "which was parked here at the curb. The trunk popped. The rest is history."

Green's car, a butt-ugly pea green square box Honda something-or-other, had suffered front-end damage. Pieces made from plastic had shattered and lay on the street.

The street had been cordoned off. Half a dozen squad cars sat at angles on either end of the accident scene.

Kovac pulled on a pair of gloves and tried to turn the nanny's head. The body was in rigor. The second-shift surveillance team had reported the girl had left the Moore house around ten-thirty. She hadn't lived long past that time. Rigor mortis would have begun to set in two to four hours after death. Full rigor was achieved eight to twelve hours after death.

The car was parked on the side street around the corner from the 7-Eleven, where Anka had supposedly gone to pick out a movie and buy some snacks, just past the alley that ran behind the store. The killer had probably initially parked in the alley, out of view. He had nabbed the girl, pulled her into the alley, killed her, put the body in the trunk, driven out of the alley, and parked at the curb. Then he had gotten behind the wheel of the nanny's Saab and calmly driven back to the Moore house.

The car would have been equipped with a garage door opener. The keys to the house were probably on the same key ring as the keys to the Saab. He could have forced the nanny to give up the security code to the house system before he killed her. Or, as Kovac had speculated earlier, David Moore had simply given it to him, along with the twenty-five thousand dollars.

"I guess we can rule out the nanny as a suspect," Liska said.

Hovney went on. "The plates come back to a Saab—"

"He swapped the plates," Kovac said. Which meant the call that had gone out to be on the lookout for the nanny's car had included the wrong plate numbers. "Whose car is this?"

"The VIN number connects the car to a Christine Neal," Dawes said.

"Has anyone tried to contact this woman?" Kovac asked.

"No answer," Dawes said. "I've sent a unit to her home."

Kovac shook his head, pissed off at the unnecessary loss of life. If Anka hadn't been involved in the plan against Carey—which she clearly hadn't been—she had been nothing more than collateral damage, just one more person to get out of the way so the plan to nab Carey could go forward as planned.

If Donny Bergen was the doer, it didn't make sense that he would kill someone to get a car. Too risky. He wouldn't have used his own vehicle, for the obvious reasons. But it wasn't that difficult to boost a car without bothering a soul.

"Was the car reported as stolen?" he asked.

"No."

Kovac nodded. "Well, let's hope Ms. Neal is on vacation."

50

The car slowed down and turned. Gravel crunched beneath the tires, and Carey's heart began to pound hard at the base of her throat. No one was ever taken to a remote area against their will for any good reason.

She tried the phone again, but still she had no signal, and her battery was starting to run low. The case of the phone had cracked when she had broken the plastic light cover. Hands shaking, she turned it off and stuck it into the front pocket of her jeans once more. The tail of her shirt would hide the outline of it . . . as long as she was wearing a shirt.

The car rolled to a halt.

She had no weapon. Her physical strength, even with adrenaline fueling it, would be no match for a man bent on harming her. The car rocked as the driver got out.

Her breath held tight in her lungs as she waited for the trunk to unlock, waited for the sudden blinding light as the lid opened, waited to finally see the face of her captor.

But the trunk didn't open.

A car door opened again, but no one got in.

Carey wondered where the hell she was. There was no traffic noise at all. No sound of human voices. All she could hear was the very faint squawking of geese flying south for the winter. She wished for their freedom, and thanked God that at least she wasn't hearing the sound of a shovel digging a shallow grave.

51

Christine Neal's cottage would have looked just as at home if it had been found somewhere on Nantucket Island. The small garage was empty. The front door of the house was locked, but a little hand-painted sign bade visitors welcome and announced, "Grandma Lives Here."

The uniformed officers had rung the doorbell and looked in the windows but had seen no sign of Christine Neal.

Dawes gave the signal. "Break it in."

The house was quiet and smelled fresh, as if it had just been cleaned.

"Well, this is weird right off the bat," Liska said.

"What?" Kovac asked.

"Look at this place," she said. "It's so—so—*neat*."

At Kovac's request, she had met them at the Neal home. They were both good detectives in their own right, but Kovac liked the way they worked a scene together. They complemented each other in the way they saw things, in the feelings they picked up, in the way they processed what they took in.

"Not everyone shares your enlightened view of organization," Kovac said as they walked around the living room, looking for any sign of something wrong.

He had sent one of the uniforms to the backyard and one to the basement. Dawes stood just inside the front door, deep in conversation with the chief of detectives, trying to explain the debacle at the Moore house.

"Not everyone has two boys and a homicide cop in the family," Liska said. "Look at the pattern in this carpet. Freshly vacuumed. I'm lucky I can *see* my carpet."

"Mmmm . . . You should tell Speed he can work off some of his delinquent child support tidying your house once a week."

"Ha. Two boys, a homicide cop, and an asshole. I would have the same house, but it would smell like sweat socks, cigarettes, and bad Mexican food."

They went into the kitchen, finding it equally immaculate.

"The boys with him this weekend?" Kovac asked.

"Yeah. I can't wait to find out what useful skill he's taught them this time," Liska said. "The last time they were with him, he taught them how to pat down a hype without getting stuck with a dirty needle."

Kovac looked out the window over the sink, into the fenced backyard. A happy scarecrow hung on a post in a vegetable garden studded with orange pumpkins.

"That's Speed, always the model father," he said.

"He's the only one they've got," Liska said. "Hey, look at this. She's a breast cancer survivor."

She stood in front of the refrigerator, looking at a collage of photographs. The life and times of Christine Neal.

"I hope to God she's visiting those grandkids," Kovac said.

The officer came up from the basement and said, "Nothing down there but wet laundry in the washing machine."

Kovac turned down the hall, checked out

the bathroom—spotless—and continued on to what he thought might be a bedroom.

The vacuum had been run in this room as well, right up to the white eyelet dust ruffle of the queen-sized bed.

Kovac looked around the room. Nothing had been overturned or disturbed.

He went down on one knee beside the bed and lifted the fabric.

Christine Neal stared at him with sightless eyes.

52

"I don't get it," Kovac said. "Why kill this woman? Just to take her car?"

"Maybe he knew her," Liska suggested. "Maybe she could ID him."

"You think Christine Neal was into porn? Is there a whole over-fifty porn movie industry out there I don't know about?"

"I don't want to know. I'm still reeling from Tippen."

Kovac huffed. "Please. Like you didn't already think he was watching porn."

"Yeah, but hearing it from the horse's mouth was too much."

They stood in the front yard, near Christine Neal's house, waiting for the ME's people to roll out the victim, cloaked in the anonymous black body bag. It would be the last private moment for Christine Neal.

By day's end the cops and the media would be dragging out the details of her life like entrails from a carcass. By the end of the next day, everyone with a television or a newspaper subscription in the metro area would know how old she was, who her family was, what her neighbors knew about her, how her coworkers felt about her.

Kovac lit a cigarette, giving Liska a warning glare. She held her hands up in surrender.

"Maybe the doer wasn't Donny Bergen," Lieutenant Dawes said.

"It was," Kovac snapped.

"Why? Because you want to pin the plan on David Moore?"

"It all fits," he insisted. "The assault Friday night, Bergen showing up at the hotel bar dressed in black like the guy on the tape from the parking garage. Moore wanted out of the marriage, but he didn't want to lose anything. Carey is kidnapped, murdered, and he's the grieving husband, the devoted single father, inherits everything via Lucy."

Dawes's phone rang. She sighed and took the call, walking away.

Liska shifted her weight to her right foot, effectively moving closer to her partner.

They stood at right angles, facing the house, their backs to the gathering mob of media and curious onlookers.

Kovac stared at the house, raised his cigarette to his lips, knowing she could see the slight trembling of his hand. Their killer had murdered twice, senselessly. There was no reason to think he wouldn't do it again. Especially if he'd been paid to do it.

Christine Neal and the nanny had been just for sport. He could have stolen either car without harming anyone. Wear a mask, tie the women up, tape their mouths shut. They hadn't needed to see him.

"Sam, there are other possibilities," Liska said.

"Maybe there are," he conceded. "But are any of them good, Tinks? You think this is going to have a happy ending? You know as well as I do more kidnap victims are murdered within the first few hours of the abduction than not. And those are the ones snatched for ransom. There's no ransom involved here. There hasn't been a call. There's not going to be a call.

"Let's say it's not Donny Bergen," he suggested. "Who's up next? Stan Dempsey?

Your boy Bobby? You think either of those scenarios is going to end well? We've looked at two dead women inside an hour."

"You need to hold it together, Kojak," Liska said firmly but gently as the ME's people came out the front door with the gurney. "If Carey Moore is still alive, she sure as hell doesn't need you writing her off."

Kovac squeezed his eyes shut and rubbed his forehead with one hand. What made a good cop was objectivity. Objectivity and dogged tenacity. He had made his career on both.

He finished his cigarette, put it out on the front step, and dropped the butt into a jack-o'-lantern.

Liska put a hand on his arm, drawing his attention back to her. The concern in her eyes touched him. "Are you gonna be all right?"

Kovac forced a smile. "Remains to be seen, doesn't it? I'd rather work ten murders than one abduction."

"You'd better not be blaming yourself," Liska warned. "That's self-indulgent bullshit. I'll have to kick your ass."

Somehow he managed to chuckle, not

because he felt any better but because that was the reaction Liska wanted.

"Let's get back to work, Tinker Bell," he said. "We've got crimes to solve."

53

The quiet lasted for so long, Carey began to think she had been abandoned. Maybe the car had been left on train tracks, and she was waiting as her death hurtled toward her. Maybe the car had been left in the back of a junkyard, and she would die of dehydration after days of suffering. Maybe anything.

She felt through the broken pieces of plastic from the light cover to find a shard she could use for a weapon in case her captor ever came to get her.

She wondered who he was. Stan Dempsey? Had he really gone that far off the deep end? He was a cop, for God's sake. How could he reconcile hurting people, maybe killing people, with having served twenty-plus years as a police officer?

Justice, Kovac had said. Dempsey was

meting out justice as he perceived it. If he was performing an act of justice, how could it be a crime?

She wished she could have seen the videotape he had made and left behind for his colleagues to find. What was his demeanor? What was his tone of voice? How did he look? How did he sound?

How about it wasn't Stan Dempsey at all? How about the note David had made to himself: *$25,000.* What if Kovac had been right from the start, and her husband wanted her out of his life badly enough to hire someone to do it?

She wondered if Kovac was looking for her. Almost certainly he was. He would have called early, or come over and helped himself to coffee. But how would he have any idea where to look? She was the needle in the haystack.

She thought about Lucy. Where was she? Was she afraid? Was she with David? Was she alive?

Shoes crunched on gravel. A key slid into the trunk lock and turned.

As the trunk lid went up, sunlight hit Carey full in the face and blinded her. The silhouette of a person loomed over her, but she couldn't make out features. She could tell the hair was shoulder length. A woman's haircut, she thought.

"You can come out now, Carey. I have everything ready for you."

The voice of a man.

He bent down over her to lift her out.

Terrified, Carey swung her arm and stabbed at him with the broken shard of plastic, driving the tip into some part of his face. He cried out and stumbled backward.

Out of the trunk! Out of the trunk!

Her mind raced faster than she could move. She had been in the cramped trunk long enough to have become stiff, and her body had already been hurting from the assault. The concussion made her head swim as she tried to scramble out of the trunk.

Her feet hit the ground, but her legs were weak, and buckled beneath her. She landed on her battered knees, pain spiking through her. Awkwardly she got her feet under her and tried to push forward, to run before she was fully upright.

The world around her tilted one way, then another. She stumbled forward, fell, tried again, stumbled, fell. The ground rushed up at her, hard-packed dirt and clumps of dead weeds that had faded to beige. She put her arms out to break her fall, and tiny stones dug into the heels of her hands.

It was a nightmare, and the worst part of it was that she knew she was wide-awake.

As she tried to rise again, hands caught her from behind, pulled her up, and held her. Carey tried to kick, tried to struggle. She didn't have the strength to fight him or pull free of him. Even if she had, she couldn't outrun him. And even if she could have outrun him, there was nowhere to run. All around was nothing but countryside and clumps of bare trees and fields of dry cornstalks.

Fear shook her like a rag doll. She tried not to cry out loud, knowing her abductor would likely find her fear exciting, arousing. But tears filled her eyes and coursed down her face, and she couldn't help it.

"You don't have to run," the soft voice said. "I would never hurt you, Carey. You're my angel."

He turned her toward him and held her at arm's length.

"Oh, my God," Carey whispered, terror rising in her throat to choke her.

The first thing that struck her was the

gaping wound in the hollow of his cheek where she had stabbed him with the shard of plastic. Blood poured from it, ran down over his jaw, down his throat, onto the brown sweater he wore.

The second thing that struck her was the makeup—the painted lips, the overdone eye shadow, the smudged mascara, the blush on his cheekbones. The stubble of his beard was dark beneath the caked foundation makeup.

He reached up with one hand and pulled the blond wig from his head.

"It's me," he said as if he were an old, dear friend. "Karl. Karl Dahl."

54

Carey stared at Karl Dahl—the bald head, bruised and scabbed over on one side where he appeared to have been struck with something; the garish makeup; the jagged edge of the bleeding wound in his cheek, moving in and out as he breathed through his mouth. The whites of his eyes were bloodred. He was dressed as a woman, in a calf-length brown skirt and low-heeled boots.

Behind him, maybe twenty yards behind him and off to his right, was a huge old burned-out brick building. Two stories high, charred black, it looked to have been abandoned for a very long time. All the windows were dark, gaping holes. She could see sunlight inside where sections of the roof had either burned through or fallen in.

Karl Dahl meant to drag her inside that building. Carey pulled back, but he held fast to her arm, his grip tight and hard.

"You don't need to be afraid of me, Carey," he said calmly.

The way he said her name was like the stroke of a lover's hand. She didn't like it.

"You should call me Judge Moore, Karl," she said, her voice almost unrecognizable to her. A dry, hoarse rasping from her aching throat. Her larynx felt the size of a fist. She had wanted to sound strong and calm as she tried to establish herself in his mind as a person to be respected.

He smiled and shook his head. "No. We're past that. You're the only one's been kind to me. You understand them things I did before wasn't bad, really."

Karl Dahl's criminal record showed arrests and time served for a variety of crimes—criminal trespass, window peeping, indecent exposure, breaking and entering. Nothing violent. No kidnap, no assault, no rape, no—

But he was on trial for the brutal murders of a woman and two children from a family who had been nothing but kind to him.

Chris Logan's words from Friday afternoon came back to her.

"It's an escalating pattern of behavior. That's what these pervs do. They start small and work their way up."

He was right. Carey knew as much about the Karl Dahls of the world as Logan did. The Boston Strangler had started out as a Peeping Tom.

As a prosecutor she had been able to knit a defendant's criminal life together that way when preparing for trial, bridging one step up to the next on the criminal evolutionary scale. And she would try like hell to get it all past the presiding judge.

Now she was the judge. And as a judge, she had to adhere to a different standard.

"I don't know very much about you, Karl," she said, her breath hitching in her throat.

She looked past his left shoulder and saw the car. Anka's car. Panic stabbed through her. She had spoken to Anka as the girl had gone out Saturday night to get a movie. Lost in thought, she hadn't paid any attention when Anka came home. She vaguely remembered hearing the kitchen door open. In her peripheral vision she had been aware of a blonde walking through the hall and going up the stairs.

That the blonde might have been Karl Dahl made her skin crawl. How long had he been in her home? What had he done there while she had been in the den, discovering the depravity to which her husband had lowered himself? Had he been upstairs when she had come up and fallen onto her bed without bothering to undress? Had he been in her room? Had he been in Lucy's room?

For the briefest of seconds, the crime scene photo of the Haas foster children flashed through her head.

"Oh, me," Karl said shyly, "there ain't that much to know."

"Sure there is," Carey said, her voice shaking. "Everybody has a story."

"I'd sure like to hear yours," he said. "Let's go inside. I have everything ready for you."

"What does that mean, Karl?"

He smiled a secretive smile made sinister by the clownish makeup and the still-bleeding gash in his face, which he seemed not to notice. "You'll see soon enough."

He started toward the building, pulling

Carey in tow. Everything in her told her not to go into the building with him. At least if they were outside, someone might drive by, and she would have a chance to escape. The odds of that happening diminished with every step he dragged her.

"C-can't we just s-stay out here for a while, Karl?" she asked. "I'm not f-feeling very well. Could I just have some fresh air for a while?"

It wasn't a lie. Even as she said it, she felt her stomach twist, and she dropped down on her knees again and vomited in the weeds. Karl held on to her hand like a lover would to comfort her.

"You need to lie down is what you need," he said gently, squatting down beside her. "You've just got yourself all stirred up."

"N-no. Could we please j-just sit here for a minute? I'm very dizzy."

"That's from that person beating on you in that parking garage, isn't it?" he asked. "On account of me. I seen all about it on television this morning. And I read about it in the *Star Tribune*. I like a good newspaper. You get more of the story.

"I'm sorry for what that man done to you,"

he said. "I seen that story, and I knew right then you was my angel."

Carey shivered as she sat back on her heels. "I'm not an angel, Karl. I'm a person. I have a family. I h-have a l-little girl. I'm a judge. I was just doing my job."

"You're cold," Karl declared. "Let's go inside. I've made a fire."

He hooked an arm under hers and lifted her with him when he stood.

"What is this place?" she asked. "Where are we?"

"My secret place. I've stayed here many times, and no one ever bothers me."

"I mean the building," Carey said, trying not to dwell on what he had just told her. "Where are we? What did it used to be?"

"It used to be a munitions dump back in the war times. WW Two. There's still some parts of shells and stuff in there, but don't nobody seem to care about it. You think they would take it away what with the terrorists and all. You know one of them Nine-Eleven boys was learning to fly a jet airplane right here in Minneapolis."

Carey was at a loss for words. The surrealism of the scene was too much for her. She had been abducted by a triple murderer, and he was calmly going on about Homeland Security.

As she stared at him, the putrid smell of sulfur came on the breeze. A refinery. She couldn't see it, but it was nearby.

"Watch your step here, Carey," he said, helping her up the worn, crumbling concrete steps and into the building.

It was a ruin. There was no ceiling, only partial walls here and there. He took her down what might have been a hallway once, turning here and turning there, working their way farther and farther from the door they had come in.

The floors were filthy and strewn with garbage and debris—broken bottles, beer cans, discarded fast-food wrappers. Bits and pieces of grit and crumbled brick bit into the soles of her bare feet.

"Where are we going, Karl?" she asked.

"You'll see," he said, a strange, boyish excitement creeping into his voice. "I'm real proud of it."

He led her around the corner of a brick wall and into his hiding place, where no one had ever bothered him.

There was more roof over this part of the building. And no windows. No sunlight. Karl had made up for the darkness by lighting candles all around.

In the flickering yellow light, Carey saw what Karl was so proud of, and a chill washed over her like a wave.

Karl Dahl had created a little nest with pillows and blankets. A small fire burned in a hibachi grill. Overturned fruit crates served as tables. There was a bottle of champagne in an ice bucket, wineglasses standing to one side. He even had framed photographs of someone's family.

Carey's gaze lingered on the photographs, realization dawning slowly. An eight-by-ten black-and-white photo from a graduation. A silver-framed photo of a baby.

Photographs of a family.

Her family.

55

"Where is he?" Kovac demanded, striding into the war room.

"Interview three," Dawes said. "You can watch through the glass."

"Fuck that. He's my suspect," Kovac said.

"Lose the attitude, Detective Sergeant Sam Kovac, unless you really want to go back to wearing a uniform," Dawes said, getting in his face. "That first word can be very easily detached from your rank. That's what's going to happen if you pull another stunt like you did with David Moore."

"I won't."

Dawes arched a brow. "This is a high-profile case, Sam. Every newsie, every politico in the city, is watching this one. I've got the chief of detectives, the deputy chief, and the chief of police breathing down my neck.

I can't risk you jeopardizing this interview by intimidating the suspect—"

"He kidnapped a judge!" Kovac shouted. "For Christ's sake! What are we supposed to fucking do? Serve him tea and crumpets?"

"You get to watch or you get to leave."

"Didn't his second wife say that to him on their honeymoon?" Tippen said, to break the tension.

Kovac kept his focus on Dawes and tried to check the storm of emotions tearing through him. He wanted to get into the interview room with Donny Bergen. Bergen had been picked up at his downtown apartment, interrupted by Tippen and friends while packing a couple of duffel bags, ready to catch a plane to St. Kitts.

"Look, LT," Kovac said, lowering his voice several decibels. "I'm the one talked to the sister. She will have warned him about me. I'm the one on top of Dickhead Moore. I've put half a dozen calls in to Ivors to rattle his cage. He's part of this too.

"I'm the one who's been dogging these creeps," he said. "You go in there, it's a whole new ball game to them."

Dawes stared at him, weighing the pros

and cons. She didn't look happy. Kovac hoped that that was a good sign. He didn't know her well enough yet to be able to predict her. This was their first high-profile case together.

She was probably considering all the things the brass had told her about him when she had taken the job. Someone had no doubt told her about Amanda Savard's having killed herself in front of him. How it had taken him months to get himself together after that. Now she saw him losing his cool over Carey Moore.

Kovac held his hands out to his sides in a gesture of surrender. "Let me go in with you. Bring a gun. If I get out of line, you can shoot me."

"Why has he never made that offer to me?" Liska asked.

"Because you'd do it," Elwood said.

"There is that possibility."

Dawes gave a long-suffering sigh. "Do you have another career to fall back on?" she asked irritably.

In the background, Tippen said, "If Donny Bergen goes up the river, there'll be a void in the porn industry."

Liska hit him in the arm. "Yuck!"

"I've been told I can flip a mean hamburger," Kovac said.

The lieutenant looked up at the ceiling and shook her head. "Lord help me. All right, Detective. We go in together. But if you put one toe over the line, you'd better go get yourself a hairnet and a spatula, 'cause you'll be working under the golden arches come Monday."

Long Donny Bergen sat at one side of the table, kicked back in his chair, his arms crossed over his chest, his legs stretched out and spread a little. A studied pose to suggest arrogance and to show off his most famous attribute, bulging in his jeans.

He was otherwise not a big guy. Slim and wiry, he could have passed for a woman if he wore a skirt. He looked a lot like his sister—the narrow face, the pallor, the perpetually red tip of the nose.

Kovac wanted to ask him if he and Ginnie got a family rate from their dealer. He wanted to walk around behind him and yank the chair out from under him. He did neither.

"Mr. Bergen, I'm Lieutenant Dawes. This

is Detective Sergeant Kovac. Thank you for meeting with us."

Dawes took the seat nearest Bergen, also sitting sideways to the table. Casual, legs crossed, one arm on the tabletop. Kovac took the seat across from Bergen. He didn't smile; he didn't speak. He just stared at the guy.

Bergen laughed. "I didn't have a lot of choice, did I? The goon squad came calling."

Dawes looked surprised. "Oh, but you're not under arrest, Mr. Bergen. I'm sorry if you got that impression."

Confusion crept in under the asshole bravado. He sat up and leaned toward the lieutenant. "I'm not under arrest?"

"No. We just wanted to have a talk with you about this business with David Moore. Apparently, you know him quite well. We thought you might be able to help us uncover something about his wife's disappearance."

Bergen looked suspicious. "I'm not under arrest."

"This is what's known as a noncustodial interview."

"So I don't have to say anything. I don't need a lawyer."

"You don't need a lawyer for this."

"So I can leave?" Bergen said. He stood up, adjusted himself, and started for the door, giving a little wave. "It's been real."

Kovac tensed, waiting for Dawes to do something. The guy he believed had assaulted Carey—at the very least—was reaching out for the doorknob.

"No," Dawes said calmly. "It doesn't really work that way. Please come have a seat, Mr. Bergen."

"Or what?" Bergen challenged.

"Or I have you held as a material witness and you can meet some new and interesting people in jail."

"Are you threatening me?"

"Not at all," Dawes said, rising from her seat. "I'm just telling you how it is, Donny," she said, drifting over to the door. "The powers that be in this city are very upset about the abduction of one of our leading jurists."

"I thought she was a judge," Bergen said impatiently. "I don't know anything about it anyway."

"Perhaps not," Dawes said. Then, just with the slightest changes of posture and expression, she was no longer the cordial hostess. Her voice took on an edge. "But you're going to go back to that table, put your tight little ass in that chair, and tell us everything you *do* know, or you're gonna need that lawyer for a whole lot of unpleasant reasons."

Kovac rubbed a hand across his mouth while he grinned to himself. She was good.

"Better listen to her, Junior," he said. "You know how big a big shot you think you are? The people she's talking about pick their teeth with little pricks like you."

Bergen's look went from Kovac to Dawes. "Does he have to be here?"

"It's his case. What's the matter, Donny? You think Detective Kovac maybe knows a little too much about your family matters?"

Bergen shook a finger at Kovac. "My sister said he pushed her around. She's gonna sue the city."

"That's cute," Kovac said. "A junkie whore takes on City Hall. I can't wait to see what she wears to the press conference."

Bergen leaned a little toward him across the safe distance of the table width. "Ginnie has friends, asshole."

"Lots of them, I'm sure," Kovac said. "Her dealer, her johns, a pimp or two . . ."

"She's not a prostitute."

"Not anymore," Kovac said. "Why fuck a hundred guys for a few bucks a pop when she can just latch on to one fat tick like David Moore? She gets his wife out of the picture, she's got it made. Nice house on Lake of the Isles, rich husband. Too bad money can't buy acceptance. To the people in that neighborhood, she'll always be a junkie whore."

Bergen was getting red in the face. "Stop calling her that!"

"Have a seat, Mr. Bergen," Dawes said, back to being Miss Manners. "Clear this up for us. If you haven't done anything wrong, there shouldn't be any problem doing that."

Bergen sat down, hooking the heel of one cowboy boot over the rung of the chair. He leaned an elbow on his knee and looked away, nibbling on his thumbnail like a rat grooming itself.

"Can you tell us where you were Friday evening?" Dawes asked.

"I thought I wasn't a suspect."

"We're trying to corroborate the statements of a third party."

"I was out," he said. "On the town. Like always when I'm here."

"You're not a permanent resident of the city?"

"It's too fucking cold."

"Where do you live?"

"L.A. Encino."

The San Fernando Valley. Smut capital of America. Kovac had read it in a magazine. Hard-core porn movies were routinely made in rented houses in otherwise normal family neighborhoods.

Picturing Long Donny Bergen there brought a whole new meaning to "boy next door."

"Yeah, look," Kovac said. "This is all nice and chatty, and I'm sure you'd be an interesting person to talk to, if I didn't happen to think you're a maggot on the asshole of life. But let's cut to the chase, Junior.

"We know you popped into the lobby bar at the Marquette Friday night to meet up with Sis and the gang. What was that about?"

"It wasn't about anything," Bergen said, belligerent. "So I stopped to have a drink with my sister. So what?"

"Where were you before that?"

"At my apartment, getting ready to go out."

"Was anyone there with you?"

Bergen turned to the lieutenant again. "How is this supposed to square someone else's story? I think it sounds like you're trying to pin something on me."

"Knowing if a particular someone was with you will be important to that other person," Dawes explained. It was a lie, of course, but that didn't matter. They were under no obligation to tell the truth during the course of an interview; only the interviewee risked a penalty for lying.

Bergen narrowed his eyes. "Who?"

Dumb as a post, this kid, Kovac thought. Good thing for him he had other talents.

"We can't tell you that, Donny," Kovac said. "If we tell you, you'll decide what story you want to tell, depending if you like this person or hate them."

Bergen turned that puzzle over and over in his narrow little head.

"That means you have to tell us the truth," Dawes said.

He frowned at that, clearly thinking he was damned if he did and damned if he didn't.

"What's the matter?" Kovac asked. "Did you have some underage girl there with you?"

"No! I don't need to do underage girls."

Kovac gave his crocodile smile. "That's not about need, though, is it, Junior?"

"I was alone."

"Between six and seven," Dawes specified. "You were home alone."

"That's what I said."

"Did anybody see you leave the building?"

"I don't know. I don't think so."

"You live in California," Kovac said, "but you keep an apartment here. You must be here a lot."

"My manager says it's a good investment."

"What do you do with it when you're not around? Rent it out?"

"What's the difference?"

Kovac shrugged. "Just curious."

"Did you speak with your sister on the phone Friday afternoon?" Dawes asked.

"Yeah. Three, three-thirty. She asked me if I wanted to stop by the hotel for a drink."

"Do you happen to know if David Moore was with her at the time?"

"I guess he was."

"How well do you know him?" Kovac asked.

"We don't hang out. Except for the fact this one has bucks, I usually don't like my sister's taste in men."

"How did you meet him?"

"Through Eddie. A year, year and a half ago."

"Eddie?" Dawes asked.

"Yeah. Eddie Ivors. I know Eddie through the business. He introduced me to Dave."

"Through the triple-X movie business?" Kovac said.

"Yeah." Bergen gave a little laugh and a smirk. "Everybody thinks Eddie made his money with theaters. Eddie made his money in porn and used the money to buy the theaters. Mr. Respectable Business-man."

"And David Moore? How was he con-nected to Ivors?" Kovac asked, his blood pressure rising again. David Moore, the crit-ically acclaimed documentary filmmaker. Kovac knew what Bergen was going to say before he said it.

"He's into it. He's directed some stuff for Eddie. Hard-core."

Kovac shoved his chair back from the table so fast, it tipped over as he stood up. Donny Bergen cringed and cowered. Lieutenant Dawes jumped and twisted around to give him her full attention. Kovac was barely aware of either of them.

That piece-of-shit, rat bastard.

He could see David Moore's photograph from his Web site, the smug, superior artiste. He wasn't any better than a pimp, no, worse than a pimp. He sopped up money making filth, and still lived off his wife.

That meant he had bank accounts no one knew about. Greedy fool. He had money of his own, but he paid for his mistress out of the family funds. Un-fucking-believable.

Kovac started to rub his temples and pace back and forth in front of the door.

Dawes looked at him cautiously. "Are you all right, Detective? Do you need to step out?"

Before Kovac could answer, someone banged on the door. Elwood stuck his head into the room.

He directed himself to Kovac in a hushed voice. "I think I might have found Stan Dempsey's hidey-hole."

56

The bottom dropped out of Carey's stomach. She felt the blood drain from her head to her feet.

Lucy's baby photo in the silver frame. The black-and-white picture of Carey's graduation from law school, her father gazing at her with unmistakable pride. These were the photographs she kept on the nightstand beside her bed at home.

She looked around the room again, slowly, recognition dawning with a sickening surety. *Her* champagne bucket. *Her* wineglasses. *Her* pillows. *Her* blankets. Karl Dahl had looted her home, taking things he thought she might want to have with her.

God help me.

"I even brung you some clothes," Karl said, pointing to where he had hung them on an old hook sticking out of a crumbling wall. Dresses. Lingerie.

He meant for her to stay. He seemed to think she should be happy and grateful for the honor.

"You're cold," Karl said. "You should have a wrap."

The perfect host. The scene was so incredibly surreal, it was difficult to believe it was really happening. Karl Dahl stood before her, blood all over the left side of his face and neck, bald-headed, wearing women's makeup, wearing women's clothes. He hadn't said one word about what she had done to his face. It was almost as if he didn't notice it.

The gold chenille throw had come from the love seat in her den. David had used it for a blanket Friday night. It smelled like cigar smoke and gin and a woman's cloying perfume. Carey wanted to throw it away from her as if it were a snake, but Karl wrapped it carefully around her shoulders.

"Please, sit down," he said, guiding her toward the only chair in the room, a cheap plastic lawn chair that had seen better days a decade past.

The chair was rusted and filthy; it was difficult to tell what color the plastic tubing might have been back when. It was the kind of chair she remembered from her teen years. She and all her girlfriends had had the lounge version, because you could make it lie completely flat, making it perfect for sunbathing.

In a brief flash she saw herself and Sandy Butler flat on their bellies on the chairs in her backyard, the radio blasting. They had been so innocent.

"I really should go, Karl," she said. "Not that I don't appreciate all you've done, but I need to go home for my daughter. She'll be afraid, wondering where I've gone."

Karl frowned at that, but he didn't say anything as he dug through a couple of grocery bags, pulling out food that had probably come from Carey's kitchen.

"She's all right, isn't she, Karl?" Carey asked, almost more afraid of knowing than not knowing.

He didn't answer. His brow furrowed as he opened a box of Triscuits.

"Please, tell me she's all right, Karl."

Without even glancing at her, he got out a summer sausage that already had a third of it missing, and a knife that had come from the block on the counter just to the right of her stove.

The sense of dread in Carey's chest was so heavy she could hardly breathe.

"Please, Karl . . ." she said, unable to keep the anxiety from her voice.

Karl stood suddenly and pointed at her with the knife. "You don't have her no more," he said angrily. "You're with me now."

Carey felt everything crumble inside her. She put her hands over her face and began to cry as silently as she could. He had killed her daughter. Her sweet, innocent child, who would never have been able to identify him even if she had seen him.

What had he done to her?

Again the Haas murder scene flashed through her memory.

It was too much. She rested her elbows on her thighs and rocked herself as she began to sob.

Her daughter was dead because of her, because of this lunatic killer who believed she had championed his cause. She wanted to die. She wanted Karl Dahl to come to her and slit her throat and be done with it. She rocked herself harder, keening.

"I didn't mean that," Karl said irritably. "I didn't mean she's dead."

He came and knelt beside the chair, putting a hand on her arm.

"Please don't cry so, Carey," he said softly. "I didn't mean for you to cry. You're my angel."

"Oh, my God," Carey mumbled behind her hands.

"It's just that you're with me now," he explained. "You're with me. You're my angel."

"Please stop saying that," Carey said, her voice trembling. "The police will be looking for me, you know."

"That don't matter," Karl said, matter-of-fact. "They got no idea where you are."

"You'll go to prison for the rest of your life if you hurt me. If you let me go—"

"They gotta catch me first," Karl snapped. "And if they catch me, I'll go to prison for the rest of my sorry life no matter what. Now, I don't want to hear no more about it."

He went to another grocery bag and pulled out one of David's exotic beers.

For Christmas the year before, Carey had signed him up for the Beer of the Month Club. That was the only thing she'd given him he hadn't had some complaint about.

The memory of a better Christmas was the two of them the second Christmas after they had married. They were having a party. Mistletoe had made the rounds, courtesy of one of their friends. She saw David laughing, trim and fit and handsome; herself laughing too, leaning against him with her hand on the flat of his belly. He was holding a poinsettia over his head and had told her that the poinsettia—being that much larger than mistletoe—meant they had to go upstairs and make a baby. And so they had, after their guests had gone home. They had been so happy.

"You want something to drink?" Karl asked.

Carey just stared at him.

He brought her a bottle of Fiji water and a couple of Triscuits with summer sausage. Hors d'oeuvres. She took a sip of the water. It went down like a rock in her aching throat. She shook her head at the food.

She probably should have eaten it. She hadn't had a decent meal in three days. She needed strength if she was going to get out of this mess. But the idea of food made her want to gag.

She pulled the chenille throw around herself, shivered, and coughed.

"You should have a lie-down," Karl said. "I know you wasn't comfortable in that trunk. I'm sorry about that. And I'm sorry I had to choke you like I did. I had to do that so you wouldn't make a fuss."

He sat on a box, eating his lunch, as if this were a perfectly normal situation for him. Maybe it was.

"Where are you from, Karl?" she asked.

"Kansas. But I ain't been back there in a long time."

"Why is that?"

He pretended not to have heard her, his little trick for avoiding a topic.

"What brought you to Minneapolis?"

"A train," he said, and laughed and laughed.

"You like moving around from town to town?"

"It suits me," he said, nodding. "Can't stay in one place too long."

"Why is that?"

His face darkened as he looked down at the knife he'd used to cut the sausage, a nine-inch boning knife Carey knew to be sharp enough to cut paper. "It's just best to move on."

Because he went from town to town murdering innocent people? The system had coughed up a record on Karl Dahl, but there was no way of knowing what he might have done and gotten away with. He was one of those people who drifted along below the radar.

No one wanted to pay any attention to men like Karl, the strange, the quiet, the disenfranchised. All the ordinary citizens, with jobs and mortgages and kids, wanted nothing more than for the Karl Dahls of the world to pass through and keep on going.

Karl might have quietly left a string of homicides in his wake as he'd moved from place to place. He could have been invisible, blending into the background, calling no attention to himself.

If not for the neighbor stupidly stepping out of his house to videotape the tornado bearing down on the city that fateful day, Karl Dahl might have walked away from the Haas massacre into the mists, hopped another train, and gone on to another state, and the Haas murders would have gone unsolved.

"Come on," he said.

He abandoned his lunch and approached her again.

Carey sat very still, like a small prey animal afraid to move or breathe. He put a hand around her wrist and pulled her up out of the chair. Not roughly, but firmly.

"I made this nice bed for you," he said. "I want you to lie down on it."

She wouldn't have thought it possible, but the sense of dread became heavier, more oppressive. She knew too much about what had been done to Marlene Haas.

Had it started like this? Karl fixating on the woman, deciding she was his angel because she had helped him out, then wanting to possess her physically and sexually, flying into a rage when she tried to reject him. The rage unleashing the demons that lived in his soul. The demons spinning themselves into a frenzy.

"Lie down now," Karl ordered her as she stepped to the edge of the nest he had made for her. The idea of his touching her, forcing himself on her, was beyond revolting.

Afraid to antagonize him, Carey lowered herself to the floor, lay down on her side, curled into the fetal position. Karl sat down and put her head in his lap and stroked her hair.

"You sleep now, angel. We have all the time in the world."

For what? she wondered. Did he think she would become his willing traveling companion? Or did he think that in death her soul would become his forever?

"You're with me now. I haven't had an angel in a long, long time."

"You had an angel once?" she asked in a hushed voice. "What was her name?"

He didn't answer the question. Finally, he said very softly, "I had an angel once."

"What happened to her?" Carey asked.

Karl looked down into her face, expressionless. "She went to heaven . . . like angels do."

57

Carey held every muscle in her body tight against the violent trembling shuddering through her. She closed her eyes and pretended to sleep while Karl Dahl continued to stroke her hair and whisper to her, *"You are my perfect angel,"* over . . . and over . . . and over.

She had no idea how much time passed. An hour that seemed like minutes. Minutes that seemed like an hour.

Questions of who his last angel had been played through her mind, the possibilities all bad. Men like Karl didn't come from loving homes with doting parents. They came from unhappy childhoods. Absent or abusive father. A mother who either blamed the child for everything wrong in her life or clung to the son because of her abusive husband.

The child learned the power of violence, and his only example of a man's relationship with a woman was a terrible, distorted story laced with hate and self-loathing.

Some people would have pitied the Karl Dahls of the world. She pitied Karl the child, but a sad story was not license to commit murder. Carey knew plenty of people with similar backgrounds—cops, lawyers, social workers—who had suffered a Karl Dahl childhood but raised themselves above it, instead of succumbing to it.

But then she was a prosecutor by nature, and prosecutors tended to think in black-and-white. Good or Evil. Innocent or Guilty.

And as a judge, she was supposed to operate with a blindfold on.

She wondered about Karl's last angel and what had happened to her. Did he consider his mother his angel, and had she died of old age or disease or her husband's brutality? Had his angel been his teenage love? Or his first victim? Or his last victim?

Marlene Haas had been kind to him, had offered him work, had offered him food. He had returned her kindness with horror. Karl Dahl was not a man destined for happy endings.

Based on a store of terrible knowledge, Carey projected what would happen to her if she couldn't escape. Karl would play out his little fantasy of loving and caring for her, but he would tire of it or feel the need to move on. Or she would do something to anger him, and that anger would be a trigger to his rage, and in his rage he would kill her.

"Can't stay in one place too long."

"Why is that?"

His face darkened as he looked down at the knife he'd used to cut the sausage. . . .

"It's just best to move on."

He couldn't take her with him. She would slow him down and draw people's attention to him. He would see only one practical and expedient solution to the situation.

Carey opened her eyes a crack. She could see the knife he had stolen from her home, lying on the makeshift table maybe six feet away.

She could feel the shape of her cell phone in her pants pocket.

Karl moved away from her, easing her head down on one of the pillows. He spoke to her in the softest of whispers, as if he believed her subconscious could hear him.

"Now, I have to step outside to relieve my-self, angel. I'm sorry, but I'm having to make sure you don't try to leave me."

Carey lay very still as he moved to her feet. He slipped a plastic cable tie around one ankle and then the other, looping the second through the first, hobbling her. Then used more cable ties to attach the hobble to a concrete block. She probably wouldn't be able to stand up, let alone run.

She listened to him move around the little room; then she couldn't hear him anymore. She counted to twenty, afraid if she opened her eyes sooner he would be standing in the doorway, watching her; but he was gone.

Shaking like a palsy victim, Carey sat up, fished the phone out of her pocket, and pressed the button to turn it on. She held it against her breast to muffle the little tune it played as it came to life, and she watched the screen anxiously as it told her it was searching for a signal.

"Come on, come on," she whispered. She was shaking so badly, she was afraid she would drop the thing.

One bar lit up on the signal indicator, then two. The battery icon in the lower right-hand corner showed only a sliver of power left.

"Come on, come on. . . ."

A third signal bar lit, and the brand name of the phone service appeared across the top of the screen. She had a connection.

Carey punched Kovac's number, listened to his phone ring on the end of the call.

"Come on, Sam. . . ."

58

"There's a cabin on one of the small lakes off Minnetonka," Elwood said. "It's owned by a Walter Dempsey. I found a reference to a Walter Dempsey in Stan's personnel file from a few years back."

"Did you call the local cops?" Kovac asked.

"They're sending three units to lock the place down, and take Dempsey into custody if he's there."

"You and Tinks go out there. See what's what. Who knows? Maybe we'll get lucky. Maybe he went back there for a breather after he finished his craft project on Kenny Scott."

"If he's not there, we pull back," Elwood said, "keep the local coppers on surveillance. They can move in and grab him when he shows."

"He's probably got an arsenal in the cabin," Kovac said.

"I already warned them." Elwood nodded toward the door to the interview room. "How's that going?"

Kovac scowled. "These people make me want to go take a hot shower. Bunch of fucking pervs."

"Literally," Elwood said.

"And Tippen recognized this asshole?"

"Makes you wonder."

"I don't want to wonder," Kovac said with disgust. "Jesus Christ. Remind me never to sit in a chair after he gets up from it."

"He's a student of the cinema," Elwood said seriously. "X-rated films are, like it or not, a subgenre, and protected by the First Amendment rights to freedom of expression."

"Somehow, I don't think the founding fathers were thinking of *Debbie Does Dallas* when they wrote that," Kovac said dryly. "Tell him he'll go blind watching that shit."

The cell phone clipped to his belt rang. He

snapped the holder free and looked at the screen.

"Oh, my God," he breathed as his heart began to pound.

Carey.

59

"Come on, Sam. . . . Come on, Sam. . . ." she breathed against the body of the phone, her eyes riveted to the opening that had once been a doorway into the room.

"Carey? Jesus God, are you all right?"

"No," she murmured, terrified to raise her voice.

"Carey, can you speak up? I can barely hear you."

"No. I can't. He's going to come back soon."

"Who? Who took you?"

"Karl Dahl."

There was an uncharacteristic beat of silence before he asked, "Where are you?"

"In an old munitions building. It's a ruin. It's burned. And I can smell a refinery of some kind. I can't see it, but I can smell it. Hurry, Sam, please."

"I'll be there ASAP. You hang on. I'll be there as fast as I can."

Something made a sound in another part of the building.

Carey turned the phone off, dropped it, snatched it up, fumbled with it, stuck it back into her pocket.

She glanced again at the door.

Don't watch the door. Get the knife.

Unable to get up because of the ligatures, she maneuvered onto her knees and scooted closer to the box/table.

Arm outstretched, leaning, even her fingers trying to elongate themselves, and still she couldn't quite reach it.

She tried a second time, leaning even further.

An inch short, maybe two.

She tried to move the concrete block but couldn't. Another sound of movement or scuffle came. Carey couldn't tell where it was coming from. The place was probably teeming with rats and mice, and who knew what else. Karl had already been gone longer than she had expected.

One last time she focused on the knife,

leaned forward, stretched, stretched until her hand was trembling. She glanced again toward the door.

Don't watch the door. Get the knife!

It was still just beyond her reach.

She pulled back six inches, regaining her balance, took a deep breath, and lunged.

She hit the end of her tether at the same time the heel of her hand hit the box.

The box scooted away.

Her fingertips caught the handle of the knife, scratched it toward her. It fell from the box.

She snatched at it again.

Scraped it toward her.

Grabbed the handle of the knife.

Carey lay there for a handful of seconds, breathing hard, then pushed herself backward and struggled to get back onto her knees. She had the knife.

Her black shirt was brown with dirt. Her face was probably no better. She did her best to brush herself off, then took the throw that had covered her and wiped her face.

A sound like metal hitting metal startled her. Had it come from inside? Outside?

Either way, she was already on borrowed time.

Pulling the throw up around herself, she lay back down on her side, hiding the knife beneath her leg.

Another sound. A crunch. Another, another. Footsteps. Karl.

Come on, Sam. . . .

Carey closed her eyes, hoping he wouldn't come to wake her, hoping that he hadn't decided it was time to make love to his angel.

She didn't want to pull the knife. There was a much greater chance that he would get the knife away from her and kill her with it than there was of her killing him. And she would have to kill him—not wound him—if she was to have any hope of getting away.

The footsteps drew closer.

Come on, Sam. . . . Come on, Sam. . . .

Kovac ran down the hall to the war room, catching hold of the door frame to stop himself. Everyone in the room turned toward him, their expressions going sober at the sight of him.

"An old, burned-out munitions plant or dump near a refinery," he called out.

Tippen grabbed his coat off the back of a chair. "I know it. Let's go."

They ran out the door of the building and down the stone steps. Colors and sounds of the media people on the stairs and sidewalk registered only dimly in Kovac's mind. A blur. White noise.

He had parked his car in the loading zone, along with Dawes's car and Liska's car and the cars of the entire task force. But he didn't go for his car. He ran up to a uniform sitting back against the hood of a squad car, watching the show.

"Gimme your keys."

The officer straightened. "What the hell . . . ?"

"Gimme your goddamn keys!" Kovac shouted.

"Detectives, Homicide," Tippen said, showing his badge. "Give him the fucking keys!"

Kovac yanked the keys out of the guy's hand, rounded the hood, climbed in the car. He gunned the engine, threw the shift into reverse as soon as Tippen's ass hit the other seat. Cars blasted their horns as Kovac shot the squad car backward into their paths. He shifted into drive and peeled out, leaving rubber smoking on the pavement.

He hadn't driven a squad car in years, but he still knew where the switches were for lights and sirens.

"Where are we going?" he shouted at Tippen.

"Thirty-five W south. I'll give directions as we go."

The speedometer swung to ninety as they came off the ramp onto the freeway. Tippen buckled in and braced himself.

"What the fuck is this traffic?" Kovac demanded as he tried to weave through without losing too much speed.

Ahead, all he could see across the lanes of traffic were taillights. Cars were trying to pull out of his way but had nowhere to go. He hit the brakes and held the wheel against a skid, and the car rocked to a halt.

"Vikings-Packers game," Tippen said.

Kovac looked at him, wild eyed. "Don't tell me this is a pack of fucking Cheeseheads going back to Wisconsin!"

He didn't expect an answer or want one.

Tippen got on the sound system, and his voice blasted out of the speaker mounted on the car.

"Move aside! This is a police emergency! Move aside!"

Drivers all around were staring at them like deer in headlights.

Kovac grabbed the handset and shouted, *"Get the fuck out of the way!!"*

Cars gave an inch here, a foot there, as he tried to wedge the squad car to the right, going for the shoulder. A sickening crunch sounded as he clipped the front end of an SUV, then the rear end of another.

When he hit the shoulder, he floored the

accelerator, and the big car lunged forward, flying past the traffic at a frightening speed.

"Exit here!" Tippen shouted pointing. "Cut across. We'll get on Fifty-five!"

Kovac touched the brakes, once, twice, took the exit too fast, just missed two cars at the bottom.

By the grace of God he wouldn't kill anybody.

And he wouldn't be too late.

61

Carey lay as still as she possibly could as she listened to Karl moving around the room.

Come on, Sam. . . .

He said nothing, maybe out of courtesy so she could sleep, as crazy as that sounded. He wanted her to get her rest.

The sounds of movement stopped. Near her. She could feel him watching her. She held her breath and kept her fingertips on the grip of the knife.

He touched her left hand, which lay on top of the blanket. It took everything in her not to jerk it away.

"You can wake up now, Judge."

The voice was not Karl's. It was lower, a gravelly monotone with an odd, slow cadence.

Carey opened her eyes and looked up, her heart stopping as she saw the craggy, homely face dark with beard stubble, the rubbery-looking too-red lips.

Stan Dempsey.

"Your good friend Karl Dahl isn't coming back in."

"He's not my friend," Carey said.

"Not anymore. You can't help him anymore."

"I never wanted to help him in the first place."

"You just don't get it, do you? You're supposed to hand out justice. The guilty have to pay. Actions have consequences."

Carey knew better than to argue or try to explain.

"Is he dead?" she asked.

"I have special plans for him," Dempsey said cryptically.

"How did you find this place?"

"Simple police work: I followed the car," he said.

"You were watching my house."

"Have been off and on for some time now. I haven't had much else to do with myself this past year," he said. "I know a lot about your life, Judge Moore. Where you live, what your schedule is, where your little girl goes to school.

"I know who comes and goes from your house, and what cars they drive. When that car came past me this morning, I knew that wasn't your nanny driving."

"Did you know it was Dahl?" Carey asked.

"We've talked enough now. Get up," he said, pulling on her arm. "Judge Moore, you're under arrest for crimes against humanity. You have the right to remain silent. Anything you say can and will be used against you. . . ."

62

"I don't think I can stand up," Carey said. "I'm tied to some kind of weight."

Dempsey huffed his impatience, snatched at the gold chenille throw that covered her feet, and tossed the end farther up her legs. He kept the gun in his right hand, and with his left he pulled a hunting knife with a wide, vicious-looking serrated blade from a leather sleeve on his belt. With two flicks of his wrist the cable ties were history. He holstered the knife.

"Now, get up."

The throw crumpled around Carey as she sat up. But with the fingers of her right hand, she managed to hold on to a piece of it to cover the knife.

"What are you going to do to me?" she

asked as she pushed herself up to her knees.

"You'll have a trial. I'll pronounce sentence and determine your punishment. Same as I did with that lawyer."

He sounded perfectly sane as he said it. He had decided that this was his job, and he was going to do it, and that was that.

"Kenny Scott?"

"Yeah, him. He got exactly what he deserved. So will you."

Carey had no idea what he might have done to Karl Dahl's attorney, but she didn't ask. She would find out soon enough, if Stan Dempsey had his way.

"You're a cop," she said. "You're a good cop. You've worked your whole life to protect and serve. How can you do this?"

He looked at her as if he couldn't believe she didn't know. "Because somebody has to."

Come on, Sam. . . .

"But you're breaking the law," Carey said. "How can you do that and talk about justice?"

"I don't see it that way," Dempsey said, the gun still trained on her in an almost casual way.

"You'll go to prison, Detective," she said, hoping in vain that using his rank might jar something in his conscience.

"No, I won't."

Carey weighed the idea of telling him Kovac was on his way. But she didn't think the information would change his course of action, except that he might feel compelled to kill her sooner rather than later.

"How long have you been a cop?" she asked. "Twenty years? More? None of it will mean anything if you do this. This is how you'll be remembered, how you'll be judged."

His wide mouth curled in a sneer. "You don't know anything. You sit up on the bench in your robes," he said with disdain. "It's just a big game with the lawyers, and you're a referee. The victims don't mean anything to you people."

"That's not true."

"Look how you treated Marlene Haas. She was a decent woman just trying to raise a family. Do you want to know the kind of hell Karl Dahl put her through?"

"I know what he did."

"Yet you give that son of a bitch every

break you can. Maybe you can't know what it is to be a victim until you are one. Get up."

Carey couldn't wait for rescue any longer. When she rose to her feet, Dempsey would make her drop the throw. Either she would have to drop the knife with it, or he would take it away from her.

"Get up," he said again, angrier.

A rumbling sound rolled over the building. Dempsey turned his head and looked up. Quickly, Carey worked her fingertips down the handle of the knife to the blade, drawing it up under the too-long sleeve of her black shirt inch by inch. She rose as Dempsey turned back to her.

"Storm coming in," he said, as if she would care.

He motioned her out of the room with the barrel of the gun.

Debris bit into the soles of her bare feet. Carey tried not to make a sound. It would probably make him angrier that she could complain about stepping on rocks and broken glass when Marlene Haas had been forced to endure unimaginable torture.

Stan Dempsey would have no sympathy for her. Justice, sure and swift, was what he had in mind. And Carey feared it would be a terrible brand of justice.

She would have to act soon. If she could do it as they came out of the building . . .

To even have a thought in her head of pushing a knife into another human being was appalling to her. She'd spent her career fighting against violence. In her entire life, she had never committed a violent act against another human being, or any other form of life, for that matter.

She didn't know if she could do it. What she held in her hand wasn't a piece of plastic that would do little damage. It was a boning knife as sharp as a razor. She tried to imagine what it was going to feel like to push the tip of it through someone's skin, through muscle, into organs. The idea made her feel sick. She was trembling to her very core.

Come on, Sam. . . .

She had no way of knowing how near or far away help might be. If Stan Dempsey put her in a vehicle and started driving . . .

Carey had prosecuted and presided over enough cases of rape and murder to know that once a woman got into a car with a man bent on violence, she as good as sentenced herself to death.

As they neared the doorway where she and Karl had entered the building, she could see that the brilliant sun that had blinded her when Dahl had opened the trunk hours earlier was gone. Heavy gray clouds had rolled in, their bellies sagging low overhead, giving the light an eerie cast as it struggled to penetrate them.

Another volley of thunder rumbled overhead.

Slowly, Carey began to let the knife slip down through her hand inch by cautious inch.

As they stepped out, Dempsey turned her to the left, and she gasped.

Karl Dahl had been handcuffed to the old iron railing on the stairs and hung limp from the cuffs, unconscious—or dead—his head covered in blood.

"That's what he had coming to him," Dempsey said. "And that's just the start of it."

"Oh, my God," Carey whispered.

Dahl's eyes were half-open, his jaw slack. He wasn't moving. She couldn't tell whether or not he was breathing. There was so much blood, it looked as if someone had poured a gallon of red paint over his head.

"Oh, my God."

This was what Stan Dempsey meant by justice. Her stomach rolled and cramped, and she leaned over, heaving, nothing coming out, her body trying to reject what she had just seen.

"That's justice!" Dempsey shouted, leaning over her. "That's justice!"

Now or never . . .

Carey came up fast, the top of her head cracking hard into Dempsey's chin. He took a half step back, straightening. Carey twisted toward him, bringing her right hand up into him with as much force as she could. The knife went into his belly so easily it shocked her.

Dempsey folded at the waist and staggered backward, pulling himself off the knife Carey still held in her hand. He looked surprised. This hadn't been part of his plan.

He put his left hand where the knife had gone into him. Blood ran out over his fingers. In his right hand, he still held the gun, but limply, as if he had forgotten it was there.

"You killed me," he said in accusation. "I wouldn't have killed you."

Carey stood there staring at him, horrified, unable to move.

Without warning, Dempsey lunged at her.

Too slow to react, Carey backpedaled, off balance, then off the landing. Stan Dempsey fell with her, came down on top of her, knocking the wind out of her. She tried to move but couldn't.

Dempsey groaned and tried to lift himself. Carey could feel his blood, warm and wet, soaking into her shirt.

Hysterical, she scrambled backward like a crab to get out from under him. Dempsey was on his hands and knees. Trying to draw breath, tears blurring her vision, Carey rolled over, got her feet under her, and ran, adrenaline pumping through her like high-octane fuel.

She ran toward the road, feeling out of control, feeling like her body was hurtling forward faster than her mind or her legs could go. Like running down a steep hill.

A gunshot blasted behind her.

She fell as if something caught her ankles from behind and yanked her legs out from under her. She hit the ground hard, bounced twice. Gravel dug into her palms, her elbows, her chin.

She landed in a heap, like a rag doll, and lay there, still.

In the back of her mind it registered very dimly that it had started to rain.

63

They cut the lights and siren when they neared the road Tippen said would take them to the munitions building. Kovac cut the speed even though it went hard against his sense of urgency. Half an hour had passed since he had taken Carey's call. A lot of bad shit could happen in half an hour.

"Karl Dahl will go into the annals of criminal psychology," Tippen said as they crept down the little-used side road. "He kills two women to get to the only woman who's done him any favors in who knows how long. Digging into the dark labyrinths of his mind for motive will be like spelunking into hell."

Kovac said nothing. It didn't matter to him why Karl Dahl would do anything. All that mattered was that he had. He had killed

Anka Jorgenson. He had killed Christine Neal. He had killed Marlene Haas and her two foster children. And now he had Carey.

"It's up here on the left," Tippen said. "What's the plan?"

"I don't have one."

"Great. What do I tell our backup units and the ambulance?" Tippen asked. "We can't go in there like the cavalry. Guns a-blazin'."

That was what Kovac wanted to do. He wanted to go in like a commando. But they couldn't risk that. If they went in aggressively and Dahl felt cornered, there was no telling what he might do. It then became a hostage situation. If they went in quietly, assessed the situation and considered their options, they had a better chance of taking Dahl by surprise, getting him away from Carey.

"There it is," Tippen said, pointing off to the left.

Kovac slowed the car. While it had gotten them out here faster than anything else would have, they couldn't drive past in a police cruiser. He pulled over to where a stand of mostly naked small trees offered some protection, put the car in park, killed the engine.

The building looked like a war ruin. It sat fifty yards or so back off the road in a wide-open patch of weeds. No cover. There was no way to go onto the property without being seen.

"Shit," he said. He rubbed his face with his hands, took a deep breath, and exhaled, trying to think. "We have to go in on foot. There's no other way to do it."

He stared at the building some more, trying not to wonder what might be going on inside even as they sat there, trying to formulate a plan.

"Sam," Tippen said. "Look up ahead. We're not alone."

An old pickup with a camper shell over the bed sat off the road on the access drive into a field down the road, partially obscured from view by another stand of small trees. Someone else who didn't want to be seen from the building where Dahl held Carey.

"Can you see the plates?"

Tippen gave him a look. "Can *you* see the plates?"

"Christ, we're old," Kovac said. "Bring the shotgun. Let's go."

They got out of the cruiser, careful not to make noise doing it. Leaving the doors open, they made a dash for the truck.

"Is this what they use for an undercover car in the sheriff's department?" Kovac said sarcastically when they stood at the nose of the pickup.

The truck had to be twenty years old. A Ford F-150. The once navy blue paint had faded over the years from sun and weather.

As Tippen called in the plate number on his cell phone, Kovac looked in the window of the cab. There was nothing in it. Not so much as a gum wrapper. He looked in through the windows of the camper shell. A couple of duffel bags, a small Igloo cooler.

He went around and opened the back to get a better look inside. One of the bags was long enough to hold a rifle. A luggage tag hung from one of the handles.

Kovac went cold as he read it.

"The truck belongs to a Walter Dempsey," Tippen said. "Safe to assume he's a relative of our man Stan."

Kovac popped the latch on the tailgate and dropped it open. He reached for the nearest of the duffel bags. It was unzipped. Inside was an assortment of tools—handsaws, screwdrivers, pliers . . . and a wood-burning tool.

"Great," Tippen said. "Double your maniacs, double your fun."

Kovac jammed his hands at his waist and paced around in a little circle. They didn't know jack shit about what might be going on in that building. There wasn't time to do reconnaissance, regroup, form a strategy. Carey was in there with two men bent on no good.

"Fuck it," he said. "Let's go in."

As he rounded the front end of the truck, he thought he heard voices in the distance. He walked faster. When he cleared the copse of trees, he broke into a run.

Someone was running toward the road.

A gunshot cracked the air.

The runner was Carey.

She tripped and fell hard.

She didn't move.

Kovac's mind was going wild. Had she been shot? Had she been dropped by Dempsey and a hunting rifle?

He didn't look beyond her to see but barreled down what once had been a driveway.

If the shooter had a scope, he was screwed, but he kept running.

"Carey!"

He dropped to his knees as he reached her.

"Carey!"

She lay facedown, crying weakly. Kovac put two fingers against her throat and found her pulse racing wildly.

He bent down close and brushed her hair back. "Carey, it's me. It's Sam. Can you hear me? Just lie still."

Feeling his way gingerly down her back, he expected his hand to come away bloody from the gunshot that had dropped her. But he couldn't find an entry wound.

Headlights washed over them. Tippen roared in with the squad car, skidding sideways to a stop between them and the building, giving them cover.

"Carey?" Kovac said. "Are you shot? Did he shoot you?"

All she could do was shake, and cry harder.

"I killed him!" she cried. "Oh, my God, I killed him!"

Kovac eased her over onto her side,

brushed her hair back from her face. His hand was shaking like an old man's.

"Shhh . . . It's okay, you're okay," he said softly.

He pulled his suit coat off and covered her with it.

Where the hell was backup? Where the hell was the ambulance?

She pushed herself up with one arm and tried to wipe her face with a hand that was covered in blood.

"Jesus Christ," he said under his breath. To Carey he said, "Lie down. Carey, lie down. Just lie down."

She shook her head. "No. I want to go home."

"Carey, lie down," Kovac said more forcefully. "You're bleeding."

She looked at her hand, confused.

"It's not mine," she said, but she sounded disoriented, maybe delusional.

"Goddammit, Carey, lie down, or I'm putting a knee into your chest and holding you down!"

Still confused, she sank back down. Kovac grabbed the lower part of the man's shirt she wore and tore it open. His hands came away bloody from the shirt, but he could find no wound on her belly.

"It's not mine," she said again, sitting up. "I killed him."

Clutching Kovac's arms, she fell against him, sobbing.

Kovac put his arms around her and held her tight while she cried, telling her again and again, "It's all right. It's over now. It's over."

He knew that that wasn't true. It wasn't over. Carey Moore couldn't just go home and walk back into her life as if nothing had ever happened. She would have to be interviewed, would have to recount and relive what had happened to her here. She would have to be checked over by a doctor for injuries. If she had been sexually assaulted, she would have to endure the rape exam.

God, he hoped that that wasn't the case. She'd had enough trauma without adding "rape survivor" to the list.

Tippen came around the back of the car. "Is she all right?"

Kovac didn't know quite how to respond, so he didn't. "What's going on? Where's Dahl? Where's Dempsey?"

"Dead and dead. Dahl was shot in the

face. Looks like Dempsey has a single stab wound."

"I killed him," Carey said, still crying against Kovac's shoulder. "I killed him. I killed a man."

Kovac stroked his hand over her wet hair. It had begun to rain in earnest. Thunder rumbled overhead. In the near distance he could hear the sirens approaching.

"Shhh . . . It's over," he said quietly. "It's over. You're safe now. That's all that matters."

64

The chaos of what had happened after Kovac had arrived at the scene was a jumbled
blur of color and activity in Carey's mind.
She remembered the police and sheriff's
cars arriving. The noise of men arguing over
jurisdiction. The carnival quality of the lights
from the cars and the ambulance. A para-
medic had given her something to calm her
down. It made her feel numb. All things considered, that was a good thing.

Instead of letting all of it swirl around and
around inside her head, she tried to focus
on the sense of relief and of being safe as
Sam Kovac had sat there in the pouring rain
and held her. That was what she wanted
now: to feel safe, to feel there was someone
right there to hold her if she needed it.

But that feeling also brought sadness as

she realized she hadn't had that kind of support in a very long time. When her father had been healthy, he had been her Rock of Gibraltar. David had never quite filled that place. He had tried to in the first years of their marriage but had gradually stepped out of that role. And she had gradually stopped wanting him to try harder.

The red-haired nurse from Friday night bustled into the room to check her IV and make notes in a chart.

"You know," she said, giving Carey a stern look completely betrayed by the kindness in her eyes, "we're getting pretty sick and tired of seeing you around this place."

"I promise this is my last time," Carey said.

"How are you feeling?"

"Numb."

"Good for you! Nothing like a little happy pill to take the edge off. I'm proposing the hospital put a gum ball machine in the nurses' lounge and keep it filled with Valium. Everyone would be so much happier to do their jobs."

Kovac peeked in the door.

"Is Casey giving you a hard time?" he asked, letting himself in.

The nurse gave him an innocent look. "Who, me?"

"The last time I was in her ER," he said, coming to stand beside the nurse, "she stapled my forehead together with an actual staple gun."

"I did not!" Casey protested, then gave him a mischievous grin. "And if I did, I'm sure you had it coming."

"I can still see her leaning over me. She came at me with that gun, and she said, 'There's no other way to put it. This is gonna hurt.' I still have nightmares."

Casey sniffed. "You should be so lucky to dream about me."

She turned back to Carey. "The doctor will be back to check in on you again later. Probably right after you've managed to fall asleep."

As she headed for the door, Kovac said, "That's Casey. I call her the Iron Leprechaun."

"But not when I'm close enough to hit him," Casey said as she left the room.

Hair wet and sticking up in all directions, Kovac stepped up to the side of the bed. He had traded his wet dress shirt for the top from a set of surgical scrubs.

"How are you feeling?"

"Dr. Kovac." She tried to smile but couldn't quite pull it off. "I don't know. I'm sure that sounds stupid."

He shook his head. "You've gone through something horrible, Carey. It'll take a while for you to process it all. And you can't do that alone. I've already been on the phone with Kate. If she wasn't looking after Lucy, she would have been down here at the speed of light."

Carey took a shaky breath. "Lucy. How is she? Is she all right?"

"She wants her mom back. She's scared."

"So was I," Carey admitted. "I was so afraid he'd done something to her, that she was hurt or—"

Kovac put a hand on her shoulder. "She's fine. Don't upset yourself thinking about what didn't happen. You've got plenty of real shit to deal with."

"You have a way with words, Detective," she said, trying again to find some small part of a smile. It was gone in the next instant. "He killed Anka, didn't he?"

Kovac nodded. "I'm sorry."

A profound sadness weighed on her. "I'll have to call her family in Sweden. How do I tell her parents their daughter is dead because of me?"

"You don't," he said. "She's not dead because of you. She's dead because Karl Dahl killed her."

Carey said nothing. It wasn't going to be that easy for her to let herself off the hook.

"So where was David through all this?" she asked.

Kovac frowned. "He was at the house when I last saw him. With his lawyer."

"His lawyer?"

"It's a long story."

"He didn't have anything to do with this," Carey said.

"He didn't have anything to do with Karl Dahl taking you," Kovac specified. "We're still looking into the assault."

Carey watched him. He was looking everywhere but at her.

"Do you know something I don't?"

"We might have found the twenty-five-thousand-dollar man," he said. "We don't need to talk about it now."

"You've just told me you've found the man you think my husband paid to have me killed," she said. "I need to talk about that.

Who is he? Can you connect him to a pay-off?"

"He's the girlfriend's brother. A porn actor by the name of Donny Bergen." He hesitated, took a deep breath, let it out. "Carey, your husband is into some pretty ugly stuff."

"I know," she said softly. "I came across some of it on his computer last night. It made me sick. I don't know who he is," she said, shaking her head. "I don't know what to say."

"You don't have to say anything," Kovac said. "I shouldn't have brought it up. You don't need anything more on your mind tonight. You need to get some rest. I just came in to make sure you're okay before I go."

"You have to go?" Carey asked him, feeling a little panicked at the thought. She didn't want to be alone with the memories of the things that had happened.

Kovac looked at her, tipping his head a little to one side. "You want me to stay?" The idea seemed to surprise him. "I'll stay. I'll stay as long as you want."

He sat on the edge of the bed, settling in. Carey looked away, embarrassed now that she'd said anything.

"I know this will sound stupid," she said. "I mean, I know I'm safe and that Lucy is safe, but . . ."

Kovac reached out and pressed a finger to her lips.

"It's all right. I know. You feel like something bad could happen at any second. You're ready to jump out of your skin. That's normal."

"I told you I don't make a very good victim," she said. "I don't know what to do."

"There's no handbook," Kovac said. "You have to feel what you feel. And it takes as long as it takes."

"That's scary," she admitted, then changed direction out of self-preservation. "What happened to Dahl? Is he dead?"

"Yeah. Stan Dempsey's last act: He shot and killed Karl Dahl. When I heard the shot, I thought he was shooting at you, but he shot Dahl. Made sure he'll never escape justice again."

"And Kenny Scott? Dempsey told me he would do to me what he did to Kenny. What did he do? Is Kenny dead?"

"No," Kovac said. "Dempsey roughed him up, tied him in a chair, and branded the word *GUILTY* across his forehead with a wood-burning tool."

He rattled that off so matter-of-factly. As if it were something he saw every day of the week. Of course, he'd seen far worse than that. So had she.

"He told me he wouldn't have killed me," she said softly. "Dempsey. After I . . . he said to me, 'You killed me. I wouldn't have killed you.'"

Kovac put a big hand over hers. "You couldn't have known that, Carey. You were in fear for your life. You did what you had to do to save yourself. For all you knew, Dempsey was gonna take you back to his nest and torture you the way Marlene Haas was tortured. I'd lay odds that's what he had planned for Dahl. He had a whole duffel bag full of stuff—a hacksaw, an electric knife, hammers, a meat fork, knives. He had all that with him for a reason."

Carey looked down at his hand on hers. Having just that much connection made her feel calmer.

"Have you ever had to kill anyone?" she asked.

"Once," he said. "I didn't want to, but I didn't have a choice. Neither did you."

Somehow that didn't make her feel any better.

"Does he have any family?" she asked, dreading the answer. She didn't want to know that he had been a father, a grandfather, a beloved husband. . . .

Kovac shook his head. "Not close—in any sense of the word. A grown daughter in Portland, Oregon, who hasn't bothered to return any of the lieutenant's calls. An elderly uncle in very poor health in a rest home. The uncle owns a cabin out on one of the smaller lakes.

"Looks like that's where Stan based himself after he split town. The property and the pickup were registered to Walter Dempsey, the uncle."

What a sad, strange little man Stan Dempsey had been. Alone. Invisible to most people, even to those who should have been close to him.

"The job was all he had, wasn't it?" she said.

"Honey, the job is all *I* have, but I don't go around disfiguring people," Kovac said. "Could someone have reached out to Stan over the years, tried to bring him out of his shell? I suppose so. Hell, I could have tried, and I didn't. But he was a grown man. His life was what he made it. Right down to how it ended."

"He didn't put the knife in my hand," Carey said softly.

Kovac hooked a finger beneath her chin and made her look up at him.

"No. He put you in a situation where you had to use it," he said quietly.

He stared into her eyes, his face the portrait of a good and honorable man. "Carey, I would give anything if I could turn the clock back. If I could have gotten to the scene five minutes sooner and spared you having to wrestle with this. 'Cause I'll tell you what: If I'd seen him threatening you, I would have blown his ass off the planet. And I wouldn't lose a lot of sleep over it."

Carey gave a little half laugh. "I don't know what this says about me, but that's the sweetest thing anyone has said to me in a long time."

He smiled back at her, touched her cheek, and said, "My pleasure. I'm going to leave you alone now and let you get some rest. And don't argue with me—you're staying overnight."

"Yes, sir."

He didn't move from the bed. He didn't take his eyes off her. He shook his head a little. "I owe you an apology."

"For what?"

"For the way I behaved at the beginning of this. I was a jerk. I was judging you without having all the facts, making assumptions. I'm sorry."

"Not so easy being the judge, is it?" she said.

"No. Turned out I was very wrong about you," he said. "You are one brave lady, Carey Moore."

"No," Carey said. "I was terrified."

"I should hope so. If you weren't, I'd be scared of you," he said. "But that's what bravery is: to be afraid and do what you have to do anyway. You can't have courage without fear."

The door swung open and the doctor walked in. Kovac eased away from the bed.

"I'll see you in the morning," he said. "But if you need me, call me. I'll be here before you can hang up the phone."

"You're a good man, Sam Kovac," Carey said.

A good man, a strong man, a man of his

word. The world could have done with a few more Sam Kovacs in it.

He blushed a little at the compliment, his mouth crooking up on one side, then slipped out the door.

65

"I'm not going to go through the motions and reprimand you for being a couple of cowboys, Detective Kovac, Detective Tippen."

Lieutenant Dawes stood at the head of the table in the war room. It was past nine o'clock, but she had gathered the task force to recap the events of the day and reassess what still needed to be done.

"I know all too well the both of you are selectively deaf anyway."

Tippen cupped a hand to one ear. "Did someone say something?"

"Instead," she said, "I'm going to ask everyone to raise their coffee cups in a salute to a job well done."

The "Hear, hears" were loud.

"Where's the beer?" Kovac complained.

"We'll get to that," Dawes said. "Work before play."

They went over the details of everything that had happened that day. Two murders discovered and cleared, an abduction with a happy ending. Happy for everyone but Stan Dempsey.

"Did his daughter ever call back?" Liska asked.

Dawes shook her head. "Not yet. The Portland PD made contact with her yesterday. I've called her directly and left messages. I'll try again later this evening. Obviously, she and her father weren't close."

"That's beyond 'not close,'" Liska said. "That's downright cold."

"It's sad," Elwood said. "How sharper than a serpent's tooth it is to have an ungrateful child."

"Thank you, Mr. Shakespeare," Tippen said dryly. "I'm personally not interested in Stan's family dynamics at the moment. Let's move on. I'm hungry.

"So we have to assume he had the Moores' house under surveillance," he went on. "But what would have made him follow the nanny's car? Dahl was dressed as a woman."

"I guess we'll never know that," Dawes said. "Maybe he was in a position to see something going on in the garage. He could have seen through the windows from the neighbor's yard."

"You're saying he would have watched Dahl put the judge in the trunk and done nothing?" Liska said.

"Why not?" Tippen said. "He gets his next two victims in a package, conveniently delivered to a remote location, no less."

"We still don't know who attacked the judge in the parking ramp," Liska pointed out. "Or are we pinning that on Dempsey too?"

"It makes sense," Elwood said. "News of her ruling on Dahl's prior bad acts had broken. Stan would have been in proximity. He was working Friday."

"And what?" Liska asked. "He'd brought his all-black mugger outfit to change into at the end of the day, just in case?"

"What did Porn Boy have to say for himself?" Kovac asked.

"Nothing," Dawes said. "He denied any knowledge of the assault. But he doesn't have anyone to corroborate his story, and I have no doubt that he's lying as to his whereabouts that night at the time of the attack."

"So he's still on the board," Kovac said.

"Why would he risk it?" Tippen asked. "The guy is a major star in his genre."

Liska rolled her eyes. "Let's not go over that ground again. I haven't recovered from the initial horror."

"O, ye of narrow mind," Tippen said. "And frankly I can't believe you haven't indulged yourself."

"That's not the point. It's the mental image of *you* indulging yourself that will send me into therapy."

"So I should be congratulated for doing a public service."

Liska snagged one of his chocolate-covered coffee beans and bounced it off his forehead.

"Ginnie Bird is Bergen's sister," Kovac said. "Maybe he's actually devoted to her. Little Sis cries on his shoulder that her boyfriend isn't going to leave his wife. Boo-hoo, can't you do something, Donny? And this is what the boy genius comes up with.

"I still like him for it. When the unis knocked on his door, he was packing and had a ticket to St. Kitts."

"Is he smart enough to know the U.S. has no extradition treaty with St. Kitts?" Elwood asked.

Kovac shrugged. "Even the dumbest criminals who flunked out of nursery school seem to find a way to know every angle how to get away with something.

"I had a mutt once who was so stupid he couldn't find his dick in a dark room. But this clown knew every way there was to create a false identity and evade the cops."

"Can we keep Bergen in town?" Elwood asked.

"Chris Logan is trying to help us out with that," Dawes said.

"Has anyone notified Wayne Haas of Dahl's death?" Liska asked.

"You have a connection with him now, Nikki," Dawes said. "I think you should take care of that."

Liska nodded and made a note to herself.

"All right, people," Dawes said. "Let's call it a night. I'm starving. Burgers and beers at Patrick's on me."

A cheer went up, and chairs were vacated immediately. While the rest of the pack went for the door, Kovac and Liska hung back.

"Jeez, Kojak, you broke one without me,"

Liska said, pouting. "I'm hurt. You cheated on me with Tippen."

Kovac smiled and put an arm around her. "Sorry, Tinks. You would have gotten sick on the car ride anyway."

"You were driving?"

"Yeah."

"I forgive you."

"Let's go to Patrick's," Kovac said. "I'll let you steal my french fries."

"Nah," she said, patting the flat of his belly. "You can have the burger I would have eaten. You're a healthy, active boy, after all.

"I'm going home. Speed's bringing the boys back tonight. I want to spend some time with them like a normal mom."

"Okay," Kovac said. "Give Speed a kick in the balls for me."

"My pleasure."

"You parked out front?"

"Uh-huh."

"I'll walk you to your car," he said.

Liska gave him a little hug. "You're a good man, Sam Kovac."

He smiled a crooked smile. "So I hear."

66

Liska pulled up in front of the Haas house. It was only a small detour on her way home to St. Paul. She felt like she owed them the visit to tell them Karl Dahl would never hurt anyone again. She could give them good news for once, instead of bad news, excuses, and accusations. She could take ten minutes out of her life for that.

There were lights on downstairs and in the detached garage. Wayne Haas's car was in the driveway. She went first to the garage, thinking father and son might be there together, working on some project. Hoping for both of them that that would be the case.

A radio was playing hip-hop, something she heard enough around her own house to have learned to thoroughly hate it. A sure sign of going over the hill.

"Mr. Haas? Bobby?" she called out as she neared the side door.

The rain had stopped, but the grass was wet, and she could feel it soaking into the leather of her shoes. *No good deed goes unpunished.*

She knocked, looking into the garage through the glass panes of the old side door. The usual assortment of junk—lawn mowers, bikes, yard tools, paint cans.

Bobby Haas was sitting on a stool at the workbench that ran from wall to wall across the end of the building. He looked up from a book, slipped off the stool, and came to the door.

"Detective Liska? What are you doing here?"

"Can I come in? It's getting really cold out here."

He stepped back from the door to let her in. Liska automatically took in her surroundings at a glance—garden tools hanging on the garage walls, fishing rods that hadn't been out in a long time. Bobby moved toward the long workbench.

"I came with some good news for a change," she said. "Is your dad around?"

Bobby frowned. "He went to bed early. He wasn't feeling well."

"Is he okay? Does he need to go to a doctor?"

"No. I think he's mostly just worn-out," the boy said, looking sad. "He's always worn-out."

"You want things to be the way they were before," Liska said.

"He doesn't even want to try. He couldn't care less about me."

"I'm sure that's not true, Bobby. Your dad's in a bad place. He feels ashamed that you've had to be the strong one in the family, when he should be strong for you."

None of this impressed the boy. He had run out of patience. Like every boy, he wanted to be the center of his father's world. There was no greater disappointment than for a son to find out that he wasn't.

"Yeah, well," Bobby said, tears glazing his eyes, "I wish he would just get over it. It's been more than a year and every day he still gets up depressed over what happened, and every day he comes home from work depressed over what happened. It's like I'm not even there. He's supposed to be my *dad*. What about me? What about what I need?"

Liska put a hand on his back and patted, offering the same silent comfort she had given her oldest boy the many times his father had disappointed him. Bobby Haas was trembling against the raw emotions rising up inside him. He was at an age when those emotions were suddenly bigger and stronger than he knew what to do with.

He stepped away from her and walked in a small circle, his hands on his hips. "He's supposed to love *me,* not a bunch of dead people he can't do anything about!"

Struggling to bat the tears back, to take the feelings that had burst free and shove them back inside, he walked his small circle, breathing hard.

Liska wondered what must have happened to spark all of this. A fight with Wayne? Or Wayne not having it in him to fight? The truth of it was, Wayne Haas was a broken man, and she really didn't think he would ever pull out of it. It looked like Bobby had come to that realization as well.

The boy swiped at his eyes, embarrassed he had lost his composure in front of her.

"So what are you doing out here?" Nikki

asked, trying for a more upbeat tone as she walked toward the workbench, where textbooks and notebooks were spread out beneath the fluorescent work light.

"Studying," Bobby said. "I can have the radio on out here and it doesn't bother my dad."

"I'll have to pass this idea on to my boys," she said, checking out his books. Advanced biology, chemistry, psychology. "Looks like you're thinking of becoming a doctor."

"I want to be a forensic pathologist."

"Smart choice." Creepy choice, all things considered, but it was better than having him say he wanted to spend his life digging graves, she supposed. With the kinds of tragedies he'd had in his young life, it made a certain kind of sense. "Your patients can never sue you for malpractice. They're already dead."

"Right," he said, managing a little smile.

"You've made yourself quite the office out here."

He had converted some of the shelves above the workbench into bookshelves. On the work surface, he had put down a number of twelve-by-twelve marble tiles to spread his work over. Pens and pencils were neatly organized in mismatched cups and water glasses. A couple of stacking trays held notebooks and file folders. The level of organization was frightening to a woman whose filing system consisted of stacking piles of paper all over her dining room table.

Bobby moved between her and the bench as if he was worried she might try to steal his chemistry notes.

Liska considered it a triumph that she had gotten Kyle and R.J. to keep a path open on the floor of their bedroom so they could escape in the event of a fire. This kid kept his paper clips sorted by size.

"I should have you come and organize my kitchen," she said. "But then I might be expected to cook."

He had "in" and "out" trays labeled for bills and family finances.

"You pay the bills?" she asked.

"If I leave it to Dad, it doesn't get done."

Even as debilitated as Wayne Haas seemed to be, she thought it strange that he would give that responsibility to a seventeen-year-old boy.

"You don't ever get to just be a kid, do you?"

Bobby shrugged and looked away from her. "It doesn't matter. I've always had to take care of things myself."

There was a bitter, ironic edge to his words.

"So what's the good news?" he asked. "You said you have good news."

"Karl Dahl was shot and killed this afternoon," she said. "He won't be hurting anyone ever again."

"Good. So it's over?"

Liska helped herself to a seat on an old riding lawn mower. "As far as Karl Dahl goes. We're still looking into the assault on Judge Moore."

"So she's off the hook for siding with him now, 'cause he's dead?" Bobby said. "She can go back to her life and do the same thing all over again?"

"Actually, she's in the hospital," Liska said. "Dahl abducted her last night. She's lucky to be alive."

Bobby couldn't seem to muster up any sympathy. "If she'd just done what she was supposed to do, none of this would have happened."

"Judge Moore didn't let Karl Dahl break jail."

"She would have let him walk," the boy said. "He was supposed to go to prison, like, a long time ago. Maybe my dad could have had some closure and moved on if that had happened."

"Life doesn't always follow the plan, Bobby. Most of the time it just happens, and we do the best we can."

Of course he wouldn't go for that, she thought. This kid probably did an outline for a grocery list. He wanted everything neat and tidy and under his control. She couldn't blame him. He'd had so little control over his own young life, he had to take it where he could.

On the wall at the far end of the bench, he had put up a coatrack and hung a variety of layers to put on when he started to get cold, in order of lightest weight to heaviest—a short-sleeved T-shirt, a long-sleeved T-shirt, a sweatshirt with a University of Minnesota logo, the black jacket he had been wearing the first two times she had spoken with him.

At least the clothes weren't pressed and on padded hangers. The shirts hung crooked. He had tossed the jacket up on the hook inside out. Nice to know he wasn't entirely perfect.

Liska stared at the coat, at the square white tag sewn into the back at the neck. About one inch by one inch. She frowned, but brought her attention back to the boy.

"Maybe your dad can have that closure now," she said. "With Karl Dahl dead, maybe he'll be able to let go some of the anger and start to heal. Maybe you can do that together."

Bobby looked off in the direction of the house as if he could see through the walls and into his father's bedroom. If he could have willed something to happen, he would have.

Liska's eyes drifted back to the clothes on the hooks. A picnic bench beneath the coatrack gave a place to sit down and change shoes. Beneath the bench were a small herd of sneakers, a pair of army boots, and what looked like a small piece of luggage partially hidden by a greasy old towel.

No, not luggage.

Liska went to the bench and pulled the towel away, revealing an old brown leather briefcase big enough to carry a bowling ball, or the files, notes, briefs, and motions a judge might carry home at the end of the day.

"Great old briefcase," she said. "My uncle William carried one of these when I was a kid. He was a real estate attorney."

Bobby Haas said nothing. He looked from the briefcase to Liska.

"Lawyers like to carry so much paper," she said. "I think it makes them feel like they must be important. Uncle William had one arm longer than the other from hauling that briefcase around."

Stamped in gold beneath the heavy brass clasp and lock was a name partially rubbed away over the years, but she could still make it out: A.H. GREER, ESQ.

"Where did you get this, Bobby?" Liska asked as she straightened up and looked hard at the boy.

"I don't remember. Salvation Army, I think."

"Really? The things you can find," she said. "This is really nice. They don't even make them like this anymore. Did you know Judge Moore had one just like this?"

"No. How would I know that?"

"I don't know," Liska said. "You tell me. It was stolen from her when she was attacked Friday night."

"Are you saying you think I stole it?" he

said, becoming visibly upset at the idea. "I didn't. That's not even her name."

"No, it isn't. But I can tell you whose name it is. Alec Greer, Esquire, is Judge Moore's father."

Red in the face, the boy said, "Well, this isn't hers. I got it a long time ago."

"Then you won't mind if I have a look inside," Liska said.

His eyes went to the briefcase again, then back to her. He was breathing faster. "Don't you need a warrant or something?"

"I can get a warrant. Is that what you want? I can call my partner, and we can stand here and wait for him to bring a search warrant. Then we can spend all night picking this garage apart, and it won't make any difference. What's in that briefcase isn't going to change, unless you have some magical powers you haven't shared with me."

He was sweating a little bit now. He didn't have an instant answer. Liska could all but see the gears in his brain racing as he considered and dismissed options.

"Bobby, the only way you have this briefcase is if you took it from Judge Moore," she said. "Turn around, spread your feet, put your arms out to your sides and your hands flat on the counter."

He did as he was told.

"Bobby Haas," she said, walking up behind him with handcuffs, "I'm putting you under arrest for the assault of Carey Moore."

As she went to put one of the bracelets on him, he jabbed back hard with an elbow, hitting her square in the sternum.

Liska staggered backward, seeing stars, the wind knocked out of her.

Bobby Haas spun around from the bench with something in his hand, something he had grabbed from the tools on the wall.

A hammer.

His beautiful face had darkened and twisted with rage. He came at her, swinging the hammer as hard as he could.

Liska caught a heel on some piece of lawn equipment, went down on her back, cracked her head on the garage floor. She rolled to one side just as the hammer's blow bounced off the concrete where her head had been.

Making it to her hands and knees, she

scrambled under the handles of a wheelbarrow and shot forward, gaining her feet.

The hammer hit the wheelbarrow and it
rang like a Chinese gong.

"You fucking bitch," he said, but he didn't
shout.

That frightened her almost as much as his
actions. He was trying to kill her yet had the
presence of mind not to shout, not to be
heard by a neighbor or by his father inside
the house.

He kept coming with the hammer.

Liska rounded a bicycle and shoved it into
his path.

His eyes were absolutely black. Flat black,
bottomless, emotionless. Like a snake, like a
shark, like a killer.

She pulled her weapon, but he was so
close she barely had it out of the shoulder
holster before he was on her.

She ducked low. The hammer hit the wall,
splintering wood.

Liska put a shoulder into the boy's solar
plexus and drove him back a couple of
steps. As she started to raise the gun, he
swung again.

The hammer struck the back of her hand.
The gun went flying.

"You fucking cunt!" He spat the words at her, full of venom.

Liska ducked away from him, darted to the side. She stuck her hand into her coat pocket and came out with her tactical baton.

With a quick, practiced move, she snapped it out to its full length and swung it like a baseball bat as hard as she could into Bobby Haas's ribs just as he pulled his arm back for another blow.

She felt a couple of his ribs give way, and he doubled over, dropping the hammer.

The second blow was a hard, downward overhand that hit his left shoulder and fractured his collarbone.

Screaming in pain, the boy dropped to his knees and elbows on the floor, fell sideways, and curled into a fetal position, crying like the child he should have been.

"Flat on your face, you little shit!" Liska shouted, the adrenaline roaring through her.

"It hurts!"

"It damn well better hurt, you rotten little bastard! On your face, now, or I'll give you something to cry about!"

Sobbing, he moved in slow motion to his

hands and knees. Furious and scared, Liska put a foot into his back and shoved him flat. She read him his rights even as she pulled her cell phone out to call for backup.

67

"I can't leave you alone for a minute," Kovac crabbed, walking across the lawn to the Haas garage. "You owe me dinner."

"Excuse me? The Son of Satan just tried to kill me with a hammer!"

"And your point would be . . . ?"

Liska scowled at him. "Don't make fun of me, Sam. I've never been so freaked-out in my life!"

Kovac gave her shoulder a squeeze. "I can see that, Tinks. I just thought a little ob-noxious levity might be in order."

"How would that be different from how you usually are?"

"Smart-ass."

To have Liska admit to being afraid took a lot. Now she would get pissy, because she had let someone see that she wasn't really as tough as she pretended to be.

"You should have seen him, Sam. When he turned around and came at me with that hammer . . ." She shivered and pretended she was cold, rubbing her hands up and down her arms. "What I saw in that kid's eyes . . . I've never seen before. And I don't want to see it again."

Bobby Haas had been hauled out on a gurney and taken away in an ambulance. And still she was more shaken than Kovac had ever seen her. She scowled down at the ground, uncomfortable with the uniforms and the forensics team crawling all over the place, lest they see through her act too.

Kovac took off his trench coat and put it around her. She could have drowned in it, she was so little. With an arm around her shoulders, he guided her to the Haases' front porch, and they sat on the edge of it. She leaned into him.

"Slow it all down, kiddo," he said. "Slow it all down."

She took a deep breath and let it out.

"I asked the unis to get Wayne Haas," she said. "I'm not telling him this. I can't. You have to."

"All the lights and sirens, and he hasn't come out on his own?"

"Bobby told me he went to bed early because he wasn't feeling well."

"I should sleep so hard," Kovac said. "If my neighbor doesn't stop banging on his roof in the mornings, I'll take a hammer to him."

Liska wasn't listening to him. She looked up at the sky and shook her head. "Oh, God . . ."

"It's because he's a kid," Kovac said quietly. "That's too close to home."

"You know, I really wanted to feel sorry for him," she said. "I *did* feel sorry for him. The poor, motherless child."

"I don't know if Bobby Haas was ever a child."

"Maybe that was the problem."

"And maybe he had three sixes branded on the back of his head," Kovac said. "Don't try to figure it out, Tinks. There's a reason that's not our job."

They couldn't do it. The toll was too heavy emotionally, and emotion took away objectivity, and one thing a detective absolutely had to be was objective.

Hypocrite, he thought.

One of the forensics people stuck her head out of the garage. "Detectives, I think you need to come see this.

"Becker took the stuff out of the briefcase to inventory," she explained. "This is pretty scary."

Inside the garage, Kovac looked over the items that had been spread across the workbench—Carey's files having to do with *The State v. Karl Dahl*. The papers she had been taking home to look at over the weekend. All of it was wet and stinking.

"Jesus, he pissed on it!" he said with disgust.

Liska had moved on to the rest of it. "Oh, my God . . ." she whispered. "Sam . . ."

All neatly contained in Ziploc bags: a journal; two clear four-pocket plastic sheets holding photos of Bobby with his father—playing catch, fishing, being happy; half a dozen large Ziploc plastic bags with newspaper clippings in them, organized by month.

MINNEAPOLIS MASSACRE

GRUESOME HOMICIDES SHAKE
QUIET NEIGHBORHOOD

CRIME SCENE "A BLOODBATH"
ACCORDING TO DETECTIVES

DRIFTER ACCUSED IN BRUTAL SLAYINGS

Kovac found the clippings only slightly weird and creepy. It wasn't unheard of for loved ones of homicide victims to keep track of the case in the media.

Then came the final, smaller plastic bag.

The bottom dropped out of his stomach, and a sudden cold sweat misted his skin.

"Holy God . . ."

Liska looked over at him. "What is it?"

In a case like the Haas murders, the detectives often kept certain details of the crime secret from the public, details only the killer would know. It helped them weed out the crackpots who always came out of the woodwork to confess to heinous crimes in a sick attempt to gain attention.

Kovac held that secret up to the light.

"Oh, Jesus!"

Perfectly preserved, vacuum sealed on a single sheet together, side by side by side—largest to smallest—the right thumbs of Marlene Haas, and Brittany and Ashton Pratt.

"Jesus H.," Kovac breathed. "Karl Dahl didn't do it."

The irony was bitter. Stan Dempsey had ruined his career and his sanity trying to see Karl Dahl convicted of the Haas homicides. He had been so convinced of Dahl's guilt. Everyone had. The strange drifter with a record of sexually oriented crimes—relatively minor crimes, but just the same . . . He'd known the victims. He'd been seen going into the victims' home on the day of the murders. He'd had no alibi. When he'd been arrested, Karl Dahl had been in possession of a necklace that belonged to Marlene Haas.

It had to be Dahl. No one wanted to think their neighbor or their mailman or their meter reader could be capable of the atrocities committed on Marlene and her foster children. No one would even have considered the boy next door.

The killer had had to be Karl Dahl. Dahl had been arrested, indicted, would likely have been convicted. Case closed.

Instead, Dahl's arrest had triggered a terrible series of events. Dahl had escaped jail, murdered two women, and abducted a third. Carey Moore had been forced to kill Stan Dempsey out of fear for her life.

Karl Dahl, as it turned out, had indeed been a murderer, but he hadn't been guilty of the crimes he had been accused of committing.

Kovac put down the vacuum-sealed bag. No one said anything. There was too much—and nothing—to say.

"Detective Liska?" One of the officers Liska had sent into the house filled the doorway.

She didn't turn her head away from the things laid out in front of them.

"Your guy in the house?" the officer said. "He's dead. Looks like maybe he had a heart attack."

"I'm sure it does," Liska murmured. "I'm sure it does."

68

The journal of Bobby Haas read like a Stephen King novel. The first entry was dated a couple of weeks prior to the murders. The boy had written about his anger over his parents' discussions about possibly trying to adopt the "two little worms," as he called them.

He wrote at length about his feelings of betrayal and rejection. Everything had been fine when it had just been the three of them. He had felt important. He'd had the undivided attention of his parents, particularly of his dad. Then Marlene had, in his mind, turned on him, rejected him. She had wanted something more—more children, *other* children. He wasn't good enough for her.

Just like before, he had written.

Women didn't love him. In his mind, every woman in his life had rejected him—his mother, the first Mrs. Haas, Marlene Haas. His vitriol directed at Marlene Haas jumped off the page. Women were selfish bitches— and worse—who ultimately became bored with him. Like a girl with a favorite doll, Marlene had tired of him and moved on to other, newer toys.

He hated her. He loved his dad. Marlene had been trying to pull Wayne's attention from Bobby, trying to ruin their father-son bond, which had clearly been the most important relationship in Bobby's life.

The details of his planning the murders were chilling. The accounts of the murders themselves were horrific. He told about feeling powerful and invincible as he watched the realization of what was about to happen to her and her "precious little worms" dawn across Marlene's face.

In the more recent entries, he had written about his attempt to kill Carey Moore, and his growing frustration that his father was paying more attention to Marlene and the foster children now than when they had been alive, and less and less attention to him. That wasn't what the plan had been.

He doesn't want to be alive. I'll be doing us both a favor. . . .

He had written pages about selenium poisoning, which conveniently mimicked the symptoms of a heart attack and wouldn't show up in the standard basic toxicology screen.

How ironic that Bobby had turned around and done the very same thing he had accused Marlene Haas of. He had tired of their presence—Marlene, the foster kids, and finally Wayne, the father he had so desperately wanted all his life. They had worn out their usefulness to him, so he had broken them and cast them aside.

The diary of a budding serial killer.

Kovac knew the journal would be valuable to the profilers and the psychologists, who were always looking for more insight into the minds of murderers. But if not for them, he would have thrown the thing in an incinerator. The book was tainted with the evil that lived in Bobby Haas, and he, for one, wanted to put it somewhere that evil could never escape.

Processing the Haas scene had gone well into the next day. By five o'clock that morning, the story had broken locally, then hit the news networks. By eight, the media feeding frenzy was on.

The chief and Lieutenant Dawes, along with Chris Logan, had handled the press conference. Kovac and Liska had gone to their respective homes for a few hours of much-needed sleep. Not even his neighbor's hammering had stirred Kovac.

He'd never felt so exhausted in his life. The job was sometimes, but not often, physically demanding. But it was the emotional exhaustion that left him feeling drained of all energy.

Why did it seem like the only time he spent with his emotions was during a crisis?

Because after the crisis had passed, he didn't want to feel very much at all. It seemed the safest way to be. And the easiest. If he didn't want to expend emotional energy interacting with people, it was easy for him to retreat. Being single had a great many advantages that way, compared to being married—at least compared to being married to the two wives he'd had.

Love just never worked out for him. His last wife had not only left him; she'd left the state, left the Midwest. At the time, she had only recently given birth to their first child, a daughter. But the marriage had been over long before the baby was born. Heartbroken, he had relinquished custody and had never seen his child again.

It wasn't often he allowed himself to think about it, and he never spoke of it. What was the point?

It was only when he got a little too close to other people's happy lives that he acknowledged the emptiness of his own.

His thoughts drifted to Carey. To Carey and Lucy, and what it would be like to be a family with them—something David Moore had stupidly thrown away with both hands. But he cut the thought short, because that wasn't his reality.

Around nine in the evening, he dragged himself from bed, showered, put on some old sweats, and went downstairs to forage for something to eat. He sat down in the living room with nuked leftover pizza and turned on the Travel Channel so he could take a vacation without leaving his sofa.

Cabo San Lucas was looking pretty good. Of course, the show had been shot at a fabulous five-star resort. Kovac pictured himself crashed in a chair on the beach under a big umbrella, listening to the surf, bikini-clad señoritas bringing him exotic drinks all day long.

He had turned off his cell phone as soon as he had arrived home that afternoon, so as not to be disturbed. According to the voice mail woman, he had twelve new messages. He started to play each, deleting most of them before the message ended. Reporter, reporter, reporter. How they always managed to weasel out his phone number was beyond him. He had the number changed after every high-profile case, and still they managed to find him.

The PR person from the chief's office called to tell him how he should dress while the world had its cameras trained on the department.

Note to self: Sell car. Buy Armani suit.

Jesus.

"Sam, it's Carey."

The final message. Kovac sat up straighter. Cabo faded into the background.

"I just wanted to check in with you."

She sounded tired and sad.

"I saw the news. . . . Just when I think this sordid case can't get any worse, it does.

"Anyway . . . I'm home," she said. "And I don't know what to do with myself. Are you sure there isn't a *Victim for Dummies* book out there somewhere?"

She tried to laugh, but failed miserably.

He played the message three times.

Just to hear the sound of her voice.

69

It seemed strange to be in the house. David was gone. Anka was gone. Carey felt their absence, listened to the silences where their voices should have been. With just Lucy in the house with her, she felt as if they were the last two people on earth.

She wouldn't be able to sleep in her bed, the bed she had been dragged from in the middle of the night by Karl Dahl, the bed she had shared with a man she didn't know. Lucy wouldn't want to sleep in her own bed either. She had clung to Carey like a piece of Velcro since Kate had brought her home.

Carey had dragged pillows and blankets into the family room. Lucy liked to pretend she was having a sleepover or going camping. Playing pretend didn't sound like a bad idea to Carey either.

Her daughter had yet to talk about what she had seen that night. Usually a chatterbox, Lucy hadn't had much to say at all. Kate told Carey not to worry, but she worried anyway.

Carey knew how what had happened would affect her own life, make her see things through a different filter, temper her feelings. Her sense of safety and security had been blown out of the water. So many things about her life she had once believed in so strongly had dissolved beneath her feet.

If she felt that way, she could only imagine how helpless a child would feel.

And Lucy had the added upset of not having her father there, and not understanding why.

How was she supposed to tackle those questions? Carey wondered. *Daddy doesn't live here now because he frequents prostitutes. Daddy doesn't live here because he's secretly a pornographer.*

What was she supposed to say? And how would any part of this make sense to a little girl who only wanted her mommy and daddy, and for her world to be safe and secure?

Lucy slept now, curled up on the couch in the family room, a blanket covering her, her thumb in her mouth. She hadn't sucked her thumb in two years.

Carey touched her daughter's dark hair and hoped she was having good dreams.

Restless, she went to the window seat that looked out on the front yard, sat down, and curled her legs beneath her like a cat. A police cruiser still sat at the curb, watching.

The police wouldn't be able to give her this kind of special treatment for long. Even though she knew the three people she had reason to fear—Karl Dahl, Stan Dempsey, and Bobby Haas—would never be a threat to her again, she still felt afraid. She felt exposed. All the world knew where she lived now. Her sense of privacy was gone.

Maybe she would sell the house. Too many unhappy things had happened here. The good memories had been pushed out by the bad. Making a fresh start sounded like a smart thing to do. She wanted to feel anonymous. She didn't want to turn on the news and see her own home fill the screen.

She wanted to be nobody, wanted no one to need anything from her. And she wished very much she had someone to understand those needs in her.

Out on the street, a car pulled up in front of the police cruiser, and the driver climbed out. Kovac.

Carey opened the door before he was halfway up the sidewalk.

"This is a surprise," she said. "I figured you would have been catching up on your sleep."

He shrugged it off as he came inside. "Nah. Sleep is highly overrated. And I would have figured you would be staying some-place else."

"Kate and John offered, but I just didn't want to be with people," she said. "Turns out I don't want to be alone either. And I didn't want to drag Lucy to a hotel. . . ."

Kovac scrutinized her appearance from head to toe. Messy hair, battered face, a T-shirt and red plaid flannel pajama bot-toms. She felt like a grubby-faced waif.

"You've certainly seen me in my finest moments, Detective," she said dryly.

"Have you eaten anything?" he asked, and answered himself. "No, of course not. Why would you eat anything? You'd only get blown over by a stiff wind. I brought food."

He held up a bakery bag, then set it aside on the hall table so he could take his coat off.

"What is it?"

"Doughnuts," he said with that crooked fraction of a smile. "What else would a cop bring?"

"You're perpetuating the stereotype," Carey said, finding a smile of her own, chuckling a little.

"Somebody has to uphold tradition. You got coffee?" he asked, heading for the kitchen.

"You know where it is."

Carey followed him down the hall, bringing the bag of doughnuts. She watched him find everything he needed to make a pot of coffee. As the machine began to gurgle and spit, he turned around to face her.

He looked different in jeans and a sweater. Younger, she thought. Less like he had the weight of the world on his shoulders.

"So, Bobby Haas, huh?" she said.

"Yeah. Bobby Haas."

Carey shook her head. "Who would ever

look at that boy and believe he could do the things he did to Marlene Haas and those children? It's like something out of a horror movie. That he would even have those thoughts in his head makes me feel sick."

"What can you say?" Kovac shrugged. "Some of them just don't hatch right."

"Do you believe that? That evil is born, not made?"

"Honey, I've seen the worst things humans can do to one another," he said. "Bobby Haas didn't rape and torture and mutilate his victims because he wet his pants when he was twelve.

"He had those thoughts brewing in his head for a long time. He had that fantasy honed like a knife by the time he acted it out."

"And he almost got away with it," Carey murmured. "You know if Dahl had gone to trial, he would have been convicted."

"Did you think he did it?" Kovac asked. "Dahl?"

"I should decline to answer that," she said. "But yes. Yes, I did. Everyone did."

"Yet you seemed to bend over backward to cut the defense a break. Why?"

"Because what if he was innocent?" she said. "And as it turned out, he was."

"I couldn't have your job," Kovac said. "I couldn't do it. I couldn't be impartial."

"And that's why you're a cop and I'm not."

He poured them each a mug of coffee. Carey reached into a cupboard, pulled out a plate, and arranged the doughnuts. The domesticity of what they were doing gave her comfort in some way. A simple, everyday kind of routine.

"Where's Lucy?" Kovac asked.

"Asleep in the family room. Let's go back. I don't want her to wake up and not have me there."

"How's she doing with all this?" Kovac lowered his voice as they went into the room.

Lucy hadn't moved, nor had her thumb.

"Her whole world has turned upside down . . . and there's nothing I can do about it."

Carey closed her eyes and put a hand across her mouth, trying to hold back tears that wanted to drown her. She had done a fair job of keeping herself together when Lucy had been awake and watching her.

But her defenses were down; she was exhausted and overwhelmed.

Without even thinking, she turned to Kovac and pressed her face into his shoulder.

Without even thinking, he put his arms around her, and held her, and stroked her hair, and told her everything would be all right. Whether it would be or not didn't matter. What mattered was that someone strong was there to take the weight for a few moments.

Sniffing, wiping the tears from her face with her hands, Carey stepped back.

"All I ever seem to do is cry in front of you," she said.

Kovac handed her a napkin from the plate with the doughnuts. "That's okay. At least you have good reason. Unlike my first wife, who would just burst into tears at the sight of me."

She managed a laugh as she curled into the corner of the couch where Lucy was sleeping. "No, she didn't."

Kovac sat down directly across from her on the big leather ottoman that served as seating and coffee table, and leaned his elbows on his knees.

"Have you heard from David?" he asked.

"No, I haven't."

Kovac shook his head. Carey held up a hand. "Let's not."

That the man with whom she had spent a decade of her life sharing intimacy, having a child, couldn't bring himself to call her and ask after her. What was there to say about that?

"I'm sorry he turned out to be what he is," Kovac said.

"Me too."

Lucy stirred and sat up, blinking and rubbing at her big blue eyes. She looked directly at Kovac, imperious, as if she was offended by his presence.

"Hello, Princess Lucy," he said.

"I'm not a princess anymore," she announced, clearly unhappy at her fall in status.

"Why aren't you a princess?" Kovac asked. "You look like a princess to me."

She shook her head and cuddled against her mother. Carey stroked her hair. "Say hello to Detective Kovac, sweetie. Be polite."

Lucy looked up at him from under her lowered brow. "Hello, Detective Sam."

"Hello." He had that look again, like he

half thought the child would leap out and bite him. "How come you're not a princess anymore?"

"Because." Lucy looked away.

"Did something happen, and you decided not to be a princess anymore?"

Lucy nodded and tucked herself tighter against Carey. "I got afraid," she said in the tiniest of voices.

"You got afraid," Kovac repeated, as serious as if he were interviewing a witness. "It's okay to be afraid. Your mom gets afraid. I get afraid."

"You get afraid?" Lucy asked, looking dubious. She thought about it and finally pronounced: "Then you're not a princess either."

"Well, no, I'm not."

"We're pretending we're having a sleepover," Lucy told him. "You can stay with us if you want."

Kovac hid his laugh behind his hand. "No, I can't," he said. "But thanks for asking. I really should be going. I just came over to check up on you and your mom. And to bring you some doughnuts."

Lucy caught sight of the plate and lit up. "Doughnuts!"

"One," Carey instructed. She unfolded herself from the couch and followed Kovac back out to the hall.

"Thank you, Sam," she said quietly. "For coming over. For the doughnuts. For everything."

Kovac shrugged into his coat. "All in a day's . . ."

"No. Above and beyond."

"You've got my numbers," he said. "If you need me, call me. I'll be here before you can hang up the phone."

Carey nodded.

He turned toward the door and started to open it.

"And what if I don't need you?" she asked. "Can I call you anyway?"

Kovac blushed a little, looked everywhere but at her, struggled to fight off a smile.

"Yeah," he said at last. "Like I said—I'll be here before you can hang up the phone."

70

The task force met the following day just before the change of shift to go over the case, which had become multiple cases. Like cancer, the evil had grown, metastasized, and touched too many lives.

"We've cleared the death of Stan Dempsey," Lieutenant Dawes said. "There will be no further action with that."

"What's going to happen with his body?" Kovac asked. "Is his daughter coming back to make arrangements?"

"No. She said to take money from Stan's bank account to—her words—take care of it."

Tippen gave a low whistle. "How sharper than a serpent's tooth it is to have an ungrateful child."

"Hey, that was my line!" Elwood complained.

"The Bard is part of the public domain, my friend. Free to one and all."

"That's not right," Kovac said, ignoring them. "Dempsey was one of us. Sure, he went nuts in the end, but he was one of us. We should take care of him. We were his family."

Dawes nodded. "I agree. I'll see what we can do. I can tell you the brass isn't going to authorize anything, in light of what happened. Talk to your PBA rep. Maybe the union can help out."

"We'll pass the hat," Kovac said. "Leave the union out of it. We'll do this for Stan like the friends we never were."

Nods and murmurs went around the table. Kovac figured everyone who had ever worked with Stan Dempsey or ignored Stan Dempsey or made fun of Stan Dempsey observed a moment of guilty silence.

Dawes then said, "Nikki, have you heard anything on Wayne Haas regarding the official cause of death?"

"Toxicology hasn't come back yet," Liska said. "The tentative COD is heart failure, but Bobby Haas goes into quite a lot of detail in his journal about poisoning his dad with selenium. Imagine he was going to be a doctor. Yikes."

"Imagine how many Bobby Haases have already graduated from med school," Tippen said. "And law school, and business school. Studies have shown that many heads of Fortune Five Hundred companies are sociopaths."

"This kid almost pulled off the perfect murders," Kovac said. "Karl Dahl would have gone to prison for crimes he didn't actually commit. And the kid would have gone on his merry way."

"Nikki, have you gone back in the case file to see what Stan Dempsey had to say about Bobby Haas?" Dawes asked.

"Bobby Haas was interviewed. He gave an alibi. It looks to me like nobody followed up," Liska said. "Stan was hot on Karl Dahl. Bobby was just sixteen, a good student, polite kid, never in trouble, seemingly despondent over the deaths. . . ."

"He slipped through the cracks," Dawes said.

"Yeah."

"Where are we with David Moore?" Kovac asked.

Dawes shrugged. "We're nowhere. He's been cleared of his wife's assault. He had nothing to do with her abduction. I'm sure a forensic accountant will have a field day digging through Moore's financial records for the divorce proceedings, but he's off the hook otherwise. We don't have anything to hold him for or charge him with."

Kovac scowled. "I don't get it. If he's so innocent, why did he lawyer up so fast?"

"Well, it might have had something to do with the way you and Chris Logan were trying to railroad him into jail," the lieutenant said dryly.

Still, Kovac didn't like it. "I want to know about the mysterious twenty-five grand, and why it had looked so clearly like Moore was up to something with Ginnie Bird's brother."

"Maybe he had been," Elwood said. "Maybe they had a plan to get Judge Moore out of the way, but Bobby Haas beat Bergen to the punch."

"Even if that was the case," Dawes said, "conspiracy charges are a tough sell. If there's no underlying felony charge, the case will never make it off the ground. And the fact remains, David Moore hasn't done anything illegal—that we know of."

Liska gave him an elbow. "We can't just throw him in the clink because you think he's an asshole, Kojak."

"The world would be a better place," he grumbled.

Whether David Moore had committed a crime or not, Kovac was going to get to the bottom of that cesspool, if for no other reason than the personal satisfaction of making Moore's life a misery. He suspected Moore had a ton of money stashed somewhere from his sojourn into the hard-core porn business. Maybe he could find a charge in there somewhere. Like Logan said: Follow the money.

"What do you know about his movies, Tip?" he asked.

Liska put her hands over her ears and began to hum.

"They're too hard-core for me," Tippen said. "Violent. Sadomasochistic. If his films are anything to judge him by, David Moore aka David M. Greer is one sick puppy, a puppy protected by the First Amendment. We might find his work socially and morally reprehensible, but he's not breaking any laws."

Kovac frowned heavily.

"All right, people," Dawes said on a long, end-of-the-day sigh. "Let's wrap it up and move on. If nobody has anything else—"

They were all half out of their chairs when Liska spoke up.

"Wait!" she said, wide-eyed, bringing everyone to attention. "Look at Kovac! Is that a-a—*new brown suit*?"

The oohs and aahs made him blush.

Kovac rolled his eyes. "Oh, for God's sake. Don't make a big deal. I buy one every decade, whether I need it or not."

He stood in front of the mirror in the men's room, trying to decide if he needed to shave again. Better not to. He would undoubtedly cut himself and show up at dinner with toilet paper on his face.

Liska walked in as he put on a fresh shirt. He scowled at her in the mirror.

"You have to stop coming in here, Tinks."

"Don't spoil my fun. This is all the action I get these days."

"Jesus."

"Where's your patch?" she asked. "You haven't given up already."

"I quit."

"Sam, you make me crazy! If you get lung cancer and die—"

"No. I mean I quit. Smoking."

The look of stunned disbelief would have made him laugh if he hadn't been so goddamn nervous.

"Wow. Just like that?"

"Just like that. It's time I started paying attention, before I end up like Stan Dempsey, living alone with an arsenal and one lawn chair in the backyard."

Liska sniffed the air. "Do I smell a midlife crisis coming on?"

"You're in the men's toilet. Chances are good you're smelling something else," he said, fumbling with his brand-new amber necktie, which a very gay salesman in the menswear store had told him brought out the whisky tones in his eyes.

Jesus H.

Liska batted his clumsy hands out of the way and tied the thing herself.

"Nice tie," she said. "It brings out your eyes."

Kovac scowled.

"So where are you off to in such a hurry, mister? Got a hot date?"

"Dinner," he mumbled, his eyes darting away from her.

"A dinner *date*?"

"Dinner."

"With anyone I know?"

"None of your business, Tinker Bell," he said irritably, adjusting the knot at his throat so that he didn't feel like he was going to choke to death.

"Well, that makes it entirely my business," Liska said with a mischievous twinkle in her eyes.

"I'm having dinner with Judge Moore," he confessed.

Liska's brows went up. "Judge Moore."

"Yes."

"Carey," she said.

Kovac huffed out a sigh. "Carey."

Liska laughed and clapped her hands. "Oh, you total liar! You're going on a date. You cad. The hubby's ass is still stinging from the door hitting him on the way out."

"It's not like that," he grumbled. "It's just a little thank-you dinner. With her five-year-old daughter. It's nothing more than that."

"Give it up, Kojak," she said. "I was wise

to you a long time ago. You don't buy a new suit to have dinner with a five-year-old child."

Kovac didn't say anything. He didn't know what he could have said. He didn't want to make too much of Carey's inviting him over. It was too soon after everything had happened. She was traumatized. That had to be the only reason she had asked him; she wasn't in her right mind.

Liska reached up and snugged the knot again. She looked up at him, somber, and patted a hand over his heart. "Be careful with this, will you?"

"It's kinda too late for that," he admitted. Jesus Christ, he was sweating like a horse. He jerked the tie loose again.

"Just bear in mind one thing, Sam," she said seriously.

"What's that?"

"That she's . . . she's . . ."

"Too good for me?"

"A *lawyer.*"

They both laughed. Liska gave him a hug.

"On your way with you, young man," she said, snugging the knot up once more. "Be polite, don't eat with your fingers, don't talk with your mouth full, and be home by curfew."

"Yes, Mom," he said, slipping on the new jacket as he headed for the door.

"And Sam?"

He looked over his shoulder. Her expression was dead serious.

"What?"

"Leave that goddamn tie alone, or I'll break your fingers."

Always with the kind word, his partner.

Kovac saluted and went out the door, moving toward something good.